Trigger Warnings

A Crown of Luminaries is a dark fantasy with heavy themes. Reader discretion is advised as this book contains:

Graphic violence

Abusive upbringing (remembered)

Blood

Death

Grief and loss

Mentions of an orphan upbringing

Sexually explicit content

Electrical play

Breath play

Bondage play

Alcohol consumption

To everyone in the trenches enduring their battles against the dark.
May you never stop fighting for hope.

The Mortal Realms of Elmoria

Blackthorn
Blackthorn Monastery
Kanoelani Forest
Vespera
Tour
Tourmaline Beach

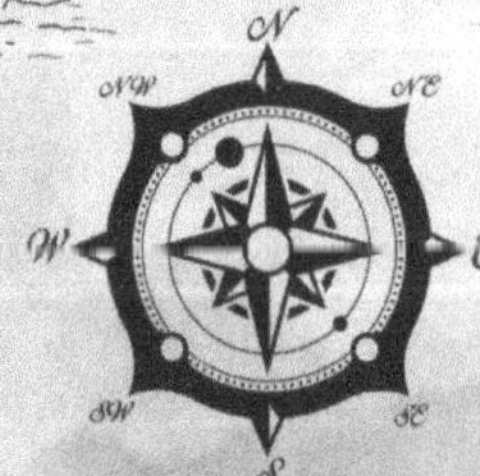

Peasant Slums

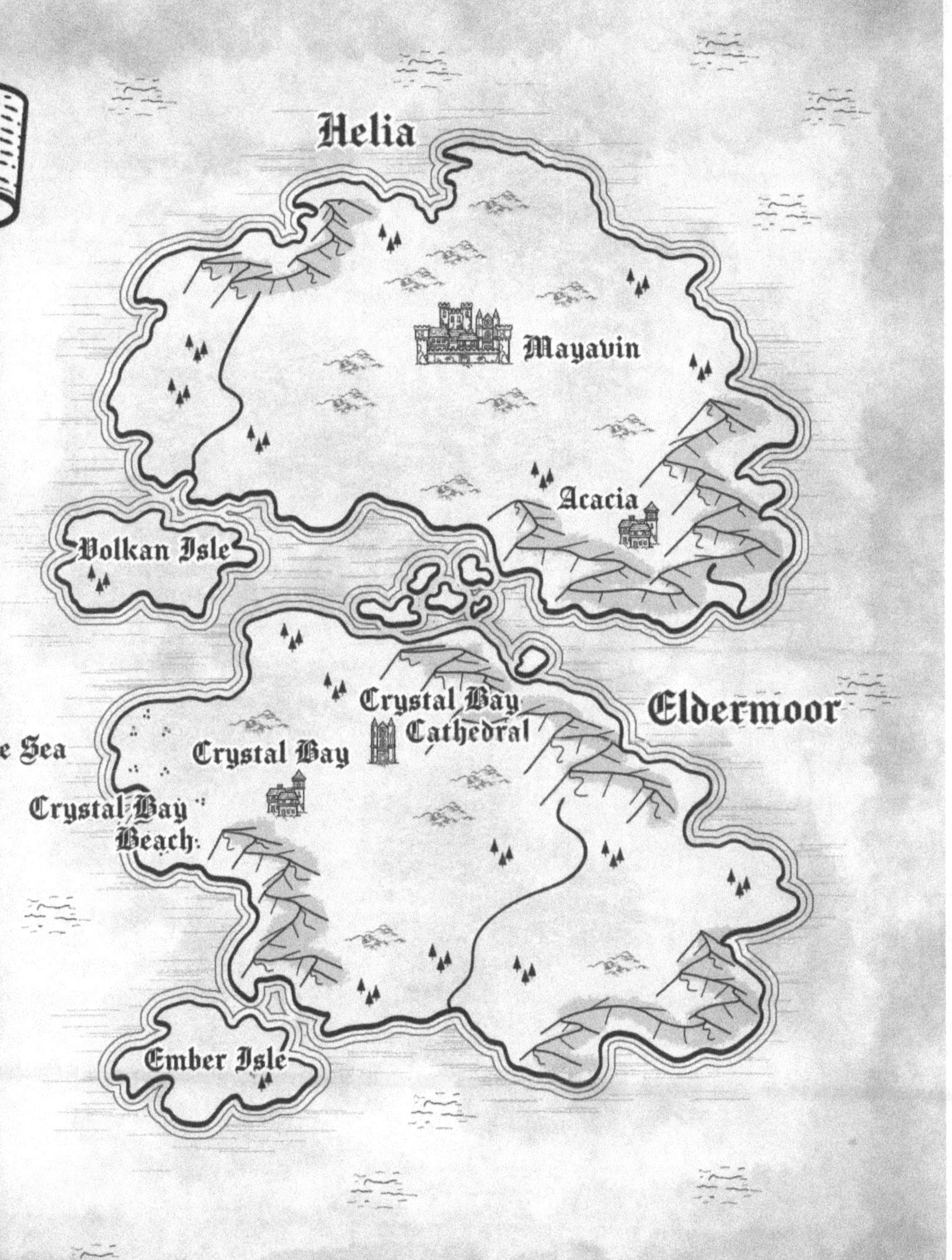

Helia
Mayavin
Acacia
Volkan Isle
e Sea
Crystal Bay
Crystal Bay Cathedral
Crystal Bay Beach
Eldermoor
Ember Isle

CHAPTER 1
The Ghost Assassin

With one of Blackthorn's most notorious gang leaders under the blade of my sword, I will likely live to see tomorrow's sunrise. Despite his successful evasion of The Knights of Blackthorn for months, tracking him through treacherous mountain passes took me only one week. One week of enduring bone-chilling snow squalls on nothing but stale bread and foraged berries to once again prove that I deserve to live.

"What are you waiting for? Finish what you started before I slice that useless head right off your shoulders. Prove your worth!"

Terror ripples down my spine in response to Rhydian's roaring threat as our prized bounty fails to parry my blade and takes a gaping wound to his abdomen. Rhydian will be the one delivering his head and reaping the benefits of the reward after I finish the job. If I'm lucky, I get to keep my head and my role as his prized ghost assassin.

Bruised, chestnut eyes stare back at me in defeated submission as blood spills from my target's wounds onto the fresh blanket of snow. His fatigue mirrors mine as our lungs gulp the thin, mountainous air, winded from the efforts of our bloody swordplay at an unforgiving altitude.

"Do you know how much silver the knights placed on that head of yours?" I chuckle, caressing his neck with my blade. Part of surviving and appeasing Rhydian means toying with my prey before finishing the job. Showing the Captain that I'm more than capable of wearing the mask of a ruthless mercenary means another day my limbs remain attached to my body.

"How does it feel to die by the hands of a lowly peasant?" I scoff.

Rhydian will *not* murder me today.

Rhydian remains close behind me, pressing his blade to the nape of my neck as a reminder there is no room for error. If my performance fails to meet his expectations or even fails to entertain him, I can expect my body to be carved like a ham and tossed to the ravenous wolves of Blackthorn's mountainside.

"How does it feel being nothing more than a trained dog of that bastard, boot-licker? Looks like he's got your tail between your legs," my target mocks. His words come out broken and stuttered in between starved gasps for air. My blood boils with rage, flushing my cheekbones with searing heat after being read by this stranger like a book.

"Last I checked, it is my blade pressed against your throat. Not a bad bite for a trained little dog," I snarl.

There is no reason for my body to be trembling with nerves other than the fact this kill has to be flawless. The cold metal of Rhydian's blade presses harder against my bruised skin, demanding an excellent performance.

"I've been gracious in sparing you despite the flaws in your form today, but I'm afraid I've run out of my mercy for the day. Show me you're capable of a perfect execution, or I'll show you to your death," Rhydian growls.

My emotions shut down on command, and I detach my mind from my body as rehearsed. The man beneath my blade becomes nothing more than just the collateral of my role as a mercenary. His eyes widen in shock as my sword severs his head from his body. By now, I've lost track of all the pairs of fear-stricken eyes that have met mine as I usher them into death. His head rolling on the ground registers in my brain like nothing more than a rock tumbling down a mountain. Still, I may never grow accustomed to the blood of strangers that stains my hands at the end of each day. A piece of my humanity dies alongside each life I'm forced to take under Rhydian's hawk-like surveillance.

Relief washes over me like the steam of a hot spring as Rhydian removes his blade from my neck and retrieves the severed head from the blood-stained snow. "Your technique is improving at a satisfactory rate, I suppose. However, hesitating is what gets mercenaries killed, Amira. It is either kill or get yourself killed. Don't make me have to waste my investments by having to take your life one of these days. I will not hesitate to slaughter you if you compromise my success."

"Maybe I wouldn't have been so hesitant without you breathing down my neck," I mutter.

Without warning, Rhydian drags the blade of his dagger across my back, driving a fresh wound into my collection of scars. I bite into the thin fabric of my scarf in an attempt to muffle my screams. Showing too much weakness will only lead to additional lacerations.

"Maybe one of these days you'll finally learn to take my criticisms with gratitude rather than with an attitude," he sneers.

* * *

Golden beams of diffused sunlight seep through the canvas walls of my tent, infiltrating my eyelids and announcing the dawn of a new day. *You survived yesterday. Today is a new day.* I rub my palms together, creating friction to warm my face. Despite the snow melting outside my tent, early spring mornings in Blackthorn are hardly distinguishable from the bitterness of winter. I'd be lying to myself if I said I've never woken up wishing I had frozen to death overnight before making it to the next sunrise.

Rhydian tells me I should be thankful for the opportunities he has given me over the years and that taking on apprentices has been a gracious mercy he never had to offer. After over two decades spent slaughtering Blackthorn's enemies, I have yet to reap a single reward or recognition for my labor.

We're expecting a visit from some knights today, so let me give you your only reminder. You've never picked up a weapon in your entire life. Got it? You so much as look like you're useful, and I'll have you chained up in a cave, starved and tortured until death mercifully ends your suffering. I have a reputation to uphold, and you will make me look like the compassionate, loving father I have always been to you. Understood? My head throbs with shooting temple pain as I recall glimpses of how I spent the twelfth anniversary of my adoption.

What I'd give to see Rhydian chained up in a cave, begging to die by my hands. Still, murdering the captain would only seal the fate of my downfall. The knights would never allow the killer of their most prolific mercenary to escape without consequences. Even if I were to spend a lifetime evading my capture, starvation would claim me instead.

An orphan, especially a twenty-five-year-old peasant entirely unaware of her bloodline, would never land a trade providing a livable wage outside of the famished peasant slums. Captain Rhydian takes advantage of such orphans by providing them with survival in exchange for training them as his mercenaries to provide for his living. Weaponizing the vulnerable as affordable hired hands for maximum monetary gain. Ingenious, despicable bastard.

I am the only remaining survivor of the twelve orphans Rhydian took under his wing. The rest have been killed in the field, or by Rhydian himself. No one has ever batted an eye when Rhydian would claim each child was just lost to illness. An easy lie to sell in the poverty, disease-ridden peasant slums.

Campfire smoke and early spring morning mist aromas engulf my tent as murders of crows caw overhead. Being surrounded by the beauty of Blackthorn's overgrown, mountainous forests is cruel irony while serving a life sentence as an exploited ghost assassin. Taking in its emerald beauty never fails to taunt me with fantasies of a lifetime spent in solitude. After experiencing all the horrors humanity has to offer, I wouldn't mind going the rest of my life without another human interaction.

I dress in one of my few blood and dirt-stained dark grey tunics, thin, dark trousers, and boots with soles hanging on by sparse threads. I sweep my tangled chin-length black tresses out of my groggy eyes and emerge from my tent.

"Good. You're finally up," Rhydian snarls. Harsh, tawny eyes peek through his unkept, auburn hair with intermittent streaks of silver. I remind my body not to flinch as he chops freshly killed rabbit over a slab on the fire. Pain never fails to radiate from the scars on my back every time he so much as touches a blade in my presence.

"Thank the gods there's still plenty of snow on the ground. Means it will be a bit before this damned head starts to reek." He shoves the blood-stained bag containing the severed head on the ground with his foot, scooting it a little farther from our breakfast.

Knowing just how much silver he will pocket for this particular kill has me mentally running through the maneuvers it would take to rip out his throat and pierce a dagger through his lungs. Picturing all the ways the knights may choose to execute me shuts the temptation down as quickly as it arises.

Rhydian hands me a plate of charred rabbit legs and a stale sourdough roll. "I have an important assignment for you today while I deliver this head to the knights. Eat up."

Reluctantly, I dig into the gamey rabbit, quickly chasing it down with my waterskin before choking on its foul stench.

"Your assignment for today does not come from the knights. Instead, you'll be taking care of a private affair for me," Rhydian tells me as I nearly choke on my breakfast.

"One of my… personal informants has gathered intel that a group of pirates has set up a temporary camp on the shores of Tourmaline Beach. They're due to deliver a shipment of supplies to the knights by nightfall, but they have a rather precious gemstone in their tow I'd like to intercept."

"Are the knights expecting this precious gemstone in their shipment? Why put a target on your back for a piece of jewelry when you're already rolling in the wealth that I earned for you?" I scoff.

Rhydian rises from his log and grazes my neck with the blade of his dagger. "First off, I'm putting a target on *your* back. Not mine. Second, my personal affairs are my business. You question them again, I'll rip out your throat. Understood?"

My stomach drops not in response to the blade against my throat but in response to Rhydian's order to steal from The Knights of Blackthorn—the hands that line his pockets with bottomless blood money.

"Understood, Captain."

"You are to return to our camp with the gemstone by nightfall. If you're caught, you are acting as a rogue thief. You've never heard of me in your life. Leave no survivors. Survivors are witnesses, and surely, the knights will have questions. Are we clear?" Rhydian uses his free hand to down a large gulp of ale. Between his sour breath churning the contents of my stomach and his blade pressing against my windpipe, I offer my compliance quickly to earn my lungs a full breath of fresh air.

"Crystal, Captain."

Rhydian takes another swig of ale and sheaths his blade.

"You best be on your way then, kid. If I catch wind of those pirates closing up shop before you even make it to the sea, you'll find yourself shackled up in that lovely little cave I spotted on our hike yesterday."

My fingers tremble as I fasten my sword in its sheath. I strap my daggers to the thigh bandoliers buckled over my trousers and take in a deep breath. At least a handful of pirates is something I could handle in my sleep. It shouldn't be much effort to make quick work of them and be out of their camp before running into any trouble.

CHAPTER 2
Tourmaline Beach

My mind drifts into a stream of fantasies on my way to Tourmaline Beach—fantasies of draining the blood beneath Rhydian's flesh and leaving his corpse to feed the crows. Throwing his bones to the wolves and then retreating far into the mountains until the traces of civilization are wiped clean from the horizon. If I knew how to sail, commandeering the pirate's ship and taking my chances running from Blackthorn on the open seas would be a thought worth entertaining. However, Rhydian would catch on to my failure to return to the camp and spin a tale convincing the knights to pursue me and deliver me back to his care. He has those noble brats wrapped around his fingers nearly as tightly as the high priestess has them.

After hours of traversing down steep mountain passes, the line where the mossy forest floor bleeds into coarse, sable sands finally comes into my sight. The thick, ashen fog seeping from the emerald mountains dissipates enough to unveil the shores of Tourmaline Beach. Grains of sand, black as a conspiracy of ravens bathing in midnight shadows, shimmer in the light of late-morning sun. The ebbing of the crystal aquamarine waves against the coal-black shore soothes me with a welcomed, brief moment of peace.

If only I could pause long enough to appreciate Tourmaline's tranquil beauty to the depths it deserves. A long moment to absorb the salty mist and allow the warm breeze to embrace me after long days up in the harsh mountains. Knowing that a squad of knights is likely nearby to accept their supplies shipment quickly brings my focus back to the task at hand.

Relying on the thicket at the forest's edge for concealment, I scout the pirate's camp and formulate an attack strategy. Thankfully, they appear to be running off a skeleton crew after I spot no more than a half-dozen men. Taking them out as quickly as possible will buy me adequate time to track down Rhydian's coveted gemstone.

A scrawny, haggard man pauses to catch his breath while unloading crates from their large vessel— certainly not a ship I could even dream of navigating without experience. Two towering masts graze the misty, overcast skies, waving flags bearing the image of Sirena, Goddess of the Sea. A pit of dread settles into my gut. If there's a chance any of these pirates can wield the water and manipulate its waves, I'm as good as dead.

After carefully observing the crew, I chalk up my concerns to irrational paranoia. Not a single member of their crew has demonstrated the slightest indication they can wield water. With what little I know of The Knights of Blackthorn, I know those who can wield the elements all serve as dragon knights. From my hazy memories of Rhydian's ramblings, mages always align their services to Blackthorn with unwavering loyalty. Their morals would likely not allow them to act as rogue pirates, shifting their loyalties to whichever kingdom or nation promises the highest earnings for their services.

Scheming of how and when to strike is interrupted by a sudden onset of splintering pain in my temples the moment a man emerges from the ship donning a bulky leather belt. I do my best to ignore the pain long enough to observe the contents strapped to his belt— an enviable array of daggers and a small iron case.

The hairs on my arms and the top of my head rise ominously as if lightning is threatening to strike nearby despite calm, sunny skies. A tingling electrical sensation infiltrates my veins as I fail to peel my eyes away from that case. The more I fixate on it, the more spasms of electrical energy dance in my veins like needles and prickle atop my skin. For the sake of my sanity, I interpret the unshakable omen as a blend of nervous jitters and instinct. The stone I am after has to lie within that case.

Another wave of sharp, stabbing pain shoots through my head as I unsheathe a couple of daggers and prepare to advance on my targets. My stomach roils as the stabbing pain now presents like dozens of mini blades digging into my skull while an overwhelming stench of sulfur wafts my senses. I need to get this over with before whatever illness this may be disrupts me any further.

I spot a crate large enough to hide behind and make a maddening dash toward its cover, keeping as light on my feet as possible. No weapons are drawn, and no one rushes to the crate, meaning my presence is still unnoticed. After catching my breath, I lock my focus on the scrawny man unloading crates from the ship. He's well within range for me to pick him off like a pesky fly without charging him. I launch a dagger into the air with as much force as I can muster and watch it rip through the air until it slices through his neck with clean precision. He immediately fumbles the crate in his arms as his body collapses into the inky sand. The sound of blood gurgling from his throat arouses the attention of his remaining crew mates. Blood pools from his body, tainting the sand with wet, shiny crimson.

A raging coughing fit sneaks up on me as a foul stench of sulfur invades the ocean breeze and takes my breath away— as if enduring the knife-like head pain isn't enough of a distraction. Sinister, obsidian clouds creep over the cerulean skies, rolling in behind the men charging after their fallen crew mate.

A heartbeat before my cover is compromised, I hurl another dagger through one of the men's biceps. It doesn't take him down, but it buys me precious seconds to return some focus to suppressing the urge to vomit.

"Bitch!" Beastly, wrathful eyes meet mine on the other side of the crate, no longer serving as my cover. Soaked in both the blood of his fallen friend and the dagger still wedged in his arm, he blazes toward me

with his sword drawn and a murderous oath fuming in his eyes.

I unsheathe my sword and prepare for our blades to meet. Twelve additional men charge behind him as electrifying pain continues to set my brain on fire. Oh, gods. I could've sworn I only scouted six. I failed to factor in any additional crew possibly occupied with tasks within the interior of the ship—a damn sloppy mistake.

At least Rhydian trained me thoroughly for high-stake encounters where the numbers work against my favor. Our swords collectively clash in a murderous frenzy as I cut through men like tall grass. It takes all my stamina to wield the weight of my sword with enough speed to counter every strike, but somehow I'm winning. Only one man remains, with an iron case strapped to his belt.

"A bitch like you belongs to Osiris. You'll make a fine whore for The God of Death," he snarls.

The livid pirate spits blood through his teeth and lunges toward me with his blade at a lethal speed. He cuts downwards, aimed for my head in a swift, reflexive attack. I immediately duck as I feel the force of his blade breezing over my head and stumble backward, finding myself choking on the sulfurous odors once again. After fumbling to regain my balance, I cut my blade upwards, lunging toward his neck. I manage to cut a slice through the side of his neck, satisfied with the amount of blood now trickling down his chest. He drops his sword and clenches his fists over his wound in a panic, buying me the opportunity to kick his sword far beyond his reach.

"Relinquish that gemstone, and maybe I'll allow you to live," I hiss through my teeth, knowing he won't be walking away from this fight either way. My limbs begin trembling with weakness as the searing pain rippling through my head blurs my vision and threatens to throw me to the ground. In the heat of the distraction, I fail to notice and deflect the blow of a dagger, now impaling my thigh. My sword drops to the ground as my arms become too weak to wield its bulk.

Rage and adrenaline course through me like wildfire. I will not die by the hands of some nameless pirate. Screaming in both relentless pain and anger, I reach for a dagger on my bandolier and drive the blade through his eye before we both fall to the ground.

Blood gushes out of my leg as I cut fabric from the sleeve of my tunic and attempt to form a makeshift tourniquet to prevent bleeding out. By the time my trembling arms finally allow me to fasten the tourniquet around my thigh, my opponent begins stirring in failed attempts to raise himself from the ground. Whoever fails to get up first between us will meet certain death.

Without warning, a sudden rupture of thunder growls through the skies, darkening the clouds in sinister obsidian. Expecting to be drenched in a torrential downpour, I'm met with nothing but the foul stench of sulfur oppressing the salty sea breeze. Tendrils of dense shadows shoot down from the clouds and wrap around my torso. The bind restricts my arm movement before I can reach for a dagger. This can't be real. Am I being hunted by a god? I violently flail and thrash against the restrictive black ropes to no avail. The bind only tightens the more I fight it. Somehow, I am hopelessly restrained like a serpent's prey, bound by some supernatural force beyond my comprehension. Amid my hopeless thrashing, my body levitates above the ground as if I'm a marionette under the control of some divine puppet master.

Before having a moment to process that I am now levitating in a strange, shadowy bind, I'm tossed through the air as if my body weighs nothing more than a piece of parchment. After a brief, violent flight, I'm thrown back to the earth shoulder-first into a stack of crates near the ship. Blood continues to drain from my poorly wrapped wound as splinters of wood fly across my peripheral. This has to be the work of a god or a goddess toying with me before escorting me to my death.

Holding onto my consciousness like a fraying thread, I attempt to survey the beach-turned-supernatural battlefield in search of the pirate and his iron case. As if finding the gemstone will magically make my wraith-like restraints disappear. It's useless. At this rate, Rhydian won't even have the chance to torture me for my failure. All I can do is hope by some miracle, whatever deity is playing with me like a cursed doll will grant me a quick and painless death.

The debris of damaged crates rumbles beneath my back as a thunderous roar rattles the skies. Before I can finish filling my lungs with my next breath, a colossal, black dragon emerges from the shadowy haze. As it barrels toward the earth, I can barely distinguish the figure of a woman atop its back.

The feminine silhouette appears to raise an arm, and ropes of shadows shoot down from the charcoal fog as if under her command. There's no way this is real. I can only recollect Rhydian's mentions of earth, wind, water, and fire mages. Not shadow mages. Hallucinating from severe blood loss and unexplainable, excruciating pain has to be the only logical explanation.

In a blurry haze, my eyes follow the trail of her shadows, tracing them down to the half-conscious pirate, convulsing in shock on the other side of the beach. "Kill me. Please," he shouts. Between the buckets of blood spilling from his neck and his gouged eye socket, it's no wonder he's begging for death after staring down that horrific beast.

The vine-like shadows wrap around the iron case and rip it from his belt. Within heartbeats, they recede and deliver the case to the dragon's rider. She catches it in her hand without taking her rage-filled eyes off me. An incinerating blast of fire pours from the dragon's maw, charring the pirate to a mound of ash to oblige his plea for death as my vision fades to black.

CHAPTER 3
The Shadow Mage

Pure darkness engulfs my weightless body as I drift through a silent void. Trapped in a state of paralysis, I find myself unable to call out to my body. A hypnotic floating sensation is all that responds as I fail to conjure any form of movement. I attempt to scream, yet no sound escapes from my lungs. Is this what it feels like when your soul departs from your body? I don't have any memories of being incinerated by dragon fire, but nothing about this state of paralysis convinces me I'm still alive.

All I know is there is no way my soul could find its way to The Immortal Realms of Niroshen with all the blood that stains my hands. Perhaps that woman and her dragon were angels of death, sentencing me to The Dark Realms to eternally punish my soul. If that's the case, I'll spend my eternity raising a hell of my own until they claim Rhydian's soul to join mine in torment.

An alluring concoction of lavender and sage slowly stirs my senses. The scent is ethereal, perhaps belonging to an angel of death on her way to escort me to Osiris. The rest of my senses slowly return to me as cold, bitter air bites my skin. A rough, jagged texture agitates the surface of my back. My weightless body begins to feel heavily restrained again. What in the realms is happening to me?

After breaking free of my paralysis, my eyes open to a flood of bright light. Frosty, crisp air abrasively caresses my skin as my hair lashes through harsh winds and stings my face like a whip. As my eyes slowly re-adjust to the light, I find myself still bound by shadowy restraints. The dagger has been removed from my thigh, and my bloody tunic scraps have been replaced with proper bandages while I was out cold. I thrash in a violent terror once I realize the ground beneath me is not the iron sand of Tourmaline Beach but rather a back of coarse, black scales. Reality finally hits. I am floating thousands of feet above the earth on the back of a dragon.

Waves of panic and shock crash through me like raging oceans. I do not understand how my heart has not yet collapsed from sprinting its marathon inside my chest. It's half-tempting to attempt a dive into the abysmal, foggy void. Taking my chances on eternity in The Dark Realms might serve me better than facing whatever fate awaits me. My restraints tighten as if in response to my temptations, allowing me no other movement other than expanding my lungs.

"Looks like you're finally awake. Try not to panic too much. Protocol states I have to deliver you to The High Priestess alive," a smooth, dark voice cuts through the howling winds.

I shift my gaze off my restraints and fixate on the woman holding the reins of her dragon, flying us somewhere likely very ungodly. Her eyes of ashen smoke cut me a lethal glare under thick, flawless brows. The slit in her left brow only makes her gaze that much more intimidating to consume. Somehow, I can't look away.

Crashing waves of long, raven-black hair perfectly contrast the tone of her porcelain skin. Black, sleeveless fighting leathers cling tightly to her curves and accentuate her muscular frame. Tattoos of dark, venomous snakes cover the lengths of her arms. The ink on her skin serves as a chilling symbolism of the serpentine shadows she possesses the ability to wield and weaponize as if she was made to become the death of me.

"Quit your gawking, peasant. I'm not your liberator from whatever pathetic life you live. I'd be surprised if you live long enough to see tomorrow's sunrise," she snorts.

"I'm no stranger to living every day sunrise to sunrise," I retort. "And try not to flatter yourself, darling. I'm only fantasizing about how satisfying it would be to hack you to pieces and feed you to that dragon of yours."

The bed of scales beneath me rumbles like an earthquake as her dragon lets out a bone-shattering roar. Bursts of fire emit from its breath and hurl toward me, barely missing my flesh. The quick, scorching blast of heat leaves my skin violently sunburned and every bone in my body trembling.

"Sarthon and I share a special bond. I'd watch what you say about me in his presence. His patience runs a lot thinner than mine."

I don't dare open my mouth with any counter remark. As much as I hate it, I have no upper hand in this predicament. There are no cards I could possibly play to turn the tides in my favor.

Rich violet, tangerine, and amber tones paint the skies as day turns to dusk. Rhydian is probably wondering where I am by now, fantasizing about how to make my death as slow and painful as humanly possible once I fail to return with his precious stone. Standing no chance in holding my own against a shadow-mage and a dragon, I can only hope whatever death awaits me will be quicker and far more merciful than death by Rhydian's hands.

My heart plummets into my stomach as we begin to make our descent. I don't know if I should feel relief that emerald foliage is becoming visible again or if I should speculate on whatever The High Priestess intends to do with me. Will I be condemned to serve a life sentence, chained up in a dungeon? Will I be publicly executed in a town square as Rhydian watches from the crowd? All I know is one way or another, Rhydian and this damned dragon knight will follow me into death. If they drag me under, I'll guarantee they sink with me.

"We're finally here. It's about damn time I can finally get you out of my hair," the woman scoffs.

Dense layers of fog begin to dissipate, unveiling a massive, snow-capped mountain. Ghostly haze weaves through its peaks and emits a strange, spiritual aura. Blackthorn has always been known as a spiritual nation, and it feels as if this mountain was formed to encourage its people to climb up to the gods and reach for their blessings.

A massive, charcoal-stoned monastery rests on the top of its highest peak. Beams of sunsetting light reflect off immaculate stained-glass windows and produce burning, fiery light. Lights flicker at the bottom of the mountain as if praising all its beauty. Vertigo taunts my head as I look down at the sights of a large, luminescent city.

"Again, quit your gawking, peasant. That's Vespera, Blackthorn's capital city. There's no place for treacherous scum within its walls."

I ignore the jeer and silently gawk at the sight of hundreds of dragons stretching their wings across the tangerine horizon. Despite being edged by death for an entire day, I can't help but gasp in awe of the mystical, terrifying beauty surrounding me. If only I could admire it from the peace of solitude.

My moment of admiration fades as our descent ends on the monastery grounds. Sarthon lands with graceful precision, digging his claws into the earth the moment we touch down. His rider dismounts her saddle and slides down a rope of shadows to bring herself to the ground. I pray to the gods that Sarthon will ride off into the sunset and buy me a fool's shot at slaying my captor and escaping to the wilderness.

Tendrils of shadows shoot up from the ground and latch onto my restraints. "One wrong move, and Sarthon and I will fight over who gets to squander you to a pile of dust."

The shadows violently tear me away from Sarthon's back and send me to the ground in a disorienting whiplash. I fumble over my footing and slam directly into the dragon knight. She looks down at me with a murderous gaze. Her ashen eyes pierce like knives as she lowers her head to whisper in my ear.

"One. Wrong. Move. That's all it takes," she smirks as I swallow the rock in my throat.

The woman yanks on my restraints and leads me down a dark, cobblestone path leading to the monastery. Its arched, stained glass windows are even more breathtaking up close. Earthy scents of old, musty books seep from its thick, stone walls.

A man with messy black hair swept between blood-red eyes meets us at the raised portcullis of the monastery's entrance. He's clothed in a crimson tunic and charcoal trousers and equipped with an exquisitely crafted rapier that puts my sword to shame.

"Felix, please be so kind as to strip this scum of her weapons. She appeared proficient with them when I plucked her from the beach." I chuckle at the condescending insult. Proficient is a gross understatement.

"Very well, Instructor Adrienne."

"Oh, so that monster has a name, and she's an instructor? How impressive!" I roll my eyes. Adrienne appears nearly the same age as me, and somehow, she's both an instructor and a dragon knight. It's amazing how drastically different life treats those who aren't born as lowly orphans in poverty-stricken slums. Adrienne reeks of noble mage privilege.

"I'd watch your tone if I were you. You're in the heart of mage territory now, so don't get cocky," Felix warns, summoning a warning flame in the palm of his hands before collecting my sword and daggers. Great. A fire mage.

"My apologies…Felix. Adrienne has been an absolute joy during our journey. I have *nothing* but kind things to say about her."

Adrienne tightens the shadows around my torso until I cough and gasp for air. "Your struggle is music to my ears," she laughs darkly before easing up on the tension.

"Felix, please inform Lady Rhonwen we are ready to meet in the interrogation chamber."

"I will send your word and begin the preparations," he responds, casting me one last disapproving glare before storming off.

"I can't wait to see what The High Priestess wants to do with you,"

Adrienne hisses.

CHAPTER 4
The Questioning

Adrienne throws me into a chair in the center of the dark, windowless room. The only light source comes from a luminous, ethereal silhouette of a woman clothed in a glistening white gown. I almost wouldn't be surprised if she were some sort of white wraith. Stranger things have happened today. Between her haunting presence, Felix menacingly guarding the door, and Adrienne standing over my chair, I'm unsure who I should fear the most.

"Lady Rhonwen. I found this peasant trash attempting to intercept a particular item from our expected shipment supply this morning. Not only that, but it appears she killed the entire pirate crew. A squad has been sent to clean up the aftermath and retrieve whatever supplies are still salvageable," Adrienne relays to the glowing silhouette.

"Thank you, Adrienne. We will get to the bottom of this atrocity."

Lady Rhonwen steps forward, appearing slightly more human the closer she approaches. An intricate crown of diamonds bright as moonlight rests atop her head of snowy, white tresses. Her glacial eyes alone are enough to convince me she's the ruler of Blackthorn.

"I'll start by introducing myself to our guest. As you have heard, I am Lady Rhonwen, High Priestess of Blackthorn. I am a descendant of Elethea, The Goddess of Truth and Healing. Your cooperation during this process will help us resolve our matters efficiently."

"Lady Rhonwen will determine the severity of your punishment. I suggest you speak only the truth. Speak only when spoken to, or I will slice your tongue right out of your mouth," Adrienne snarls.

I let out a flat, emotionless chuckle. "Doesn't a room full of sacred half-mortals have anything better to do than harass lowly peasant trash, as you like to call me?"

A rope of shadows forms around my neck and threatens to crush my windpipe as Adrienne's fingers curl into white-knuckled fists. "There are much better ways I would rather be using my time right now. Perhaps I should start with crushing your lungs first." My blood burns with electrifying rage as I gasp for air. I will not die at the hands of pretentious mages.

"Adrienne! Control yourself. Do not allow your short temper to compromise this interrogation," Felix warns.

"Like you're one to talk," she mutters under her breath. The rope disappears from my neck, allowing me to gasp for air.

"What is your name, and why did you murder a group of pirates on the shores of Tourmaline this morning?" Lady Rhonwen asks.

"My name is Amira, and I should be considered innocent of whatever charges you wish to pin against me. I was just following orders assigned to me by Captain Rhydian. If you don't want to waste your time, you should be going after him instead."

Felix extends his fist. At his command, a ring of towering flames encircles my chair, burning my skin with smothering heat. "Your full cooperation is a demand. Not a request. I won't hesitate to command my fire to swallow you alive. If you are telling the truth, what in the realms did Rhydian order you to do?"

"What was it that you said about temper?" Adrienne retaliates.

Felix reels back his rage and smothers his flames.

"Don't be shy, my love. Why don't you share the specifics?" Adrienne drops to her knee, meeting me at eye level. I swallow the rock-solid lump in my throat and clench my trembling knees together, refraining from looking directly into her silver irises. Gods, I wish my heart wasn't sprinting out of my chest in response to the taunting way she said my love. The sooner I can secure an opportunity to kill the shadow mage, the better.

"Rhydian is one of our most reliable contractors. Last I heard, he hasn't been given any new assignments. What did he ask you to do for him?" She asks.

The sooner you cooperate, the sooner you can plot your escape, I tell myself with a deep sigh. "I was ordered to retrieve a gemstone for him and to leave none of the pirates alive so they couldn't be questioned about the ordeal."

"You mean…*this*?" Adrienne reaches into her pocket for the iron case and pulls out a sparkling, white stone. Excruciating, sharp bolts of pain shoot into my head and blast down my spine. My body thrashes in unrelenting waves of agony. I fall backward in my chair and collapse to the floor. This pain is somehow worse than what I experienced on the beach. Now, it's as if I'm being electrocuted from the inside out.

"Make it stop! Make it stop!" I scream from the top of my lungs.

"Adrienne! Enclose that luminary and deliver it to me at once!" Lady Rhonwen orders, her eyes widened in bewilderment.

Adrienne returns the stone to its iron case and hands it to The High Priestess. The excruciating, electrifying pain stops when Lady Rhonwen conceals the case in her gown.

"Gods above, how is that possible?" Felix mutters under his breath with a stunned expression behind his fire-red eyes.

"It appears the light luminary may be calling out to Amira," Lady Rhonwen answers. "Her pain appears to be genuine."

"Luminaries only call out to half-mortals who wield the element of its design. Adrienne, I thought you said she was just some peasant. Did you suspect she could be anything more?" Felix asks in a perplexed panic.

"How could I have? She hasn't displayed any indicators she can wield an element. My astonishment is no greater than yours," Adrienne hisses.

"That's enough." Lady Rhonwen reigns in control over the room. "It is possible Amira may be a light mage. That would make her a descendant of Kallik, The God of Light. Blackthorn hasn't seen a light mage in centuries, so her heart and soul must be examined. If she truly can wield Kallik's light, she could pose as a great hope or a lethal threat to all Elmoria. I hereby sentence Amira to Trial by the Kanoelani Forest first thing tomorrow morning. The Spirits will condemn her to The Dark Realms if they deem her existence a threat to The Mortal Realms."

"It's also entirely possible she's just feigning her reaction to the stone as a ploy to get off the hook long enough to plan an escape," Adrienne interjects. "There's no way that scum is a descendant of Kallik," her cheeks flush in crimson rage.

"Can someone help me off the ground here and explain what this is all about?" I shout, still tipped over in my chair, bound by Adrienne's shadows.

Felix reluctantly picks up my chair and continues the conversation like I'm not in the room. "Speaking from a tactical standpoint, if the light luminary truly calls her, and she's truly a light mage, she would become an invaluable asset to our forces. With Eldermoor on the move, we need all the dragon knights we can acquire," Felix suggests.

Adrienne shoots him a fuming glare. "Don't get your hopes up so easily. Even if the Kanoelani Spirits reveal she is a true light mage and not a threat, that doesn't mean she will automatically fly out of her trials on the back of a dragon. It's still possible the forest decides she is not worthy of becoming a dragon knight and executes her on the spot. Half-mortal or not."

"I couldn't imagine a world where the spirits decide a light mage isn't worthy of becoming a dragon knight," Felix counters.

"Enough of this useless bickering," Lady Rhonwen orders. "We've accomplished all that we can for tonight. Adrienne, assign and escort Amira to a room for the night. Fly her to Kanoelani first thing in the morning. In the meantime, I will commission a squad to retrieve Captain Rhydian and bring him in for questioning. Interfering with our supplies shipment alone is an act of treason, and if his sights were truly set on the light luminary…that is gravely concerning. You are all dismissed."

Adrienne releases the shadows from my torso, replacing them with a new rope around my wrists. After losing track of how many hours I spent in that bind, my body feels lighter than a feather.

"Warming up to me now, are we? How brave of you," I sneer.

"Any longer in your old bind, and you'd eventually pass out. Unfortunately, The High Priestess would not be pleased with that. I'll remind you one last time today: don't try anything stupid. The monastery is surrounded by elite knights, ruthless dragons, and their half-mortal riders. Any cute little sparring tricks will get you nowhere against anyone within these walls." Adrienne escorts me out of the interrogation chamber through a dark labyrinth of torchlit halls.

"While you have me here, I think it's my turn to ask a few questions. What is this Kanoelani Forest trial? Do you really think even if I were some half-mortal brat, I would automatically swear my allegiance to you? Working for you knights indirectly through Rhydian has been insufferable enough."

First Captain Rhydian, now this pretentious shadow-wielding brat. I am done offering my service to anyone. Maybe getting sentenced to some forest trial is exactly what I need. If surviving its alleged spirits purchases my long sought-after solitude, this could be my pathway to freedom.

"The chances of you ever emerging from that forest are next to none, so least I can do is allow you to die with a morsel of dignity." Adrienne scoffs.

"The Kanoelani Forest homes the hatching grounds of Blackthorn's dragons and the ancient veradis spirits. Veradis Spirits are capable of shifting into whatever lethal form they desire. There are endless possibilities of how they may choose to kill you tomorrow."

"For such deadly spirits, how is this the first time I'm hearing anything about them?"

"Because you're a lowly, uneducated peasant who clearly never studied any religious texts," Adrienne snorts. "The veradis spirits are eternally bound to The Kanoelani by order of the gods to protect and care for the hatchlings while mature dragons defend Blackthorn with their riders as dragon knights. The spirits also serve Blackthorn by judging the hearts and souls of every half-mortal born into this world. Every half-mortal born into this world is subjected to The Kanoelani Trials. It's part of how we preserve the balance of all Elmoria," she explains.

"If the spirits deem them a trustworthy, dependable ally, they will present the half-mortal before an un-bonded dragon of their discernment. The dragon, chosen by the spirits, then makes the final decision. They can bond the half-mortal or incinerate them on the spot if they feel the spirits made a lapse in judgment."

"So, half-mortals are either fated to serve as dragon knights or assumed to be a lethal parasite and sentenced to death?" I scoff.

"Elmoria rests on a very delicate balance. By nature, the very existence of half-mortals either protects that balance or threatens to destroy it. The gods possess infinite power beyond our comprehension. Any soul containing even a morsel of that power must be evaluated to preserve life as we know it," Adrienne explains, her tone reeking of boredom.

"And if it turns out I'm not a half-mortal?" I ask sheepishly, finding it impossible to believe I'm some half-mortal descendant of a god. Surely, any powers would've manifested by now. I would've slaughtered Rhydian in a slow, torturous death if I could wield whatever powers manifest from a light mage.

"If you're fully human, you'll be weeded out by the trials and killed as an intruder of a sacred forest. A full-blooded mortal cannot survive the trials by design, and the spirits don't take kindly to mankind." Adrienne flashes me a sadistic smile, fully expecting the trials to claim my life.

Apprehension slices through my nerves and stabs me in the gut. There is no winning. There is no escape. Either I'll be sentenced to death for one reason or another, or I'll be fated to serve as a dragon knight due to some divine, unrevealed bloodline I've possessed my entire life. If somehow my death would be mercifully quick, I would much rather prefer an execution over a lifetime in servitude to The Knights of Blackthorn.

We finally arrive at my room for the night, heavily guarded by armed sentries. The idea of sleeping in a bedroom is uncomfortably foreign. I can't recall if I've ever slept anywhere other than in a flimsy tent out in the elements. Even back on Rhydian's property, none of his adoptees have been permitted to rest within the warmth of his cabin. We all slept in tents, relying on each others' body heat for survival during the blistery winter months.

A bed draped in thick, ivory blankets rests beneath a large arched window. A dark wooden armoire marked with floral carvings is tucked in a corner at the opposite end of the room. A goblet of water and a plate of steaming hot food are waiting for me on a tiny desk adjacent to the botanical armoire. The amenities are so luxurious I wouldn't be surprised if it's a trap. As if sensing my hesitation to enter the room, Adrienne shoves me right through the door.

"Those sentries posted at your door are earth mages. Try anything funny, and you'll slowly asphyxiate in an encapsulation of stone. Unfortunately, that food isn't laced with any special poison, so you can scarf it down worry-free. The High Priestess graciously orders that every trial participant receives nourishment and rest before entering The Kanoelani. Sleep tight, my love." Adrienne gives me a mocking wink before slamming the door shut.

At least I finally get a moment of longly-desired solitude. I give in to my grumbling stomach and dig into the juicy, smoked turkey leg and steamed potatoes at my tiny desk. This meal was undoubtedly prepared in an adept kitchen rather than scraps hastily cooked over a campfire. Whenever Rhydian's pupils, including myself, have taken down a turkey, deer, or any sizable kill, he has always reaped the bulk of our efforts. We were always left to feed off his table scraps.

Never sleep with both eyes closed when out in the field. Never fall prey to the element of surprise. Captain Rhydian's voice rings loudly in my brain as if he is breathing down my neck. The earth-wielding sentries guarding my door don't stop me from scanning my dark room for his presence. Rhydian haunts me like an incurable disease.

I muse on how long a squad of Blackthorn's knights will take to track down the blood-lusting bastard. He is certainly no fool. That vile mastermind has skillfully hidden measureless atrocities from them for decades through his skillfully deceitful mask of charm. His charm seduces the wives of nobles and paints him as the savior of the slums. Until tonight, the knights have only known him as a loving, adoptive fatherly figure with a heart for orphans.

The Knights have practically entrusted the fate of the peasant slum villages to his care. They commission him to clean the streets of the slums and keep the heart of their focus on Vespera and Blackthorn's wealthier, flourishing cities. As much as I vehemently despise the knights, I pray for their success in his capture. I envy whichever coddled knight that will get to deliver his execution. I envision Rhydian dying by my hands instead until falling into a deep sleep with both eyes closed.

CHAPTER 5
The Kanoelani Trials

Faint traces of sulfur mixed with Adrienne's haunting scent of lavender and sage begin slowly arousing my senses. A bitter wind greets my face and ripples through my hair. I half-consciously pull my blankets over my head to block it out. Tendrils of thick, black haze throw the blankets to the floor and wrap around my torso. A moment later, I'm thrown through my bedroom window and crash into a sea of dark, spiny scales. Sarthon.

"Rise and shine, peasant." Adrienne's silver eyes greet mine in a threatening glare. The wind tosses her raven-black hair against her face like ocean waves to the midnight shoreline. She appears as an angel of death, leading me to my execution with a beaming smile.

"Eager to get rid of me, I take it?" The twilight sky suggests she couldn't wait until sunrise to deliver me to my death.

"You have no idea," she chuckles.

If Adrienne is escorting me to my death, I refuse to go down without a fight. Foolish of her to leave my legs unbound. I wait for Adrienne to take her eyes off me and return her focus to the horizon before making my desperate move. I rock my body back and forth until I create enough momentum to rise to my knees. Then to my feet. Driven by rage and the knowledge my death is inevitable, I charge down Sarthon's back, intending to push her over the edge with me. If I'm lucky, Sarthon will let out a blast of fire in panic and incinerate us both.

As expected, Sarthon releases a thunderous roar followed by a blast of flames. However, I failed to account for how the intensity of his roar would impact sprinting across his back in a lethal balancing game. Seismic-like vibrations throw me into a foggy abyss before I get anywhere near reaching Adrienne. My lungs struggle to grab the crisp, early spring air as I rapidly free fall. I can't collect a single coherent thought amongst the loudness of the rushing winds terrorizing my eardrums.

A thick, black rope latches onto my restraints, halting my descent to death in a violent jolt. Adrienne slowly hoists me back up through the air until I am returned to my scaly seat.

"You're damn lucky I'm under direct orders to make sure you arrive to the Kanoelani Forest alive." Adrienne's ashen irises morph into pools of obsidian as black smoke seeps from her flared nostrils. My throat tightens, nearly choking me as I swallow. Ropes of shadows wrap down the lengths of my legs until my entire body is bound in a wraith-like cocoon. "Just a little further, and hopefully, we'll never see each other again," she snarls.

* * *

The dense fog that blankets Blackthorn's mountainous skies intensifies beyond its usual thickness. I can't get rid of the sensation of being watched. Intimately. It feels as if mystical entities are already analyzing my every heartbeat. The rise and fall of my chest feels as if under strict surveillance. I've grown accustomed to the feeling of being watched behind my back between the years of Rhydian's threats, the consequences of letting my guard down, and in the villages of the enemies I have slain. However, nothing can compare to the feeling of being watched internally, as if hoards of creatures are staring down my soul.

Strange, golden lights twinkling in the cloudy haze help me shift some focus off the discomfort of my unforgiving restraints. The lights appear to be dancing in a mysterious, choreographed disarray. Their melodic swirling patterns invite me to dive deep into mesmerization. I'm mostly convinced they could pull me into an alluring state of hypnosis if I stared at them for too long. Sarthon lets out a gentle, rumbling growl as if communicating with the lights.

"Welcome home, Sarthon," Adrienne whispers to her dragon. We begin to descend deeper into the dense, ethereal mist. There isn't a single inch of my existence that doesn't feel vulnerable. I try my hardest to shake the feeling and remain alert to the strange surroundings. The golden, dancing lights are the only objects that can be seen clearly. Despite clearly descending into an enormous forest, thousands of trees only appear as dark silhouettes hiding behind the fog.

We finally land into thick layers of glowing moss, blanketing the ground. Adrienne reels me down from Sarthon's back by the ropes of my restraints before setting me free of the bind. She knows by now I've learned challenging her only humiliates me further.

Adrienne grabs a fistful of my hair and yanks my head back, tilting my head up to her soul-crushing eyes. Before I can tempt myself to fight against her grip, she forces a potent elixir down my throat. Warm, metallic liquid slithers down my esophagus and throws me into an instant state of vertigo. It takes all my strength to refrain from stumbling to the ground. Returning to my feet might be next to impossible if I do collapse.

"That's my girl. I hope you're ready to face your demons."

Adrienne winks at me before she jumps into the air. Black smoke forms beneath her feet and propels her up to her mount on Sarthon's back. Before they entirely disappear into the fog, my sword and daggers drop from the sky as Adrienne's sinister laugh trails off in the distance. At least I'm no longer defenseless.

I awkwardly fumble to secure my daggers to my thigh bandolier and hold onto the hilt of my sword. It takes a copious amount of effort to assess my surroundings in my intoxicating haze. An endless labyrinth of foggy forest surrounds the small clearing, inducing mild claustrophobia. The mystical frequencies that harmonized with the winds of the sky have gone silent since landing on solid ground. Dead silence in a forest engrossed in ancient spirits and ruthless dragons is an alarming flag for concern. I shouldn't be able to hear the blood circulating throughout my body.

Rustling leaves and snapping twigs interrupt the deafening silence. My stomach roils at the thought of being hunted. I tighten my grip on the hilt of my sword and hone my focus on the dense, whispering thicket. Waves of vertigo and nausea compete for my attention as I attempt to locate the source of movement.

Despite my disorientation, it doesn't take long before I notice glowing blood-red eyes stalking me from the darkness of the brush. Every muscle in my body stiffens. Upon further observation, it appears the eyes belong to the body of a massive wolf. It steps into the clearing, coated in smoky, obsidian vapor rather than fur. A demonic, ear-shattering scream escapes from its maw as it begins charging after me.

"Heed my voice if you wish to survive," A faint, airy voice seeps into my mind. *"Walk away. Walk briskly, but do not run. Never turn your back on a vapor wolf."*

Am I hallucinating? Having no time to prepare an attack against a creature I don't understand, I listen and obey. Without turning my back on the ghostly, smoke-swirling wolf, I begin to inch away as slowly as I can manage.

The creature lets out another agonizing shriek, sending electrifying shivers down my spine. It takes every morsel of discipline not to sprint upon catching a glimpse of razor-sharp fangs drenched in blood. By some divine miracle, the wolf's charging sprint has transitioned to a slow, stalking prowl. Listening to this strange, hallucinogenic voice seems to be working to my advantage so far.

"Do not run."

I obey, walking backward until I trip over a branch and fall to the ground. No. Not a branch, but a shackle of chains. What is a shackle of chains doing in the middle of a forest? The vaporous wolf, triggered by my abrupt movement, stops dead in its tracks— pools of saliva now frothing from its bloody maw.

"You are going to grab those chains and rattle them. Before you even dare getting back up."

Listening to the external voice inside my head now feels like a mistake. I aim my sword, blade pointing in the direction of the wolf. Won't creating more racket aggravate it? I think to myself. I need to defend myself, not dig myself into a deeper grave.

"Choose your actions wisely. I suggest you rattle those chains," the voice responds as if it read my thoughts.

The vapor wolf takes off into lethal pursuit. A wolf-like body of black smoke and gleaming red eyes thunders towards me, licking its feral fangs. Knifelike claws dig into my shoulders, drenching my tunic in my blood as I let out a scream. A choir of trilling shrieks echo from the thicket as if a response to my scream.

A pack of vapor wolves emerges from the hazy brush, sprinting towards us. Bile rises in my throat as I realize I'm about to be devoured by a pack of wraith-like wolves. I began slicing with my sword to no avail. My blade cuts right through their ghostly bodies without dealing a trace of damage. These wolves will tear the limbs from my body within seconds unless I can figure out an effective way to slaughter them.

"Heed my warning or your death will be inevitable. Rattle those chains. NOW."

Having only a moment to define either my death or my victory, I choose to rattle the chains and put down my blade. I pray to the gods my blood loss won't send me into shock. Heavy wolf paws drive claws deeper into my skin, further incapacitating my movement. I rattle the chains again, as violently as I can manage, with my shoulders pinned to the ground. The wolves let out another round of agonizing shrieks as they begin violently convulsing. They convulse like a violent exorcism until vanishing into thin air.

I take a moment to collect my breath before prying my bruised, blood-soaked body off the ground. I cut through the fabric of my trousers to create tourniquets for my most severe wounds. The last thing I need is a trail of my blood alerting any more spirits…or dragons, that I am injured and vulnerable.

With the majority of my legs now exposed, the cold spring air stings my skin. My vision is dizzied and blurred between the effects of blood loss and whatever vile elixir Adrienne shoved down my throat. If I have any hope of survival, I'll need to learn how to kill anything that comes after me.

"The veradis spirits cannot be killed. Those vapor wolves you encountered still patrol the forest elsewhere, along with countless creatures far more powerful," the anomalous voice creeps into my mind once more.

"Who are you? What do you want with me?" I'm not entirely sure why I'm calling out loud to a voice inside my head. At this point, I'm convinced I'm starting to lose my sanity.

"I may answer your questions if you survive long enough to find me."

"Find you? Do I even want to find you? How do I know you aren't just leading me into a trap?" I continue arguing with the voice as if it's more than a hallucination.

"Answering your questions would result in the automatic failure of your trials. You don't want that now, do you?"

"I don't know what I want. I don't even know if I want to survive. I'll deal with you later." There's no point in exerting more energy arguing with this voice inside my head like a madwoman.

I scan the layers of forest that surround the clearing of glowing moss. Searching for anything that might help me decide the wisest path to tread. No flocks of birds flying overhead. The sun is not rising yet to help me discern which way is east. Moss seemingly consumes the entire surfaces of the rocks and trees it touches, making it impossible to discern which way is truly north. The dead silence of the Kanoelani creeps back in, exposing every beat of my heart. Every path that leads into dark labyrinths of trees clothed in fog feels identical.

"No! Please! Stop!" A panicked voice shouts from the depths of the woods, different from the other voice I've been hearing.

"Help! Please!"

I debate if I should investigate, or if I should take off in the opposite direction before becoming the next victim.

"Amira! Please! Help me, please!"

My blood goes cold. The cries become familiar. They're the cries that frequently plague my nightmares and wake me in vicious fits of dry heaving and tears.

It has been five years since any voice has brought warmth into my life. Since any voice has served as a beacon of hope worth fighting for.

"Amira!"

Hearing my name cried out in such familiar desperation brings back an ocean of memories that will haunt me to my grave. Memories I had to bury as deep as possible to find any hope in numbing the eternal hole in my heart. Tears blur my vision. I rattle the shackle of chains now fastened to my belt to ward off any additional vapor wolves and sprint toward the painfully recognizable cries.

I blindly race through the fog, weaving between evergreens and jumping over mossy rocks. I pump my legs past towering vines rooted intermittently amongst the trees. I don't care if my sprinting draws the attention of any new threats or dragons. I am a force of violence to contend with.

If my next trial is somehow a second chance to save my love, to somehow bring him back from the dead, I am not failing this time. I will singlehandedly face every horrific creature these trials throw at me if reviving Casimir and returning him to my arms is the prize.

A trail of fresh blood freezes me dead in my tracks as waves of suppressed nightmares send me drowning in my own brain. *"Amira! Do something! Please!"* Casimir's cries grow louder and louder. The only logical explanation my brain can conjure is some damned spirits rose Casimir from the dead just to torture him all over again. My trial must be to succeed in saving him this time. Adrenaline pushes my exhausted body forward as I resume sprinting along the trail of spilled blood.

Five years without Casimir might as well have been an eternity. I slam the images of his lifeless body lying limp in my arms to the back of my mind. Somehow, fate is giving us a second chance. The Veradis Spirits will be begging for my mercy until they return him to me.

I find his bruised and battered body lying prone on the ground. His bludgeoned face appears just as horrific as it did five years ago. I can't breathe. My stomach twists into irreversible knots as the worst day of my life repeats itself in front of my eyes. Casimir is in the same fatal condition I found him in during the final moments of his short life. No spirits or dragons are found towering over his dying body. Instead, I find Helmar. Helmar, the wanted serial killer Casimir was assigned to dispatch. I butchered his body to pieces that night. How could the spirits have orchestrated all this?

"You were a damn fool for letting him out of your sight. Sweating out your fever back at The Captain's camp rather than accompanying your lover on such a deadly assignment. He would've stood a fighting chance if you didn't hesitate to join him," Helmar taunts.

I was far too late by the time I finally decided to track Casimir's tracks through the snow that night. I should've gone after him when he failed to return by dusk rather than waiting until nightfall. When I finally found him, his entire body had been carved to shreds as his body lay limp outside Helmar's camp. I threw my blade against Helmar relentlessly until I gained the upper hand and tore his body apart. Casimir then sputtered his final words in my arms. I love you, my sunbeam. Fight for hope, Amira. Fight for a brighter Blackthorn. I am always with you.

My vision is blurred through stinging tears at the sight of Casimir dying before me. Again. "You are not taking him from me again!"

Seething hatred sears my blood as I charge down Helmar with daggers aimed for the kill in each hand. I killed him once, and I will kill him again. He throws his fists equipped with spiked knuckle gauntlets in a series of quick maneuvers as I dodge each blow. I slide my body between the wide stance of his muscular legs and slice a blade through his left achilles. He loses his footing as he takes another swing at me. I deflect it with one of my blades.

"Amira! Watch out!"

As quickly as I regain my fighting stance, I'm met with a blow of spiked gauntlets to my cheek. I can feel the warmth of my blood trickling down my neck as Helmar pins me to the ground.

"You know what I've always hated about that conniving bastard you call your captain? He sends his dogs after his prey rather than fight his own battles. What a shame I have to kill one of the useless pups he sent after me."

An electrifying surge of energy charges through my veins as I drive a dagger through his chest. I escape from beneath him and repeatedly stab him over and over again. Sparks of white light dance on the tips of my blades, sending him into a violent convulsion before his body vaporizes. Before I release my breath, his body reappears over Casimir's and drives his gauntlets straight through his chest with brute force. Blood spews out of Casimir's mouth.

Whatever was left of my fragmented soul is now gone. No words form out of my mouth. Just a guttural scream as I charge Helmar with inhuman speed I did not know I could possess. I throw my entire body weight into vengefully piercing my daggers through his chest. He attempts to rip the daggers from his chest, but I grant him no opportunity. I throw countless punches to his face.

A raging electrical current begins flowing through my veins, charging my punches with literal shocks. With tiny bolts of lightning dancing on my fingertips, I continue to throw my rage into pummeling his face, sending him into another round of convulsions before his body suddenly vaporizes from beneath mine.

I scan my surroundings, waiting for him to reemerge. Nothing. Just the eerie stillness of the woods. It becomes clear Helmar, or whatever that thing was, will not be making another appearance.

"Casimir," I whisper through my breathless sobs. "It's okay, Casimir, it's okay. Stay with me, okay? We're getting out of here together. We can find a way to heal you somehow." I examine his critical condition. Multiple cracked ribs. His entire body is laden with lacerations as he continues coughing up blood.

"I'm sorry Amira, I'm afraid I won't be coming. You know what I ask of you though. Remember?" Casimir struggles to form his words in between coughing up bursts of blood.

"I love you, my sunbeam. Fight for hope, Amira. Fight for a brighter Blackthorn. I am always with you," he chokes.

"Don't talk like that. You're going to be okay. We're going to get you help." I pull his body in as tight as I can against mine. I embrace him like our lives depend on how tightly I can hold onto him, starved for his soul to face this world with mine. I rest my head on his chest, seeking the comfort of his heartbeat. His pulse vanishes. Casimir's body vaporizes out of my arms, vanishing into the dense, spiritual fog.

I collapse into a sea of uncontrollable sobs, cursing The Kanoelani from the top of my lungs. Adrienne wasn't joking when she said I would be fighting my inner demons. Nothing could have prepared me for getting lured into such a sickening, soul-shattering illusion.

"You have fought valiantly, daughter of Kallik. You have shown you

are capable of confronting your darkness with a heart of courage and that you're worthy of wielding the light."

I want nothing more than to silence the voice calling out to me and never hear it again. What good is wielding light when all hope for my life has vanished? Without hope, there is no light.

"Stop! Please, stop! What do you want from me? Name your price for leaving me alone and I'll pay it!"

A blast of warm steam spills out of the trees and rustles my hair like a summery breeze. Two vibrant, violet eyes slice through the fog, towering far, far over the trees. The ground rumbles beneath my feet. I unsheathe my sword in a startled panic. If I'm going to die by dragon fire, I'll at least go down with a blade in my hands.

"Lower your weapons, child."

Without hesitation, I obey and sheathe my sword. If I have learned anything in this forest, it's to obey the commands of its voices. I stoop to one knee and lower my head in a reverent bow, surrendering that I am nothing but a guest in the spiritual domain of dragons.

"Great darkness plagues your heart, yet you have shown you can still call upon the light. You are a worthy warrior, Amira. Daughter of Kallik, please rise."

My knees buckle, and I nearly lose the contents of my stomach, but I obey. Shock threatens to throw me back to the ground the moment it fully hits that I am standing in the presence of a colossal, opalescent dragon. Her scales are white as snow, casting glints of rainbow light. She's equally as terrifying as she is mesmerizing.

"My name is Lumithra. I sense the great potential that flows within you, Amira. You have the potential to emit beams of hope from the light that you wield. Much is at stake not only for The Nation of Blackthorn but for all the lands of Elmoria. The world needs a light mage to join the fight for its balance."

"I-I'm afraid I don't understand," my voice wavers, fretting to find an appropriate response. A response that won't turn my body to heaps of ash. "Blackthorn has its weaknesses, but overall, our nation is at peace. Is this another trial I must face?"

"Your next trial extends far beyond The Kanoelani, my child. Close your eyes and empty your mind. There is much you need to see."

I slam my clamorous thoughts into quiet numbness to quickly bring my mind to a blank state— a survival technique I've practiced for as long as I can remember. My body simultaneously becomes heavy and weightless. I'm both floating and sinking as six luminescent gemstones flicker in a dark void.

"Eons ago, six elemental gods came together to forge the luminaries. Six luminaries were created to bring Elmoria to existence. Water, fire, wind, earth, shadow, and light. Each luminary is a divine pulse of pure power that circulates life throughout The Mortal Realms of Elmoria. The Elemental Gods built our world upon the foundations of their magical, powerful stones. They are the sculptors. The stones, their clay. Elmoria, their divine masterpiece," Lumithra explains.

The luminaries gravitate towards one another in the center of the dark void before my eyes and forge a crown. As the final piece of the crown comes together, an astronomical mass of blinding light explodes, and a world is born. The explosion disperses the luminaries to great lengths, planting them in hidden alcoves scattered throughout Elmoria's blank canvas. The luminaries settle into their alcoves and then emit explosions beyond my comprehension. Sacred bursts of power sculpt layers of mountains, carve out bodies of water, and sprout infinite trees and varieties of vegetation. Darkness and light take shifts, covering Elmoria in day and night.

"Each luminary is a vital heartbeat essential to sustain life in Elmoria. Due to their gods given power, the luminaries pose a catastrophic threat if they are to be brought together. Uniting all the luminaries provides one with the power to forge The Crown of great authority. The Crown

of Luminaries. A crown meant only to be worn by gods and grants its wearer access to omnipotent magic and power. The Crown submits to the authority of whoever places it upon their head, granting their deepest desires as universal, Elmorian law. The Crown that created Elmoria will grant its wearer enough power to rival The Gods of Niroshen."

Lumithra then shows me glimpses of a battlefield. Mortal men and women equipped in full body armor clashing swords on horseback. Arrows flying through the air, knocking soldiers to the ground. Wounded civilians and sobbing children are rushed to barricaded shelters, screaming the names of their loved ones. Dragon Knights engage in aerial combat against Eldermoor's witches and their massive, ink-feathered raven-griffins, spilling blood from the skies like rain.

"The kingdoms and territories of Elmoria spent thousands of years in harmony, respecting the sacred powers of the luminaries, until six hundred years ago. Eldermoor, a nation founded on the worship of Osiris, plotted to unite the luminaries to expand their ideologies across Elmoria. Eldermoor believes The God of Death is to be worshipped and revered above all other gods they believe to be weaker. They believe their collective purpose is to see Osiris worshipped exclusively in every nation and kingdom. The Nation of Blackthorn, The Kingdom of Helia, and Eldermoor fought for the future of Elmoria in what became known as The Luminary War.

"The Luminary War ended after years of bloodshed on Blackthorn's soil after Eldermoor lost the means to carry out their campaign. Blackthorn and Helia threatened to cut Eldermoor off from all their trades and declare war upon them if they were to seek out the luminaries again. For centuries, Blackthorn and Helia's alliance has remained steadfast and has kept Eldermoor's hands tied. However, intel now suspects Eldermoor may be mobilizing to pursue the luminaries again. Tensions are brewing among the lands, and Eldermoor has been gnawing away at their ropes."

Lumithra releases me from glimpses of The Luminary War, and I awaken to the eerie stillness of the Kanoelani. Her violet eyes glow with both unwavering authority and alarming concern.

"A second Luminaries War is brewing on the horizon, my child. Tensions are rising, and Eldermoor's forces are growing in power, preparing to bite back despite the consequences they would face. I also sense a great power and a great hope slumbering within you, waiting to come alive. I choose you, Amira, daughter of Kallik. I choose to form a bond with you and take up the fight for Elmoria alongside The Dragon Knights."

What choice do I have in the matter? I have no desire to join the Knights of Blackthorn. Picturing Adrienne as a comrade on a battlefield twists my stomach into constrictive knots. Fuming heat collects under my skin at the thought of aligning myself with the knights who have treated the peasant villages as a problem not worth their time.

I don't even want to begin exploring my newfound hatred of Kallik. How could a god allow his daughter to be raised by such a monster and never attempt to commune with her? I could easily lose myself in fantasizing over how to possibly bring suffering to a god. However, as callously bitter and empty as I have become, even I can't turn a blind eye to Lumithra's revelations. It's time to swallow my pride and accept my fate.

"I accept the bond. I'll fight with Blackthorn." My thoughts burn like a pungent, yet necessary medicinal elixir.

"I'm proud of you, my child." Lumithra's voice seeps inside my mind and responds to my distress with a gentle, compassionate embrace.

"Save your praise. I do not accept my fate for the interest of The Knights of Blackthorn. I don't care if any of them live or die on a battlefield. I accept my fate to live to see the next sunrise. To fight for the chance to one day run to the refuge of the woods and seek the comfort of solitude," I respond.

"Regardless of why you accept your fate, I'm proud of you. I see what you can become. For now, let's see you to the next sunrise together."

Lumithra lowers her elongated neck until she brings herself to a height I can climb, inviting me to board her back. I hoist myself up her shimmering scales and find a saddle already waiting for me.

"How do you have this?" None of this feels real. A small part of me still questions whether or not the elixir I force-fed induces hallucinations.

"The magic of The Kanoelani works a multitude of mysterious wonders. I ordered the spirits to start crafting your saddle the moment you arrived for your trials."

Lumithra rises and bolts into the sky in a swift ascension that leaves my stomach on the ground. My lungs seize in a brief panic as they adjust to the thinness of the air. The rippling winds sting against my exposed skin and make quick work of drying my bloodied wounds. I can resent the knowledge we're headed back to the monastery later. For now, I relish in the satisfaction I am no longer a captive entangled in shadows. I am soaring through the skies on the back of a dragon that chose me. For the first time in my life, I savor the slight, warm buzz of freedom.

CHAPTER 6
The White Empress

Lumithra's opal scales collect beams of sunlight, dispersing iridescence into the smoky, mountainous fog. I welcome the cool mist onto my skin, soothing the stickiness of the dried blood caked onto my arms and face. Scents of evergreen pine sap and blooming wildflowers wash away the lingering odor of vapor wolf breath.

Savoring the taste of freedom is short-lived before the silhouette of the monastery etches its way into the horizon, basking in the sunrise. Vespera's shimmering beauty below is breathtaking, yet I can't shake the knotted pit swelling in my stomach. I don't think I could dread serving alongside the knights and running into Adrienne any more than I already do. The High Priestess only ordered her to deliver me to the forest alive, as far as I know. Does that mean she'll be waiting to kill me upon my return?

"You're returning to the monastery as an indisposable light mage. If anyone treats you as anything less than, I will remind them of who chose you." Lumithra flares steam from her nostrils as if to reassure her breath of fire serves in my defense.

Adrienne awaits as we descend into the botanical courtyard of the monastery, blooming with rows of black roses and wisteria trees. My heart palpitates as I prepare to confront darkness herself. I want nothing more than to strangle that smirk off her face for everything she put me through over the last twenty-four hours.

"I'll be damned to the gods." Adrienne lets out a wickedly sinful laugh the moment we make our landing. "Not only does the peasant survive The Kanoelani, but she bonds the White Empress. Unbelievable." Shadows seep from the inked serpents on her arms as if preparing to lunge for my neck.

Lumithra flashes her fangs with a low, threatening growl.

"The White Empress?" I question Lumithra down our new bond.

"I was planning on saving that detail until you've had a chance to settle in some. I should've known the shadow mage would be fuming about this the moment we arrived," Lumithra lets out a grumble of agitation.

"You have no idea who decided you're worthy of pursuing the path of the dragon knight," Adrienne scoffs. Tendrils of shadows now also seep from her clenched fists, along with the shadows emitting from her serpents. I can practically feel the heat radiating from her flushed cheekbones.

"I wasn't exactly dragged into this whole mess by choice. You can either choose to enlighten me, or I'll leave you to your brooding." I attempt to walk away, but Adrienne grabs me by the shoulder before I move past her.

"Six hundred years ago, that dragon of...yours...channeled Kallik's powers to create the shields that extend over the entire Nation of Blackthorn. Lumithra, The White Empress, is responsible for the impenetrable fortress of Kallik's light that prevents The Crown from forging within our borders. Lumithra bought Blackthorn and Helia the means to subdue Eldermoor in The Luminary War. And now, she's somehow yours," Adrienne seethes.

"You were there? Six hundred years ago?" I ask Lumithta in baffled astonishment.

"Like I said, I was hoping to save this conversation for later," she grumbles. *"Dragons are immortal, my child. I was there during The Luminary War."*

"General Verona, one of Eldermoor's most powerful crones at the time, gained total possession of the luminaries during the bloodiest battle of Elmorian history," Adrienne explains. "According to our historical records, Lumithra and her rider, Nuri, reached for Kallik's power together. They channeled enough power to erect shields posing the strength to repel the luminaries from forging The Crown. That power manifested as a breath of white flame that stretched over the entire nation, creating an invisible shield of his divine light."

"*Your former rider was a light mage,*" I piece together. Lumithra doesn't comment.

"The torrential surge of Kallik's power claimed the lives of Nuri and General Venora in the heart of the blast. The luminaries re-dispersed to hidden ends of the earth. The casualties were cataclysmic, but The White Empress absorbed enough of Kallik's power to save Elmoria from entering an age of darkness that day." Adrienne speaks as if she's recited the story thousands of times. As if she witnessed it herself.

Chills scuttle down the length of my spine and settle inside my chest. I can feel the color draining from my face as nausea delivers repeated punches to my gut. Lumithra is an immortal, legendary savior. She bonded a nameless, feral mercenary when her previous rider paid the price of her life to save the fate of Elmoria. I somehow defiled a timeless, sacred piece of history simply by existing. No wonder Adrienne hates me.

"Bonding to The White Empress is an honor I do not hold lightly." I finally manage to break my silence. "I-."

Adrienne slams me against the trunk of a weeping wisteria tree before I can form another sentence. "You are the first light mage the world has seen since Nuri. Do not blemish her legacy. You do anything to embarrass her name, and I'll forget all about Lady Rhonwen's orders to keep you alive. I'll have the time of my life defying her orders with you." Thick ropes of obsidian smoke dance predatory circles around my neck.

Lumithra releases a warning blast of flame, barely missing Adrienne by a narrow margin. Embers flicker like diamonds in the blackened patch of grass behind her hack. Adrienne backs away reluctantly, bowing before The White Empress in an apology.

"That serves as her only warning. Next time, I won't miss," Lumithra promises me.

Our mutual fear and respect for The White Empress prevents us from going for each other's throats for now. If Adrienne wishes to challenge me, she'll now have to wait for Lumithra's absence.

"I truly do not take the honor lightly. I promise I will give all that I can and then more to honor the legacy of Nuri's sacrifice." I extend a light bow before Adrienne. My words are meant for Lumithra, but expressing them out loud to Adrienne might purchase me a more civil interaction with her. I'm far too drained to endure any more of her hostility. I'd at least like an opportunity to scrub away at the bloody filth painfully itching my skin first.

I also truthfully mean what I tell Adrienne. While I have no desire to appease her or anyone else, I worship nature like Blackthorn worships its gods. Nature didn't place an orphan abandoned by a deity and a nameless, faceless mother into the arms of a sadistic mastermind. Nature didn't raise me to kill or be killed. Blackthorn's emerald, fog-laden beauty has given me the strength to endure Rhydian, and something about Lumithra makes me want to survive. Our strange, newly formed bond dares me to thrive, and that curiosity is worth my investigation. Just for that glint of hope, I owe The White Empress my very best. Perhaps that is how I will survive and stomach my path as a dragon knight.

Adrienne lets out a long, exasperated sigh. "That's enough for your little history lesson today, peasant. The rest you'll have to learn from whichever fortunate instructor that gets to take you under their wing."

Before I can respond, Lady Rhonwen enters the courtyard, approaching us with a sway of intimidating authority and grace. Her gown glows so bright I lose my train of thought. Her bodice clings tightly to her dainty features, followed by a loose silhouette that drapes over the cobblestone path like a blanket of glistening snow. Her luminous hair glows like a winter solstice full moon, complimenting her glacial eyes. In every way Adrienne's devastating, obsidian beauty emulates death, The High Priestess emulates life.

"What a curious sight to behold," she gasps in awe at the sight of The White Empress. She takes Lumithra in with a long pause as if confirming her eyes aren't deceiving her. "I hope by now you have been informed of what a spectacular dragon has chosen to bond you. The Kanoelani must have discerned you as a source of great potential."

Lady Rhonwen's eyes trail back and forth between Lumithra's mesmerizing opal scales and the wounds covering the lengths of my body, still processing her disbelief. "I hope you can find it in your heart to forgive the harshness of our prior manners towards you. But by now, I trust you have an understanding of our intentions during these tense times." The empathetic warmth in Lady Rhonwen's tone is a stark contrast to her infuriating tone during my interrogation.

"If the White Empress has found favor in you, I would be a fool not to welcome you to begin your training. Lumithra has sought you for a reason, and I am eager to see that reason develop to fruition. Adrienne, I will be assigning Amira to your squad. From one unique mage to another, you are our most capable instructor in helping Amira hone her skills."

"If I may respectfully remind you, Lady Rhonwen, there hasn't been a descendant of Kallik since records of Nuri six hundred years ago. I am no more equipped than any other instructor. Besides, my current apprentices are among the most promising of the monastery. I would hate to hinder their growth by taking on a new project."

I almost laugh at Adrienne's struggle to maintain her professional composure. The tone of her voice sounds as if it requires all her self-control to refrain from lashing out on The High Priestess in passionate protest.

"If your apprentices are the most promising, then they can handle the distraction better than the others," Lady Rhonwen counters. "If I may remind you, Adrienne, you are the only known shadow mage and descendant of Kamaris among Blackthorn's mages. If anyone can bring out Amira's full potential, it's an anomaly like you."

Kamaris. The Goddess of the Night. Adrienne is a flawless metaphor for darkness, death, and night. Menacing, spine-chilling, and dangerously seductive. This comes as no surprise to me.

"Please be so kind as to show Amira to the bathing chambers and provide her with a fresh change of clothes. From here on out, she is to be treated as a respectable apprentice, taking up the path of the dragon knight. I trust you will lead her well." Lady Rhonwen and Adrienne exchange a silent bow before she continues on her walk through the courtyard gardens.

"I trust you'll settle in well enough for now. Adrienne's hands are bound from harming you, and I have further business I must tend to in The Kanoelani. I will return when it is time for your training."

My heart speeds up in anxious dread as Lumithra plans her departure. I'm amazed by how quickly I've gone from fearing she'll turn me into heaps of charcoal to finding comfort in her presence.

Lumithra expands her immense, snow-white wings and takes flight to the hazy skies. Her body quickly becomes a trail of sparkling gems— ruby, sapphire, emerald, and topaz seeping through the layers of ashen fog. I can't help but envy her gift of flight. I would give anything to distance myself from civilization in less than a second.

"How many times will I have to tell you to quit gawking at the sky?" Adrienne hisses. "Come with me. I can't stand your vapor wolf stench any longer."

CHAPTER 7
The Squad

Adrienne leads me down the garden path. I admire the twin rows of weeping wisteria trees creating a shaded tunnel of lavender blooms. I remain a few steps behind, studying the sway of her gait. If I could catch her without her shadows on guard, it would take two simple maneuvers to bring her to the ground. To make her pay for everything she put me through is a delicious temptation.

"Do I also need to ask you to quit gawking at me? You're not as sly as you think you are, my love." Gods, what I'd give to gain the upper hand on this woman— to instill fear into her tempestuous gray eyes.

"As much delight as I would consume witnessing Adrienne swallowing some of her pride, she is your instructor now. You'll need to devise civil means to prevent her from getting under your skin," Lumithra advises down our bond.

"Where's the fun in that?" I shoot back.

"You're not here for fun, child. You're here to learn how to wield your light, and The High Priestess is right. Adrienne is best equipped to train you. You two owe each other your respect."

I have no experience growing up with a mother, but from what I can assume their qualities must be like, Lumithra sure sounds like one.

The path ends at the entrance of a dark stone building annexed to the monastery. Large pendant flags displaying Blackthorn's crest wave proudly in the wind atop large watch towers. I've only ever seen the crest on the uniforms of knights in their brief exchanges with Rhydian, and never bothered to study its details. While I've known the crest bears the image of a large diamond, I never noticed the runes etched on the inside of the diamond before. Upon closer observation, the runes appear to represent the elemental gods.

"Welcome to the training quarters," Adrienne says drily, sending shadows to open the large, arched latticework doors. Floors composed of checkered black and white marble tiles cast reflections of my blood-stained boots. Reverberations of sparring blades and weapons slicing into wooden targets jar memories of sparring with Casimir and all Rhydian's late orphans who shared my fate through childhood. I can only hope they're all resting in peace in Niroshen.

"This is where dragon knights and ground soldier apprentices spend most of their time around the monastery. Training, bathing, dining, repeat. You'll spend a lot of time getting your ass handed to you here," she sighs with a smirk.

"Sounds like you're speaking from personal experience," I mutter.

"About time our instructor shows up," a warm, friendly voice interrupts before Adrienne can respond to my jeer.

A woman with cascading braids of aquamarine hair descends the dual staircase, making her way to greet us. Her brown leather corset fits tightly over a flowing ivory tunic, flattering her dark hazelnut complexion. An impressive collection of knives and hand axes adorns her belt, fastened over olive green trousers. The clicking of her boots against the steps pulsates like a steady metronome.

"Looks like I get the honor of meeting our new apprentice before the rest of the squad." Her voice flows as smooth as a low tide. "You must be Amira. It's a pleasure to meet you; I'm Irvette." Irvette greets me with gentle warmth radiating from one sea-foam, green eye framed by a faded scar. An eye patch conceals her left eye. Her soothing aura is dramatically contrasted by the fierceness of her features as if she is the dynamic nature of the ocean personified.

"Irvette is the daughter of Sirena, Goddess of the Seas, and engaged to wed Felix. She is one of the strongest water mages I've been privileged to train. You have quite the prestigious roster to live up to among my squad. There are no weak links, and I will not allow you to embarrass us," Adrienne warns in a threatening tone.

Irvette nervously twists the ruby gemstone on her left finger, seemingly uneasy with the tension between us. "I hear you're the daughter of Kallik and managed to bond the White Empress," she interjects. "Adrienne has been a little more tense than her usual self since Sarthon informed her Lumithra was on her way back to the monastery after choosing to bond you. Maybe now I can see why. She failed to mention to us that you're stunning." Irvette winks as she smiles warmly at me.

Adrienne rolls her eyes and shoots Irvette a threatening glare. "Irvette, please inform the squad we'll meet up with them for breakfast momentarily. They trained their asses off yesterday, so they earned a heads-up before meeting their new class pet."

"Don't worry. Give it a day or two, and she'll warm up to you," Irvette mutters to me with a smirk before heading off down the halls.

Adrienne waves her off as we make our way up the stairs. I catch myself holding my breath, avoiding breathing in her enticing fragrance of lavender sage. I admittedly already made the mistake of noticing the way her black leather armor flatters her curves while envisioning throttling her in the gardens. For an infuriating dragon knight, Adrienne is unfairly intoxicating.

"You're not stepping foot anywhere else until you wash up." Adrienne shows me into a large washroom filled with steaming bathing pools. She pulls a fresh gray tunic, black trousers, and a clean set of training armor from a linen wardrobe and hands them to me. "You have fifteen minutes. Be dressed and ready by the time I come back to show you to the dining hall."

"You mean you're not going to force another elixir down my throat or restrain me with your shadow tricks? Maybe Irvette is right about you warming up to me." I wink at Adrienne as I tauntingly close the distance between us.

Adrienne's cheeks flush nearly as wine-red as her lips. She takes a long, deep breath and releases a puff of black smoke upon exhale. "No more tricks or trials for now. I'm just doing my hard-working students a favor before they have to meet you," Adrienne states sharply. Gods, flustering her is so fun.

"Well, I do clean up quite nice. You'll likely warm up to me even more by the time you return," I tease as I begin peeling off my shredded, bloodied clothing. Perhaps my familiarity with deadly games is why flirting with Adrienne is so entertaining. I don't know how to thrive outside of a constant state of danger.

Adrienne presses her body against mine, lowering her lips dangerously close to my ear. Dark, snake-like shadows weave around my neck, lightly choking me. "I mean, sure. You're pretty, love. I'm not afraid to admit what's undeniable," she whispers darkly. She pins my shoulders to the wall, sending heat down my neck. My heart is thundering in my chest, anticipating whether I should draw a blade or embrace a kiss. Should I try to figure out how I managed to wield that light in The Kanoelani? For some reason, I choose to refrain from any attacks and decide to flirt with danger a little longer.

"You're my pretty little sparring partner that will be begging for my mercy later this afternoon. You'll regret the way you've been looking at me all morning," Adrienne croons. A sultry half-smile burns into her lips. "Fifteen minutes, my love." The snakes release from my neck as Adrienne pries herself off me. She storms off with a mocking, exaggerated sway of her hips without saying another word.

I finish removing my clothes and soak my body under the steamy water, now wishing it was cold. I hate the part of me that decided against knocking Adrienne off her feet and delivering a satisfying punch to her face. I could've easily sliced a scar into her back for toying with me like her prey. What I hate even more is the reckless, danger-craving part of me that wants to be at her mercy.

*   *   *

Adrienne doesn't say a single word to me as we make our way to the dining hall, appearing to be lost in thought. Being forced to take on the mercenary peasant she finds unworthy of The White Empress as one of her students must be crushing her spirits. I smile at the satisfaction of humbling an instructor of nobles.

"Over here!" Irvette waves Adrienne and I down from a long, crowded dining table. We weave our way through the tight rows of jam-packed tables to fill the empty seats she saved for us.

"I went ahead and made you one of my infamous lattes." Ivette smiles playfully as she hands me a warm, wooden mug filled with red steam. I glance down at my mug, caught off guard by the thick, ruby-red liquid that looks more like a mulled wine and less like coffee.

"Oh! I almost forgot!" Irvette twirls her fingers over my mug, and a frothy, white dragon appears in the red brew. She then pulls a small spice jar from her pockets and sprinkles what looks like crushed jasper fragments atop my frothy dragon. "Couldn't forget the garnishing touches. I brewed everyone my signature red jasper latte this morning," she explains. "Knowing Adrienne, we're going to need it today."

The mention of Adrienne and drinks in the same sentence makes me hesitant to take a sip of whatever concoction is steaming in my mug. The last thing I need is to ingest another intoxicating atrocity before an afternoon of training on the back of a dragon.

The man sitting across from me dressed in a low-cut, beige tunic stifles a laugh as if picking up on my hesitation. His tawny, earth-toned eyes meet mine through long curls of thick, chestnut hair. "Don't worry. Contrary to its questionable appearance, you can trust your drink. Irvette likes spiking her lattes with red jasper elixirs as endurance and stamina enhancements." He draws a sip from his mug and lets out a sigh. "I'm Arden, by the way. Descendant of Kun."

I could've easily assumed Arden to be a descendant of the Earth Goddess. Simply observing his burly stature is enough to conclude his body is his own most proficient weapon. The definition of his muscles is a dead giveaway that he fights primarily in a brawler-type style. I would expect none less from a descendant of Kun's.

He may be over twice my size, but I'm no stranger to taking down large opponents. The sooner I can learn how to summon and wield my light on command, the sooner I'll stand a fighting chance against him if the need arises.

"Remember that you are among allies, not enemies, my child. Arden's bloodline allows him to mold earth into sturdy, lethal weapons. He may very well save your life on a battlefield one day," Lumithra assures.

"I've only ever witnessed blind trust result in death. Forgive my lack of willingness to trust any organization that fails to recognize the monsters under their noses," I scoff.

"The knights aren't without flaws, but you must learn to trust them with your life if you want to survive the trials you'll inevitably face together."

I shift my attention back to the wine-red coffee in front of me and its rose-scented, ruby steam. Irvette has been nothing but warm and kind since we've become acquainted, but it still feels foolish to trust anyone without hesitation.

Arden takes a small sip from my mug to assure me of its innocence. "You won't last one second as a dragon knight if you can't learn to trust your squad with something so trivial as a beverage," he scolds.

"At least try to understand my reluctance," I counter. "You endured the trials of The Kanoelani, so I'll assume you remember that pungent wolfshit you're forced to drink beforehand."

Arden's expression is filled with confusion rather than empathy or understanding. "I'm afraid I don't know what you're talking about," he confesses.

Adrienne half-chokes on her drink with a snort, then meets me with a sly smirk.

"Weren't you forced to down a gods-awful elixir that tastes like rotten blood and causes violent bouts of vertigo?" I ask. Arden and Irvette look at me as if I'm speaking in a foreign tongue.

"Adrienne, don't tell me you put sweet Amira through an unnecessary hazing before her trials, did you?" A man with long, jet-black hair sitting across from Adrienne questions.

"Don't let those big blue eyes fool you. Amira is anything but sweet," Adrienne mutters. "She just needed a little something to adjust her cocky attitude. None of you entered your trials hours after being captured as defiant treason suspects."

If I weren't in a room full of elemental-wielding half-mortals, I'd lunge across the table and rip out Adrienne's throat.

"Well, Amira, you seem rather sweet and well-mannered to me. I'm Zephyr, son of Cael, The God of Wind." His bright, cerulean eyes beam with pride as he mentions his divine lineage to Cael. He carries a pride that could only come from someone who has grown up aware of their spiritual heritage and given plenty of opportunities to connect with it properly.

Zephyr flashes a sultry smile to a couple of knights walking past our table. His one, subtle head nod is followed by soft giggles and flushing cheeks. "Don't get too friendly with me unless you want swarms of knights sizing you up as competition for my affection," he chuckles as he levitates his knife with a small gust of wind to peel the skin off his pomegranate.

"It's a little early for you to be acting like a smug ass already Zeph,"

Irvette sighs.

Zephyr winks at Irvette and continues cutting the food on his plate with his levitating knife trick. "Speaking of smug asses, why isn't your beloved joining us for breakfast?" He asks.

"Likely doing his morning meditation out on the flight field. Grounding himself in sacred moments of solitude rather than listening to you running your mouth," Irvette retorts. If that's the case, Felix is a wise, wise man.

I tune out the jeering banter and finally sip the rich, velvety coffee in front of me. Surprisingly, it tastes like a blend of fiery spices, rose, and dark chocolate. It doesn't take long before a jarring surge of energy pumps through my veins and over-activates my nervous system. After only a couple sips, my nerves are begging my body to run laps, sprint up a mountain, spar…anything to alleviate the sudden onset of restlessness. How is everyone else so seemingly unfazed by the effects of this drink?

"You grew up in the peasant slums, did you not? Then, this must be your first time experiencing such a potent delicacy," Zephyr says with a soft smile.

All eyes lock onto me with soft amusement as I fail to mask my restless discomfort. I feel as if I'm rare creature trapped within an enclosure being gawked at for entertainment. Memories of Rhydian laughing as my body thrashes under the cruelty of his blade creep to the front of my mind and threaten to throw me into a rage.

Adrienne glances down at my leg, restlessly shaking under the table, and laughs. "You better hope you learn to manage that energy effectively, or you'll embarrass yourself miserably in today's exercise."

I wait until Adrienne takes another sip from her mug before grabbing the bottom and tilting it with just enough force to cause her to choke on her drink. I laugh as she works through her sudden coughing fit, taking small satisfaction in my small victory.

"And you better hope you learn to manage me effectively, or you'll embarrass yourself miserably," I mock.

Adrienne yanks me by my ear and pulls me in close. "We'll see if you even survive the afternoon. I may not have to manage you for long," she whispers with a smirk.

CHAPTER 8
The Light Mage

Restless waves of suppressed energy continue to race through my veins and beg to be released from my body like a caged beast. I need to work this red jasper out of my system before my heart implodes inside my chest. Irvette places a hand on my shoulder and meets me with an empathetic gaze in her eye.

"I shouldn't have given you a regular dose for your first exposure to red jasper," she confesses apologetically.

"No need for apologies. I'm sure I'll be thankful for it once we begin." With my body still adjusting to the high altitude of the monastery and the exhaustion from getting nearly mauled to death in The Kanoelani, a healthy adrenaline rush may be what I need to survive today's training.

The High Priestess and Felix stand waiting for us near the precipice of the flight field. Irvette runs up to Felix and greets him with a soft kiss. He smiles as her lips press against his and reels her body in against his chest. For a second, I'm staring into the past, watching Casimir embrace me after a sweaty sparring session. I shift my attention to Lady Rhonwen to refrain from losing myself in an unexpected wave of grief.

The High Priestess glows like a beacon of moonlight shining atop the monastery's dreary, fog-laden mountain. Her light is a bright contrast to the rich sea of dark evergreens, hidden caverns, and cascading waterfalls slumbering peacefully on the horizon.

"Good morning, apprentices. I will be observing your aerial sparring this morning. While I pray and trust that you fervently pursue deepening your relationships with the gods, I must also ensure you are all prepared to excel in enemy combat. Today, I challenge you to unlock greater depths to reach for the potential you possess. Great power dwells within the fibers of your unique existence. Have the courage to call upon your gods-given magic and the wisdom to wield it effectively," Lady Rhonwen encourages.

Hopeful optimism glistens in her eyes like a fresh blanket of snow. Meanwhile, her words sting my chest like a dagger, twisting my stomach in constrictive knots.

"Am I really expected to spar against skilled mages when I have only summoned sparks in The Kanoelani? I don't even know how I called those sparks, let alone wield them into any useful attacks." I reach for Lumithra, flooded with dread. The thought of engaging in aerial combat on the back of a dragon against elemental mages with nothing but my blades throws me into a trembling panic.

"Are you doubting what I, The White Empress, sense within you? Your magic merely awakened in The Kanoelani and has been stirring within you ever since. Learn to recognize its flow. If you can find its source, you will learn to pull from it abundantly," Lumithra answers.

"And how exactly am I supposed to do that?" Lumithra sounds like she's describing how to find a body of water in the wilderness rather than how to weaponize my newly discovered abilities.

"You have spent your entire life focused on nothing other than survival. Focus on becoming familiar with your soul, and you'll learn how to call upon your magic."

"Sounds easier said than done," I mutter.

Adrienne reels in our focus, interrupting my conversation with Lumithra. "You will take turns sparring one on one. Today's training aims to evaluate your ability to control and wield your element against an opponent during flight. As dragon knights, you must learn to master aerial combat. I don't think I need to tell anyone wielding the elements on dragons is a lot different and more difficult than wielding them on the ground."

Nothing in my years of training could have possibly prepared me for sparring half-mortals. Sadistically, I miss the simplicity of being a peasant mercenary controlled by Rhydian's puppet strings. At least I had the element of control on my side when fighting for his blood money.

"Stop doubting yourself before you even touch the skies. I promise you will figure it out. We'll be arriving in just a few minutes. I'm almost there," Lumithra rumbles.

I take a moment to retreat into one of my few happy memories to take the edge off my panic. Sparring with Casimir alongside a whispering creek on a balmy summer morning. We spend the morning training one-on-one before Rhydian awakens for the day from his drunken slumber. I gain the upper hand in a crafty waltz of skillful footwork and blade against blade. It doesn't take long for me to pin Casimir up against the trunk of a grand oak tree with the tip of my sword. Sweat is dripping from his tawny brown curls and down the muscles of his chest. His laugh is stifled by heavy breathing as I lower my sword and press my body against his.

"You're damn brilliant, Amira," he pants as I blush. I grab him by his dirt-stained tunic and press my lips against his. I begin-

"Amira! Unless you want to piss off a legion of dragons, I suggest moving your ass out of their landing zone!" Adrienne's orders whiplash me back to the present as seven dragon silhouettes break through the silver fog and rapidly approach the flight field. I immediately clear the landing zone, unable to peel my eyes off the sky. I'll never adjust to the presence of such magnificently stunning and horrifying creatures. Dragons will always leave me in a trancelike awe while simultaneously fearing for my life.

Lumithra leads in front of the legion's triangular flight formation. Seven sets of knifelike claws longer than my arms dig into the earth one at a time— a cascade of thunderous waves rippling into the ground. I straighten my posture, aligning my legs with my shoulders, and fix my gaze solely onto Lumithra's luminescent, violet eyes. How The Nation of Blackthorn celebrates and worships the gods in higher regard than literal dragons will never cease to baffle me.

"First up will be Irvette and Tsuna against Arden and Hyrix," Adrienne announces. Not going first feels like a suffocating weight of debris has been lifted off my chest.

"As a brief reminder of our rules, the first opponent to fall from their seat or find themselves too compromised to strike back is obliged to yield. I will also remind everyone that you are not aiming to kill your opponent. Honorable dragon knights never kill their own." Adrienne's eyes lock directly onto mine in an intense glare. I wink back at her, reveling in the small satisfaction that no one is permitted to kill me today.

"That doesn't mean we're liable to save your ass if you can't hold your own," she whispers in my ear. "There are no weak links among The Dragon Knights."

Irvette raises her fists to her ribs, summoning pools of water to encapsulate her arms. She slams her water-immersed arms toward the ground, creating two geysers that propel her body upwards as she twirls her way into the saddle of her sapphire-blue dragon. Arden then stomps the ground, and a massive boulder emerges directly underneath his feet. He raises his arms, and the boulder lengthens until it carries him to his seat atop his emerald dragon. As Arden takes position in his saddle, he punches the boulder with one fist, disintegrating it into nothing but flying shards of gravel.

"I'll try my best not to humiliate you too badly," Irvette winks as she sends a spiraling wave of water through her aquamarine braids, twisting them into a tight bun.

"Forgetting the outcome of our last match so soon, are we?" Flashes of sapphire and emerald take to the sky, leaving behind waves of flesh-burning heat from twin blasts of dragon steam.

"Climb aboard, you're going to observe this match up close." Lumithra lowers her head to the ground, inviting me to board her back. As I awkwardly fumble into my saddle, I roll my eyes at how effortlessly Adrienne mounts Sarthon. Her shadows propel her with an elegant, spiraling grace I wish I didn't admire.

"Take all the notes that you can, my love. Gods know you're going to need them," she taunts.

We ascend into dark, charcoal skies consumed by stormy clouds. Masses of earth and blasts of water are tossed back and forth through the storm-brewing skies surrounded by mountain peaks. Sarthon takes Adrienne to the heart of the brawl, allowing her to observe every move exchanged between Arden and Irvette as closely as possible.

Arden channels hundreds of micro-blasts of sharp, projectile rocks through his fists, aiming them like lethal arrows toward Irvette as his target. Irvette throws up watery shields as Tsuna carefully evades each blow, weaving her long, sapphire body in and out of the jagged spears of earth. She spirals like swirling waves of deep sea across the hazy skies.

"Playing hard to get only gets you so far, you know," Arden bellows across the howling winds.

"Oh, is that what I'm playing?" Irvette lets out a hearty laugh. While maintaining her balance through Tsuna's acrobatic maneuvers, Irvette stretches the palms of her hands to the skies. She conjures a tornado of ferocious waves, siphoning the rain from the heavy cumulus clouds. She then directs her hand-crafted cyclone in a hasty pursuit after Arden and Hyrix.

Arden extends his reach towards a nearby mountain, and a massive bulk of granite extracts itself from the crest. The enormous mountain stone follows the commands of Arden's movements, blocking the trajectory of Irvette's violent funnel of waves.

"How is any of this possible?" I ask Lumithra, hardly believing what I'm witnessing.

"Descendants of the gods can either extract their element directly out of nature or produce the element themselves out of their own energy. Both techniques demand costly energy and focus," she explains.

No wonder Irvette spiked all our coffees with an energy and stamina-enhancing elixir this morning.

"Using too much power too quickly could even drain all the life from its mage. Not only will you have to learn how to call upon your magic, but you must learn your limitations. Pushing yourself too hard can and will lead to lethal consequences." An icy wave of shivers invades my body in response to Lumithra's sobering warning.

The tower of funneling waves crashes into the colossal mass of granite with an explosive force. As Irvette's cyclone dissolves on impact, Arden's boulder obliterates into shards of projectile stones sharp as dragon fangs. Arden and Hyrix retreat from the flying shrapnel, and Irvette seizes the moment. She stands atop Tsuna's saddle with delicate, calculated balance. Through rhythmic steps of graceful dance, Irvette carefully crafts spheres of water into the shape of a giant lance.

Irvette remains standing as she holds the giant aquatic lance above her head. Tsuna is now hot on Hyrix's trail. Arden turns backward in his seat, rapid-firing stone arrowheads toward Irvette to no avail. Irvette dodges each blow as Tsuna fully closes in on Hyrix. As she lowers her lance and points it dangerously close to Arden's chest, Tsuna pauses.

"There's no way that lance is sharp. It's made of water. He still has a chance to deflect and strike back," I comment to Lumithra.

"The sheer water pressure pent up in that lance is more than enough to lethally blast Arden off Hyrix, thus costing him the duel," Lumithra explains.

"Any last words, Arden?" Irvette asks playfully, savoring her victory.

"I yield," Arden mumbles under his breath. Realizing he doesn't have the time or space to craft a worthwhile counterattack is written into the disappointment on his face.

"I'm sorry. What was that?" She taunts.

"I yield!" Arden yells, frustration flooding his tone.

"Irvette wins match one," Adrienne confirms.

After descending to the flight field, Adrienne debriefs the duel, reviewing notes of critiques and praises. Irvette receives praise for maintaining the balance to stand mid-flight, maximizing the power of her attacks. I tune out while Arden gets his feedback, fearfully dreading when my name is called.

"For the next duel, I will be putting Felix and Zephyr to the test," Adrienne shouts, projecting her voice over the increasingly turbulent winds.

"Fire versus wind. A recipe fueling disaster, If I say so myself. It is my pleasure to demonstrate my strengths in front of our new lovely apprentice," Zephyr smirks, winking in my direction.

Adrienne creeps up behind me like a sinister wraith. My heart falls out of sync as I choke on the rock-sized lump in my throat. "That means I will challenge you next, my love." She smiles darkly, drinking my fear like a glass of fine wine.

I should've expected Adrienne to want to assess me personally. Anyone else would have likely gone easy on me. Adrienne won't be showing me any mercy. My blood boils at the thought of dying as an inexperienced, clumsy mage rather than as a ruthless mercenary.

"Remember, Amira, this is not a duel to the death. It's just a test of strength and skills. Dragon Knights do not kill their own, and Blackthorn needs its only light mage alive and well-trained."

Adrienne will not humiliate me today. I will learn to recognize the flow of my magic and learn to pull from its source within me.

"One way or another, the student will humble the instructor," I promise Lumithra. I pray to the gods that my burning desire to make her proud will awaken the power I need to win.

"Now, that is the courageous demigoddess I bonded in the forest,"

Lumithra praises. *"You have the heart of a fighter. I have full confidence in your potential, my child."*

"All right, Sylphira, Let's put on a ravishing spectacle." Zephyr produces a commanding gust of wind with a sweeping kick, propelling his body to the top of his blue-eyed, golden dragon. Sylphira trails into the skies like a swirling stream of sunlight.

"This won't take long, Fieryn," Felix whispers to his scarlet dragon with eyes of glowing magma. He uses nothing other than agile muscle power to board Fieryn. However, once he reaches his saddle, he lets out a blast of fire from his breath in perfect sync with Fieryn's blast.

My head spins as Lumithra takes me to observe violent collisions of roaring flames against suffocating, stormy winds. At least the heat of the fire warms my skin, chilled by the bitter winds. It quickly becomes difficult to discern which winds are coming from Zephyr and which are coming from the storm clouds. Regardless, Zephyr is using them all to his advantage.

"How can Eldermoor find any success in rivaling the powers of these half-mortals?" I ask Lumithra. After witnessing catastrophic forces of nature wielded as lethal weapons, I find it impossible to believe anyone could pose a real threat to half-mortals.

"Half-mortals are indeed extraordinarily powerful by nature. The witches of Eldermoor, however, are not to be underestimated. Osiris has gifted his most devout followers with dark, blood-wielding magic in exchange for their worship. Blood mages turn the bodies of their enemies into vulnerable puppets and laugh as they snap their bones like twigs."

Lumithra's voice raises the hairs on my skin. I always thought of Rhydian as a puppet-master, controlling me with invisible strings. Gods forbid if he ever sought after Osiris and learned to wield blood.

"As I explained earlier, Eldermoor has been testing its limits with Blackthorn and Helia as of late. While all borders are open to foreigners throughout Elmoria, Eldermoorian activity in Blackthorn and Helia is

becoming increasingly suspicious. We haven't found hard evidence they are mobilizing in pursuit of the luminaries yet, but at this rate, I wouldn't be surprised. The likelihood they will weaponize their practices against us in another luminary war is a threat we must treat as an inevitable future."

"If we suspect Eldermoor is pursuing the luminaries, why hasn't war been declared already? Why do our borders remain open to Eldermoor?" I ask Lumithra.

"Lady Rhonwen believes the gods wish to see Blackthorn ruled with compassion, grace, and mercy. The High Priestess isn't ready to close our borders and spill our blood based on mere suspicions. The King of Helia operates with similar convictions and typically mirrors Blackthorn's decisions in external affairs," she explains.

"What a deplorable pity," Zephyr scoffs. "I…I yield." I realize I paid zero attention to the match between Felix and Zephyr, having no recollection of how they sparred one another. All I know is Felix must have made quite the statement based on Zephyr's theatrical brooding.

I barely notice when Lumithra takes me back to the ground for the debriefing of match two. I haven't been able to stop imagining the number of ways blood mages can inflict torturous deaths upon their enemies. Just days ago, I was under the impression Blackthorn's most significant threats were limited to organized crime leaders who primarily preyed on the vulnerable peasant slums. I should know by now that the more I learn of the world, the more monsters emerge from the darkness to challenge the light.

"Amira! Ready to begin?" Adrienne asks eagerly.

Speaking of monsters, I will not let Adrienne make a fool of me. If I can persuade her to respect me or, even better…to fear me, my time at the monastery may become much more palpable.

Roaring drums of thunder reverberate through the ominous, onyx clouds, releasing the anticipated heavy rainfall. "Match three. Amira versus Adrienne," Felix bellows over the deafening downpour.

Sarthon roars in sync with the next outburst of crackling thunder. Lumithra responds with a roar perfectly aligned with a strike of lightning branching across the sky. Lightning. I close my eyes and take a deep breath, inhaling courage.

"Guide us well, Lumithra," I plea as I exhale my fear, discarding it to the earth as we bolt into the thunderous atmosphere.

Adrienne draws the palms of her hands together along with a deep breath. She then extends her arms, releasing a cauldron of shadowy bats bearing razor fangs and wings as long as the blade of my sword. I draw my blade from its sheath, slicing through the swarming cauldron set on throwing me off Lumithra's back. Knife-like talons dig into the scalp of my head, my shoulders, and my thighs, fighting to tear my flesh in far too many different directions. My attacks yield fruitless results as each bat respawns completely intact within seconds of being sliced in half.

"Examine your soul, my child. Where does the river of your power flow?"

"Can't exactly focus on anything right now," I snap.

Adrienne's bats multiply and multiply, obstructing my vision as they lunge at me through the heavy, slanted downpour. The rain spews from the skies with such a violent force I'm almost convinced the gods are trying to drown me. I still don't have the slightest clue as to how to call upon magic I never knew I even possessed. The only thing we can do now is focus on flying out of the swarming cauldron.

Lumithra hastily whips her opal body through the seemingly eternal stream of Adrienne's obsidian bats as Sarthon gains on us. The freezing rain lashes at our bodies like whips striving to slam us down to the ground. It takes all my physical strength to avoid slipping and falling out of my drenched, slippery saddle and to hold on to its handle despite my body's relentless shivering. With one hand death-gripped on the handle, I continue to use my free hand to slice my blade through as many bats as possible.

"We can't keep retreating forever. You must call upon your magic at once!" Lumithra growls.

Adrienne and Sarthon disappear into an abysmal black wall cloud, and the entire cauldron of bats vanishes instantaneously. The calm before her next storm of deadly tricks. Thunder clamors throughout the tourmaline skies as Lumithra and I find ourselves engulfed within the confines of a thick, circular cloud. Dense walls of dark smoke surround us as Adrienne emerges like a wraith-like creature of the night.

"I'm feeling rather generous. Why don't you yield now before I unleash your next nightmare?" She taunts.

I say nothing. I focus on steadying my breath despite shivering through the merciless downpour. Breathing through the tingling numbness of my drenched tunic cemented to my icy, wet skin while maintaining balance on the back of a dragon consumes all my stamina. Adrienne breaks my silence with a bone-chilling laugh.

"Can't say I didn't warn you, love."

Adrienne extends her arms above her head, reaching toward the walls of black smoke. She brings her reach down towards me like a conductor commanding the crescendo of an orchestra. A midnight-black, vaporous cobra the size of Lumithra hurdles towards us with a blood-thirsty hiss. Lumithra attempts to break through the walls of the cloud but crashes into the abyss of smoke as if it were an impenetrable fortress.

"What half-mortal can possibly restrain a dragon?" I ask Lumithra, sensing the color drain from my face as the massive, shadowy cobra quickly closes the distance between us.

"You don't even know half of who she is and what she is capable of," Lumithra gasps in exhaustion from her futile efforts to escape the vast chrysalis of darkness.

The shadowy serpent reaches us within seconds, entangling us in suffocating, constrictive knots. My hands begin slipping from Lumithra's handle as the monstrous cobra begins to cut off the airway from my neck slowly. Lumithra lets out a wall of blazing flames from her breath in an attempt to shake us free. It's no use.

"Amira! Yield NOW unless you have a death wish for you and your dragon!" Raw, raging fury seizes control over my lightheaded body. All my life, I've been treated as a caged animal to prod and manipulate. I will not accept defeat. Never again will anyone's power weigh me down.

My primal rage feels electrifying as burning heat sears my veins. I feel Rhydian repeatedly lashing his blade through the dirty, raw flesh of my back. I feel the blistering fevers from my infected wounds. I see Casimir's final, dying breath once more. I see the blood of Rhydian's targets soak my hands, drowning out my childhood. I feel my hunger pangs flood me with fatigue on the brink of starvation.

I let out a feral, blood-boiling scream as the world around me comes to a pause.

"AMIRA! Control yourself!" Lumithra lets out a pleading roar of panic.

A massive bolt of lightning deviates from my body's natural electrical current through my fingertips, striking a near-direct hit to Adrienne and Sarthon. Any closer, there would have been no chance of surviving the strike. My vision blurs as Sarthon releases a seismic, shattering roar, potentially reaching the ends of Elmoria.

The impact of my spidering branches of self-produced lighting throws Adrienne from Sarthon's back. For a moment, I can hear the curses spewing from her lips as she falls rapidly through the rain and the perimeter of her cloud disintegrates. My stomach descends into free fall with her as the slamming rains go silent.

"Adrienne yields." My ears regain their ability to process audio stimulation again as I hear the faint trace of Felix announcing my victory over the harshness of the storm.

Adrienne is back on Sarthon as they're headed toward the ground, meaning he must have caught her while I was lost in my trance. I never once doubted Adrienne's ability to survive the fall, yet I still struggle to contain the contents of my stomach. The first time I intentionally wielded my magic, I nearly killed a dragon knight.

"You certainly found the source of your power and wielded it beyond even what I was expecting," Lumithra confesses. The tone of her voice sounds equally baffled and proud with a hint of concern. I struggle to hold on to her with my tingling, deadweight limbs as we begin our windy descent back to the ground.

"I promise I wasn't going for a kill. I-I don't know what happened," I stutter.

"I can sense the source of your power flows from great anger and pain. Now that you've learned to identify and pull from the source within you, you must learn to control what you wield," Lumithra responds firmly.

The storm dissolves by the time we return to the ground. I clumsily dismount from Lumithra's back, tumbling to the ground on my hands and knees. On top of the absence of feeling from my glacially numb skin, an inhuman wave of fatigue devours me whole.

"Is it normal to feel this exhausted after wielding an element?" I ask, struggling to catch my breath. We couldn't have been in the sky for more than a few minutes, yet I feel as if I just spent several hours sparring with Rhydian on an empty stomach.

"You'll learn to adjust," Lumithra assures. *"However, you did manage to exert quite an extensive blast of power for your first time wielding it intentionally. Remember my warning on over-exertion. You don't want to risk lethal burnout."*

No one says a word as everyone looks at me with expressions of terror. Every eye locked onto me, a trembling arrow waiting to fire as I fail to control my shivering. Good. I haven't survived the last twenty-five years fiddling my thumbs like some meek, humble damsel. Instilling fear into the hearts of every soul I've encountered is how I've kept myself alive. Even Rhydian learned to fear me to an extent. He wouldn't have kept me on such a short leash and felt the constant need to subdue me with violent threats if a small part of him wasn't afraid of me.

"Taking down the instructor on your first day, huh?" Arden is the first to break the silence. He looks at me as if struggling to convince himself I'm real and that what he witnessed actually happened. "That is certainly a feat none of us have ever accomplished. Welcome to the squad, Amira. Welcome to the squad, indeed." I feel as if every freezing bone in my body is about to shatter as he gives me a hearty pat on the back.

The High Priestess makes her way over to me with an expression of gasping awe. If any part of her is angered that I nearly cost her one of her instructors, her beaming smile fails to show it. "Daughter of Kallik, you have extracted extraordinary, destructive power from your sacred bloodline. Well done, Amira." Lady Rhonwen covers me with her snow-white cloak, immediately restoring some warmth to my frozen limbs.

"With all due respect, Lady Rhonwen, my apprentice has demonstrated she has zero control over her power. She needs to be critiqued. Not coddled. The only thing remotely impressive about her little lightning tricks is that she didn't strike me directly," Adrienne protests.

Lady Rhonwen seems to wave off Adrienne's concerns as her attention remains fixated on me. "The first light mage Blackthorn has seen in ages has shown us she possesses a power that can turn the tides of battles if adequately trained. Your duty is to train her to shape and control that raw power. My duty is to praise the gods for such a hope-laden blessing."

Something about being referred to as a *hope-laden blessing* churns my stomach and fills me with unease. Regardless of my new fate, I will always be a merciless, jaded mercenary at heart. My soul is damned to The Dark Realms the day I die. Being praised and celebrated by The High Priestess is so wickedly ironic that I have to stifle my laughter.

"Let's get you out of the cold. The last thing we need is for you to get sick." Lady Rhonwen pulls me into her arms as I pray I don't look as uncomfortable wearing her robe as I feel. We make our way back through the damp, brisk gardens as her words continue to haunt me.

CHAPTER 9
Playing with Darkness

Lumithra and her legion of dragons have dismissed themselves to the woods to pick off packs of wolves for their next meal. Thank the gods they all respect and fear The White Empress as much as the knights do. I imagine that's the sole reason Sarthon hasn't torched me to stains of soot for nearly frying both him and Adrienne out of the sky. Between my lethal lack of control and the draining fatigue from wielding a single bolt of lightning, I have much to learn before relying on my newly discovered magic. At the same time, I would be lying to myself if I said I didn't savor the exhilaration of wielding such divine, chaotic power.

After returning to my room to change into a warm set of dry clothes and scarf down a hot bowl of beef stew in solitude, I decide to venture to the monastery's library. Over the years, I developed a habit of stealing books off my targets when possible to gift myself small, luxurious escapes from reality. As stinging electricity still sizzles in my bones, I feel long overdue to escape my current reality, if only for a bit.

A black diamond chandelier composed of flickering candlesticks gently sways from the ceiling in the center of the library. It swirls and sways like an articulated dance, suspended by creaking chains. The flickering candle flames emit echoing, ethereal harmonies throughout the tall, tower-shaped room. Singing. The flames are singing.

I lightly slap myself in the face, expecting to snap me out of some strange hallucination. Beautiful, chilling harmonies with worshipful tones for the gods and goddesses continue to flow freely from the dancing flames.

Perhaps their magic is somehow a byproduct of the holy atmosphere of the monastery. Never have I ever imagined I would feel uncomfortable in a room full of books. I have never been one to reflect on the gods, let alone worship them. Despite my unease, I will gladly take the singing candle flames and floating dust clouds over any interactions with Adrienne or her squad.

The candlelight choir casts a delicate ambiance upon several stories of walnut shelves overflowing with books blanketed in dust. I browse my fingers over rows of leather-bound religious texts, scanning for any interest-piquing titles. Desperate to find any title unrelated to any deity.

"You've been avoiding your classmates like a plague since we landed," Lumithra probes into my mind.

"Don't you have wolves to hunt or something? Why does it matter to you?" I scoff.

"You can't avoid them all day. Eventually, you'll need to adjust to their acquaintance," she insists.

"We'll see about that," I mutter.

I pull a text from its spot titled *The Luminary War War of Elmoria* and head to a table decorated with a golden vase of freshly trimmed black roses. Of all the books I have managed to steal from Rhydian's endless list of expensive enemies, very few have referenced this monumental war. Historical texts have proven difficult to come across in the peasant slums.

"I'll give you credit where it's due. Not a single one of my apprentices has ever claimed victory in their first duel against me," A dark voice taunts. Adrienne appears at the library entrance like a stalking ghost in the night. She leans against a pillar dressed in her curve-clinging, black leather armor as her obsidian hourglass haunts the entire room. If she's here to kill me over our little incident, her looks alone could do it. What is it with my reckless attraction to such dangerous beauty?

"Then again, they were all in skilled control over their magic and never once came close to killing me." Adrienne glances uninterestedly at her black nails, masking any hint of what she wants with me from her expression. I've been so occupied with staring at her that I hardly realize I've been restlessly fidgeting with the hilt of a dagger.

"As much as we have gotten off on a horrible foot, I swear to the gods I wasn't out for your blood." Just as the effects of the red jasper elixir have finally worn off, my heart is again slamming against the walls of my chest. My lust for danger sets my mind swirling in an intoxicating haze. It's impossible to discern how exactly I hope she intends to destroy me.

She slowly approaches my table, laced boots clicking against the checkered marble floors— the rhythm of a moth who could effortlessly smother a flame. Adrienne leans forward on the table, staring me down with her eyes of gray, shimmering moonstones. "Don't worry, my love, I'm not here to pick a fight. I'm here to give you a little lesson in controlling that spark of yours."

"A lesson?" I scoff. "Everyone around here has been suffocatingly clear I'm the first light mage in centuries. Do you even possess the credentials to teach an anomaly like me, instructor?" Admitting to myself that a one-on-one lesson with Adrienne would intrigue me as much as it would terrify me is a humiliating poison to swallow.

Adrienne's porcelain complexion shifts to a ghostly pale I didn't think possible. Her hands curl into fists on the table as smoke sifts between her knuckles. "My *credentials* are none of your concern. What is your concern, is learning how to control yourself out there. Understood?" She snarls.

"What's the matter? Did I dare...*strike* a nerve?" Testing how far I can push her before she breaks grants me a strange sense of security to explore how and why I'm hopelessly fascinated by her. Testing the ice I'm about to tread is how I have learned to explore the world around me, horrors and wonders alike.

The eyes of the serpents inked into Adrienne's arms glow like bright obsidian flames. I flinch back in my seat, almost expecting them to release a smothering blast of heat. "Is this all a joke to you?" She growls in a deep, wraith-like tone. "This is your last warning. My experience is none of your concern. None." Spiraling shadows swirl around her fists, ready to be molded into bats, dragon-sized serpents, or whatever nightmares she may desire to wield against me. Message received.

"We've wasted enough time. Let's get our lesson started, shall we?" She extends her shadows toward the library doors and slams them shut. My stomach drops as I hear the click of the locks.

"Lumithra! Are you sensing this? Do something! Please!" I reach for The White Empress, suppressing my panic to the best of my abilities. The ice suddenly feels dangerously thin, and I suddenly feel dangerously under-prepared to tread these deadly waters.

"Relax, Amira. The descendant of Kamaris is more than capable of leading a light mage through some basic control techniques. If you ask me, she should keep those doors secured until the two of you learn to get along," Lumithra responds.

"Well, you're no help evidently," I scoff. Maybe it was a mistake to trust motherly compassion from a dragon as a life-preserver.

"Why are we doing this now? Lady Rhonwen wants me to attend a religious studies seminar before too long, right? I recall her requesting I attend a study on the elemental pantheon as she escorted me back inside. Should we just save this for later?" I ask Adrienne. Despite dreading the seminar, it may be what spares me from whatever torturous lesson she has in store for me.

"Now that you have fully awakened your magic, I'm not allowing you to go *anywhere* until you at least grasp how to control the deadliness of your abilities. What good is studying the elemental pantheon if you pose a risk of frying up the whole monastery?" Adrienne asks. "Now, come with me," she beckons with her index finger.

Adrienne motions me to follow her through the depths of the library, stretching back much farther than I anticipated. As we reach a dead end, she pulls a dusty book from a large bookshelf, and the shelf swings open like a door. The hairs on my neck rise as a dark, hidden passageway is unveiled before my eyes.

"There is no way I'm following you down that hallway," I protest. Whatever secrets hide in the alcoves of hidden passageways in religious monasteries can't possibly be harmless.

"I'm afraid you don't have much of a choice." A thin, cruel smile curves on Adrienne's lips, and my heart fumbles its steady rhythm. The bookshelf closes abruptly from behind, submersing us in pitch black.

Darkness swallows us whole as I fail to make out the details of my hands in front of me. For a moment, I wonder if I've gone unconscious until I notice the warm, musty library air shift to damp, moldy, and cold. Sulfurous drops of water leak from above and splash to the ground in a steady, reverberating cadence.

"Godsdamn, it's gotta be around here somewhere," Adrienne mutters, rummaging through the darkness. "Ah, there we go." A soft glow of candle flame dispels some of the darkness as she closes the door to a small, iron lantern.

"We could've spared the trouble by asking you to light the way, but not at the risk of any electrocutions or burning to death," Adrienne scoffs. "Just a little farther, at least. We're almost to our destination." She leads us down a dark, narrow stretch of cavern walls until we reach a small, cramped room.

"Have a seat," Adrienne commands as she lights the torches lined on the stone walls, filling the room with an eerily ambient glow. Whatever dark, torturous ritual she may be plotting, I won't allow her to have her way without a proper fight.

"I defeated you once today already, and I'm prepared to do it again," I snarl. Adrienne intercepts my hands before I can reach my daggers or make an attempt to summon my light.

"Relax, my love. Whether we like it or not, it's my duty to instruct you now." For the first time since we've met, Adrienne's eyes meet mine with empathetic sincerity rather than menacing cruelty. "We're on the same side. You're going to have to learn to let down some of that impenetrable wall of yours. Trusting your comrades is essential for survival in the ways of the dragon knight."

"Why exactly did you bring me all the way down here if you're not plotting to harm me?"

"With the dark, undisturbed stillness of the earth, these little caverns are the perfect place to learn how to ground. Centuries ago, earth mages developed the art of grounding as means of controlling their flows of lethal power. Grounding is the art of reaching for the flow of your magic and forcing it to your submission. It gives you the means to block the flow of your magic like a dam and only release what you intend to release."

"Follow my lead, and I'll lead you through the steps. In time, you'll eventually learn to ground more quickly, but it can be quite the process at first. Let's get started, shall we?"

I reluctantly join Adrienne, mirroring her cross-legged position rooted on the ground. She shifts her body until her legs gently rest up against mine. I pray she doesn't notice the lightning-fast pulse pounding in my wrists as she takes hold of my hands. My reaction to her touch is nothing short of humiliating.

"Your first time can be dangerous if practiced without careful, disciplined focus. If you don't want to destroy us both, I will need you to trust me as your guide through this practice."

The proximity of her lips to mine might pose the most significant threat to us both. I would be lying to myself if I denied that the thought of them colliding crossed my mind at least once. Gods, why do I find this woman so seductive?

"Take a deep breath. Close your eyes as you become acquainted with the surrounding stillness. Allow yourself to adjust to this space."

Adrienne speaks in an alluringly soothing tone, naturally easing the tension of my muscles as I allow my eyes to close.

"Focus your attention on each sensation you notice. Permit yourself to acknowledge and process each feeling that arises." My attention is drawn to the sensation of Adrienne's toned, muscular legs partially resting on top of mine. I feel her smooth palms in my hands and imagine the dangerous places I want to see them drift. This likely isn't what I'm supposed to be feeling. Am I bound to destroy us?

"If you catch your mind drifting, reel it back in. Take another deep breath. Now, I want you to ask yourself what your soul longs to consume. Notice the desires that surface, aching within your heart."

What does my soul desire? Survival? Peace? Solitude? Nothing truly surfaces other than crippling numbness. I wouldn't be surprised if I'm no longer human enough to have any real longings buried in my soul. The more I search my soul for any trace of real desires, the harsher the numbness stings.

Adrienne sits in patient silence as I fail to feel anything rather than nothing. After what feels like hours of sitting in silence, my numbness shifts to anger. Anger that my soul has no tangible hope to crave or desire despite my focused, desperate searching.

"I feel nothing. Nothing other than anger," I finally admit in defeat.

"That's okay. We can work with that," Adrienne calmly assures. "What sparks your anger? Focus on that for now."

My anger sparks a gravitational yearning to feel anything other than the numbness that callouses my severed heart. Yearning for my body to forget the pain of every scar carved into my back, every blistering infection, every hunger pain of starvation. To forget the faces of each child-turned-mercenary that died before my eyes. To forget the sounds of their final breaths and the memories of their suffering. Our suffering. I yearn to forget Casimir's beaten, unrecognizable, lifeless body.

I long to feel warmth in place of icy abandonment. Warmth in place of shivering out long winters in thin tents. Gentle warmth in place of burning my throat with boiling water to prevent freezing to death on blizzardy mountains. I long to feel the weight of each life I have slaughtered in place of feeling nothing. I long to love again. To feel love in place of loneliness. To feel purpose in place of aimless, meaningless survival. I long to fight for hope.

Searing currents of electrifying heat rip through my veins— the same agonizing heat that manifested when I nearly struck Adrienne with lightning. This is the same hellish wave of heat that manifested in the light luminary's presence while I feared my head would split in half. Jolts of adrenaline kick in, and I attempt to withdraw my hands from Adrienne's grasp. She firmly holds them in place, refusing to let go.

"Have you lost your mind? Let go so I don't fry us both! Get the hell out of here!" I scream as my vision blurs.

"You're doing great, Amira. You have found the flow of your magic." Adrienne's voice remains soothingly calm despite the storm threatening to explode from within me and transform this room into an electrocution chamber. "Acknowledge your power. Respect its existence within you and command it to submit to your will. Take a deep breath, and imagine an impenetrable wall holding back its lethal flow."

It's no use. All my mind can conjure is a paper-thin wall against a raging flood of power from The God of Light. Kallik's divine power demands to break free from my paper-thin dam and flow without seizing in the form of lightning. My limbs tremble under the weight of power coursing through me, threatening to make a cataclysmic escape. It's only a matter of when lightning finally escapes from my fingertips into the small confinements of this room and kills us both.

"Adrienne!" I whimper in panic. I know by the rattling of my bones that I can't hold my surging power back any longer. It has to go somewhere, or my body will explode. Our lives are over if I can't immediately redirect its fatal flow.

Adrienne speaks with authoritative calmness. "Stay with me, Amira. I want you to envision a portal. A portal to a place where you can easily find stability. Imagine that place."

"Stability? What about me makes you think I've ever known stability?"

My hands are now convulsing and burning in sizzling heat. Not a single location that remotely symbolizes stability comes to mind. My soul frantically searches for an image of stability and comes up with nothing other than the dragon knight instructor in front of me. The portal Adrienne commands me to imagine turns out to be my lips crashing into hers. Her thighs wrapped around my back. Escaping my demented reality in the waves of her touch.

I lunge forward, throwing myself into Adrienne's lap. I kiss her with crushing force, knowing our lives depend on it. Her lips are silken against mine, supernaturally cleansing my distress with euphoric peace. Without hesitation, Adrienne throws her arms around my neck, parting her lips slightly, inviting my tongue to slip inside. I pull her tongue deep into my throat, pulling her body up against mine as I run my hands down her long, slender back. The closer I reel her in, the farther the fatal threats of my power recede.

"*Amira,*" Adrienne softly moans as she grabs a handful of my hair, pulling it backward, leaving my neck vulnerably exposed. Throwing myself to Adrienne's mercy is somehow the key to redirecting the lethal force of nature I have become.

The warmth of Adrienne's lips tracing their way down the nape of my neck nearly sets me over the edge. Her breasts crash into my chest, sending tantalizing waves of tingles between my thighs.

In this moment, Adrienne is no longer the noble brat who kidnapped me and forced my service to The Knights of Blackthorn. She is no longer the horrendous monster who drugged me and left me to fight for my life in the Kanoelani. In this moment, Adrienne is the peace that calmed the storm. The stability that shattered my world as I knew it and altered the course of my fate.

By now, it's clear we are no longer at risk of lightning releasing from my body. It also becomes clear she is not ready to release me from the dangerous fire we are fueling. I surrender to her beautiful, enticing mystery as she takes the lead.

Adrienne pins my shoulders to the ground and pulls her body on top of mine. "Gods, I hate how badly I want you," she whispers. Her heartbeat on top of mine has me desperate to feel nothing but her bare skin against mine. For a moment, I debate unlacing her leather corset and throwing off our clothes, but I don't dare interrupt the perfection of this moment. Part of me fears it will be all over if I move another muscle.

Adrienne's lips trace down my jawline, venturing lower and lower. She rips the neckline of my tunic, working her kisses down my chest until the warmth of her breath grazes over my breasts. I gently rock my hips back and forth, chasing after dangerously satisfying friction as she swivels her hips in response. The flawless flow of her hips combined with her kisses across my breasts is a near out-of-body experience.

"You're not asking for more, are you?" Adrienne asks in a low, breathy tone between waves of unrelenting kisses.

"*Please*," I beg pathetically.

Adrienne's nails dig into my thighs as she starts slowly pulling down my pants. She sends a trail of firm, pulsating shadows, cruelly taunting my clit. I grind against the rhythm of the shadowy vibrations as pleasure floods every inch of my body. I'm far too breathless to beg for more. As if reading the desperation on my face, Adrienne sends her shadows inside of me, increasing the intensity of their pulsations. She curls the vibrations in and out, faster and faster.

"*More*," I moan as my body shakes beyond control.

Adrienne laughs darkly and gives me a sinister smirk, eager to oblige my request as cruelly as possible. She covers my mouth as she increases the intensity until her shadows feel nearly seismic. Release consumes me as I can't help but let out a feral scream.

"Who's power is in control now, my love?"

We freeze in silence, unprepared to process what in the realms just happened between us. I awkwardly comb my fingers through my tangled, sweaty hair and do my best to destroy the evidence of our grounding exercise turned explosive…chemistry.

"Something tells me that wasn't what those earth mages had in mind when they developed their grounding technique," I dare to break the uncomfortable lull.

Adrienne looks at me and erupts in laughter. Honestly, I don't blame her and can't exactly hate her for it. Just days ago, she plucked me off the shores of Tourmaline and wished to see the spirits of Kanoelani execute me. Just days ago, we both wanted each other dead.

"Oh, I'd be lying if I said I expected any of that. Magic flows from the soul. Our souls determine how much force we can withstand wielding before burning out, along with what grounds us. Apparently, your soul perceives mine as your source of stability. You left me with very little choice but to play along." Adrienne smirks as she reels in her composure.

"I—I…can't believe I lost control like that." A scarlet sea of guttural embarrassment floods my cheeks. We wouldn't be here right now if I had suppressed my impulses. My soul finding its grounding stability in Adrienne couldn't possibly be a larger shot to my pride.

"If that's what you call losing control, you're in for a wild ride with me, my love," Adrienne winks. "That was pretty tame for my standards. I could have had a lot more fun with you, but we can't have you incapacitated for the rest of the day."

My heart flutters like swarms of insects, and I nearly trip over nothing. "So…what does this mean for us? Does this mean we have to do that every time I lose control of my powers?" I ask apprehensively as the heat on my face intensifies.

"If my suspicions are correct, any amount of physical contact would do the trick to ground you. Sorry if that's not the answer you were looking for," Adrienne taunts. Gods, she's never going to let me live this down. Dealing with her is about to become insufferable in ways I never imagined.

"But…maybe if you're good and remain on your best behavior, you'll still see more of those tricks you seemed to really enjoy."

My heart rapid-fires at the mention of Adrienne's rippling currents of pulsating shadows. I never would've suspected shadows capable of wielding horrific death would also be capable of such earth-shattering pleasure. What does it say about my life that Adrienne is my closest source of stability?

"It says it's a good thing fate led you to the light luminary, leading you to the Knights of Blackthorn. Only the gods know the disastrous trajectory of your life when Adrienne found you on that beach," Lumithra interjects.

"Now is not the time for you to intrude into my headspace!" I retort.

"When I said Adrienne should lock the two of you up in the library until you could get along properly, that's not exactly what I had in mind. I give you much credit for exceedingly over-achieving, however".

"I don't have the capacity to be mocked by a dragon right now. Go do whatever it is that dragons do with their spare time," I snap.

"Seems like The White Empress isn't going to let you live this down. It's written all over your expression," Adrienne sneers. I take a deep breath, hoping that somehow prevents my face from turning any redder than it already is.

"Don't worry, it's cute when you're flustered," she teases.

"It's not going to be cute if I have to ground myself again so soon…so I suggest you don't test me." Electrifying currents boil beneath my skin once more, promising deadly threats if I don't get myself under control.

"Oh, I think we both know it is going to be cute if you have to ground yourself again," Adrienne taunts as she grabs my wrists. My magic obeys her touch, instantly returning to a state of dormancy.

Why didn't my soul settle for picturing myself alone in the dark evergreen forests, sharpening my knives under the shade of its trees, surrounded by nothing but Blackthorn's comforting blankets of fog? Why did my soul gravitate to Adrienne over solitude? A dragon knight instructor, as the grounding source for my raging magic, has to be some sort of cruel punishment from the gods. I suppose it's a relatively merciful punishment, considering I nearly fried the only descendant of Kamaris and her dragon right out of the sky. Knowing how much Adrienne will enjoy holding this over my head is enough to churn the contents of my stomach.

"The last thing I need is you allowing this to go to your head. I'm fairly certain the stench of your ego is enough to cover the borders of Blackthorn and beyond," I remark.

"Well, I do most certainly delight in the power I hold over you, my love. I won't deny that. However, it would be recklessly foolish of me not to give you a little warning. The last thing either of us needs is for you to fall in love with me. I am a rather dangerous creature. It's best for us both that grounding you never leads to romance." Adrienne's tone quickly shifts from prideful sneers to that of a sincere warning.

"You're joking, right?" I can't help but laugh at the absurdity of Adrienne's warning. "You're giving yourself a lot of credit if you think I'd fall for you so easily. I can swear on my soul that will not be an issue. Also, I think you and I both know I'm more than capable of handling dangerous. Frankly, I'm a little insulted," I retort. As if I wasn't born an orphaned, ruthless killer raised by a blood-lusting, drunken mercenary. As if I wasn't a light-wielding demigoddess, a descendant of Kallik.

"I think you've learned by now that I am nothing like any lowly, mortal criminal you've ever assassinated with merc blades and fists," Adrienne counters.

"I know you're the sole descendant of Kamaris. Is that all there is to be afraid of?"

Adrienne's ashen eyes fade into a haunting gaze resembling how I'd imagine an ancient wraith. Her playful, taunting smile has been replaced by a dark, solemn expression that sends chills scuttling down my spine. "If only that were all there was to fear, my love." She winks as she cloaks herself in a swarm of shadows, hastily disappearing as far as she can from the dim, candlelit room.

"What exactly am I supposed to be afraid of?" I ask Lumithra, hoping her divine trove of knowledge may provide some insight.

"It is against the code of dragons to pry into the personal affairs of half-mortals with whom we did not bond. We have all sworn an oath to The Elder Spirit of The Kanoelani to prevent such affairs from distracting us from our purpose— to defend Blackthorn's sacred grounds. Whatever Adrienne chooses to disclose or not disclose is entirely her decision. I will not stray from my duty to dabble in her affairs," she answers firmly.

"So...you're seriously not going to offer any insight? What if Adrienne is a threat? Can't you share anything? If her touch grounds my magic, I have a right to-"

"My duty is to guide you along your path of the dragon knight and defend Blackthorn. Dragons are not gossip partners. I have known Adrienne much longer than you have, and despite the skeletons in her closet, she is not a threat. This discussion ends here," Lumithra cuts me off.

I still can't help but shudder at what Adrienne is withholding and for what reason. Based on the sudden transformation of her demeanor, whatever she isn't disclosing is enough to trouble a terrifying shadow mage that manipulates the darkness. Maybe it's safer being left in the dark. Perhaps the less I know about a descendant of The Goddess of the Night, the better. All I can do is hope grounding myself in her touch won't be the death of me. The more I allow myself to think about her, the more I invoke death to my peace of mind.

"I'd like to remind you that your seminar is starting soon. Powerful mage of light magic or not, your service and your training are still requested

by The Knights of Blackthorn," Lumithra nags.

I take a deep breath, hoping my exhale will dispel the lingering chills raining down my spine. Somehow, I have to cram more information regarding this new way of life into my overcrowded head.

"Yes, mother."

CHAPTER 10
The Accolades

I fail to shut my brain off while strolling through the halls heavily decorated in murals of Niroshen and the gods who occupy its holy, immortal realms. Spectrums of romantic, vibrant colors paint glorious stories of power, prosperity, and peace. Stories that will forever be nothing more than distant myths the peasant slums will never find relatable. Walking around the monastery in warm, dry clothes, free of hunger pains, and a massive roof over my head churns my stomach with roiling guilt.

If half-mortals were born and raised in the slums, Blackthorn would've likely lavished them with its bountiful riches and resources. The peasant slums would instead be crowned jewels as brilliant as Vespera rather than neglected, infected scabs. However, the gods of Niroshen are known to only invite residents of Blackthorn's flourishing cities to The Immortal Realms to conceive their half-mortal offspring. The peasant slums must have been damned to endless cycles of poverty since the creation of Elmoria. Did the power of the luminaries fail to extend to that region of Blackthorn? Or did the elemental gods decide part of their world needed to contain persistent suffering to entertain them for eternity?

My promise to Lumithra and Casimir to fight for a brighter Blackthorn is the only reason I haven't acted on delicious temptations to flee the monastery. Blackthorn won't be brighter until its bleakest crevices are illuminated with the power, prosperity, and peace portrayed in the murals of Niroshen.

I shuffle my way into a lofty, overcrowded seminar hall and weave through vacant-less rows in search of an empty seat. While I wasn't sure what to expect walking into a religious seminar, I wasn't expecting aromas of burning frankincense clashing with the stench of sweaty training armor. I wasn't expecting knights and apprentices to vastly outnumber Lady Rhonwen's priestesses.

"Amira!" Irvette shouts over the crowd, signaling to the empty seat beside her. After nearly striking her instructor out of the sky just a couple of hours ago, I'm surprised to see her greeting me with a warm, hospitable smile.

"I'm glad to see you here!" she reels me in with a hearty, welcoming hug. Her scent of sea salt and citrus is at least a preferable contrast to the sweltering sea of sweat-stained fighting leathers and steel. "Zephyr and Arden may or may not have placed wagers on whether or not you'd show up," Irvette confesses.

Zephyr elbows Arden in the ribs. "Well, well, well. Looks like someone owes me ten copper coins," he crows, waving a hand in front of Arden's face.

"Yeah, yeah. You still owe me a pint from our last bet, remember? Buy me a round tonight, and then we'll talk," Arden writes Zephyr off dismissively.

"Ignore them," Irvette sighs. "It's just nice to see Adrienne didn't hand your ass to you after this morning. Now that you've both been accounted for in one piece since your duel is all that matters."

Nothing about me is currently in one piece. Not after feeling the weight of Adrienne's lips crushing mine. Not after my soul reacted to her touch as my source of grounding stability.

Before the squad can question me further, Felix takes to the altar. He smothers the burning candle flames, and the chattering room falls silent as if rehearsed.

"What is Felix doing down there?" I ask Irvette.

"Felix holds many titles around here," Irvette beams with supportive pride. "After passing his Kanoelani Trials, it didn't take long before The High Priestess realized his gifts extend far beyond just fire-wielding. She made quick use of his diplomacy, appointing him as Blackthorn's Emissary. He's also due to receive his accolade as a formal dragon knight, but as tensions have been building overseas, he's been too preoccupied to make it official as of late," Irvette whispers.

"Does he normally lead religious seminars at the monastery too?" I ask.

"No. This is not one of his regular tasks. Today's seminar must be a little different." Irvette fidgets in her seat apprehensively, as if knowing more than she is letting on.

Lady Rhonwen, Adrienne, and two dozen knight instructors file into the room, standing at attention in an orderly row behind Felix. A woman cloaked in black with a hood concealing most of her face stands at his right-hand side. This feels cryptically excessive for just a routine seminar. Quiet gasps and whispered conversations cascade down the hall like dominoes.

"My apologies for disrupting your hour of studying the gods today," Felix bows. "I know you are used to one of our lovely priestesses or Lady Rhonwen leading our seminars. However, we must use this hour together to discuss urgent matters. Please kindly adapt to today's anomaly with grace and respect. In a few moments, I will hand the floor over to General Cyrina, a descendant of Solaris, to deliver an important address."

Felix signals to the woman standing to his right. She lowers the hood of her cloak, revealing a pair of fiery, crimson eyes nearly identical to his. Her beaming red hair of scarlet flame, woven into a waterfall braid, shines like a beacon against her dark fighting leathers. She doesn't just look like a fire mage. Her very essence is fire.

"General Cyrina is a master fire mage," Zephyr whispers. "The most brilliant descendent of Solaris Elmoria has seen in centuries. She commands elite squads filled with Blackthorn's strongest mages. If she cleared time to make an address-"

"Quit your jabbering before you get our squad assigned scullery duty," Irvette interrupts.

"General Cyrina will now address the monastery regarding developing tensions beyond our borders. You are to show her critical respect," Felix commands.

"Now is not the time to drift into the catacombs of your mind. Your undivided attention is of the essence," Lumithra claws into my mind with a concerningly stern urgency.

"You know what this is all about? I thought dragons weren't gossip partners," I retort in a mocking tone.

"Correct, my child. We are defenders of Blackthorn. Now, pay attention."

Felix steps to the back as General Cyrina takes to the altar. The murmuring whispers dissipate, infiltrating the lecture hall with an eerie silence rivaling that of a graveyard. My head is spinning. With hardly one training session under my belt, I'm about to listen to a general deliver an address. After just one training session, I'm about to hear an official declaration of war.

"For the past six hundred years, Blackthorn, Helia, and Eldermoor have peacefully respected one another's borders, abiding by the settlements forged out of The Luminary War. That torrential bloodshed has served as our sobering reminder that the luminaries are to be undisturbed by the hands of mortals and half-mortals alike. The luminaries are to slumber unprovoked, only to be touched by the divine hands of their original artists- The Elemental Gods. With grave sorrow, I must report Elmoria's delicate balance is now officially under attack." General Cyrina pauses to allow her words to marinate through the crowd— graciously gifting us a brief moment to prepare ourselves for the bomb she is about to drop.

"At the break of dawn, Eldermoor launched raven-griffin battalions on Volkan Isle, Helia's largest trading port. The city quickly surrendered to Eldermoorian occupation after facing catastrophic fatalities of blood mage attacks. We suspect they have secretly acquired at least one of the luminaries to pull off such a large-scale attack, but intel has yet to confirm that. Regardless, we must act under the assumption that Eldermoor seeks to expand its occupation across all of Helia in the name of Osiris and will then set course for Blackthorn. Helia has declared war on Eldermoor, and Blackthorn will answer their call for aid."

I lower my head between my knees as if that would somehow stop the room from spinning like threads of raw fibers running through a hand spindle. As if taking my eyes off General Cyrina will make every problem magically disappear without a residual trace. My pulse slams in my eardrums as the blood rushes to my head. Too much. This is all too much to process.

"Take a deep breath," Irvette gently coaches in an instinctive tone as she places a hand on my back. She calmly presses the weight of her hand against my shivering spine as if she recently received the same form of comfort. How long has she known about this? How long has Felix known? Did anyone know the civilians of Volkan Isle were being brutally slaughtered before breakfast? My stomach can't afford to speculate any longer.

"Lady Rhonwen, along with Felix and I, will coordinate with Helia's Royal Court this afternoon to strategize our response," Cyrina continues. "We have already imposed an embargo against Eldermoor, restricting all imports and exports. Between fighting Eldermoor's forces in Helia, and defending our own borders from their advances, we will no choice but to fight this war on two fronts. All apprentices will be enrolled in active duty to reinforce our battalions effective immediately."

The silence of the room erupts into volcanic havoc among the apprentices. Questions spew through the room like sputtering fountains of lava, heating the room with molten panic. Clamors regarding Helia's pegasus knights, how none of our spies were tipped off to the attack, speculations on the whereabouts of the luminaries, the power of blood mages, and curses to Osiris bounce off the echoing walls, making the vast room feel suddenly very, very small.

"How was such a vital trading port silently occupied under everyone's noses? Why the sudden boldness despite understanding the consequences?" I ask Lumithra, still in disbelief that Helia's largest trading port has fallen under enemy occupation so quietly and effortlessly.

"Eldermoor's increasing but quiet, peaceful presence in Helia gave no valid reason to disrupt our centuries of harmony by opposing them. Their sudden surprise attack was nothing short of a shocking act of betrayal to Elmoria's peace and a tragic oversight on our end. As far as the embargo, Eldermoor must assume they have the power to end this quickly before their people suffer extensive consequences."

"SILENCE!" General Cyrina bellows, releasing a wall of fire from her breath, reeling the clamors of the room to controlled silence. "Save your questions for your direct reports and your dragons. They will tell you everything you need to know. Using this time together to engage in mass panic is fruitless! Prepare to receive battalion assignments from your instructors. Apprentices on the path of the dragon knight, this seminar is now a mass accolade ceremony. In our hour of darkness, with The High Priestess as our witness, you are all Dragon Knights of Blackthorn. Your instructors are all now promoted to the status of Wing Commanders."

Every face in the room blanches in somber unison. For Lady Rhonwen and General Cyrina to permit such a dramatic notion, they must suspect Eldermoor as a far more substantial threat than they anticipated. Blackthorn's half-mortals pull from the powers of six elemental gods. Helia's Pegasus Knights pull from the magic of Aisling, The Goddess of Illusions. Seven gods against Eldermoor's blood mages in service to Osiris, The God of Death. Why are our leaders acting as if we are severe underdogs?

"I practically have zero training. This decision couldn't possibly be any

more asinine. What in the realms are they thinking?"

"You are correct. This decision is utterly asinine. However, it is necessary. The consequences of not enlisting every capable soul in Blackthorn would be far more disastrous. When fighting those who call upon Osiris, you must always assume they're operating with hidden artilleries up their sleeves. The day we underestimate the power of The Dark Realms is the day we hand the fate of Elmoria and its sacred luminaries to Eldermoor's will."

Lumithra's omen rattles my bones. Just a few sunrises ago, I was fighting my way through Rhydian's list of scoundrels to evade as much torture as possible and line his pockets with precious blood money—blade against blade. Now, I'm expected to fight my way through enemies who summon their powers from an ancient, immortal god of death to evade the end of our world as we know it. Magic that manipulates the forces of nature against magic that manipulates the blood beneath our skin.

One by one, Adrienne and all the dragon knight instructors of the monastery receive Wing Commander patches over their hearts. A white dragon defending three mountain peaks with a breath of shimmering flame reaching toward Niroshen. Symbolic of Blackthorn's commitment to safeguard its borders with its dragons, to preserve the harmony and balance of Elmoria's three lands, and to serve while revering The Gods of Niroshen.

"To conclude my address and our ceremony of accolades, I now leave you with a parting message from our high priestess, Lady Rhonwen," Cyrina announces.

The High priestess, luminescent with her moon-white tresses and alabaster silk gown, is the tranquility that smothers the flames of spiraling panic. The entire room responds to her presence as a wounded child seeking assurance in the healing kisses of a steadfast mother before she utters a word.

"My beloved, courageous warriors of Blackthorn. Do not be dismayed. There is no denying the hour of darkness eclipsing over our lands. However, there is no denying the light of Niroshen shines in our favor. I am confident our trials will mold you into the valiant, noble defenders of hope you were always destined to become. May the light of the gods and goddesses guide you well. It is their light that burns within you. It is their light that goes before you. Go in the confidence gifted to us by the companionship of our sacred, unwavering, eternal warriors. You are now dismissed." Lady Rhonwen bows, maintaining a calm, fearless composure.

Rows of apprentices solemnly file out of the seminar hall as if exiting after a funeral recessional. I can't help but wonder how many of us will be marching to the frontlines of our death sentence. How many empty seats will haunt this room with grief the next time we are due to gather?

"I hereby decree a mandatory squad outing to The Wretched Owl tonight as our first act as official dragon knights. First round of ales on me," Zephyr declares, throwing an arm over Arden's shoulders with a mocking smirk.

"Gods, I hate that I'm on board with this," Irvette mutters.

To my surprise, I can't find it in me to decline the invitation. It's nearly impossible to believe that a night on the town downing ales might pose a better distraction than solitude. Leaving myself alone in the company of my tortured brain screaming in silence is now a dangerous gamble. Now that my inner chaos poses the risk of triggering deadly outbursts of lightning storms, I need a distraction that will prevent me from relying on Adrienne's touch. The last thing I need is to rely on the touch of a seductive, gorgeous monster to ground my sanity.

CHAPTER 11
The Wretched Owl

Blackthorn's iridescent capital city is even more breathtaking when explored on foot than seen from the skies on Lumithra's back. The amethyst cobblestone beneath our feet sparkles with beaming hues of violet, sapphire, ruby, and opal, mirroring the star-laden night sky kissed by mountainous silhouettes. The streets are lined with the bustling shops of Vespera, along with cottages swallowed by towering ivy vines and private gardens of arctic thyme and mountain avens.

I wonder how many knights may never return to their little mortal slice of Niroshen. How many peasants will beg to join the ground forces for the promise of food rations to face any death other than starvation?

Aromas leaking out of The Brine and Bone Butchers, Fauna's Florals and Elixirs, and The Blackthorn Bakery compete for the mountain-crisp air space and interrupt my thoughts. Vast window displays showcasing weapons forged by The Molten Ember and precious diamond jewelry illuminating the displays of The Goddess Trove starkly contrast the diseased, trash-littered streets where I grew up fighting for my survival.

Zephyr quickly whirls into Fauna's Florals and Elixirs, leaving a trail of winds behind him. We watch from the windows as he drops a few copper coins into the shopkeeper's hands and whirls back out of the jingling doors with a single black rose.

"Oh, for me? You shouldn't have!" Arden jeers, stroking his stubbled jaw.

"In your dreams, darling." A smug expression forms on Zephyr's lips as his glacial eyes narrow with amorous plotting. A young woman with hair rich as aged mahogany clad in a cerulean, busty dress steps out of a bookstore several shops ahead of us. Zephyr clenches the rose between his teeth as he winks at us.

"Here we go again." Irvette runs her fingers through her aquamarine braids, pulling them over her eye as if preparing to look away from the scene of an unfortunate accident. Zephyr squats, drawing a blast of wind from the ground beneath him with the calculated circular patterns of his hands. He launches himself into the air, exhibiting unnecessary demonstrations of his wind-wielding magic.

"Does he do this sort of thing often?" I ask. Is this how a town of half-mortals entertains themselves when they've never known stomachs bloated with hunger? Waltzing into shops and buying gifts to swoon strangers for fun?

"What do you think?" Arden scoffs.

Zephyr executes an intricate, spiraling descent right in front of his target of desire. Bowing before her, he delicately places the black rose atop the stack of books in her trembling arms. "A gorgeous rose for a gorgeous, ravishing maiden. Would you care to grace Blackthorn's newest dragon knights with your company at The Wretched Owl?" He inquires with a dark, smug tone.

"Oh, I hate that I can't look away from this," Irvette sighs.

"I'm on my way to grace my husband with my company in our bed, thank you very much." The gorgeous, ravishing maiden shoves the rose back in between Zephyr's teeth before strutting away with her books. Arden and Irvette join together in unified snickering as Zephyr walks back to us in shamed defeat.

"I'll care to grace you with my company as your lovely suitor this fine evening," Arden taunts, linking his arm with Zephyr's. Zephyr shakes free of his grasp.

"I would rather choke on cold, undercooked porridge than accept you as a suitor." Zephyr retorts. I am very much regretting my poor decision for the night.

After strolling through the vibrant streets painted with rainbows of overgrown gardens, illuminated by starlight and flickering ember candle flame, we arrive at a shanty stone pub hidden in the city's alcove. Despite the charm of the moss invading the weathered stone exterior, the pub is considerably an eyesore compared to the rest of Vespera's glistening beauty. A sturdy trunk of an immaculate oak tree emerges through a hole out of the center of the dilapidated roof. The tree is occupied by a parliament of spectating owls perched amongst its branches, deeming The Wretched Owl a fitting name for the ornery haunt.

Arden holds the large iron doors open as we cram into the overcrowded Wretched Owl. A small, wooden stage encircles the massive oak trunk rooted in the center of the noisy, dim-lit pub. Drunken patrons dance without rhythm across the stage, lost in the folky sea shanties provided by a group of novice bards. We sift through the lively, bantering crowds like tightly packed sardines to snag a small vacancy at the bar.

"Four pints of Golden Dragon Ale, please." Zephyr waves down a freckled, green-eyed barkeep with curly locks of auburn. The skirt of her ivory frock cascades from underneath her chestnut corset as she sways her hips to the tunes of the bards, overfilling our mugs with crisp, frothy ale.

"Thank you, darling." Zephyr pays the barkeep with a generous tip and his previously rejected black rose. Her cheeks flush like pink carnations.

"Is-is this for me?" She asks in flustered confusion, picking up the rose.

"It's all yours—just a small token of my appreciation for your sweet smile."

The soft, pink blush of the barkeep's cheekbones is now bright enough to fill every darkened corner of the pub with crimson light. "My shift ends in an hour if you'd like to stick around," she informs Zephyr with a sultry smirk.

"Unbelievable," Arden mutters, downing a gulp of ale.

"Leave it to Zeph to forget about Volkan Isle and our new promotions by seducing strangers." Irvette rolls her eyes at Zephyr, but he doesn't take notice. He appears long gone in a trance of admiration, conversing with his pretty little distraction.

"Tell me more about yourself," Irvette shifts her attention toward me. "I don't know much about you other than that you're a descendant of Kallik, mysteriously hailing from the unnamed villages in the South. I'd love to hear more of your story."

Irvette means well with her soft, sweet enthusiasm, but her words make me feel like a cornered, wild beast waiting to be probed. I choke as I swallow my drink too hard. "It's going to take me a lot more than a pint of ale to entertain that discussion," I grumble.

"If we're going to be covering each other's backs in a war together, shouldn't we get to know each other a little better? You don't have to share anything that would be painful to discuss. Just start with something small," she gently encourages.

I can't help but chuckle at the thought of fishing my brain for a story to share that isn't rooted in pain. Memories of administering and witnessing morbid deaths, Rhydian's brutal punishments, nearly freezing to death, starving to death, and daily fights for survival are all that arise. Irvette may have been nothing but kind and hospitable toward me since we met, but that does not entitle her to the knowledge of my vulnerabilities. Just the thought of casually sharing my nightmares over drinks in a noisy pub rattles my bones with jarring, electric sparks.

"I could have spent the night alone in my room, but I had to opt for a night on the town with nosy, noble mage brats," I vent to Lumithra in an effort to blow off some steam.

"The water mage means well. Loyal, unbreakable squad camaraderie is valued directly under their sacred service to Blackthorn. Perhaps start

with discussing your love for nature. Something small. You are in control of where this conversation leads," Lumithra advises.

The room suddenly feels smaller and louder, as if the walls are closing in on me. As if every eye in the room is on me, waiting to see how the beast will respond when provoked. My throat goes dry, and I freeze, failing to conjure any plan to execute simple small talk. "I don't understand how my upbringing is relevant to my abilities as a dragon knight," I snap cruelly.

"I promise you can trust me." Irvette seems frustratingly unbothered by my cruel tone. "I promise you'll be safe with our squad. If we're going to be serving our nation together as an unfaltering unit, you'll have to learn to trust us," she implores.

Trust. I've only known trust as a weapon of lethally honed deceit, ripping through manipulated, vulnerable pawns. Trust is a gift I will never give to the knights who fail to recognize gluttonous monsters and hire them as unquestioned mercenaries. Trust is what gifted Rhydian with innocent, orphaned infants to craft into inhuman, murderous weapons to wield until I watched them all break. How much longer before his last remaining weapon finally breaks too?

"Don't lose yourself, Amira. You can rise above this." Lumithra's voice is a faint, distant whisper as my blood stirs with searing heat.

My vision blurs, and I'm suddenly no longer at The Wretched Owl. I'm fourteen years old, delivering Rhydian the severed head of a crooked courtesan caught making deals with fathers selling their daughters. My limbs are frozen from the hours spent trekking through a wintry blizzard in nothing more than a thin, ragged tunic and loose cotton trousers. I no longer feel the snow seeping through the holes of my boots. I trek past my tent, barely clinging to its stakes in the howling winds, and barge through the doors of Rhydian's cabin.

"What in gods' realms took you so long?" Rhydian bellows in volumes that could provoke an avalanche as he snatches the bagged head from my ghost-white, trembling fingers.

"I carried out my campaign to completion. Is that not good enough?" The heat emitting from Rhydian's hearth is the only reason I can even form words through the lingering chattering of my teeth.

"Good enough? Is that what this is about? Just being good enough? Gods, I can't stand adolescents. You know the faith I lose in you every time you delay. How are the knights going to continue commissioning me if I can't swiftly cleanse their lowly scum? How am I supposed to trust you?" Rhydian draws the hilt of his favored dagger for my punishments.

With one brutal kick, Rhydian knocks me off my feet, leaving me prone underneath the weight of his boot. His suffocating weight presses down into my back, starving my lungs of air. My veins are now possessed with blazing currents of raw, electrical flames as I anticipate the sound of my ribs cracking. My blood is boiling, screaming for my body to unleash white flames of lightning from the confinement of my fingertips.

"Amira!" Lumithra's voice faintly calls out to me as I relive Rhydian's blade cutting through my skin, carving a cavernous slice into my frozen back. I reach for one of my blades and roll onto my fresh wounds as I slice through the back of his ankle.

"Bitch! Give me one good reason I shouldn't carve into your chest and rip out that sloppy, ungrateful heart of yours."

Rhydian disappears, and all I can see is a vision of white, electrical fire, begging to destroy and devour every inch of the pub. A premonition of white-lightning flames burning bodies to ash. I am no longer in control of my body, trapped somewhere in the in-between of reality and one of my countless nightmares.

"Amira! Amira!"

My internal flames recede to nothing as smothered by the familiar, dark voice screaming my name. A familiar scent of lavender and sage draws my awareness back to The Wretched Owl. As I slowly readjust to my surroundings, I'm met with Adrienne's stormy grey eyes studying mine with fierce concern. Her arms are tightly wrapped around me, grounding the lightning force within me that nearly swallowed this place in electrical, alabaster flames.

"Thank gods she's back to normal," Irvette sighs heavily in relief, peering over Adrienne's shoulder. It takes a full moment before I realize I'm on the ground, with my chair tipped over beside me.

Back to normal? What is that supposed to mean? Guttural humiliation from a room full of eyes plastered to me like bricks on mortar prevents me from asking out loud. There's no evidence I caused the slightest trace of any damage, so why is everyone staring at me like they just witnessed an exorcism?

"This is certainly not how I envisioned you screaming my name," I whisper to Adrienne, attempting to shift any of the attention off how close I came to incinerating The Wretched Owl in flames of lightning. Her eyes narrow in on me, unamused by my pitiful attempt at humor.

"This is certainly not how I envisioned having to leave in the middle of a council meeting. Do you have any idea what just happened?" Adrienne asks, her tone low and demanding. Not a single patron dares to take their eyes off me. Even the musicians are staring at me with aroused hyper-vigilance as they continue nervously strumming their folk melodies with a little less free-spiritedness.

"Based on how everyone is staring at me as if I just summoned a wraith out of The Dark Realms, I guess I don't know everything. Any of your speculations are as good as mine," I snap defensively.

"I witnessed the whole thing. I can explain it... I think," Irvette answers, lacking confidence in her voice. "We were mid-conversation, and out of nowhere...she just froze. Her eyes transformed into blinding orbs of white light. Looking at them was like looking at the sun. She went into a trance-like state, fell out of her seat, and started thrashing on the ground. No one was able to snap her out of it. Not until you showed up and threw your arms around her," Irvette mutters. Her blanched complexion suggests it isn't normal for a mage to be thrown into a trance-like state while struggling for control over their powers.

"Thank you, Irvette." Adrienne returns her focus back to me, refusing to release me from her arms. While fully expecting to be met with eyes filled with fury, her gaze is that of a surprising empathy, catching me off guard. "Can you please share what you can recall from your experience?" She asks me gently.

I allow myself a deep breath before answering. The sooner I cooperate, the sooner I can get the realms out of here and rid myself of all the eyes latched onto me like bloodsucking parasites. "All I know is that at some point during our conversation, I was pulled into an old memory. Like I was treading water, and something pulled me beneath the surface. At times, I could faintly hear Lumithra call out to me, but I had little to no grip on my present surroundings. The deeper the memory dragged me under, the further removed from reality I became. The harder and harder it became to suppress my power from releasing beyond my control." Power I still hardly understand. Power that apparently has manifestations I have yet to discover. Am I ever going to be able to venture anywhere without Adrienne ever again?

"Mini bolts of lightning sporadically sparked out of your skin, forming white flames," Irvette adds. "I've seen countless mages fighting for control over their elements. I've fought for my own control before. Yet I think I can safely speak for the whole room when I say none of us have witnessed anything quite like this before."

"You've never experienced a light mage before or any of the ways their magic can manifest," Adrienne scoffs as if speaking from experience. Gods, her arrogance is insufferable.

"From the sounds of it, Amira love, your magic was charging to take the shape of lightning flames. That power of yours sure is eager to manifest into new forms. For the safety of every living creature that comes anywhere near you, it looks like I'll have to keep a much closer eye on you." Adrienne flashes me a taunting smile as if she just defeated me in a game of chess and has no plans of letting me live it down.

No one was able to snap her out of it. Not until you showed up and threw your arms around her. My brain mocks me with Irvette's words. How in the realms of the gods did my soul gravitate toward Adrienne as the source that grounds my powers? The brazen dragon knight instructor, now Wing Commander, who practically forced me into this new life without a choice? Not that giving up a life under Rhydian is anything to grieve, but at least I knew what to expect. At least my trials with Rhydian were predictable.

"Now that I saved all your asses from flames of mass electrocution be sure you're all out of here at a decent hour. We're dragon knights at war now and should expect to be ready to receive assignments at a moment's notice. You'll need all the rest you can get while it's still available," Adrienne warns.

The color drains from Irvette's rich hazelnut complexion as if tonight's events distracted her from our jarring reality a little too effectively. Arden places a hand on her shoulder, offering her a light, empathetic smile. If any part of him feels unsettled about the inevitable roles we'll be serving in war, his calm composure certainly doesn't express it.

"I'm heading back now to squeeze in some training. Bloodying up my knuckles a bit would be nice before calling it a night." Arden leaves a tip next to his empty mug for our barkeep, who's blushing and giggling at Zephyr's banter between taking care of her patrons. At least, it appears they've already moved on from what happened with me tonight.

"I will ensure Zephyr receives your word, Wing Commander," Irvette lets out a tired sigh.

"You can skip the formalities. I'm not partial to elaborate titles." Adrienne addresses Irvette curtly as she offers me a hand, helping me off the ground. "As for you, my love, you're coming with me."

CHAPTER 12
Tolerate It

Serene melodies of chirping crickets and the owls perched above are a welcomed contrast to the cheery, shrilling fiddles accompanying the drunken singing and rowdy banter confined within the tiny pub. Emerging out of the stale, stagnant air brings a soothing relief to my lungs.

"Looks like I won't be able to leave you too far from my sights for the time being," Adrienne breaks the silence of our walk to gods-knows where. "Especially now that our services could be requested on the battlefield with a moment's notice. I've got to hand it to you, though. Your power contains a lot more rawness than I expected. It appears to be fueled by more darkness than I truly anticipated."

"What is any of that supposed to mean? How did you even know to come after me tonight in the first place?" I question. Between a violently vivid memory leading me to nearly frying everyone in The Wretched Owl and becoming a dragon knight with zero training out of vast desperation, I've hardly had time to question how Adrienne knew I was about to break without being anywhere near me.

"Always so eager for answers. You truly do need me for everything," Adrienne mocks. I bite my tongue and follow her silently along the shimmering amethyst cobblestone until we reach Vespera's city gates. She greets the sentries as we venture into the fog-laden forest. We don't stop until we're far removed from any traces of a nearby bustling city.

"We should be safe to hold our discussion from here," Adrienne decides.

"Must you always whisk me away to dark, cryptic locations where I have to fear what you'll do to me?" I protest despite knowing it's of no use.

"Don't pretend you don't enjoy the thrill of it, light-bringer. I know you can't thrive without a sense of danger," she smiles cruelly. The slight curve of her dark, satin lips, paired with the alluring storms surging behind her silver eyes nearly takes my breath away. Unfortunately, she's right. Not only can't I thrive without a sense of danger, but apparently, I'm hopelessly attracted to it.

Adrienne grabs the collar of my tunic and tilts my chin up to meet her concentrated, threatening gaze. "Listen carefully. What I am about to share with you does not leave this forest. Understood? You speak of this to no one. Not unless you want me to feed you to Sarthon in exchange for you feeding anyone this knowledge worthy of a death sentence." The tone of her voice is nearly as dark as the tendrils of smoke sifting between her fingers.

I swallow the rocky lump in my throat, praying my heart doesn't leap out of my chest in anticipation of whatever Adrienne had to drag me out in the middle of the woods to disclose. "Understood."

"My soul is the only force that grounds yours. As we know now, especially after tonight, you'll never be able to venture too far from my touch. Unfortunately, that also means some of my secrets aren't exclusively mine to keep anymore. There are things we will have to understand about one another to fight effectively in this war together." Adrienne takes a deep breath, exhaling a cloud of dark smoke, blowing off the steam of her apprehension.

"You want to know why I knew to rush after you and throw my arms around you in the middle of The Wretched Owl? How I knew you were on the verge of losing control over your power despite being out of my sight? I sensed your distress from the monastery. Not only could I sense your distress, but I also saw the entirety of your memory vividly play out in my own mind," she confesses.

The chilling sincerity in her voice tells me this isn't a joke, yet I hardly believe her. Half-mortals manipulate and weaponize the elements of nature to defend the lands created by the gods. They're elemental mages, not mind readers. I fail to form any adequate response to Adrienne's claim, hoping she'll elaborate further rather than waste our time ridiculing me.

"I am darkness herself, my love. I wield it in the shapes of shadows, and I can read it in suffering minds. For what it's worth, I will stop at no ends to see that The Captain pays sufficient atonement for his atrocities committed against you. As soon as Rhydian is delivered to the monastery and I get my hands on him, he'll be begging me to kill him. I'll never be able to forget the look on your face as he lashed into you in his cabin, and the look on his face I will contrive will be much, much worse," Adrienne growls like a wraith as onyx smoke seeps from her fists.

My heart stops as Adrienne recites details from my flashback as if she had witnessed the events right alongside me. I struggle to decide what is more mind-boggling— the fact she can read memories or the fact she now has a passionate hatred for Rhydian over how he treated me. "So, you mean to tell me you can read into peoples' minds, and you want to personally handle Rhydian's execution based off what you saw?"

"We may have gotten off on a terrible start, but even I am not a total heartless monster. You see, I have a problem with anyone who preys on the vulnerable. Rhydian is a total monster, and if a heart somehow exists behind his breastbone, I fully intend on ripping it right out.

"Regarding my abilities, I can't just read minds as if they're books. I am, however, able to read darkened memories and emotions plagued with pain and suffering. I'm ever-so-blessed with front-row seats into the dark memories that haunt mortals and half-mortals alike and the gift of sensing the emotions those memories contrive."

For a moment, I find my heart aching for Adrienne. I struggle to fathom what it must be like to be sucked into such intimate trenches of raw darkness suppressed within everyone she encounters. To share such a millstone of a burden with her newest recruit, who depends on her touch to prevent lethal disasters, must be complicated shoes to walk in. "And this ability of yours is what I am not to disclose to anyone?" I ask sheepishly.

"Reading into the minds of others has never been a reported trait of half-mortals. As far as all of history is concerned, I am the only mage with such an ability. Wisdom says it is best to keep that a secret. Especially during war times."

Adrienne's revelation leaves a giant pit swelling in my stomach. Anytime my past decides to haunt me and throw me into a spiral of distress, she'll be watching my pain from her own mind. There is no hiding from her. To be known so profoundly, to be seen so intimately, may very well be my biggest fear. One of the few fears I am in no condition to confront.

"So, does this mean you'll be in my head constantly now? Reading through my nightmares? Keeping me on a short leash? Am I expected to calmly accept I can no longer keep any of my pain to myself anymore?" I shout as searing heat flushes my cheeks. Even more infuriating, if Adrienne wasn't right here next to me, nothing could prevent my rage from setting scorching white flames or deadly bolts of lightning to this forest.

"Do you think I read into the suffering of other souls for leisurely pleasure?" Adrienne clenches her jaw. "Do you think I enjoy sensing the darkness that plagues other's nightmares? Normally, I can at least ground myself and shut others out when prying into their memories isn't necessary. I can shut their pain out when I don't need to see or sense how it may influence their actions. I can shut it all out when my head just needs some quiet.

"However, I can't shut it off when it comes to you. It's been impossible since your soul grounded to mine. I've already seen into the darkest depths of your soul without having much of a choice. Yet, at the same time, I have only seen a fraction of the bottomless well of your power. Until you mature in your practice, you are a storm no one will stand a chance of surviving without me as your shadow, whether we like it or not. So, at the bare minimum, I suggest we learn to tolerate it."

"Pretty sure we've experimented with tolerating it already," I daringly remind her.

Adrienne chuckles as her lips curve into a smug, wicked grin. It's probably for the best that I don't know exactly what she's thinking about right now, but I'm afraid I still have good enough of an idea.

"We truly are going to be the death of one another," I sigh. I nearly immediately forget how deeply I want to hate Adrienne the moment I notice her thick, raven-black hair luring in reflective beams of moonlight. Flickers of starlight shimmer in her silver irises as if she were made for the night. Or, as if Kamaris created the night just to worship her beauty. The more I trace the lines of her curves with my mind, the more I forget how hopelessly exposed my vulnerabilities are to her. If Adrienne has the ability to explore the depths of my darkness, then maybe I too, should explore every inch of her soul.

"How do you suggest we learn to tolerate it?" I challenge while carefully closing the space between us as if any sudden movement would scare Adrienne away like a deer alerted to danger. My heart violently flips within my chest, anticipating the thrill of what I'm potentially asking for.

Adrienne throws her arms over my shoulders, interlocking her fingers as she reels me in like a siren of the night. "If I was thinking rationally, I'd say we shouldn't escalate our touch to such extremes again so soon. However, the more I think of you squirming beneath me in the chamber, the more I'd very much like to see you so desperate for me again. If you think you can tolerate me," she whispers, delicately brushing her lips against my ear. There is something wildly dangerous about the way I want her. About the way I need her. "I think we're both damned by enough darkness and could use a little distraction. Don't you think, light-bringer?"

I answer by playing with fire in the form of a kiss, claiming Adrienne's lips with mine in a ravenous frenzy. Her breath hitches as she drives her nails down the nape of my neck, inducing euphoric waves of sharp, icy chills down my spine. "You make it damn near impossible to keep my hands off you," she growls. The low, rich tone of her voice heightens my arousal as she traces her fingers down the small of my back.

Our chemistry shouldn't make sense, but it does. Atoms of rivaling elements, siphoning explosive rage into carnal desire. Darkness and light taking turns between acting as devouring forces and relinquishing control to the other.

Adrienne sinks her canines into my neck, adding fuel to the flame as the heat of her breath ignites my skin. I fail to hold back a pitiful moan as she works a trail of hot, breathy kisses down my neck, working her way down to my breasts. Tendrils of shadows make quick work of unlacing my tunic as she flicks the tips of my nipples with delicate sweeps of her tongue.

"I'm afraid your notorious lack of control is contagious, my dear." Adrienne snarls as she lifts me, slamming my back against the sturdy oak tree behind me. I wrap my legs around her hips, locking them in place as I throw my arms over her shoulders and cling to her with all my trembling strength.

A rush of helplessness takes over as her satin-like lips once again meet mine with devastating force. I close my eyes as the world melts away more and more with each passionate kiss. There is no war. No threats to the balance of Elmoria. No concerns regarding the luminaries. There is nothing other than exhilarating bliss consuming my body as I plunge my tongue into Adrienne's mouth, electrified by the little moans that she lets out as our tongues entwine.

There is no Rhydian. No knights, no blood mages. No kingdoms, nations, no borders. No nobles, no peasants. There is only my carnal desire to intensify Adrienne's moans and explore what drives her wild. I would love nothing more than to pleasure her with little tricks of my own. I unwrap my legs and slither my body against hers as I plant my feet back on the ground. My heart pounds violently at the thought of tasting her arousal on my tongue and how sexy she would sound, screaming for me, begging me for more.

The ground beneath us quakes as hundreds of dragon knights blaze across the midnight sky overhead, interrupting the heat of our moment. Adrienne and I grudgingly untangle our bodies as we watch tightly knit formations of dragons and their half-mortal riders disappear into the night with urgent haste. "That's no training exercise." Adrienne hisses as she spews curses under her breath.

At least it's encouraging to see the disappointment in her eyes matching my own. Her eyes filled with thirst, and her cheekbones flushed crimson, indicating she had no plans of cutting us off anytime soon. The jarring return to reality stings like a freshly honed blade to a blistering wound. "Consider yourself lucky. You likely wouldn't have survived what I had in store for you next," I tease, attempting to savor our moment, if only for a little longer.

Within seconds of the battalion fading out of sight, Sarthon and Lumithra descend from the sky as if sent to collect us. Sarthon's molten ember eyes lock onto Adrienne's with a grave, fierce focus. Whatever pressing conversation is taking place between them certainly isn't one of positive news. "Lady Rhonwen wishes to speak with me immediately. I wouldn't be surprised if our squad is among the next batch to receive orders," Adrienne mutters another string of curses as she takes her mount on Sarthon. They dart off into the sky without elaborating any further.

Lumithra helps me take my mount, and the forest quickly becomes tiny specs of emerald trees, barely distinguishable from the ink-black sky. Our swift ascension leaves my stomach on the ground below as we hastily soar over Vespera's sleepless city lights.

"Any idea why we just watched hundreds of dragons hurdle across the sky just now?" I ask Lumithra as my hair lashes across my face in the stinging, chilled breeze of flight.

"Eldermoor's forces are now making substantial advances inland from Volkan Isle. They're continuing to mobilize much more quickly than we anticipated. Lady Rhonwen ordered a battalion to reinforce Helia's defenses. Get whatever sleep you can tonight, if any. As Adrienne stated, I would be surprised if we're not among the next wave of squads to be deployed into action," she responds.

Just moments ago, my heart was pounding with devious schemes to flood Adrienne with pleasure. Now, it pounds in dreadful anticipation of going from mercenary to half-mortal dragon knight.

"I had one session of aerial sparring. I attended one seminar turned general's address. Now, I'm expected to function as a well-prepared dragon knight with a squad I just met. I'm expected to wield magic I barely understand. How is that not going to lead to disaster?" I ask in a humbled panic, unable to recall the last time I felt ill-equipped to take on an assignment. No amount of mercenary training will matter in a war fought with powers inherited from the gods.

"Consider yourself gifted with an abundance of in-field experiences that will strengthen and grow you by necessity. If anyone is capable of adapting quickly to adverse circumstances, it's you, Amira. As under-prepared as you may be in the ways of the dragon knight, you're well prepared for tho pressure. Survival is in your nature. Adrienne will also help you grow in your magic, which, apparently, you won't seem to mind one bit. Now that you get along so well."

"You truly have a gift of delivering reassurance while being a pain in the ass in the same breath," I mutter.

Lumithra snorts, releasing a puff of steam from her breath as she picks up her speed to ascend the mist-laden mountain. The abrupt acceleration leaves me nauseated, clenching the handle of my saddle with white-knuckled fists and a disorienting sensation of lightheadedness. Enduring the physical tolls of flight is a grueling adjustment that I hope will get easier with more experience.

* * *

Upon returning to my room, I find the doors to my armoire wide open, overflowing with sets of fighting leathers and a collection of satin nightgowns. My cheeks flush with embarrassment at the realization I probably entered the wrong room. Before hightailing it back out the door as quickly as possible, a folded-up note with my name on it catches my attention and stops me in my tracks.

Amira,

I wanted to ensure that every member of my squad would receive their official dragon knight armor in a timely matter. Fighting leathers are to be worn while serving on all campaigns and assignments. Their design allows for maximal mobility while still providing optimal protection. The nightgowns, however, are a personal gift from me to you. The least I can do is ensure you're comfortable when you're thinking of me in your bed. Rest while you can, my love.

Yours truly,

Adrienne

Pretentious asshole. When in the realms did she even find the time to fill my closet like this?

"Looks like your Wing Commander has you well taken care of,"

Lumithra snorts.

"Shouldn't you be sleeping?" I fire back. I hate admitting to myself wearing more than scraggly tunics and thin trousers for the first time in my life is a luxury I've always been curious about.

"Dragons don't need nearly as much sleep as humans and half-mortals. I've been reviewing wartime procedures with the veradis spirits responsible for guarding our nesting grounds. As you know, it has been six hundred years since they've had to protect the Kanoelani from such threats. You, however, need all the rest you can get," Lumithra grumbles.

Despite being intrigued by my new collection of fighting leathers, I shudder. Days ago, I was just Rhydian's dog— an anonymous mercenary peasant invisibly suffering while stuffing the Captain's pockets with blood money. Now, I'll be flying into battles conscripted by the nation that failed to protect me, along with all the children who didn't make it out alive. Conscripted to the nation that grotesquely neglects its villages lacking a presence of descendants of the divine.

"Even the most beautiful of roses are not without their thorns. As sacred as Blackthorn's lands may be, this nation is not without inexcusable wickedness. Your anger is valid, my child. Allow it to drive you to fight for hope. Fight for a brighter Blackthorn," Lumithra consoles. How a dragon has the capacity to be a terrifying, death-wielding creature of nightmares while also possessing the ability to comfort with insightful wisdom will never fail to astonish me.

There won't be any fighting for hope if my mind shatters from fatigue. Tonight, survival to the next sunrise looks like allowing myself a small distraction from the world outside my window. I strip my clothing and slip into a smooth, silken black gown with a sheer, lacy bust and a high-thigh slit. Despite feeling absolutely ridiculous, it's surprisingly the most comfortable fabric I have ever worn. The lightweight satin feels cool and soothing against my skin, extending me an invitation to cave into my exhaustion and crash into peaceful unconsciousness.

I stare at the ceiling under the warmth of my ivory duvet, pleading with my brain to acknowledge the heaviness of my eyes and surrender to the lure of sleep. I can never give Adrienne the satisfaction of knowing I'm wearing one of the gowns she gifted me, lying in bed now thinking of her. I may never understand how or why my soul gravitates toward hers. How her touch grounds the rage of my magic and leaves me desperately craving more. It's cruel that transporting myself back to those flawless, seductive moments alone with her is what allows me to drift off into the waves of deep, restful slumber.

CHAPTER 13
Strange and Unprepared

"Amira!" Half-disoriented, I slowly awaken to Adrienne's voice, assertively shouting my name and loud pounding knocks on my door. "Amira! Get your ass up! Now!" I untangle my way out of my sheets and fumble to open the door, half-sleepwalking and heart-palpitating.

Adrienne's jaw drops in silence as I open the door. Her eyes widen as she takes me in. I look down, having nearly forgotten my silky black nightgown and its plunging neckline. Heat instantly floods my cheeks and pulls me out of my mental fog. "Gods, Amira. Are you trying to destroy me?"

I throw Adrienne a sinister smirk, basking in the satisfaction of inducing her panic. "What brings you hounding down my door like a depraved wolf at this hour? Picking up where we left off?" I lean against the doorframe, shifting my weight to accentuate my curves. Deep sapphire saturates the skies behind the stained glass windows, indicating Adrienne has once again thrown me out of bed before sunrise.

"Unfortunately, I'm not here to make any more deliciously reckless decisions. I'm here to inform you that Lady Rhonwen is expecting our squad in the conference hall in ten minutes. Throw on your gear, and don't be late," Adrienne snaps curtly, struggling to maintain her restrained composure.

"You can stay while I get dressed if you'd like," I taunt. If I'm about to get dragged into serving Blackthorn before dawn, I might as well indulge in Adrienne's flustered panic first.

"Don't be so asinine. If I stick around for that, you and I won't stand a chance of making it to the conference hall," she hisses. Before I can respond, my door is slammed shut with a gust of shadows as she storms down the corridor.

I quickly dress myself in a set of fighting leathers and exit my room, taken aback by the commotion of the corridors despite the early twilight hours. Novice knights who were nothing more than apprentices just yesterday afternoon swarm the halls, preparing to receive their first orders of war. Today, under-trained humans will take up the swords, axes, and arrows of Blackthorn's ground forces, and half-mortals will take their elements to the skies with their dragons. Tomorrow, the crowds in these halls will be significantly thinned.

"Amira, wait up!" I turn my head and spot Irvette running toward me, weaving through the madness while re-adjusting her eyepatch after brushing shoulders with scrambling, tunnel-visioned knights.

"I never got the chance to apologize for last night. I shouldn't have probed you so persistently. If I had known—"

"No need to blame yourself," I interrupt her breathless apology. "My magic is somehow even more unpredictable and sensitive than I originally thought, and I have no clue how to control it. Perfect time to serve in a war, right?" I chuckle. After how startled Irvette was by what she witnessed last night, there's no need to make her feel any worse. Especially not before walking into whatever orders we will be receiving today.

"Unpredictable and sensitive, huh? I guess that's one way to describe how the rest of my evening went last night," Zephyr gloats as he catches up to us.

"Did I invite you to join our conversation? Beat it before I encapsulate you in an ice chrysalis," Irvette hisses. "Anyways, give yourself some grace. It took me months to figure out how to ground properly. I lost track of how many times I accidentally transformed the training halls into rooms of raging rapids," she confesses.

Zephyr snorts. "Or the time you nearly caused a tsunami at Tourmaline Beach. We were lucky Adrienne had a more experienced water mage on standby to save our asses that day. You were quite the force of chaos." Irvette shoots Zephyr an icy glare, daring him to test her patience further.

"Zephyr, surprisingly, has brought up a good point. I had access to a handful of master water mages who assisted me in my training. Zephyr, Arden, and Felix all had access to masters in their elements to guide them along their path. You are the first light mage Elmoria has seen since the first Luminary War with no masters to seek for specific guidance. Give yourself some grace."

"Adrienne is the only shadow mage in Elmoria, and we've never seen her fumble control or threaten large-scale disasters," Arden scoffs as he finds us. "Amira, if you're going to be releasing bolts of lightning or walls of scorching white flames, you better not stray far from Adrienne today. Our success today, as well as our survival, depends on it. You are to stay near the Wing Commander. Understood?" Arden's eyes narrow as he talks to me like the younger sibling he's reluctantly forced to look after.

"Well then, that means our success today, as well as our survival, depends on you not being a condescending ass to me, or I might just snap. Understood?" I snarl, flashing my teeth at Arden. No one utters a word as Irvette flashes me a smile of amusement.

Felix and Adrienne barely acknowledge our arrival as we file into the conference hall. Despite seeing Adrienne hardly ten minutes ago, they appear lost in thought, deeply engrossed in the map sprawled out across a large oak table. By the dark bags under their eyes, I wouldn't be surprised if they'd been studying it for hours rather than sleeping. Guilt suddenly pangs me in the chest for taunting Adrienne so shamelessly when she came to wake me this morning.

Lady Rhonwen illuminates the darkness with her ethereal, white glow as she enters the room. Her glacial eyes are red and puffy as if she spent the night reviewing strategies through mournful tears. "Thank you for getting here as quickly as you could. We have much to discuss in as little time as possible. Adrienne, please briefly bring your squad up to speed on all we've discussed as concisely as possible."

Adrienne bows to The High Priestess as she turns her attention to her squad. "To sufficiently prepare you for your assignment, allow me to backtrack and review the most recent developments. We deployed forces to Volkan Isle to aid Helia in reclaiming their city but experienced a catastrophic defeat. Eldermoor slaughtered through our forces, taking no prisoners. Blackthorn hasn't seen such a monumental loss of life since the battle that ended the first Luminary War." Adrienne leaves hardly a second of pause for us to process before continuing with her summary, silently communicating there is no time to mourn.

"Additional raven-griffin battalions have been sent further inland. Their exact numbers are unknown, but we expect at least thirty thousand. Based on reports of gathered intel, we can now officially confirm they are attempting to overthrow Helia to claim the land as an offering to Osiris, and plan on utilizing the luminaries to establish his will as totalitarian Elmorian law."

"Even with slews of blood mages and raven-griffins at their disposal, why start fighting to expand their territory without acquiring all the luminaries first?" Arden asks.

"Eldermoor knows all Elmoria is now in a desperate race to retrieve the luminaries. They can't afford to wait until they acquire them all before making their advancements. Helia not only neighbors Eldermoor, but it's also Elmoria's largest land mass, along with its numerous substantial trading ports. Claiming it before having all the luminaries provides a strategic advantage in fighting two armies at once. Helia also doesn't contain any shields defending against summoning the imperial magic required to forge The Crown like there are in Blackthorn, making it the perfect location to execute their objectives," Adrienne explains.

"Eldermoor must also suspect that a handful of the luminaries are hidden within Helia's borders," Felix adds. "That would explain why the bulk of their efforts are being sent to Helia while leaving skeletal crews to search their own lands. Due to the defense of our shields, our elemental-wielding half-mortals, and our dragons, they also won't shift their attention on invading Blackthorn until they either have The Crown of Luminaries or are just shy of a single stone."

"Now that everyone is up to speed, on to today's assignment," Adrienne interjects. "Our squad is needed to carry out a rescue and retrieval operation. Water mages sensed the presence of the water luminary while flying over the Tourmaline Sea on their way to assist Helia. Four water mages received permission from their Wing Commanders to break from the battalion to seek it out. They flew their dragons down into Mount Neritas, the underwater volcano leading to the Maren Caverns, where they suspected it to be located. It's been several hours since any of them have been seen or heard from. We will be flying into the Maren Caverns and will not re-surface until our comrades and the water luminary are located and safely in our care."

Irvette rolls her shoulders back as if warding off shivers shooting down her spine. "Irvette, I'm sure you can understand we will be heavily relying on your abilities and expertise for this assignment. Are you going to be okay?" Adrienne places a hand on Irvette's shoulder, assessing her like a wounded warrior.

The light drains from Irvette's eye, transitioning from sea-foam tranquility to darkened, whirlpooling rage. She grazes the scar slicing through her eye, sucking air in through her teeth. "I refuse to allow the sea wraiths to claim any more of my people. It will be my honor to blast their skulls to nihility," she growls.

"*Sea wraiths?*" I ask Lumithra. I've only vaguely known of sea wraiths as cryptic campfire tales of folklore created to scare children into obeying their elders. An irrational childhood fear that surfaces near large bodies of water until outgrowing the fables.

"It's in your best interest that I do not describe them to you for now," she warns. I shudder and take her word for it, no further questions asked.

While I had no clue what to expect from receiving our first assignment as dragon knights, I at least assumed most of our operations would take place high in the sky. Orders to plunge into the depths of the sea on a rescue and retrieval mission were certainly not a thought in my mind. By the looks on every strained expression in the room, it's at least safe to assume I am not the only one feeling overwhelmingly unprepared.

CHAPTER 14
Troves of Tragedy and Riches

Surges of knights become nothing more than blurred flashes of black as we burn our lungs sprinting for the flight field. "Water breathing can only be sustained for twelve hours. The missing mages and their dragons have already been out for at least six hours, and Mount Neritas is a two-hour flight from here. We can't afford to spare another second," Irvette shouts, utterly unfazed by the swiftness of our pace.

Within seconds of mounting our dragons on the flight field, Irvette throws her fists together, crafting an orb of opalescent, shimmering water. She kneads the orb and stretches it to great lengths above her head. Like an eclipse of darkness sweeping over the earth, the orb engulfs our entire squad in its celestial waves. Irvette throws her arms toward the ground, commanding her waves to come crashing down, drenching us and our dragons before we launch into flight.

My skin glistens with cobalt-blue sparkles, stinging every inch of my body like icy blades— an unpleasant sensation combined with taking flight to the brisk skies, shivering in soaking wet fighting leathers. It almost feels as if hundreds of wasps are repeatedly stinging my skin with a glacial venom so wickedly frigid that it burns.

"Any uncomfortable side effects from the concoction I just conjured are only temporary. Once they subside, that's confirmation you will be able to breathe and wield your elements underwater," Irvette shouts across the wind-tossed skies. Part of me is amazed that water mages can manipulate their element with magic that safeguards against drowning and defies the laws of nature. The other part of me silently curses Irvette for having to drench us in an icy hell at the very start of a long flight.

I shift my focus on admiring Tsuna as she flies adjacent to Lumithra in our formation. Her scaly indigo and sapphire blue body blending into the twilight sky is a breathless sight that distracts me from my chattering teeth and frozen limbs. Her glowing eyes of emerald appear deeply focused on Lumithra, leaving me curious about whatever silent conversation they may be having.

"You appear to be deep in conversation with Tsuna," I pry.

"You assumed correctly. In fact, we were busy discussing how you forming deeper emotional ties to our mission will help you summon greater depths of your power since your wielding appears to be deeply connected to your emotions. With the threats lurking in the caverns, our mission will only be successful if everyone functions at the height of their abilities," Lumithra responds.

"Everyone seems to be more concerned that I suppress it," I scoff. *"It sounds like you're suggesting we provoke me, which is quite the opposite."*

"The stakes we're facing demand that we grow your power as quickly as possible. This isn't a training exercise, and Adrienne will ground you if the need arises. Connecting your emotions to the ties of this mission will ensure you can extract enough power to rival the threats that managed to compromise four master water mages and their dragons, and help us secure the water luminary."

"How do you suggest I connect my emotions so quickly, then? You're working with quite a numb, calloused subject, I'm afraid." From growing up on streets littered with bloated, starved corpses while learning how to slaughter men more than twice my size before learning how to read, death has been a daily part of life for as long as I can remember. After losing Casimir and becoming the sole survivor of Rhydian's sadistic ploys, death and tragedies may never be able to faze me ever again.

"You're not as hopelessly calloused as you may think you are," Lumithra counters. *"Your heart still fights for the light, whether you see it or not.*

Tsuna has informed me that Irvette has graciously permitted me to show you some of her memories of Maren Caverns. When you close your eyes, Tsuna will send Irvette's memories to me to show you through our bond. You must allow the pain you will witness to guide your soul to greater depths of your power."

"Irvette?" I almost forgot how her dark complexion blanched and how she shivered in horror when we received our orders. Adrienne did mention we would be heavily relying on her expertise for this mission.

"Close your eyes and open your mind, my child. There is much to show you."

Irvette gives me a silent nod of approval, confirming my permission to view what our dragons wish to show me. My vision fades to black, and Irvette's memories flow into my mind in a sea of vivid detail.

*   *   *

"There's the ol' beaut! Lower the anchor!" A gangly old man with a silvered beard shouts down from the crow's nest of a large ship to the rest of his crew mates below. On command, a burly man with broad shoulders strikes the anchor chains with his sledgehammer, sending the anchor plummeting to grip the sea floor. A small girl, appearing no older than twelve years old, restlessly fidgets with her hands, stirring the waves of the sea. Her seafoam-green eyes beam with delight as her waves rock the ship back and forth, to the annoyance of the crew mates. Her rich hazelnut complexion and aquamarine braids catch the beams of sunlight reflected off the waves twirling in her hands.

"You promised to let me accompany the dragon knights this time. Remember, Father?" The girl pleads with the broad-shouldered man, tugging on his thick belt strapped with fishing knives as he sets his

sledgehammer down.

"You're a tad bit young to be plundering for sea herbs and sea glass worthy of a ruler's ransom, Irvette. Blackthorn has a serious shortage of precious supplies for medicinal elixirs. Besides, at the rate disease is devouring the peasant slums and threatening to spread like wildfire, the knights cannot afford you slowing them down on their assignment. Maybe next time," her father suggests.

"But you promised! I also already received that magic that allows you to breathe underwater, and it hurts! Did I really let the knights give it too me for nothing?" Irvette protests.

A legion of sapphire blue dragons and their water-wielding half-mortal riders mirror the rippling waves of the sea from the skies above. One of them descends through the rainbow mist and delicately lands in the sea parallel to the ship. "Relax. She'll be with me the entire time," the dragon's rider reassures. "We have twelve hours worth of breath beneath the surface, and I can't possibly imagine us needing more than two. She's one of us. As a descendant of Sirena, resilience is in her blood."

Irvette's father lets out a reluctant sigh. "Alright, kid. You can go as long as you stay with Kai the entire time. You listen to everything she tells you to do. Got it?"

"Got it. Thank you, thank you, thank you for letting me go!" Irvette squeals with excitement as she hugs her father goodbye.

Kai extends her hand to Irvette and helps position her in the saddle. "I got you just in time to review our objectives with General Muir. You're in for a real adventure," Kai promises.

"Knights of Blackthorn! Today, we end the supply shortage limiting the healing aid of our apothecaries. We put an end to the rampaging disease claiming the lives of our children in the slums. The answers to our desperate prayers lie within the depths of the Maren Caverns." General Muir addresses her specially designed team of fifty water mages with a spirit of confidence. "These caverns are the only home in all Elmoria to Sirena's sea herbs and

sea glass. The precious resources we seek receive their potency directly from the sacred water luminary hidden within the seas. Fill your satchels to the brim, empty them onto the ship, and repeat until the caverns are bare."

"Furthermore," Muir continues, "Nobody travels alone. Understood? Any sighting of sea wraiths or their hydrafangs means immediate retreat. Mortal knights! Remain at the ready with your steadied ship to receive the resources as we resurface. Be sure to pack the sea glass and herbs with delicate care."

"Dragon Knights! Prepare to descend into Mount Neritas single file," General Muir orders. Irvette's father takes one last anxious glance in the sky at his daughter before dragons begin plunging into the volcano's crater with their riders.

White-capped waves crash against the charcoal, jagged volcano, partially peaking out of the sea. One by one, through carefully crafted maneuvers, dragons and their riders dive down the narrow crater of Mount Neritas single file as instructed.

"Hold on tight!" Kai warns as their turn approaches. Irvette clings to the saddle's handle with Kai seated protectively behind her. Darkness blurs past them as they plummet into the crater in a stomach-dropping, vertical descent.

They finally reach the end of the seemingly bottomless dive, spilling into a vast cavern system. Irvette gasps in awe as she takes in the labyrinth of chambers bathed in the depths of iridescent blue waters.

The dragon knights start dispersing into small groups of two or three as they venture into the endless passageways to begin their search. Kai pairs up with Cordelia, one of Blackthorn's strongest master water mages, to further ensure Irvette's safety.

"Your father told me you've been practicing your water spear technique diligently," Kai breaks the silence as they traverse through a narrow cavern. Irvette swallows the lump in her throat. She knows her father likely also mentioned the numerous times she lost control of her water spears, coming *close to killing her sparring partners, and how easily she burns out.*

"Will it ever get any easier?" Irvette asks sheepishly. "I only manage to wield about twenty spears before I end up creating blasting rapids or completely burning out. No dragon will ever bond me with such laughable limits. I have no hopes in surviving The Kanoelani Trials when I'm due to be tested," Irvette huffs.

"You're already wielding twice as many spears than what's average for your peers," Kai consoles. "Cultivate that roaring passion in your heart, and learn to shape it. Your magic and sense of control will strengthen with time, especially with that tenacious drive of yours."

They continue to venture deeper into the cavern until the appearance of luminous, turquoise herbs rooted in a glistening, rocky sea floor stops them in their tracks. Kai gracefully dismounts her dragon and immediately begins stuffing her satchels.

"We just struck a trove of riches," she gasps. Kai invites Irvette down to the sea floor to assist in foraging bountiful heaps of Sirena's healing herbs and sea glass. Cordelia remains mounted atop her dragon, assuming the role of their party's watchful guard.

After just a few minutes of peaceful foraging, a guttural, panicked scream for help echos throughout the caverns, followed by a blood-curdling, monstrous shriek. Color simultaneously drains from Cordelia and Kai's faces as they exchange grim expressions. Irvette freezes. A mournful, maddening roar coming from one of the dragons rattles the rocky walls of the caverns. The roars of the dragon and the screams of the mage intensify until they grow gravely silent. Cordelia spews archives of rancid curses.

"We need to retreat! Immediately!" Cordelia bellows.

An astronomical, serpentine beast hurtles out of a narrow passageway, and barrels straight toward Irvette's company with ravaging yellow eyes. Hydrafang. Towering in an abundance of height over Kai and Cordelia's dragons. The sides of its murky, scaly face are composed of tentacles oozing in clumps of freshly drawn blood. Sitting atop the horrible creature is a ghastly woman with amphibious, slate-gray skin and massive webbed ears. Her eyes are nothing more than soulless, ancient pools of obsidian.

With the force of a surging geyser, Kai grabs hold of Irvette as she blasts them to the top of her dragon, Zhaleh's back. The party retreats with their filled satchels in a frantic pursuit, barely evading the reach of the hydrafang's tentacles. Cordelia erects shielding walls of dense ice from the back of her dragon, Aegir, only buying seconds of retreat at a time. The hydrafang and sea wraith slice through each towering wall of ice like a knife through parchment.

"I'll hold them off as long as I can. Kai, you and Irvette focus on getting the realms out of here!" Cordelia shouts, throwing up new walls as quickly as they break.

The hydrafang extends its tentacles, grabbing hold of Cordelia before she can form her next wall of ice. Gluttonous, smothering tentacles crush her body as she is whipped from Aegir's back with lightning speed. The moment Aegir whiplashes in the direction of the hydrafang is the moment it reels her suffocating body to the clutch of its lethal jaws. Cordelia's chest is instantaneously impaled with venomous fangs.

"Cordelia!" Kai cries out in terrorized shock, having no time to process the gruesome murder of her fallen comrade.

Aegir roars in tumultuous rage as Cordelia is devoured whole. He charges the hydrafang with scorching flames, charring its skin as he sinks his claws deep into the murderous beast.

The sea wraith pounces from her perch atop the hydrafang's head and latches onto Kai with webbed, suctioned hands. The hands wrap around Kai's throat, threatening to crush her windpipe as she struggles to shake herself free.

Irvette begins wielding as many piercing water spears as she can toward the wraith. Wielding water spears while struggling to balance atop a soaring dragon proves hopelessly futile. She fails to land a single spear into the wraith while struggling not to fall to her death.

Irvette's attention shifts as Cordelia's dragon lets out a gut-wrenching roar. The hydrafang drives its venomous fangs into Aegir's neck with its final breath before succumbing to its fatal burn wounds. Both Aegir and the charred hydrafang collapse lifeless to the bottom of the seafloor.

Kai, driven by adrenaline and the totality of rage, breaks herself free of the wraith's lethal clutch and implodes her skull with the force of raging water at her fists. Before she catches a breath, another hydrafang pummels through the cavern walls.

"Irvette! Take Zhaleh and get out of here! Now!" Kai screams. Before Kai can launch another attack, the hydrafang launches its fangs into Zhaleh and devours Kai with its tentacles in one sweeping motion.

Aegir and Zhaleh's once majestic, sapphire bodies now lay lifeless on the sea floor, pale as winter sunlight. Tears flood Irvette's eyes as she summons waves from the kicks of her legs, propelling herself out of the cavern with haste as the hydrafang feasts upon the flesh of the dragons.

It doesn't take long before the hydrafang catches up to Irvette with fangs drenched in dragon blood. Irvette kicks her legs as fast as her body allows, refusing to discard her heavy satchels loaded with sea glass and herbs. While dropping the weight of her satchels would increase her speed, she refuses to allow her fellow descendants of Sirena and their dragons to die for nothing. She will continue the work of their mission even if she dies trying.

Irvette exerts precious amounts of draining energy to summon another forceful blast of waves to distance herself from the hydrafang. She turns down a narrow passageway after successfully throwing the hydrafang off her trail before collapsing from exhaustion. Her limbs tremble with fatigue as lethal burnout threatens to overtake her body.

A lone sea wraith emerges from the darkness as Irvette fades in and out of consciousness. Having nearly no energy left to call upon her magic, nothing stops the wraith from driving a lance directly through her eye. Excruciating pain and fury possess Irvette's body, consuming her with just enough goddess-given stamina to put up one final fight.

Her comrades will not die for nothing. As blood gushes from her eye, she rises to her feet. She channels a rapid-like current of waves through the wraith's head, channeling greater and greater force until the wraith's head implodes in the same fashion as the wraith Kai executed right before her death.

"For the fallen." Irvette's vision fades to darkness as she collapses onto the sea floor of slaughtered, color-drained dragon and water mage corpses.

✶   ✶   ✶

"Grab the lead physician. She's waking up!" Irvette awakens in a hospital bed surrounded by apothecaries, medics, and a dark, itchy patch of fabric concealing her eye. She grabs it in panic, without knowing where she is or if her soul has departed from The Mortal Realms into Niroshen.

"No, no, don't pick at that! We don't want your eye socket getting infected." Irvette traces her fingers under the patch, finding fresh scar tissue where her eye once was.

"Should we sedate her?" A voice asks.

"Give her a second to adjust! The poor girl has been through enough, for the gods' sake."

"Where am I? Where's my father? The satchels? The survivors?" Irvette asks in panic, on the verge of hyperventilating.

"Irvette," a medic audibly gulps down a massive lump in her throat. Her tired eyes flooded with grief. "You are in Vespera, currently recovering in an infirmary. You are the sole survivor of the entire expedition. The hydrafangs and sea wraiths slaughtered every dragon and every knight, along with every human aboard your father's ship. After those...creatures retreated from the attacks, you were retrieved and brought to us by a lone

dragon."

That lone dragon was none other than Tsuna, who detected a faint pulse beating beneath the sea during a hunting flight. Tsuna dove into the crater of Mount Neritas and retrieved Irvette from the wreckage.

A bleak void of shock blanches Irvette's heavily bruised face as the light from her eye retreats into a state of dormant hiding. Her body tremors worsen as sweat pours from her forehead. Her rapid breathing no longer draws any effective breath into her lungs.

"Sedate her before her panic summons her magic. She still poses a high risk of burnout.

CHAPTER 15
The Maren Caverns

Blood-orange blankets of light sweep across the skies as Lumithra pulls me out of Irvette's stream of memories. Flanked between Sarthon and Tsuna, with Adrienne on standby. I draw in a deep inhale and release a breath that feels like blistering steam. Despite the briskness of soaring above the clouds in the morning air, my insides feel like they are screaming with fire. Alabaster flames of electrifying lightning fire, begging to be unleashed to devour and destroy.

Adrienne rises from her seat and leaps from Sarthon to Lumithra as if jumping over a small stream. She wraps me in her arms faster than I can process, immediately willing my magic back to a state of dormancy. "Save that ferocity stirring in in your eyes for the caverns. We're going to need it," she tells me. No judgment. No snide remarks. I lean into her embrace and lean into the safety of allowing myself to feel the weight of Irvette's pain.

Glancing over at Irvette, the blinding rage swallowing her eye puts the intensity of flying into direct sunrise to shame. Did Tsuna know she was rescuing her future rider that day? Did she hold out, refusing to bond a single soul who entered the Kanoelani Trials until sensing her once again? With such an unfathomable display of courage and determination at such a young age, Irvette's dragon knight spirit is pure and true. If every knight had a fraction of her heart and resilience, Blackthorn's future would be undeniably brighter.

I want to promise Irvette that not a single soul will be lost to the caverns today. That we will prevail. What I can promise, however, is for my wrath to join hers to forge an unstoppable force. Irvette is an ocean of fury, waiting to wield the powers of The Goddess of the Seas, and I get the privilege of fighting by her side.

"Do you think the missing mages and their dragons have a fighting chance?" I ask Adrienne. After witnessing hydrafangs and sea wraiths tear through an entire expedition party without much of a struggle, I can't fathom how a much smaller team could possibly survive.

"Since the tragedy, The Knights of Blackthorn have invested in rigorous training programs to strengthen their underwater operations. Elixirs have since been developed to slow the speed of paralyzing hydrafang venom and are now carried by every dragon knight as a precaution for flying overseas. We're looking for well-trained knights who likely consumed doses of the elixir before their plunge. While the elixirs aren't strong enough to prevent paralysis, they delay it significantly. They buy the inflicted just enough time to attack before the paralysis starts taking possession of their bodies. If I remember correctly, the elixir delays venom from reaching the heart for nearly twelve hours," Adrienne recalls.

"There's a strong chance the mages we're after were able to ward off the hydrafangs and wraiths or even kill them before paralysis settled in if they're still alive. Hydrafangs are blind and have a keen sense of hearing. Ironically, the paralyzing stillness would give them a fighting chance until rescue," she continues.

"You didn't happen to receive any of those elixirs since that mass accolade ceremony, did you?" I ask Adrienne nervously.

"Every last vial was distributed amongst the battalions sent overseas to Helia. Due to the time needed to allow the elixirs to ferment, the apothecaries won't have more to distribute for at least a week. All the more reason I need every member of this squad ready to wield at the height of their abilities. We cannot afford a single marginal error," Adrienne warns.

"Even at the height of our abilities, how is this mission not a guaranteed death sentence? Irvette was amongst an expedition of fifty master water-wielding dragon knights, and that still wasn't enough. How-"

"I won't allow death to claim any one of you under my watch," Adrienne interrupts in a low, authoritative tone. "I would open a portal to The Dark Realms and confront The God of Death if that's what it would take to ensure every soul on my team walks out of this with rhythm to their pulse and breath in their lungs," Adrienne growls. I refuse to let you die at all costs. Certainly not before we address the fires we've been playing with; her eyes seem to scream at me. I decide it's for the best that I don't ask if opening portals to The Dark Realms is even possible before Adrienne returns to Sarthon.

*　*　*

The crater of Mount Neritas strokes the silver-blue horizon as solemness thickens the frosty spring air nipping at our faces. A squad of prematurely commissioned dragon knights summoned by the blood-spill of war, willing to risk their lives for fellow defenders of Blackthorn. Willing to search treacherous, watery graves for the sea luminary in the fight for Elmoria's preservation.

"Before we make our descent, we need to run over a few important logistics. Listen closely," Adrienne shouts to her squad over the crashing winds and waves.

"Number one. Hydrafangs are highly vulnerable to flame. We will predominantly rely on Felix's firepower and Amira's electric flames to inflict the most significant damage in the event of any encounters.

"*Assuming I can actually summon them successfully and without frying our team,"* I gulp.

"I can sense the great power stirring within you, Amira. It is more than ready to be summoned at your will. Do your best to keep your thoughts in the present, remain close to Adrienne, and you will succeed," Lumithra consoles.

"Number two. Hydrafangs may be blind, but their sense of hearing is impeccable. We will traverse the caverns without our dragons to provide us with maximal stealth and our best shot at keeping them safe despite our lack of elixirs. Our dragons will resurface after dropping us down the crater and remain on standby above Mount Neritas should we need their assistance.

"Number three. Sea Wraiths are ancient pawns of The Dark Realms. The only way they can be killed is by blunt head trauma. Aiming for anything else is a precious waste of your energy.

"And lastly, no one gets left behind. We fight as one. If any one of us goes down, we all go down. There is no retreat until every member of our squad, every missing mage and dragon, and the sea luminary are safely accounted for."

Adrienne and Sarthon take the lead plunge into the crater, followed by Felix and Fieryn, and then Irvette and Tsuna. I brush my sweaty, wind-tossed bangs out of my eyes and take a deep breath, reminding myself that Irvette once took this plunge on the back of a dragon at the age of twelve. Surviving the vertical dive is the least of the horrors that await us in these abysmal depths.

Lumithra tucks her wings to her side, plummeting straight down the narrow, pitch-black chamber in a heart-dropping free fall. My death grip on the saddle and clenching the muscles of my thighs against my seat serve as the only prevention from tumbling over Lumithra's head. My spine shudders at the thought of testing our ability to find each other in the obsidian void before crashing to my death.

As soon as the narrow chamber spills into vast, phosphorescent cavern walls, Lumithra expands her wings and guides us to a gentle landing on the sea floor. The flawlessness of her execution leaves my mouth agape in awe.

I hold my breath until the remaining members of our squad safely break out of their free falls and stick their quiet as possible landings in one piece. Each safe, uneventful landing earns a sigh of relief.

"We won't be far. We'll be able to pick up on the slightest hint of distress before it is even called out. Be careful, my child. I have complete confidence in the magic stirring within you, but know that I will still be worrying fiercely," Lumithra rumbles.

She lowers her head as I gently stroke her luminous opal scales, taking in her piercing violet eyes. *"What fun would it be if I'm not around to gray some of your scales? I'm not going anywhere,"* I comfort her.

"Dragons are immortal, immaculate beings. It would take a lot more than a reckless half-mortal to gray our scales even if doing so were possible," she huffs. *"Just be careful, Amira. I refuse to lose another rider."*

We watch our dragons launch back up Mount Neritas one at a time. Due to the narrow chambers preventing the expansion of their wings, they're forced to rely on nothing other than propelling blasts of steam to guide them as they climb back up to the mouth of the crater. We spend the first moment of their absence scanning our surroundings and thank the gods that the repeated blasts of dragon steam miraculously didn't summon any hydrafangs.

Irvette winces, hunching forward as she frantically massages her temples with her fingertips. "Gods, this is vile," she groans before falling into a brief fit of violent dry heaving, undoubtedly sensing the nearby presence of the sea luminary. By the strength of the searing head pain the light luminary inflicted upon me, I'm impressed she's still standing at all.

"The mages were definitely right," she mutters. "Following whatever pathway increases my pain will likely lead us to the missing dragons and mages." Irvette takes a deep breath, signaling with her finger there's more she is trying to say. "However, that is no guarantee. It's possible any hydrafang or wraith encounter would've thrown them from pursuing its path," she winces.

"How should we proceed then? Follow your lead as a group, or split up to cover more ground more quickly?" Arden asks.

"It's only a matter of whether the magic allowing them to breathe down here wears off or if the venom reaches their hearts first. Or gods-forbid if any creature decides to come back and finish them off before we can find them in time. While it poses a major risk, I'm afraid we don't have time to stick together. We will need to break into groups. It is still your call, Adrienne. How should we proceed?" Irvette asks, dipping her chin to her chest as she struggles to breathe through her searing agony.

"I trust your intuition. We will split into two teams. Felix and Arden will go with Irvette to follow the path of the water luminary. Amira, Zephyr, and I will search the remainder of the caverns as quickly as possible. Remember to tread stealthily. The greater the chances we don't alert those ancient terrors, the better," Adrienne commands.

Facing the catacombs laid before us, Irvette takes off, leading Felix and Arden down the path that intensifies her pain the most as Zephyr and I follow Adrienne down our first search route.

"How exactly do we plan on extracting half-conscious, paralyzed dragons out of these catacombs? There's no way those dragons will be able to make it back up to the crater. With all due respect, has that been thought through at all?" Zephyr asks as we trek through clusters of jagged stalagmites, luminescent rocks, and decomposing carcasses.

"You and I will have to create and sustain clouds large and strong enough to support their weight as we fly them the realms out of here. We'll have to search for an opening in these cavern ceilings or have Arden create one large enough to fit them through as an alternative route to the surface. It's far from a perfect plan, but it'll have to suffice,"

Adrienne answers.

"With anyone other than you, that plan would be unspeakably absurd," Zephyr chuckles. "However, the strength of your magic puts every other mage I've witnessed in action to shame. Although, Amira might have the potential to rival your strength. Anyways, I trust your plan, Wing Commander."

"Drop it with the formalities," Adrienne hisses as she rolls her eyes.

*　*　*

An hour of searching the alcoves of countless caverns passes by without detecting any other forms of life. The deafening silence looming over all the catacombs is a good indicator that Irvette's team has also yet to come across any of our comrades or the water luminary. "By now, the team we're searching for has less than an hour before their magic wears off and their lungs fill with water. We may need to reevaluate our-"

"Hold that thought!" I interrupt Adrienne upon noticing the arrowhead of a spear poking out of a pile of rubble. I pull the spear out of the rocks, examining its nearly mint condition.

"That's a standard spear water mages rely on when they're forced to fight on the verge of burnout," Adrienne confirms.

"Based on its condition, it hasn't been beneath the surface for long. If you also look closely, you can see fresh blood spill," I add. How I noticed the blood blended into the midnight-blue, bioluminescent cavern walls and rocks is nothing short of a miracle.

"Well done, light-bringer, well done," Adrienne praises. "We've got no time to lose. We're following that blood trail."

Adrienne leads the way as we climb over piles of crushed boulders and head down the narrow passageway, barely wide enough to fit the width of a dragon. "I'm smelling traces of sulfur. Stay vigilant," she warns, wielding knife-like shadows to pierce through chunks of debris obstructing our path.

One moment, I'm trekking through the glowing catacombs in search of wounded mages and dragons. The next, my mind takes me through memories of searching for Casimir through labyrinths of evergreen forests under the moonlight. The crunch of sea glass beneath my boots becomes the sound of Casimir's cracking ribs. The sound of breaking his ribs through desperate chest compressions the night I failed to get his pulse back sends a deluge of electrified blades sizzling under my skin.

The warmth of Adrienne's fingers interlocking with mine disrupts the flow of lethal power boiling in my blood. "Save it," she whispers gently.

Our brief moment of grounding touch is interrupted by faint cries of labored, disgruntled breathing. We collectively hold our breaths, silently searching for the source of distress.

"Hang on a second," Zephyr whispers as he hones his focus on a layer of rock-filled walls to our left. "Stand back," he orders.

Zephyr summons a large gust of turbulent winds, blasting through the wall of rocks with tornadic force. As the dust settles, a limp dragon tail protrudes through the rubble.

Adrienne curses under her breath as we leap over the debris, finding an entanglement of ghostly pale, half-conscious dragons. Heartbeats later, we find their paralyzed riders scattered like lifeless rag dolls amongst the debris-littered ground.

"Amira!"

Casimir's blood-gurgling cries infiltrate my head in an invasive flashback. I rub my eyes, and one of the mangled, battered faces of the water mages before us morphs into his face. The rest of the faces before me recast into my brain as the bloodied faces of my beloved childhood friends— the patron orphans slain on Rhydian's lethal assignments. The faces then take on the form of thieves, crooked courtesans, and a slew of criminals who died by my blades. The scars across my back flare up in excruciating heat as if they're being grazed by a blade of flames.

"Amira!"

Casimir's cries bring tears to my eyes as my vision fades to blinding white light.

The deep indigo waters of the caverns now appear glacial white, and I lose sight of Adrienne and Zephyr. I sprint across the rubble in a blurred haze, frenziedly attempting to reach any of the mages. Some bizarre, unfamiliar instinct tells me if I can get to them, I have what it takes to save them. After blasting through a large boulder with a bolt of lightning, I finally reach one. His breathing is rapid and shallow. His bloodied flesh is pale as a corpse, but I refuse to let death have the victory. No one dies today.

"Amira!"

My name sounds muffled as if I'm hearing it from the surface while drowning in a sea of terrors I can't navigate. Nightmares from the past and the current horrors before me fight for my presence. Orbs of glowing white lights engulf my hands, charging my nerves with an energy that feels vitalizing rather than life-crushing. That bizarre, unfamiliar instinct is now unshakeable, urging me to place my hands on the dying mage's chest.

Energy flows through me like surging rapids. I feel it depart from the well of magic within me and transfer into the half-mortal lying limp in my arms. Movement slowly returns to his fingers, to his hands, and then to his arms. Despite my distorted vision, I can see the rich color returning to his flesh as vibrant life returns to his body. It's now clear that screaming instinct led to a new manifestation of my light-wielding—the power to heal.

With healing magic encapsulating my hands, the world around me does not exist. All my focus pours into the desperation to reach the remaining mages and dragons before it's too late. No one dies today.

"Amira! Stop!"

The voice calling out to me is no longer Casimir's, but Adrienne's, distant and faint. It's impossible to distinguish if her cries are real or imagined. I slam them out of my thoughts and return full focus to making use of my newfound power. A power to finally rid myself of the chokehold death has had on me my entire life.

Spine-rattling, guttural roars bellow through the caverns, drawing fragments of my focus back to my surroundings. Bone-shattering roars, growing louder and louder. Getting closer and closer. Through the corner of my peripheral, I catch a glimpse of a colossal hydrafang emerging at the entrance of the cavern and the figure of a ghastly sea wraith atop its back.

With my hands transferring surges of my energy to the half-mortal currently in my arms, I catch glimpses of Adrienne dodging lashing tentacles, blasting her way to the top of the hydrafang to wrestle the wraith. My heart violently plummets into my stomach, witnessing Adrienne spar hand to hand, wielding shadows against a pawn of The Dark Realms.

An ocean of knots swells up in my stomach, knowing I don't have the slightest clue how to quickly channel my healing energy into an energy of destruction to rush to Adrienne's aid. As the woman stabilizes in my arms, I spot Zephyr rushing to confront the wraith battling Adrienne.

I sigh in relief and rush after the next dying mage. No one dies today. Everyone will surface from these treacherous caverns victoriously.

The next mage in my arms stabilizes as a wave of weakness hits me. Waves of roiling nausea and fatigue threaten to crush me as I move on to heal the last half-mortals and then work my way to the pile of dragons. I can push through it. I can do this.

Within heartbeats, Felix emerges through the rubble behind the hydrafang with a lethal blast of fire. As the hydrafang collapses, four more come charging in behind him. I vomit as my brain processes the sight of four monstrous, serpentine beasts with faces composed of festering tentacles. The hope of emerging from these caverns victoriously suddenly feels gravely bleak.

I reach deep into the well of my magic, demanding more. If I can call upon enough magic to somehow heal the dragons before me, maybe we can still get out of this.

As I begin my work on the pile of dying dragons, my lungs feel heavier than bricks. Shades of sapphire blue begin coloring one body of blanched scales, and I crawl my way to the next in tremoring, feeble movements. I'm weightless as a feather and heavy as the dragons I'm healing all at once.

It takes all my strength to lift my neck to catch glimpses of the battle raging around me. Through my hazy white vision, Zephyr and Felix pour the elements of fire and howling, stormy winds into weakening the hydrafangs. Adrienne makes quick work of the wraiths as she leaps from head to head of each hydrafang. Severed, bloodied heads of slaughtered sea wraiths drop like flies to the ground.

"Amira!"

Adrienne's scream is no longer muffled and rings through my head with jarring clarity. My vision fades to a brief moment of darkness as unconsciousness threatens to take over. Darkness threatens to drag me deep into a void I fear I won't return from if I let it take me.

"Amira!"

Adrienne's scream snaps me out of its luring call, and I find her coiled in slimy tentacles pulling her dangerously close to rows of bloody, venomous fangs.

"NO!"

The scream that escapes my lungs exerts almost enough force to shatter me. In less than a second, the healing energy of my magic shifts into its lethal form. I summon blasts of electrifying flames from my fists, aimed for the hydrafang. Adrienne breaks free from its death grasp as its charred body drops to the ground. I attempt to raise myself from the pile of dragons as they start to slowly regain small movements in their muscles, but my limbs don't obey. Splotches of darkness flicker in my vision as I fight to hold onto my fading consciousness.

Lumithra's fierce roars rattle the stalactites above us, shaking them to the ground. I can sense her presence several caverns away as the roars of dragons and hydrafangs threaten to shatter my eardrums.

"Amira! What in the realms have you done?" I can sense her guttural cry of panic as our dragons fight through swarms of hydrafangs to rush to our aid.

The world around me spins too fast to process any of the battles around me. I think I hear Arden's voice. Adrienne's screams. I think I hear blasts of earth pummeling into hydrafangs, and I think I can feel the heat from explosions of flame. It's hard to tell while it feels as if I'm gently floating above the clouds. I feel the life drain from my body. Feeling my soul fight to cling to my body. It's failing.

Tranquil, serene weightlessness, and suffocating heaviness devour the remains of my existence as I lose all equilibrium to the violent bouts of vertigo. I want to scream for Adrienne, to grip her hand, as if holding onto her will tether my soul to The Mortal Realms, but I am hopelessly stifled by unrelenting paralysis.

The last image my body allows me to fully witness is Irvette storming the cavern on the back of Tsuna with a glowing blue stone around her neck. The sea luminary. Devastating whirlpools command the death of every remaining hydrafang and sea wraith as they're crushed to oblivion. With the collapse of the final hydrafang, I draw one last breath before finally falling into the void of darkness.

CHAPTER 16

The Maren Caverns: Adrienne

My heart stops at the sight of white pools overtaking Amira's eyes. The same torturous trance that overtook her just last night at The Wretched Owl. With her focus intently honed on the dying mages and dragons in her trance-like state, she has yet to notice the hydrafang that just barreled through the cavern walls.

"Take care of it while I handle the wraith!" I order Zephyr. Zephyr begins his attacks, hardly evading its tentacles as I blast my way to the top of its head to make quick work of its damned sea wraith. Amira has no hope of surviving in her vulnerably distracted state if I let it get anywhere near her.

"Aren't you a lovely sight to behold," the wraith growls. "Let me carve into your flesh. I would love nothing more than to offer your organs to Osiris as a token of my fruitful labor."

Distracted by my inability to shut out Amira's current raging turmoil, I take a gash across my face from the wraith's razor-sharp nails. It's impossible to shield my mind from each bloodied, mutilated childhood friend that she sees in the marred faces of each water mage. The faces of the lives she was forced to take as a young child. I can't shield my mind from the daggers piercing her heart as her first love dies in her arms all over again. I deserved that laceration. Nonetheless, I will not let Amira die today.

"Damn fool. You have *no* idea who you're talking to," I hiss through my clenched teeth. Commanding my shadows to take on the form of a vapor wolf, I release it to feast upon her skull, watching waves of black blood seep from her skull as my vapor wolf sinks its fangs into her amphibious flesh. Damn pity it made such quick work of her. I didn't have an opportunity to hear the ancient whore scream in agony due to obliterating her so quickly.

I shift my attention to Amira to find her hands drenched in orbs of white. Her limbs tremble as she exerts heavy surges of healing magic into the mages. At the rate of her exertions, it won't be long before she's on the verge of burnout. Healing magic drains twice as quickly as wielding destructive attacks, but it's an incredibly rare manifestation. Of course, Amira's light-wielding would take another new, dangerous form before I'm given a chance to teach her about it.

"Amira!"

I pump my legs toward her as fast as I can, only to be halted by a wave of hydrafangs and sea wraiths now severing my path. Reaching Amira will be impossible until they're all dealt with.

"Amira!"

Screaming her name is futile. There's no hope of getting through to her in her current state. Especially not while she's hopelessly beyond the reach of my touch. Vast, flailing tentacles lunge for her as she feebly makes her way to the pile of dragons. I hone careful focus on my shadows, shaping them into knife-like blades. My blades drive through the tentacles, spilling pools of inky blood to the sea floor, drawing its attention on me.

"Amira! Stop!"

Ghost-white scales slowly return to vibrant shades of sapphire blue as I continue morphing my shadows into slews of deadly forms to ward countless attacks away from Amira. None of it will matter if I can't reach her in a matter of seconds.

"Amira!"

Her pain is mine as the nightmares plaguing her brain infiltrate my mind in haunting, vivid clarity. My vision blurs as I fight to keep my focus on remaining present in the fight before me. While fighting Amira's inner demons along with the sea wraiths, I horribly miscalculate the reach of those damn hydrafang tentacles and find myself in their clutches. Breaking myself out of this will be only mildly tedious but will still cost more time than I can afford to spare.

As I am on the verge of breaking myself free of its grip, repeated blasts of white, electrified flames incinerate the hydrafang's flesh, dropping it to the ground as a corpse of charred flesh. My heart vaporizes into nothing more than the black mist of an immortal wraith, and the world goes still. The raging battle between dragons and hydrafangs ceases to exist to me as Amira's life rapidly drains before my eyes.

Days ago, Amira was nothing more than a ruthlessly trained mercenary fixated on no other survival other than her own. Today, she drained her life by pouring it into dying dragons and half-mortals, refusing to allow death any more tragic victories. Today, I sensed the agonizing, heart-wrenching terror she felt as she feared she was losing me. The sight of me wrapped in those tentacles devastated her soul. Now, the fear of losing her devastates mine.

A luminous, ethereal blue light breaks through the cavern entrance as I sprint after Amira. Irvette emerges on the back of Tsuna, wearing the sea luminary around her neck. Through the power of the sea luminary, she commands turbulent whirlpools towering over the hydrafangs. Her waves distinguish enemies from allies as they obliterate every last vile creature to obsidian, bloody mist.

I finally make it to Amira's side, paying no attention to the recovering water mages and dragons finally regaining the majority of their strength. Simply being in their presence raises bile in my throat, knowing the price that was paid for their survival.

"Zephyr! Give us a lift! Now!" I shout as I expose Amira's chest and begin stable compressions, pumping her heart as if both our lives depend on it. Zephyr forms a cloud beneath us, skillfully lifting us to Sarthon's back as I focus on keeping Amira's body alive. "You are not leaving me like this! Damn it! Come on, Amira!"

Black electrical burns cover the surface of her skin, revealing the severity of her burnout. Her skin beneath the palms of my hands burns as her body breaks into a fit of convulsions. My hands flinch in response to the scorching heat, and what they uncover nearly stops my own heart. The rune of Osiris etches between her breasts in thick, claw-like marks. As the last line is drawn, her convulsions cease.

"*Osiris has staked his claim on her soul. While the girl's physical condition is nothing Lady Rhonwen's healing magic can't handle, there's nothing she can do to challenge The God of Death,*" Sarthon growls.

"*I'm more than fit to challenge the old bastard. Amira's soul does not belong with him. He'll have no choice but to return her soul to The Mortal Realms by the time I'm through with him,*" I seethe.

"*Don't tell me you plan on summoning a portal to The Dark Realms. Do you really think Osiris will just happily return Elmoria's only light mage to your arms? Don't let your attachment to the girl make you so rash. Even for you, confronting him is far too dangerous,*" Sarthon protests.

After what feels like an eternity of solitude, surrounded by the damned, inescapable darkness of my existence, Amira has become a gravitational beacon of light. I'm the foolish, cursed moth, devastatingly drawn to it. Funny how I was the fool who warned her not to fall for me when I'm the one who knows I can't endure The Mortal Realms without her.

"*I need Amira alive. I'm getting her back, no matter the cost.*" What a stupid, damned fool I am.

*   *   *

After an agonizingly long flight, glimpses of the monastery finally peak through the dense, ashen haze. Black veins slowly begin branching out from under the rune of Osiris etched into Amira's chest, throwing her body into sporadic fits of violent thrashing. That bastard is going to pay.

"Take me directly to The High Priestess's chambers," I order Sarthon. *"Hurry!"*

Sarthon takes me right to Lady Rhonwen's window carved into the monastery's tallest tower. I wield her windows open, scooping Amira in my arms as we dive through the opening to find The High Priestess ready to receive us.

"Osiris," Lady Rhonwen growls with the rage of a mother, her hands already glowing with the same blinding white that engulfed Amira's hands. Her eyes fill with piercing animosity as I quickly lower Amira onto the bed.

"She doesn't have much time left before Osiris forges her name into the scrolls of The Dark Realms. I need you to keep her body alive and tend to her burn wounds while I go after her. Do you think you can do that?" I ask in a panicked burst, throwing all formalities out the window we barged in through.

The High Priestess lowers her hands to Amira's chest, instantly restoring her heart to a normal, steady rhythm. A brief wave of relief is brought upon my muscles, aching from the hours spent throwing my body into keeping hers alive. "Amira is in the best possible hands. You need not worry about her physical state," Lady Rhonwen gently assures.

Until today, The High Priestess has been Blackthorn's only half-mortal capable of healing magic as a descendent of Elethea. Descendants of Elethea are given the gift of healing rather than elemental wielding. They're only born into this world when the days of the current high priestess are numbered, making them next in line to rule over Blackthorn.

Somehow, Amira manifested both elemental wielding and healing. Osiris certainly won't surrender her soul without a fight. If it's a fight the old bastard is looking for, I'll oblige his request tenfold and then some.

"You know that through The Goddess Elethea, I'm more than capable of keeping Amira stable. The bigger question is, are you ready to face The God of Death?" She asks in a wavering tone.

"I'll make him suffer every taste of his own realm if he refuses to release her to me," I snarl. It takes all the discipline I can muster not to shift into a demon of shadows on the spot at the thought of what Amira must be enduring as we speak. I'll save that for The Dark Realms. "I am no stranger to the darkness. I know how to play my cards. I owe it to The White Empress and Blackthorn to ensure we do not lose our light mage." More importantly, I owe it to myself.

Lady Rhonwen lets out a long, contemplative sigh. "If anyone is capable of returning Amira's soul to her body, I have no doubt that it's you, Adrienne. That's why I already have sentries posted outside these doors as we speak to keep vigil while your soul ventures to The Dark Realms. You may summon your portal whenever you are ready."

"Thank you for allowing me to use your chambers for such a dark ritual. I do not take your grace lightly," I thank The High Priestess as I stoop before her in a deep bow.

"May Elethea's light clothe you in her protection upon your travels. May all The Gods of Niroshen grant your safe returns," Lady Rhonwen prays out loud.

I position myself in the farthest corner of her chambers and prick the palm of my hand with the blade of my knife, letting my blood spill until I have enough to smear it into a circle on the pristine marble floors. I seat myself in the center of the circle and begin my incantation.

"With the spill of my blood, I grant my soul permission to wander from its confines of flesh and bone. With the breath in my lungs, I voice my permission to enter through the gates of The Dark Realms. With the fire in my heart, I grant my soul permission to traverse the lands of Osiris until my task is complete." Black, sinister gates open before me, inviting my soul to storm through the entrance of The Dark Realms.

CHAPTER 17
The Dark Realms: Amira

I awaken in writhing agony to scorching hot chains around my neck, my wrists, and my ankles. Chains with the glow of molten lava, branding blistering, black burns into my flesh. If it weren't for the excruciating pain shattering my mind and my body all at once, I would assume this was a dream. This is far too real to be a dream. My lungs burn as I thrash and flail in a frenzied panic, to no avail. My screams do nothing more than rouse murders of crows, rustling in gnarled branches of black, barren trees. Trees scraping a sky darker than the midnight of a new moon.

Something cold and slippery slithers across my legs. I tilt my head down as far as my molten collar allows to find a serpent sliding over my legs to a ground composed of bones, skulls, and coals. Nothing should be able to sprout from such cursed ground, yet luminescent violet mushrooms are scattered like weeds as far as my eyes can see.

I'm no longer in The Maren Caverns. I'm no longer in Blackthorn. I am in The Dark Realms. Eternity would be the only explanation as to why my lungs haven't yet burst from my relentless screams and why my skin isn't melting to my bones. My current state of torment must have been designed for eternity.

"Lumithra!" I cry her name in choked sobs, only to be met with silence.

"Lumithra!" Her grave silence confirms I truly am in The Dark Realms, far beyond her reach. My tears spill onto my chains, now crackling and sizzling. I broke my promise to The White Empress. She has lost another rider.

If a dragon can't reach me, then no one is coming. Certainly not any of The Gods of Niroshen, who would never step foot into The Dark Realms. I am a forgotten soul in a pitch-black forest of death. Damned to burn on the forest floors of rotting carcasses, hidden within the sickly, twisted trees scraping the charcoal skies.

How long will it take before Adrienne forgets me entirely? Months? Years? Or is she already moving on, sparing no time to grieve me with a war to fight? Adrienne was the culprit responsible for rearranging my life as I've known it, and has somehow quickly become the only sense of home I've ever truly felt. The first time my raging magic responded to her touch, my heart felt like it found safe shelter in a roaring blizzard. I could deny it all I wanted, but nothing could change the way my soul was drawn to hers. The way my soul is still drawn to hers, even in death. None of that matters now. Never again will I feel that sense of home.

"There you are, Amira, descendent of Kallik."

Chills claw down my sweating spine as a demonic growl rumbles through the forest, interrupting my internal spiral. A faceless, cloaked figure emerges from the shadows and approaches me faster than I can blink. Towering over me like an angel of death. Where his face should be, I see nothing more than a black, shadowy abyss shielded under his cloak, drenched in the scent of rotting corpses. There are no eyes to greet me. Staring into his face is staring into bottomless depths that seem to have no end. All that greets me is a pit of unshakeable dread, branching out to consume every fiber of my being.

"I've been looking to stake my claim on your soul for a long, long time. Welcome to The Dark Realms, light-bringer. Welcome to my kingdom."

Despite my apathy towards the gods, I've always prayed this fate would never come to me. I've always prayed that, by some miracle, my soul would find Niroshen. Turns out Osiris was more eager to claim my soul for his realm than my so-called father. In a state of irrational panic, I make a pitiful attempt to run as he fastens a rope of shadows to the collar around my neck.

"No need to delay the inevitable, child. You belong to me. Let's go make it official now, shall we?" The tone of his voice is the scraping of long, bony nails down a slab of granite. His laughter reaches into my stomach and twists it like a wet towel to be wrung out.

Osiris grabs hold of the rope fastened to my blistering collar, leading me through the dismal woodlands. "You proved to be quite the natural talent in The Mortal Realms. All the more reason I had to claim you first. The Gods of Niroshen must have grown tired. Kallik's first descendent in centuries, yet his presence was nowhere to be found as you were burning out like a dying star."

I'm unable to form a response as my molten chains deprive me of the energy to form words. Infuriation sears through my boiling veins as he digs his claw-like fingers into the small of my back as if he owns me. Killing a god has to be next to impossible, but if I can wield just enough power to break free from his clutches, perhaps I can scheme a way to cheat my fate.

I call upon my magic, inviting my rage to manifest as destruction. Inhale fury, exhale anguish. Inhale vengeance, exhale hopelessness. Despite the intensifying rage burning in my bones, not even a spark escapes from my bound hands. The incinerating heat of my pent-up magic only adds to my excruciating suffering without an outlet of release. I can't take this anymore. I just want it to end. I wish I could vaporize to bloody mist like the monsters of the Maren Caverns. I'd pray for my lungs to shrivel up and burn to crisps, but The Gods of Niroshen all have their backs turned to these damned immortal wastelands. No one is coming to bring me mercy.

Osiris lets out a menacing laugh. "Did you really think you would have free reign over your magic in my kingdom?" He growls, tracing the scars of my back with his skeletal claws. "You half-mortals are all the same. Nothing more than entitled, spoiled fools. You belong to me now, remember? Your magic can only be wielded to my will. Not yours. I'm going to have fun playing with such a feisty puppet for all eternity. Your stupid, foolish recklessness has reaped a satisfying reward for me today."

We reach the end of the woods and arrive at the bottom of a long, winding staircase leading up to the entrance of a large obsidian castle. Each step onto the creaking, half-rotted planks triggers horrific, reverberating screams and shrieks of agony. With every step I take, tortured cries quake beneath my feet, making me feel as if I'm traversing over graves of souls buried alive.

"There's a prison underneath these stairs, you know. It's where I like to keep the most deplorable swine of The Mortal Realms after they enter through my gates. I wonder how many of them were brought to me by your blades?" Osiris chuckles. I shiver and fumble over my footing, wondering if I'll be next to join them.

After our nauseating ascent, we finally enter the castle gates and step foot into the throne room of The Dark Realms. I try shutting my eyes to shield myself from this never-ending nightmare, but the throbbing burn of my eyelids forces me to keep them open. Osiris leads us up a dais composed of skulls to a throne of flaming embers. The only source of light in The Dark Realms other than the iridescent fungi of its forests seems to be the molten glow of its throne and shackles.

"Such a shame The Mortal Realms never got to reap the reward of your true potential before you were given a proper chance to bloom. You will flourish vibrantly under my command," Osiris sneers. The God of Death takes his seat on his throne, kicking me to the floor to sit beneath him like his pitiful, emaciated dog.

A wraith hisses as it enters the throne room, carrying a glowing, ember muzzle in its bony hands— a muzzle perfectly matching the chains that already bind me. "Our ceremony will commence briefly," it snarls as it stoops into a reverent bow.

Osiris chuckles as he takes the muzzle from his wraith. "What good is a dog with a pestering bark? Now, go fetch my scroll for me so we can make Amira's new residence in The Dark Realms official."

"Very well, My Lord." The wraith bows again as it's dismissed to collect the requested scroll.

"Once we get your name written into my scroll, you're mine forever. We can't have you objecting to that now, can we?" Osiris bends down from his throne to strap the scorching muzzle over my mouth.

Agonizing, tortuous flames prevent any sound from escaping my lungs. My screams are stifled. In a matter of minutes, my unendurable suffering will be inked into eternity. No one is coming. No one is coming. Minutes feel like years as I sit in silence, bound by muzzle and chains at the feet of The God of Death, wishing my soul could cease to exist altogether.

"Servant! What is taking so long? Where is my scroll, you useless mutt?" Osiris shouts. Silence creeps back in as the echoes of his voice fade. "Bring me my scroll at once before I throw you under the stairs to join the mortal swine!" He bellows. Despite the concealment of his eyes beneath his hood, I can feel his scorching gaze setting his vacant throne room ablaze.

A seismic blast of thunder answers his demands as the doors to the throne room fling wide open to a plume of thick, black smoke. "Looking for someone?" Adrienne appears amid the smoke, holding the severed head of the wraith who failed to fetch the scroll. My heart stops. This has to be some sort of wickedly cruel hallucination. There is no way a half-mortal would be powerful enough to venture into the throne room of Osiris.

"You took something very precious to me. It would be in your best interest to return her to me at once." Adrienne growls as swarms of shadows weave around her hourglass silhouette clad in black leather.

The severed head vaporizes to bloody mist in her hands as tendrils of smoke seep through her nostrils. Even if only a hallucination, her fierce, devastating beauty quenches the raging wildfires devouring me from the inside out. Vividly imagining her is a rainfall of respite for my parched soul. It satiates the blistering heat just enough to allow tears to stream down my cheeks.

"Adrienne, darling. It's been too long. I'm rather surprised you decided to pay me a visit, child. Remind me to dispose of those useless servants who failed to keep you from barging in so unexpectedly."

"Already taken care of," Adrienne growls in a vastly threatening tone that I've never heard from her before. Osiris seethes, driving his claws down my back, tracing the lines of my scars with my freshly drawn blood.

Adrienne shifts from her half-mortal form into an unrecognizable demon-like form. She transforms into a demon of shadows. A demon of obsidian vapor, nearly towering the heights of the throne room. She lunges for the fiery throne and drives the claws of her demonic form into Osiris's chest, drawing black, ancient blood. "You touch her again, and I'll break every finger of yours, one by one, and nail them to your throne. Forever reminding your wraiths of the day you picked a battle you couldn't win," she roars.

Osiris secures my chains to his throne as he rises to his feet, staggering in lethal muscular strength honed by an eternity of ruling his domain. "Don't worry, Amira. This little disruption will be over quickly," he snarls.

Osiris conjures swarms of swords out of the darkness of his shadows, hurling them straight toward Adrienne's demonic form. Thousands of shadow-forged swords fly across the throne room, desperate to draw her blood.

I am unable to scream. Unable to beg this nightmare to disappear. Unable to look away or force my hallucination to take on a different form. Adrienne summons a massive shield of shadows, blocking the volley of piercing blades. Every blade disintegrates as it crashes into her shield. She intercepts the last sword before it vanishes into her shield and grabs hold of the hilt without breaking a sweat.

"You know damn well that we are equals in power, Osiris. Fighting is futile. As long as I reside in your kingdom filled with your weak, useless wraiths that cannot control me, not a single revision is being added to that scroll of yours."

Osiris scoffs. "You are right about one thing, child. We are equals in power. Why not form an alliance? Together, the three of us could put an end to Elmoria's worship of The Gods of Niroshen. I know you particularly don't care for them," he sneers. "Regardless if you decide to join me or not, I'm not relinquishing the light mage. She's far too valuable, and I'm growing rather fond of her company."

Osiris forges a massive blade to rival Adrienne's, engaging her in a deadly dance of blades forged by darkness. Matching parry after parry, Adrienne holds her own against the God of Death as if he's a casual sparring partner. They fight like equals. They fight as if they've both had centuries to study each other's moves and know exactly what to expect. Their blades clash as if rehearsed in a meticulously organized choreography— as if it could take an eternity to determine a victor.

"I'm growing tired of this. We'll be at this for years at this rate," Osiris yawns. Without warning, he whips his hand off the hilt of his blade to conjure a dagger. He aims it for Adrienne but shifts course at the last possible second and hurls it toward me instead. His ink-black blade penetrates my shoulder, spilling my blood as I collapse from my knees onto the ground.

"Finally. Something interesting is happening," Osiris chuckles as he glances toward my muzzled screams with a hearty satisfaction in his laughter. Adrienne lets out a blood-curdling roar of fury as my blood pools to the ground and trickles down the dais. She sheds her demon form and, in a plume of black smoke, shifts into the form of a massive dragon composed of shadows. I am definitely hallucinating. There is no way Adrienne is actually in the form of a dragon, launching bursts of obsidian flames directly toward The God of Death.

"No need for such theatrics, child! Just give it up already. I refuse to put up with your tantrums all day!" Osiris's growls rattle the floors of the throne room as he shields himself against Adrienne's wraith-like dragon flames.

"You know I refuse to leave without the girl," Adrienne rumbles in fierce protest. "You know I can do this for all eternity, and I'm more than happy to if that's what it takes. Your little followers in Eldermoor, however, don't have eternity. The longer you're distracted, the longer you'll fail to provide them with the provisions they need to expand your pathetic kingdom. They don't stand a chance fighting against two nations without your aid. The longer you fight me for Amira, the more strength you relinquish to Blackthorn and Helia," Adrienne growls.

"You spoiled, entitled bitch!" Osiris bellows. Plumes of smoke emit from his lungs and his fists as he screams in shattering defeat. "I'll release your precious girl to you, but she won't be released unscathed by her time with me. She's paying a price. A price that punishes you both. Her… curse if that's what you want to call it…will stick with her forever as a result of your failure to leave her soul to rest in The Dark Realms. Is that really what you want, child?"

"Name your terms. Nothing could possibly be worse than leaving Amira to serve as one of your dogs for eternity. Try me," Adrienne snarls. The room suddenly goes deafeningly silent. Adrienne's dragon eyes lock into The God of Death's dark, faceless cloak with burning intensity. It appears as if they are conversing through a bond similar to the one I share with Lumithra. Is that even possible?

Osiris scoffs. "I am not to be held liable if the girl grows to resent you for these terms. Remember, you are the one permitting this. Take the girl and get out of my sight. Like you said, I have my followers to tend to and realms to conquer."

"Gladly. After I do one last thing," Adrienne rumbles. Her wings expand to the lengths of the throne room as she quickly grabs Osiris by her talons, plucking him off the ground. Giving him no time to counter her attack, she slams him back into his throne, pinning him down by the crushing weight of her dragon form. I tilt my head as far as my collar allows to find severed, skeletal fingers flying to the ground as Osiris's grueling screams threaten to shatter my eardrums. One by one, his fingers fall to the ground. As quickly as they fall, Adrienne collects them and fastens them to his throne by tendrils of shadows. As the final finger is secured to the throne, she releases him from her clutches as he thrashes and flails upon his throne in writhing pain.

"Apologies. You harmed something precious to me, and I'm a woman of my word. I'm sure they'll grow back just fine, but not before your servants get to see how pitiful you look, screaming in defeat upon your own throne," Adrienne growls.

Adrienne shifts out of her dragon form, back into the familiar half-mortal that has become my sense of home in The Mortal Realms. She races to the top of the dais and scoops me in her arms as Osiris spews curses faster than blood. For the first time since her arrival here, she finally feels real. The lavender sage infiltrating my senses, the tangible, soothing touch of her skin, the familiarity of being held in her arms, it's all too real. She feels so real I find myself hyperventilating, fearing if I take my eyes off her, she'll somehow disappear.

"Amira! It's me. I promise it's me. It's Adrienne. Everything is going to be okay." Threads of black smoke unbind me from my chains and muzzle as she buries my face against her chest. The sound of her heartbeat is home. Her fingers sweep through my sweat-drenched, knotted black tresses as she allows me a moment to take her in. Gently allowing me a moment to process that she is real. "I've got you, I've got you, my love," she whispers. "You're coming with me. You're coming home."

I cave at the sound of her gentle voice and find myself sobbing in her arms like an unraveling, broken mess. Adrienne stormed the gates the gods would never dare touch. Adrienne faced down The God of Death and gave him a taste of his own poisonous torture. She came after me. She came after me, and now we're going home. I allow myself to trust those truths and sink deeper into her arms, bracing myself to enter into the portal of pitch-darkness that swallows us whole.

CHAPTER 18
The Awakening

After a few brief heartbeats devoured by darkness, I feel my back melting into the comfort of a soft bed as my eyes adjust to brightly beaming daylight. Floor-length cerulean curtains sway in the breeze of open windows, welcoming the fragrance of floral spring air into a spacious room. My blurred vision stabilizes as I find the glacial eyes of The High Priestess looking down on me with an expression of profound relief. My fingers are interlocked with Adrienne's as she stands quietly at my bedside.

"Welcome back to The Mortal Realms," Lady Rhonwen whispers delicately. Despite the careful tenderness in her voice, taking in my new surroundings is a jarring awakening. I quickly sit up to inspect my body, finding no evidence of my time spent in the Maren Caverns or The Dark Realms. No piercing dagger wound from Osiris's blade. No molten chains, collar, or muzzle inducing excruciating suffering. My heart thunders in my chest. Can I trust this is all real? Can I trust I didn't just finally slip into unconsciousness in The Dark Realms?

I attempt to fumble out of the bed in a disoriented panic, but Adrienne holds me back. "Amira! I promise you are safe! We're back at the monastery. We are in Lady Rhonwen's chambers. Your body and soul are safely tethered to The Mortal Realms, but you need time to recover." Adrienne's tone is firm and reassuring, slowly grounding me to reality. "As long as you are with me, not even death has enough authority to hold you down," she growls.

Digesting the reality of all that has transpired during my time spent in The Dark Realms is as difficult as digesting the healing elixir Lady Rhonwen is coaxing me to drink on an empty stomach. "This will help reinforce the healing work done to you and should also take the edge off some of your pain. It will go down easier if you chug it quickly," she insists as I put a vial of pungent blue liquid to my lips. A sharp, acidic bitterness stings my throat as I reluctantly chug every last drop of the vial as instructed.

"Never, and I mean never, pull off such a reckless stunt of that magnitude ever again," Lumithra claws into my mind as the healing elixir roils in my stomach. Her shimmering, opal scales bounce beams of rainbow light into the room as the thunderous beat of her wings alerts me to her presence right outside Lady Rhonwen's window.

"Lumithra! Thank gods I can hear your voice again! I thought I lost you forever!" Hearing and seeing Lumithra once again feels as if an insurmountable weight has been lifted off my chest, almost bringing me to tears.

"We nearly did lose each other forever. You owe your life to Adrienne for pulling you out of an eternal contract with The God of Death. I am infinitely grateful she also refuses to live without you," she sighs with a blast of steam.

Chills scuttle down my spine as I recall that long, drawn-out silence between Adrienne and Osiris as they discussed the terms that pulled me out of that eternal contract. I'll release your precious girl to you, but she won't be released unscathed by her time with me. She's paying a price. A price that punishes you both…I am not to be held liable if the girl grows to resent you for these terms. My mind races with dread, failing to come up with any speculations of how my time in The Dark Realms may have altered our fates.

"My release came with a price!" I blurt out.

Adrienne's eyes widen as if she wasn't prepared for me to recall any details from those conversations. She looks at me like I just launched an attack she wasn't ready to counter. "Osiris said I would not be released unscathed by my time in The Dark Realms. He said something about you having to live with the burden of knowing I'd forever altered if you decided to take me back to The Mortal Realms. What does any of that mean?" I ask without caring to hide the panic in my voice.

Adrienne takes a long moment of pause, carefully plotting her response. "Your name wasn't penned into that scroll. That is all that matters." Her tone is low and curt, conveying she has no intentions of discussing this matter any further. Defensive anger swirls in her ashen irises as if I'm prying into a trove of secrets I have no business exploring.

"If Osiris did something that affects us both and only you hold the details, I think I have the right to share that knowledge with you," I protest. Lady Rhonwen quietly listens to our back and forth, contemplating if she should intervene or withhold her input and allow more details to unfold naturally.

"What he did to you, to us, is a very fragile, complicated subject. For now, the best I can do is promise we are both safe and far beyond his reach. Disclosing the details right now is too risky for your stability. Even my touch might not be enough to ground you if I disclose the details now, and I am not willing to risk your safety or the safety of everyone in Blackthorn. I promise you, Amira, I will not withhold this forever. I can't withhold it forever. You'll have to trust me in the meantime that you are safer not knowing everything. As far as you Lady Rhonwen, you must trust that the less you know, the safer. I refuse to risk giving you any information that may make you an even more valuable hostage to Eldermoor than you already are."

Lady Rhonwen studies Adrienne's gaze intently before letting out a long sigh. "I trust your judgment, Wing Commander. Although it pains me that I'm left without knowing how I can properly guide you through this, I trust that the gods will ensure you do not tread this path without their wisdom. Amira, it is in your best interest that you also trust Adrienne's decision. Your top priority for the time being needs to be rest. You've already been through enough."

If it weren't for being in the presence of The High Priestess, I'd be tempted to slam Adrienne against the wall and demand her to elaborate further. How in the realms are they both easily agreeing to drop this discussion so suddenly? After more careful thought, I realize my actions would just take an entirely different direction than intended. I blush, reluctantly taking Adrienne at her word for the time being.

I run my fingers through my hair and dip my chin to my chest. Silky strands of *white* fall in front of my face, causing me to flinch. I audibly gasp and grab more handfuls of my hair, finding all my tresses as white as a full moon. Not a single strand of my raven-black hair in sight.

"Oh! Oh, Amira, we should have shown you this before getting carried away in our discussion. I'm so sorry for the fright!" Lady Rhonwen apologizes with a light, flustered panic in her voice. I prop myself up against the plump, ivory pillows and scoot toward the floor-length mirror positioned near the bed. I'm met with a reflection of shoulder-length strands of wavy, snow-white hair. I process my reflection in disbelief, struggling to comprehend how my hair is now strikingly similar to the ethereal tresses of The High Priestess.

"We suspect your transformation is a permanent side effect of your healing. Every inch of your body was covered in blistering electrical burns. I had to pour a great deal of my magic into your wounds to ensure your soul would have a body to return to at all. As a result of how much of my healing magic your body absorbed, the pigmentation of your hair has been altered," Lady Rhonwen explains.

I'm met with pounding head pain and sensory overload as I attempt to take everything in, and the foreign reflection staring back at me in the mirror is the least of it. Adrienne storming the gates of The Dark Realms and confronting The God of Death with unexplainable displays of power. My rescue involving alleged forever life-changing altercations

I have yet to discover. The events of The Maren Caverns. Oh Gods, The Maren Caverns!

"Wait…what about the rest of our squad? The mages? Their dragons? Did everyone make it?" The last thing I remember from the caverns was the vibrant blue light of the sea luminary around Irvette's neck and horrible creatures vaporizing to black mist. I never saw if the others managed to make it to the surface before I was dragged into The Dark Realms.

"Everyone is fine. They're currently resting off minor injuries nowhere nearly as deadly as yours," Adrienne answers. "As furious with you as I am for your recklessness…I take full responsibility for your burnout. I should've taught you how to recognize the signs before throwing you into the midst of your first assignment with practically zero training. But you still owe me an explanation as to why in the realms you didn't slow down the moment you felt yourself weaken," she hisses as hazy streams of black smoke coil around her fists.

"I'm going to go make my rounds and check on the others," Lady Rhonwen interjects. "Take as much time as you need in my chambers. I have a day's worth of battle reports to catch up on, so you two can have all the time you need to debrief today," she sympathetically offers.

"Thank you again for everything, Lady Rhonwen," Adrienne bows. She waits for The High Priestess to dismiss herself before returning her attention to me.

"Now, where were we? Oh yeah, that's right. Why didn't you, at the very least, listen to your body when you felt yourself draining? Light mage or not, you're not a goddess. You're a half-mortal. You're still breakable. Consider this our first formal lesson on the subject of burnout. When you feel your energy rapidly drain, you slow down!" Adrienne seethes.

"How could you expect me to just slow down?" I challenge. "You saw my memories. You felt my pain. I've experienced enough death for hundreds of lifetimes. A lot of them I've inflicted. A lot of them I've witnessed, unable to do a damn thing to prevent any of them. The moment I learned my wielding can manifest as healing magic, I wasn't going to let that go to waste, even if that meant pushing myself to my limits. And if only you knew what I felt when I saw that hydrafang launch at you-"

"Believe me, Amira, I get it. I truly do," Adrienne interrupts. "In more ways than you know. I promise I get it. How do you think I felt watching you die beyond my reach? You aren't playing with just mortal-crafted weapons anymore. You are playing with lethal, divine-given magic. Calling for as much magic as you did within such a short period is what got you killed, and I am never losing you again."

Adrienne stops herself in her tracks, regaining her composure as her smoke dissolves into the specs of dust floating in the sunbeams. "We will have this fight later. Trust me," she sighs. "You're in no condition to be riled up right now. We're fortunate I was able to bring you back. Never, and I mean never, scare me like that again." Adrienne looks at me softly, running her fingers through my strands of hair.

"In other news, this color suits you quite well, my love."

Quite well indeed, I have to agree as I examine my reflection in the mirror once again. My hair is as white as my lightning flames— flames capable of facilitating both life and death. I am both a blessing and a curse. A monster and a healer. My heart leaps as I watch Adrienne crawl into the bed and wrap her tattooed arms around me. Her embrace is both exhilarating and calming.

"You are a beautiful fire, and I fear I am a moth hopelessly caught up in your light," Adrienne whispers. Arousal throbs between my thighs as I watch her nibble on my ear and thread kisses down my neck in the reflection.

"I thought I wasn't in any condition to be riled up right now," I playfully protest, daring her to explore me further.

"Mmm, I suppose you're right," Adrienne sighs. "In that case, my presence will do us far more harm than good right now." She gently pries herself away and gets out of the bed, leaving me desperate and furious at myself for opening my damn mouth.

"I should be exchanging reports with the Wing Commanders on site, and you should be heading to the bathing chambers after all you've been through. We'll just have to rile you up later," she taunts with a cruel smirk.

Adrienne crashes her lips to mine in a brief, tantalizing kiss before making a swift exit. She leaves me with no opportunity to retaliate. Part of me has to wonder if she rescued me just to be the death of me. Between the art of her seduction and her secrets from The Dark Realms, it's only a matter of time before she pushes me to the edge of my sanity.

CHAPTER 19
The Adjustment

The lingering, foul stench of the rotten corpses of The Dark Realms and dried hydrafang blood threaten my ability to refrain from vomiting as I lower my body into the pool of warm, soapy water. Adrienne was right. I was in desperate need of a trip to the bathing chambers. I sink deeper into the warmth and begin washing away the caked layers of grime. I exfoliate my filth vigorously as if the harder I scrub, the farther I can keep my thoughts from those cryptic conversations between Adrienne and The God of Death. Gods, I wish I could cleanse myself of those memories. What could possibly lead Adrienne to a fear of losing her ability to ground me?

Whispers of racing Eldermoor to the luminaries, murmurs of their recent attacks, and talks of the rising death tolls spill in from the halls, providing quite the sufficient distraction from my intrusive thoughts. I shouldn't be able to distinguish words with such a keen, crystal clarity through such dense stone walls.

"Are you able to tell if I am hearing these conversations correctly or if I am just imagining them?" I ask Lumithra. Perhaps I'm just imagining things as a result of my exhaustion.

"The conversations you are overhearing are not figments of your imagination. You are hearing them correctly," she answers. There's a reluctant tone in her response, as if she dreaded my question.

The more thought I give to my enhanced hearing abilities, the more acutely aware I become of all of my senses, seeming explicitly heightened. Vibrant blends of perfumes, musty-scented dust, weapons of various metals, metallic-scented bloodstains, crisp leather armor, sweat, and misty mountain air invade my senses like an overpowering army. The citrusy-pine soap in the bathing pool is so overwhelming that I find myself increasingly dizzy the more I focus on the scent currently seeping into my pores.

"I'm not experiencing any side effects of that healing elixir, am I?" I ask Lumithra again. I feel embarrassingly paranoid, reaching out to her over every little sense my body detects. What is wrong with me?

"What you are experiencing has nothing to do with that healing elixir. If anything, I suspect the time you spent in The Dark Realms may be the culprit of your heightened senses," she answers.

Despite the warmth of the bathing pool, I find myself shivering at that possibility. I've had about all I can take for the day. I exit the pool, dry, and dress myself as quickly as possible, succumbing to the vast overstimulation. The quicker I can get back to my room for a moment to collect myself, the better.

The hues of the paintings that line the halls, the ambiance of the torchlights, and the stained glass windows are now more vibrant than ever before. My eyes can hardly withstand the vivid intensity of my surroundings. Is this what Adrienne was so insistent on withholding from me for now? Something tells me there's still far more to all that transpired in The Dark Realms I have yet to learn about.

* * *

I let out a heavy sigh of relief upon approaching the door to my room. If these heightened senses are here to stay, I need a long moment of privacy to adjust before putting myself at risk for any more uncontrollable outbursts of my magic.

The moment I open my door, I'm met with a man I've never seen before, looking at me with a confused expression in his beady brown eyes. "C-Can I help you?" He asks nervously as he looks up from a stack of partially unpacked boxes. I peer around the corner and glance into my armoire, finding none of the fighting leathers and gowns it was filled to the brim with just yesterday.

For a moment, I wonder if I have mistakenly barged into the wrong room. No. That can't be right. I've trekked the lengths of Blackthorn's mountains and back through squalling blizzards and torrential downpours without ever failing to find my way back to the peasant slums. I wouldn't have gotten myself turned around in a monastery as intricate as its halls may be. My doubts are further erased upon noticing the letter Adrienne left for me crumbled up on the floor beside my bed.

"I'd like an explanation as to what you're doing in my room and what in the realms you did with all my belongings. Last I checked, I never agreed to any roommates," I scathe.

"I-I apologize; I'm not sure what you're talking about. This room was just assigned to me. You must be mistaken." He reeks of sweat and smoked sausages. His heartbeat is pounding in my ears like a pestering branch tapping against a window in the middle of the night. This is the last thing I need right now. I desperately need this man out of my sight.

Anger sizzles through my veins as fragments of my lethal electricity begin charging up under my skin. I am in no mood to put up with whatever wolfshit this is. After suffering through The Dark Realms and back with every bone in my body still aching, my heightened senses making it feel as if all the walls are closing in on me, the last thing I need is some strange man in my room staring at me like a lost puppy.

Before I can even attempt to reel myself in, a bolt of lightning escapes from my fingertips and strikes the glass of my bedroom window. The bolt grazes right past the stranger, missing him by a thin sliver of sheer luck. He shields his head and ducks, dodging projectile shards of jagged stained glass until the blast resolves.

The shaken expression of shock on his face matches my own. I nearly killed the man. "I'm sorry! I'm sorry! I swear I didn't know this was your room. You can have it back! I'll sleep in the training hall, I swear!" He cowers, trembling in fear.

"What are you doing back here? I thought you were in the bathing chambers!" Adrienne exclaims as she appears from around the corner. Her eyes narrow with a looming darkness as she focuses on the shattered glass and the hyperventilating stranger.

"I was, but I couldn't take another gods-damned second of every sense smothering me with suffocating intensity! Can you tell me what this man is doing here?" Of all the things I could've said, that is what escapes from my mouth rather than leading with an apology for the explosive disaster I just created. Apparently, I can still make this mess even worse. I would've been much better off riding out my anxiety in the bathing chambers after all.

"I was on my way to collect you in between making my rounds as soon as I was informed Lady Rhonwen requested new sleeping arrangements for you. Forgive me for expecting you would've still been there after hardly ten minutes," Adrienne scowls, raising her slitted eyebrow.

"Y-you must be the l-light mage everyone is talking about," the man interrupts as he struggles to steady his breathing.

"And you must be a brand new recruit based on your inability to reel in your composure. Good luck with that in combat," I scoff.

Adrienne glares at me as she firmly grabs my wrists, likely a preventative measure to avoid any more spontaneous lightning bolts. "What am I supposed to do with you?" She mutters under her breath as sweeping shadows collect the shards of glass into a pile and crush them to specs of harmless, floating dust.

"Apologies, sir. I'll see that your window is replaced by nightfall," Adrienne promises before shutting the door to the room that is no longer mine.

"As for you, you're coming with me," she hisses. "Now would be an excellent time to show you to your new arrangements."

"Where will I be staying now, and why the sudden change?" I ask as I follow Adrienne through the halls, hoping to the gods my new room will be quiet and unoccupied.

"Given the frequency of your outbursts, The High Priestess requested I find you a room closer to the only source capable of grounding you. Closer to yours truly."

At this rate, I'd be surprised if Adrienne lets me out of her sight ever again, especially after my journey to The Dark Realms. After witnessing her bite the fingers off The God of Death and tether them to his throne in guttural rage over my capture, I somehow seem to mean more to her than I can comprehend.

"Would my heightened senses have anything to do with what happened in The Dark Realms?" I ask. Adrienne looks at me with pause, biting her lip as if deciding whether or not to tell me anything beyond what she's already shared so far. "Please, tell me something. Anything. How am I supposed to have any hope of controlling the raging flow of my magic if I don't have the slightest clue why it feels like my senses are so strong my mind could shatter?" I plead.

Adrienne's eyes soften as she gives me an empathetic glance that could melt me to my knees if I allowed it. "Far more than just your senses have been heightened, I'm afraid," she confesses. "You'll soon discover you are more than twice as powerful as you were before Lady Rhonwen and I resurrected your body and soul, so there's no point in withholding that information from you. You're now more than twice as deadly and more than twice as unstable. Even in your sleep, the smallest of nightmares could very likely induce catastrophic disasters, hence…your new sleeping arrangements. We can't afford to worry about the threat of your powers while Eldermoor is busy committing mass bloodbaths in search of the luminaries."

Shivers trickle down my spine like freezing rain in response to Adrienne's words. I've hardly adjusted to the half-mortal blood running through my veins and the reserves of light wielding magic from a god I've never connected with in my entire life. Now I have to learn to adjust to twice the chaos. "Can you explain why?" I ask quickly and casually, attempting to test my luck further.

Adrienne half-chuckles. "Nice try, my love. I may have a soft spot for you, but that's the very reason this conversation ends here for now. You're still quite far off from being able to handle that just yet," she pushes back.

I should know by now there's no point in trying to win when it comes to Adrienne. There's no point in trying to win against a creature of devastating, goddess-level beauty that can put even Death himself in his place. We turn down a small, quiet corridor with no rooms other than whatever lies behind an ominous pair of large, sable black doors at the end. Intricate carvings of ravens and black roses cover the entirety of the woodwork.

"We're finally here," Adrienne sighs. These doors appear more like they lead to a strange seminar hall than a bedroom. Something tells me this new room won't resemble my former one in the slightest. I guess I should also know by now when it comes to Adrienne; she'll never fail to lead me down paths beyond what my imagination can conjure.

CHAPTER 20
Tethered

"Welcome to my lair," Adrienne announces as she leads us through the elaborate doors to a bedroom that feels more like a palace. Massive, arched windows carved into black garnet walls provide immaculate, clear views of the fog-laden mountains. Rose-gold pots filled with long, dramatic black vines and emerald ivy hang from the ceiling. Shelves line the portions of the walls not covered in windows, filled with black rose succulents and ancient bottles of rare liquors and trinkets.

The noticeable absence of religious artwork may be as mesmerizing as the room itself. The heavily praised, worshipped, and admired gods haven't so much as touched The Mortal Realms of Elmoria since their luminaries created the world. Yet Lady Rhonwen, the vast majority of her knights, and the people of Blackthorn sing their praises with the fibers of their very beings. To finally catch a break from the fervent worship culture is the very rest my tired soul is craving.

"This is a lot larger than what I was expect-wait a minute. Did you say your lair?" I've been so occupied admiring the beautiful, dark work of art this room is, it just dawned on me that Adrienne referred to it as hers.

"My apologies. You're right. I guess it's technically *our* lair now," Adrienne says as if correcting herself.

"Wait, wait, wait. Are we going to be sharing this room? This is really what Lady Rhonwen requested? For me to share your room?" My heart flips and twists and thumps violently in my chest. This has to be a joke. Heat flushes to my cheeks faster than I can hope to suppress.

"All she asked was that I move you closer to me. She didn't exactly specify how much closer," Adrienne smirks. "You sleeping in my room gives me the best shot at keeping you and everyone in this monastery safe. And selfishly, it provides me some peace of mind."

I hate admitting to myself that I can't find any arguments against her logic. I hate admitting to myself that sharing Adrienne's room also provides me with peace of mind. There is no point in trying to come up with any rebuttals or protests when my heart screams that I am home. I am home, and there is no point in fighting against it.

"Not the religious type, I gather?" I try awkwardly changing the subject, not quite ready to show Adrienne how relieved I am with my new sleeping arrangements.

"Don't let my close work with The High Priestess fool you. You're correct to assume I'm not the religious type," Adrienne confesses. "I've learned how to wear my masks quite well over the years. As far as Lady Rhonwen is concerned, my soul is unconditionally devoted to the beloved gods without hesitation. She has no clue I hold personal grievances against them. She has no clue I couldn't care less about those distant, immortal assholes."

I'm glad I changed the subject. Confirming Adrienne despises the gods as much as I do makes me feel even safer in her presence. I want to pry further about her own personal resentments against them, but the tone in her voice and the expression on her face indicate she has no desire to elaborate further. I can settle with our established common ground for now.

"I don't know about you, but I could use some fresh air now," she sighs. Adrienne walks the length of her room to a set of floor-length glass doors. She flings them open, unveiling balcony mountain views so stunning my jaw drops. Floral spring mist and the woodsmoke of Vespera's campfires pour from the balcony into her bedroom like welcomed party guests. Dragons, winged courier foxes, and crows sweep against the foggy, ashen horizon like brush strokes of watercolors onto a canvas.

My eyes are then drawn to glimpses of the mountains reflected in her pristinely polished black marble floors. Reflections of flickering candle flames weave throughout the marble floor mountains, accompanied by the sound of flowing bath water. I look up to find crystal clear water pouring into a large, tourmaline basin surrounded by candlelight, tucked in the alcove of Adrienne's balcony.

"Do all wing commanders get such luxurious accommodations like this?" I ask as I feel my mouth gape in shock, finding it hard to believe rooms like this exist within a monastery.

"Instructors, wing commanders, emissaries, and Lady Rhonwen's lower priestesses all get quite a few generous amenities as part of our compensation. I would be lying if I said there weren't some perks to serving so closely under The High Priestess," Adrienne smirks.

"Anyways, you've hardly had a proper bath earlier, and I don't believe either one of us can endure your lingering stench any longer. Get in before I throw you in myself," Adrienne orders. After leaving the bathing chambers in such a hurry, there are still quite a few splotches of dried, inky hydrafang blood accompanying the vile odors of The Dark Realms. Again, I'm frustratingly unable to come up with any worthwhile arguments against her.

"Ever so charming, as usual," I scoff as I undress and sink into the crystal waters. Finding myself immersed in the mountainous soundscapes melts away the tension in my muscles as the cool spring air soothes my lungs. I allow myself a moment of blissful floating, soaking in the views of the evergreen, snow-capped peaks in a warm buzz of weightlessness. For the first time since stepping into an awareness of my heightened senses, I feel alive. Alive with the hope I may learn to thrive rather than merely survive.

Adrienne peers over the balcony, admiring the views with her arms stretched out over the railing—the staggering beauty of a queen watching over her domain. I'm no longer at the monastery. I'm in a queendom ruled by a full-blooded goddess, as far as I'm concerned. If Adrienne can subdue The God of Death to a state of writhing agony upon his throne in his immortal kingdom, I have no doubt she could rule over a land of her own. Should I be terrified by how effortlessly she shifted into the form of a demon that could rule above those wraiths? A dragon that nearly resembled a spitting image of Sarthon? The more I try to understand this woman, the more she feels like an undiscovered element without any laws of nature that can properly define her.

"You know I can sense you contemplating just how much you should fear me," Adrienne's lips curve into a taunting smirk.

"Then you should know it's a fear that fascinates me rather than terrifies me. Sorry if that disappoints you," I taunt back. "Tell me, though, how did you shift into such powerful forms in The Dark Realms? I don't think I realized wielding can manifest as shapeshifting."

I may not have spent much time around half-mortals, but I've seen enough to gather that was no ordinary display of wielding. "The more time you spend in the art of your element, the easier it becomes to shape it to your desires. The abilities of mages are also heightened when naturally surrounded by their element. The Dark Realms was a fitting playground for me, just like that thunderstorm was for you during our little sparring match that nearly struck me out of the sky."

"Why didn't you just shift into a dragon or something when I nearly hit you? Considering how dark that storm was, I'm sure it would've been easy enough."

"True. However, It was much more fun to turn it into a spectacle and enjoy your panic when you thought you nearly killed your instructor. You gave me a good laugh," Adrienne chuckles as she exits the balcony to gather fresh towels and clothes.

I bite my tongue to avoid throwing knives of curses her way and sink deeper into the water to keep my mind off the sizzling flames heating up under my skin. Not only did she let me think I nearly killed her, but she allowed the entire squad to think it as well. All for entertainment.

"Easy now, my love. We both know what happens when you get too worked up," Adrienne taunts in her alluring, dark tone as she returns to the tub. "Mind if I join you?" She asks.

"Pl-Please do." I nearly forget how to speak as she begins slowly shedding the layers of her dragon knight uniform. A beautiful serpent shedding her skin into a much, much deadlier form.

Gods, I hope she can't hear my pulse thundering in my chest at the sight of her. She strips down to nothing more than a black bra and matching, lacy underwear. Her flawless, porcelain skin glistens like a fresh snowfall under luminous moonbeams. She lingers over the tub and throws her voluminous raven-black tresses into a bun atop her head. I may need to sink beneath the surface before she notices my scarlet flushed cheeks. Before she realizes how easily she can break me with her perfection alone.

Adrienne's ink serpent tattoos cascade down the rippling muscles of her arms as she continues fixing her hair, releasing a couple of wispy strands to frame her high cheekbones. I try not to panic upon noticing her toned abs. The muscles honed by a deadly warrior full of secrets and battles I have yet to uncover. Gods, it's all too much to take in— the fullness of her breasts, the curves of her hips, and her firm, well-defined thighs. There is nothing half-mortal about her beauty. Adrienne might as well be a full-on goddess.

She slowly bends over the pool, flashing her cleavage dangerously close to my face as she brings her lips to my ear. "Are you feeling up to picking up where we left off earlier?" She whispers.

"I was beginning to worry you would never ask," I respond. Gods, I'm really done for. My heart drops right along with the underwear that drops down Adrienne's towering, long legs. She unclamps her bra and lowers herself into the warm, crystal water. I swear the temperature immediately rises.

"Can I ask a question you may be up for answering?" It takes all my damn wits to form my words and maintain my composure as Adrienne inches closer, and closer. She grabs an elixir vial from the side of the tub and empties it, filling the water with humming bubbles.

"It better be a damn good question," she snarls. If my heart races any faster, she may need to retrieve my soul from The Dark Realms again.

I swallow the boulder in my throat, shooting the shot that could potentially fire right back at me. "What exactly are we to each other?"

Adrienne slithers onto my lap, swiveling her hips in disarray as she wraps her arms around my neck. Her slippery, bare skin sliding on top of my upper thighs sends my nervous system into a roaring adrenaline rush. Her soaking-wet breasts pressed up against my chest, threatening to send me into cardiac arrest.

"I warned you not to fall for me," she whispers. She grabs a fistful of my hair, pulling it back as her warm, velvet lips caress my neck in a stream of heavy, passionate kisses. I place my hands on her hips to feel her body sway with the waves as she dances on my lap.

"Turns out I was warning myself," she growls into my ear. Adrienne works her kisses up my neck, making her way to the corner of my mouth as she bites my lips. "I've fallen quite hard for you, my love. I'm afraid I've fallen far beyond the point of return." Adrienne's silken lips claim mine with an immeasurable yearning that melts me beyond reality. I match her desperation with equal force, crashing my lips into hers in deep admiration of how she tethers my soul to this world.

"See how we fit together so perfectly?" Adrienne wraps her legs around the small of my back as she pins me against the side of the tub. "My soul was destined to find yours," she growls against my lips. Electrifying currents tingle on the tip of my tongue as it entwines with hers. She flinches at the initial shock, then lets out a soft moan, embracing the sparks dancing on our tongues with wicked desire.

"I'm afraid I've fallen quite hard for you as well," I confess as I flash Adrienne a taunting smirk, forging schemes to take her over the edge in pleasure. I take a moment to close my eyes and focus on the flow of my magic, channeling more of those tingling sparks to my lips and my tongue. As soon as I feel ready to give my plan a shot, I turn the tides, pinning Adrienne up against the wall of the tub as I take my seat on her lap.

"We're fortunate I can't actually destroy you since your touch grounds my magic, and I'm about to have a whole lot of fun with that." I flick my tongue around Adrienne's nipples, sending my electricity prickling around her dangerously sensitive nerves.

"Amira," Adrienne moans as I continue my arousing her with light, throbbing shocks. Hearing my name moaned so desperately in response to my actions may be the epitome of euphoria. "I want this moment to last, Amira. Gods, you need to slow down," she moans again.

"You need me to switch things up? I will gladly oblige. Sit on the side of the tub. Now," I order.

Adrienne complies, and I position my head right between her thighs. The intoxicating scent of her arousal nearly makes me forget how to breathe. "I've been torturing myself, wondering what you taste like. May I?"

"Please," she whimpers. Adrienne is now at my mercy. Exactly where I want her. With electric, pulsating currents vibrantly dancing at the tip of my tongue, I skillfully stroke my tongue around her vulva. Gripping her thighs tighter, the louder she moans. "More," she pleads with me.

"You taste exquisite, my dear," I moan as I slowly pull away. Adrienne gasps in frustration, thrusting her hips as her thighs shiver over the side of the tub.

"Please!" She begs again, whimpering.

"Look at you, begging so nicely for me. Since you asked so nicely, maybe I'll continue until you come for me," I tease.

I go back and forth between licking circles around her clit and sucking on it, changing up my patterns each time I fear she's getting too close. The heaviness of her breath and her gasps of desperation guide my pacing. My heart flutters at the sound of Adrienne's intensifying moans, leading me to realize edging her is as cruel to me as it is to her.

"Don't be shy, love. Take what you need and hold nothing back," I coax, knowing full well I'll allow her to go over the edge this time. I glide my electrified, throbbing tongue up and down her clit as she thrusts her hips against me. Adrienne's moans turn to screams as surging pleasure releases from her body— pleasure that washes over me in soul-cleansing waves of oxytocin.

Adrienne lowers herself back into the water and brings her lips to mine in a tantalizingly gentle kiss. "I'm never going to forgive you for that. Consider yourself damned when I decide to retaliate," she warns with a smug grin.

Adrienne breaks her lips off mine, melting me with her eyes, smokier than the foggy mountains surrounding us. With our heartbeats pressed against each other, perfectly aligned in a chaotic rhythm, I can barely distinguish where my body stops and her's begins. We take each other in with a stillness rivaling the eye of a hurricane. By the restless look in her eyes, something tells me this stillness will be short-lived. Something tells me she has to shatter it. Perhaps I can tell simply by knowing we both thrive in the heart of the storm rather than in the lull of the eye.

"I love you, Amira," she blurts out, stirring up the winds once more. "Since the moment your soul found mine as your grounding stability, I feared falling for you would become inevitable," she confesses.

My mind spirals with meteoric speed, struggling to process how what I'm hearing could possibly make sense. Adrienne can read emotions and memories plagued by darkness, and when it comes to me, she can't shut it out. We essentially share my inner demons. How could she possibly love someone bound by such life-draining, internal parasites?

"Knowing everything that I know, having been exposed to everything I've been exposed to, I swear I would've still fallen for you in every lifetime," she responds as if knowing the exact trajectory of my inward spiral. "Your soul grounds mine in pathways I never thought could exist for me. It's a harbor of respite amongst the sea of darkness that comes with my existence. Even amid your own darkness, your light shines brighter for me than the lights of the gods ever did. Yes, I have seen the depths of your scars, and at the same time, my soul still finds yours to be home. Never for one second believe those monsters ever smothered your light. I will spend an eternity helping you realize the miracle that you are if that's what it takes, light-bringer."

Overwhelming surges of peace, relief, and elation consume me like wildfire, leaving me nearly too stunned to speak. "I hope by now, it's clear that I love you too, Adrienne. I fear my love for you may far exceed my half-mortal lifespan. So, with every heartbeat I have left, I'm yours. And when it's time for our souls to part from The Mortal Realms, I vow always to find you just as you found me in The Dark Realms. Our souls were made for each other, and I refuse to allow any change of fate, any death god, or any abysmal darkness to rip us away from each other. Deal?"

"Deal," Adrienne smiles, sealing our deal with a firm, passionate kiss in agreement.

Never in a million years could I have imagined falling in love again after losing Casimir. Not after every harsh, glacial spear I've taken to my heart while serving as Rhydian's favorite weapon and then as his only weapon. Never in a million years could I have imagined falling in love with a dragon knight. Not after all the knights have put me through simply by overlooking the practices of their favorite mercenary. Yet here I am, hopelessly in love with Adrienne. Wing Commander, shadow mage, daughter of Kamaris.

I savor the moments entangled in her immaculate beauty, longing for simpler times I've never known. A time when the luminaries could be left in peace without wicked hearts lusting after their catastrophic power. When every man, half-mortal, and every creature could respect Elmoria's delicate balance in symbiotic harmony. A world with no impoverished peasant slums, no disease, no bastard mercenaries forging orphans into lethal, tortured weapons. A world where souls could fall in love without the need to sleep with one eye open. Every moment spent home, spent in Adrienne's arms, teases me with a taste of such a world.

"What a disastrous storm we will be," I mutter nervously, miserably unprepared to face the realities of Elmoria's current threats. Not with now having much to lose.

"No. What a disastrous storm you will be when I'm through with you," Adrienne laughs darkly.

"Retaliating so soon?" I ask, embarrassingly too eager. I'm more than thoroughly prepared to savor this taste of glorious distraction just a little longer.

Adrienne smirks as she slams me against the side of the pool, fastening my arms behind my back. Shadows wrap around my wrists, binding them in place. "I decided we're not finished here quite yet."

Too full of fluttery nerves to take in her eyes piercing me like daggers, I lower my gaze until the fullness of her breasts sends me into a panic. I fight against my restraints, desperate to feel their weight in my hands. My binds grow increasingly tighter and tighter in response to my pitiful attempt to break free.

"Oh, you're not going anywhere, my love," she taunts. With my hands bound behind my back, I'm nearly driven to the edge of my sanity as she teases the throbbing need between my thighs with tendrils of caressing shadows—an extension of her masterful touch.

"Gods-damnit, you're so unfair," I moan, thrusting into the shadows in desperation to let them touch where I need them the most.

"Do I need to silence that tongue of yours?" Adrienne asks as a band of thick, black rope wedges in between my teeth in the form of a makeshift gag.

Adrienne slams her body against mine as she bites my ear, nails clawing into my back. The friction of her hips thrusting against my own, combined with the warmth of the pleasurable pain running down my back, stifles a moan through my gag. "I could get used to the sound of your muffled moans," she whispers darkly. The heat of her breath sends electric currents of my magic pulsing down my spine. Gods, I need nothing more than to break free and run my hands over every inch of her divine perfection.

Her lips curve into a satisfied smirk as she kisses down my jawline to the corner of my mouth. "You don't get to play with magic and expect me not to make an immediate retaliation. Don't you dare underestimate the effect that your pleasure has on me," she warns in an icy tone. A cluster of trembling shadows forms at her fingertips as she lowers her hand beneath the water. Gods, I am done for.

Her shadows pulsate around my dangerously sensitive nerve endings, inching just close enough to nearly set me over the edge right before ebbing away from the brink of release. Adrienne's magic devours every last nerve with exhilarating ecstasy as I thrust my hips back and forth against the expanding and contracting rhythm.

"More," I attempt to mutter through the thick rope clenched between my teeth.

"I'm sorry, love, what was that?" Adrienne taunts as she casts her shadows inside me, swirling them in unpredictable patterns that send me closer and closer to the edge. After graciously allowing me to grind against the palpitating waves, she pulls them out, leaving me panting and pleading for more.

"Oh, are you asking for more? I can show you much, much more," Adrienne warns with the raise of her slitted eyebrow. Within seconds, she launches her shadows to depths I never realized were accessible. The intimacy of her reach, combined with my overwhelming vulnerability, forces me to scream into my gag as I ride the biggest wave of pleasure in my entire life. It takes me several full seconds of blissful weightlessness before I realize tears are streaming down my face.

"That's my girl," Adrienne smirks as she unbinds me from her restraints. Too stunned to speak, I focus on catching my breath and regaining control over my hopelessly heavy legs. "You took that so well," she praises

"You're…you're-" Why do I even bother trying to form words right now?

"Good? You can leave it at that while you recuperate. I'm sure you'll remember how to speak soon enough," Adrienne jeers as she hands me a towel.

I feel pieces of my calloused, ice-laden heart melt into a glacial puddle as she offers me a hand out of the tub. Every heartbeat spent at her side slowly fills the hollow shell of my heart with light, one torch at a time. I do not deserve this restoration, nor do I deserve Adrienne. However, fighting for a brighter Blackthorn and a harmonious Elmoria without her at my side is not a task I am capable of or willing to endure. Our souls are now irrevocably tethered in love and chaos.

CHAPTER 21
New Pathways

Adrienne dusts off a bottle of whiskey from her eclectic liquor collection as I dry off and change into the plum tunic and soft, chestnut linen trousers set out for me from my new armoire. Despite slowly recovering feeling in my legs, I don't think I'll ever truly recover from the chemistry-altering pleasure that sent me to a realm of pure euphoria.

"This one is particularly smoky and spicy, so I'm more than confident you'll enjoy it," Adrienne smirks. "Aged in ember oak barrels by a team of earth mages and Eldermoorian apothecaries, back in simpler times," she sighs reminiscently. She hands me a charcoal-colored mug with a hand-carved crescent moon as we take our seats on the bench on her balcony. She takes a sip from the emerald mug she selected for herself, covered in hand-carved evergreen trees.

"Where did you get these mugs? They're beautiful," I ask, admiring the intricacies of the wood carvings.

"You're not the only one who knows your way around your blades. Sometimes, my sleepless nights compel me to spend the quiet hours of twilight carving wood," Adrienne casually responds. How much do I still not know about this woman?

Thumping dragon wings scatter the stench of sulfur amongst the rain-scented mist as rain breaks free from the dense clouds. Raindrops drum against the sable stone awning in a palpitating cadence as the smoked whiskey burns the back of my throat. Adrienne blows shadowy rings of smoke into the air upon releasing a drawn-out sigh. "As reckless as you were, I really should've taught you how to recognize the signs of burnout before we got assigned to that mission," she says before taking a swig of whiskey.

"You're still hung up on that?" Guilt pangs my stomach upon noticing her eyes weighed down with exhaustion as heavy as the rain clouds. The weight of love accompanied by the fear of loss in a world growing more hostile with every heartbeat is a heavy burden to carry. "You haven't even failed me once. My body was a paper-thin dam holding back rapids of magic demanding to be channeled, and you had no way to reach me," I attempt to comfort her, knowing I'm failing.

"Exactly. I allowed you to slip from my reach your first time on an assignment without access to my touch. It's not happening again," she seethes. A plume of thick smoke escapes from her breath and disperses into the dense layers of fog. "Here I was promising myself not to tell you too much too soon, yet here I am about to share more. You're well on your way to being the death of what remains of my sanity, my love." Adrienne downs another shot of whiskey, preparing herself to share whatever she clearly doesn't want to share.

"As much as I would love for you to tell me everything right here and now, I'm not asking for more. You can let it go for now," I offer gently.

"Since when did you become so sweet?" Adrienne taunts. "Anyways, considering how it might save your stubborn ass on the battlefield, we might be better off taking our chances on you losing your only grounding source rather than you potentially losing your life. I'm afraid there's not much I would be able to do against all the Gods of Niroshen, and Osiris will never be coming for your soul again. I made sure of that."

I lay my head on Adrienne's shoulder as she silently twirls strands of my moon-white hair between her fingers. "Do your worst," I challenge with a soft smile. After everything I've been exposed to in the last few days alone, I don't know what it would take to surprise me anymore.

"Be careful what you ask for, love."

I nearly choke on the whiskey lingering on my tongue upon hearing

Adrienne's voice in my head.

"Before you even ask, no. You're not imagining things. I'm communicating with you through a new...pathway of sorts." Without a doubt, Adrienne's low, satiny voice has somehow infiltrated my mind despite the silence of her lips.

"How? How are you in my head right now?" I reply, my head whirling with bewildered panic. Oh, Gods. *"Does this mean you can read my mind now? What is even happening?"*

"Typically, half-mortals can only communicate through internal pathways like this through their bonds with their dragons. You and I, however, were also gifted with a bond after our encounter with The Dark Realms. And no, I still cannot read any thoughts that exist outside of your distress or your dark memories," Adrienne answers.

My blood turns to ice. None of this makes sense. The God of Death does not appear to be one to hand out harmless parting gifts. I have still yet to learn the catch. The catch that Adrienne fears could cost her ability to ground my soul from spreading death like wildfire.

"What in the realms did you agree to, Adrienne?" What else did she agree to to get Osiris to part with me? She clenches my hand, pulling me in close, sending the rising currents of my lethal electricity back to a state of controlled dormancy.

"I swear on my life, Amira, we are both safe, and that's all that matters. Osiris knows if he ever touches you again, I will spend my entire lifetime wasting and draining all his precious time and energy so he can't effectively lead his war. He can't afford to come after us. As much as he wants you, he wants full reign over Elmoria more, and I played that to my advantage."

My stomach plummets. "You truly could have stalled him to the point of costing Eldermoor the entire war if you simply fought him long enough?" I ask sheepishly.

"Yes. I could've bought our forces and allies more than enough time to crush Eldermoor's armies and force their surrender. Osiris was so drunk on his fixation with keeping you in his realm that he didn't even realize it. I did him a favor and brought it to his attention. Once he realized he could choose between you or focus on invading Elmoria, he released you to me with zero hesitations. However, he chose to permanently alter you out of spite. It's not every day The God of Death doesn't get everything that he wants. And allowing you to suffer for a moment longer was not an option," Adrienne seethes.

Adrienne could have cut The God of Death off from supplying his blood mages with their magic and commanding his armies. She could've delayed Eldermoor's immortal warlord long enough for Blackthorn and Helia to acquire all the luminaries and end the torrential bloodshed. Instead, she chose to snap him out of his hyper-focused frenzy. She chose me over an opportunity to end the war.

Adrienne sweeps a strand of my hair out of my eyes and looks at me as if admiring a trove of all the riches the world has to offer. *"I'm aware my logic is tragically flawed, but I'll never regret the choice I made. I hope you can understand without you, there is no Elmoria worth fighting for."*

I let the rain and gentle rumbles of thunder fill the silence between us while processing the weight of Adrienne's words. Lightning strikes the sky in branches of bright light, inspiring me to channel as much passion as my soul can conjure into kissing Adrienne like it's the last opportunity we'll have. Her lips part for mine, reciprocating my zeal and reiterating the reality that no grave contains enough authority to separate us.

I allow my words to flow into our bond to communicate without breaking her lips from mine. *"If my heart were noble, I would resent you for your decision, but it isn't. If the tides were turned and it was you in the clutches of death, I would've chosen you over the world in a thousand lifetimes,"* I truthfully admit, accepting our new pathway as a sacred gift.

CHAPTER 22
The Dragon's Glade: Lumithra

The melodic songs of the Veradis Spirits pull me out of my deep slumber as diffused beams of sunrise trickle in through the blankets of fog covering the towering vines and evergreens. The spirits hum their morning song, letting me know I've been out since yesterday afternoon. Recovering from nearly losing Amira has proven more draining than all that transpired in The Maren Caverns. If it weren't for today's council meeting, needing to gather reports on the hatchlings, and my restless need to keep frequent tabs on my recklessly stubborn light mage, I could easily sleep for an entire week.

I swear I spent most of my slumber lashing out at Kallik for failing to retrieve Amira's soul before Osiris got to her and giving her nearly twice the power he granted to Nuri. The gods haven't always been so apathetic regarding the half-mortals that share their blood. Why are they growing careless now, especially during a war over their precious Mortal Realms?

A surge of energy ignites my bond with Amira, signaling that she's also finally up for the day. She's awake and in one piece, much to the credit of spending last night sleeping in Adrienne's arms. Despite the insufferable annoyances of young, angsty love, I am elated Amira is finally over despising the only source capable of grounding her powers.

"When you train with Adrienne after breakfast, you are to follow her instructions precisely with zero deviations. If she warns you are approaching burnout, you stop what you are doing, and you listen to her. Understood?" Knowing just how much magic Kallik has gifted her makes my two stomachs roil. I could sense its depths before Sarthon lowered

her to the ground for her Kanoelani Trials. Now, with the irreversible mark Osiris placed on her, Amira's magic rivals the strength of the gods.

"Did you even eat breakfast before you began nagging me first thing in the morning? Maybe a meal to curb your hangry mood would serve you wonders," Amira snarks through our bond.

"You following Adrienne's orders verbatim is what would serve me wonders," I hiss back. I swear the gods intended for our mages to test the limits of our patience to keep our spirits young. They're nearly as bad as hatchlings.

"I promise I will be fine. It's just training. My soul won't leave The Mortal Realms again anytime soon, Lumithra."

She's right. I know she is right. I release a blast of fire to the sky to exhale my fears. However, much of my apprehension is rooted in grief, and grief will be as everlasting as my immortality. After six hundred years, I still mourn Nuri's death. I still feel the weight of the decision we made. I knew reaching for the amount of Kallik's power required to raise shields against imperial magic would result in her burnout. However, Nuri insisted we make the sacrifice, and I decided to allow it. I ended the first Luminary War at the expense of her life, and I don't think I would have it in me to make a decision like that again.

Veradis claws dig into the earth, snapping twigs and crunching leaves as the presence of Choilleich, The Matron Spirit, draws near. I rise from the ground and shake the shrubbery from my scales, preparing to stand presentable before her. Now is not the time to lie in a coiled half-slumber, consumed by grief and worries. Now is the time to tend to my duties as The White Empress and meet with the elder of the veradis spirits.

Choilleich's luminescent green eyes glow through the dense fog as she steps out of the haze and into my thicket. The Matron Spirit bows before me. "Good morning, Lumithra," she bows before me. Fireflies dance around the dark, sage green and amber leaves composing Choilleich's mossy fur while butterflies come and go from their perches upon her knobby, branch-like antlers. She stands hardly shorter than the dragons, possessing the body of a massive wolf and the antlers of a mature stag. As the heart of the Kanoelani, the forest's spiritual aura follows her every step.

"Good morning, Choilleich," I greet as I return her bow. "You're here with the hatchling report, I take it."

Choilleich shakes her antlers, commanding the fluttering butterflies to rest quietly on their perches as she prepares to speak. "One of the dragons bonded to a descendant of Kun had all six of her eggs hatch during your assignment in the caverns. Each of the hatchlings appears to be in perfect health and taking well to their feedings," she reports.

"And what of the mother?" I ask

"Her earth mage is among the many squads sent to reinforce Helia's forces, so she is missing her hatchlings furiously," Choilleich sighs empathetically. "Nonetheless, her health is in excellent condition, and I've been reassuring her that my spirits have been very tentative to the needs of her hatchlings in her absence."

"I'm happy to hear all are doing well," I sigh in relief. There have been numerous stillbirths during this spring hatching cycle— likely a result of the stress Elmoria's threatened balance is imposing on egg-laying mothers. To hear of six healthy, thriving hatchlings in times of war is almost unheard of.

"I can only hope this war somehow ends long before it reaches anywhere near the Kanoelani and our hatchlings," I add. "For Eldermoor to make such drastic advancements in such little time, I would be foolish not to fear the possibility their power may come to exceed that of my shields over Blackthorn." Icy shivers scuttle down the lengths of my wings at the thought. I grip the soil between my claws, tilling the earth beneath me, praying the days of peace upon our sacred land aren't numbered. Praying if all the luminaries reach the borders of Blackthorn's protection, my shields will still hold firm against whatever Osiris may be forging to wield against us.

"You know we will defend the hatching grounds and join the fight for Elmoria's balance if the gods unleash our spirits from our confines. If our spirits are summoned to spill the blood of our enemies, then so be it," Choilleich growls.

"I hope it doesn't come down to seeing one of my oldest friends on the frontlines," I reply, masking as much fear in my voice as possible. I have no doubts that Choilleich is more than capable of handling herself and leading the veradis spirits into battle. The gods entrusted them with the sacred task of protecting the future generations of dragons for a reason. It's the thought of how dire Elmoria's condition would have to become if the Matron Spirit and her kin were released from their realm, taken from their role of guarding the Kanoelani, that twists my stomachs into knots.

"Not all hope has been diminished, my dear friend. No powers of Osiris, whether ancient or unrevealed, could ever hope to match the unrelenting spirit of dragons. Regardless of the fires that spawn from The Dark Realms, your flames will outlast them all. Even if shadows come to blanket every last inch of our lands, we will prevail." The soothing words trickle from Choilleich like a peaceful river of healing waters.

"Spoken like a tried and true Matron Spirit. Where would I be without your guidance, my friend?"

Choilleich smiles as a gentle breeze ruffles through her leafy coat as if the gods sent the winds to echo her wisdom and majesty. "You have a council briefing this morning, if I'm not mistaken. Get along to your meeting now. I'll see that the spirits feed the hatchlings before they set the forest ablaze," she chuckles.

We exchange bows before I launch to the sky and head for The Dragon's Glade. It's the most spacious clearing the Kanoelani offers, making it the perfect location for holding our council gatherings. The flight is brief, but I welcome stretching my wings and feeling the sun on my scales as glimmers of bliss before the briefing. Glimpses of the glade's vast stretch of moss-laden terrain peak through the fog, and I descend back through the towering vines and evergreens.

Sarthon greets me with a menacing glare and a scoffing breath of steam as I land in the space next to him. "Nice to see you too," I hiss.

"You're fortunate Adrienne emerged from The Dark Realms unscathed when she went after your precious little light mage. If Amira steps out of line one more time, I won't hesitate to incinerate her on the spot for all the trouble she's caused. Consider this your first and final warning," Sarthon grumbles.

Either he woke up on the wrong side of his thicket this morning, or he's entirely forgetting who he's talking to. "I'm sorry. Can you remind me who raised the shields that ended the last Luminary War? If that was you, then by all means, feel free to test me. Otherwise, I strongly suggest you don't come at me with threats against my mage. You so much as look at Amira, and I'll have no problem with borrowing a torrential downpour of power from Kallik again," I growl.

"Don't test me, White Empress. You know the weight of war better than any of us here. If Adrienne's energy has to be critically diverted from our enemies to keep your mage's powers in check, the blood of any resulting casualties will be on your claws, not mine. Maybe find a way to discover a new grounding source for Amira's lethal explosions and let my mage focus on her own invaluable assets," Sarthon seethes.

"You know it doesn't work like that. Not even the gods hold authority over what grounds a mage's soul. Maybe talk Adrienne into coming clean to everything with Amira before taking any further jeers at my mage if you're that worried about any distractions," I fire back.

"You know damn well the deal with Osiris complicates the situation," Sarthon growls. "Since your mage has ever so conveniently chosen Adrienne as the grounding source to all the magic Kallik has gifted her, Adrienne can't reveal her cards too soon. You know there's no telling what mass exodus of white flames will ravage our lands before our enemies even have the chance to destroy us if Amira's heart severs its recognition of Adrienne as its grounding source."

Withholding Adrienne's secrets from Amira has been as painful as icy talons piercing my underbelly, but Sarthon is right. Even if his argument wasn't valid, it is still against the code of dragons to meddle in the affairs of mages, especially Adrienne's. My duty is to defend Blackthorn and the Kanoelani with an unfaltering focus.

"We've both voiced our grievances. Arguing any further at this point would lead to us violating our codes. Guide Adrienne well, and I will guide Amira well. We're honored to be bonded to Blackthorn's most powerful mages despite the complications."

Sarthon ignores me, rolling his eyes as he turns his attention to the other dragons of our council. I'll take that as a sign I sufficiently put him in his place.

Before my next breath, the stillness of the atmosphere is interrupted by the cerulean celestial body of scales breaking through the dense haze. Eir, bonded to The High Priestess, swoops down from the sky, descending to the center of the glade. The gusts of her wings stir the glowing, viridian moss upon her elegant landing.

"Good morning, council," Eir bows before us, her alabaster eyes glowing bright as the constellations. I lower my head and return her bow in unison with the dozens of dragons in attendance. "As I'm sure you're all aware by now, Blackthorn is now in possession of two luminaries— Kallik's light luminary and Sirena's sea luminary. You have Lumithra's squad, especially the light mage, to commend for rescuing and healing the members of our council along with their water mages in The Maren Caverns. You have Tsuna and her water mage, Irvette, to commend for retrieving the sea luminary and ridding the caverns of its imposing threats."

Tsuna's aquamarine eyes beam with pride at the mention of Irvette.

"The sea luminary reflected the purity of Irvette's heart, magnifying her powers and fulfilling her desires of prevailing justice, rather than a heart tainted by the malice of greed. You should be proud the heart of your half-mortal is even more noble than it was the day you bonded her," Eir praises.

A single luminary on its own provides its bearer with unfathomable power as it magnifies the intentions of their heart. When they're all gathered into The Crown that The Gods of Niroshen forged to create Elmoria, the desires and intentions of its bearer become the ruling force of all the lands. The goal of gathering every luminary within the safety of Blackthorn's shields is a necessary evil that will always chill me to my bones. There is no room for my shields to fail, and the gods designed them to scatter to the ends of the earth for a reason.

"As much as I wish we had nothing more to discuss than our recent victories, we have more pressing matters to attend to," Eir continues. "Our intel has gathered that Eldermoor is currently in possession of both the wind and the earth luminaries. Having the power of two luminaries at their disposal, Helia is falling dangerously close a state of total Eldermoorian occupation."

"Eldermoor has two luminaries they're clearly using to reinforce the strength of their armies. Why are we just hiding our luminaries rather than using them to strengthen our attacks as well?" Amira asks. Based on what I'm sensing down our bond, it appears her training session with Adrienne was interrupted by a briefing among the knights at the monastery.

"I can only suspect The High Priestess wishes not to risk losing the light and sea luminaries to the enemy," I respond.

"Pardon my interruption, Eir, but could you possibly convince The High Priestess to allow The Dragon Knights to wield our luminaries against Eldermoor? If Irvette could single-handedly wipe out every remaining hydrafang and sea wraith in the caverns wielding the power of the sea luminary, imagine what an army of our water mages could do to turn the tides of this war. Imagine what more Amira could accomplish with the light luminary," Tsuna implores.

"The High Priestess does not wish to risk bringing the luminaries into battle. Considering the fatalities our forces and Helia's pegasus knights have faced so far, she isn't willing to risk Eldermoor gaining possession of four luminaries. Lady Rhonwen believes the gods will grant us favor if we defend our luminaries rather than exploit their power," Eir explains.

"I don't see how not using all necessary means to fight for Elmoria's balance will grant us the gods' favor. Adrienne informed me she attempted to persuade Lady Rhonwen to reconsider, but she won't budge," Amira seethes.

"While I have my hesitations regarding Lady Rhonwen's decision, she is The High Priestess of Blackthorn, and our code binds us to support her leadership. We will have to trust that the gods will deliver their favor as she senses they will." Hopefully, the gods haven't gone as silent on The High Priestess as they have with me.

"I don't want anyone here questioning the logic of The High Priestess," Eir growls. "The Eve of Eleodora is just two months away. Lady Rhonwen plans to launch a large-scale attack on Eldermoor's forces to seize possession of the earth and wind luminaries before dawn after the sacred holiday. Our fire and earth mages experience heightened powers during the first twenty-four hours of summer, meaning nearly half of our mages will be invading during a surge of great power," she explains.

"Taking advantage of The Eve of Eleodora gives me more confidence in Lady Rhonwen's decision," I tell Amira.

"What exactly gives the fire and earth mages heightened powers during the first day of summer? The High Priestess is also convinced the fire and earth mages will be able to sense the luminaries with exact precision rather than being limited to a general idea of their locations. What makes her so confident?" Amira asks skeptically.

"Eleodora, the goddess of the sun, holds an intimate relationship

with the earth goddess Kun and the fire goddess Solaris. When Eleodora is ushered into her summer season with celebration, her joy infectiously spreads to Kun and Solaris in the form of explosive bursts of energy they can hardly contain. For the first day of summer, they transfer much of that energy to their descendants to ease the load," I explain.

"So essentially, the energy that comes with that level of joy is so immense it becomes a burden. Must be tough being a god," Amira scoffs.

"Chances are high all your mages will be sent out on a multitude of assignments in the weeks leading up to the attack," Eir warns us. "However, encourage them to train profusely at every given opportunity. This operation has the potential to be a critically pivotal moment in this war. Also, do not let your guard down for even a heartbeat. The shields over Blackthorn may prevent The Crown of Luminaries from forging within our borders, but our land is not immune to bloodbaths. Keep your senses keen and your firepower ready. With that, I conclude today's briefing. May the Gods be with us all," she bows.

Whether or not the gods will heed our cries and prayers, I am more than prepared to take up the fight for Elmoria with or without their attentiveness. Amira will survive this war. Between Adrienne and myself, there is no alternative. Her survival means more to us than she may ever know. The Kanoelani will hold strong as the unwavering refuge for our hatchlings by the protection of Choilleich and her veradis spirits. The God of Death can gift every last Eldermoorian with his power, and he still won't have an army vast enough to contend with the wrath of dragons and our mages.

CHAPTER 23

The Shores of Tourmaline: Amira

Lady Rhonwen dismisses us from our briefing, and our squad congregates as we wait for Adrienne to arrive with our instructions for this afternoon's training. If it goes anything like my one-on-one training with her this morning, gods help us all. I'm beginning to fear I may never be able to blast blood mages from the skies without striking slews of allies down with them, based on the hundreds of charred birds I left littering the clearing behind the monastery.

"If it's any consolation, chances are a dragon thoroughly enjoyed those birds as a post-breakfast snack before any of the knights found them. Mastering control takes time, child. I have all the confidence you will get there," Lumithra consoles.

"Unfortunately, time is not exactly one of the amenities I received when becoming a dragon knight," I mutter.

"How long did it take you to master control over your element?" I ask Irvette, trying my damndest to mask the nervousness in my voice.

"It took me about a full year before I could control my surges of waves without nearly drowning everyone within my vicinity," she admits. "Don't sweat it though, Amira, you seem to be a fast learner. Dragons don't choose hopeless mages in the Kanoelani. You've already more than proven that you're capable," she assures me with a gentle smile.

"Dragons also only choose the fiercest. Resilient mages capable of sculpting their elements into masterful, beautiful art," Felix adds, smiling at Irvette in admiration before planting a soft kiss on her cheek.

Despite Irvette's encouragement, my breakfast starts immediately roiling in my stomach. I don't have a year. We only have two months until the Eve of Eleodora. Two months until we launch a massive attack that could turn this war in our favor, and this morning proved I have yet to master a sliver of control over the trajectory of my lethal outbursts.

"Not only did you cheat death long enough for Adrienne to pull you from The Dark Realms, but you returned looking like you've been kissed by the full moon. You returned with beauty rivaling the starlight. What can't you do light-bringer?" Zephyr asks with a smug smirk.

Arden scoffs as he leans against a pillar, keeping his thoughts to himself. I'll take the fact that he isn't interjecting with lectures on how dangerous of a liability I am as a sign that he's slowly coming around to me.

"Oh, please. Isn't suffering through The Dark Realms exhausting enough? Pretty sure the last thing she needs right now is putting up with your shameless flirting," Irvette sneers, elbowing Zephyr in the rib.

"What? All I'm trying to say is with Amira's razzle-dazzle, she's an unstoppable, beautiful badass," Zephyr fires back. "Who could argue with that?"

"Oh, I certainly wouldn't dream of arguing with that."

My heart palpitates uncontrollably as Adrienne enters the room and throws a wink in my direction. "However, I'd listen to Irvette if I were you and refrain from flirting with members of our squad," she warns. We lock eyes, and my face instantly flushes. I trip over nothing and stumble into Irvette. I did not prepare myself to maintain a calm and collected composure after how we spent the majority of last night.

"I'm going to need you to bring me up to speed on whatever is happening between you two as soon as possible," Irvette whispers.

"A proper lady doesn't worship and tell," I whisper back, unable to contain my smirk. Irvette's eye widens as she covers her mouth to stifle her laughter.

"Ask your dragons to meet us at the clearing," Adrienne orders our squad. "We're taking this afternoon's training session to Tourmaline Beach."

*　*　*

Nothing could have prepared me for the stunning aerial view of the emerald mountains outlining the iridescent, obsidian shoreline. It will forever amaze me how Tourmaline Beach can still take my breath away with its rich, haunting beauty despite the chilling nightmares I've collected here over the years. Every time Rhydian's assignments have led me to these shores, the high tides would cleanse the buckets of blood I've spilled into its sands. A haunting cycle of kill, wash, repeat.

As our dragons descend through the salt-scented mist, I'm reminded of the night Casimir and I dared to sneak away for a night swim like it was only a few nights ago. My scars burn as I remember the brutal punishment Rhydian dealt when he awoke in the middle of the night and tracked us to the beach. Casimir received a bludgeoning punch to the head before Rhydian tied his hands behind his back. All he could do was watch my punishment as he slipped in and out of consciousness. All he could do was scream in terror as he watched Rhydian slice his blade down my back, bind me, and throw me into the salty sea with my fresh, gaping wounds. I was convinced death was on its way to claim me as I inhaled buckets of water, frantically fighting through the burning pain to break free of Rhydian's ropes that nearly sent me to a watery grave. Adrenaline saved my life that night, and my escape impressed Rhydian enough to allow us both to live to see the next sunrise.

"Rhydian can't hide from the knights forever. He can't run from his atonement forever. Learn to master some control over your magic so you can deliver his death blow by the time he's in custody. As much as I would

love to kill the bastard myself, his death belongs to you if you want it," Adrienne growls.

"As long as you don't object to me taking my time and drawing out his suffering as long as possible, consider the job mine," I tell her.

"Gods, I'll never stop falling more in love with you," she responds with longing admiration in her tone.

Lumithra's claws dig into the iron sand as the other dragons follow suit. I slide down her long, scaly back, hoping to execute this training session without any catastrophic errors. As long as I don't kill any more wildlife or strike anyone in the squad, I'll consider this afternoon a success.

"We're taking off to hunt for lunch. Once again, pay attention and follow your instructions closely. I'd like to return finding you all in one piece," Lumithra grumbles.

"Yes, mother," I reply in a mocking tone. The blast of wind nearly knocks me off my feet as our dragons launch back to the skies. I take a deep breath, telling myself over and over again that I am not hopeless. Kallik's magic may flow like a wild, unpredictable beast in my veins, but taming it isn't impossible.

"Everyone, gather around," Adrienne orders. "Each of you has proven capable of wielding large sums of your raw power. You have all proven you can naturally recognize your wells of magic and extract natural disasters that can win battles. Today, we focus on aim and control. While some of you may be better at controlling your magic than others, none of you have wielded your elements within close proximity of thousands of allies. Show me you can take a landslide and effortlessly channel it into mere pebbles. Summon monsoon-like waves and craft them into dagger-like raindrops. There will be times on the battlefield when you will have to quickly alter the flow of your magic within a moment's notice to avoid friendly fire. I asked Felix to prepare a demonstration as an example of what I'm looking for."

Felix reaches for his supply pack and pulls out a candlestick, placing it atop a large stone. He widens his stance, squaring his hips as he slowly fills his lungs with air. Sweat begins to trickle down his chest as he looks to the sky, ready to summon the fires of Solaris.

Irvette's hazelnut cheeks turn pink as carnations as she fidgets with her engagement ring. Her thundering pulse sounds like the hooves of excited warhorses. "You okay over there?" I ask her softly.

"Oh, I'm perfectly fine. Watching Felix wield fire always makes me want him in a way that would make the gods turn their backs on me," she whispers.

Thankfully, my laughter is silenced by crackling flames as Felix forms a ring of raging fire outstretched above his head with the release of his breath. Maintaining his firmly planted stance, his arms flow in a rhythmic cadence, and the ring of flames takes on the shape of a massive phoenix. My jaw gapes in awe as his flames become a phoenix with molten talons and wings of blazing ember. Felix bows, and his phoenix hurdles through the sky toward the candlestick.

"Are you out of your gods-forsaken mind?" Zephyr shouts as he shields himself in an orb of howling winds, bracing himself for impact. Irvette clenches her fists, diminishing her hurricane-sized waves into a light, drizzling rainfall over Zephyr as he releases his shield with an exasperated sigh of relief.

Irvette surfs the sea waves back to the shore, landing mere inches from Zephyr. "I hope I was a bit more mindful this time," she says in a mockingly sweet tone as she straightens the collar of his tunic and brushes dirt off his shoulders.

"Never piss off a water mage. Especially mine," Felix snorts.

"Excellent work, Irvette. Way to demonstrate the heart of today's exercise," Adrienne smirks. "While Zephyr works on regaining his composure and recovering from nearly wetting his pants, Arden, let's see what you've got."

Arden rolls up his sleeves and distances himself from the rest of the squad. He stomps the earth beneath him, and a massive tourmaline boulder shoots out of the ground with the force of a geyser. Arden twists his wrists, sculpting the boulder into the shape of a giant, clenched fist. He extends his arms, sending his boulder-sized fist hurdling straight for Zephyr.

"Seriously? Again?" Zephyr cries, throwing up another shield. Arden drops his arms to his sides a heartbeat before impact, and the massive fist disintegrates into gritty grains of sand that return to the ground below.

"Amira, you're next," Adrienne facilitates, paying no attention to Zephyr as he struggles to regain his composure.

Everyone, except for Felix and Adrienne, begins slowly retreating, inching as far away from me as they can manage. They refrain from making any hasty movements as if fearing Adrienne will call them right back if they draw too much attention to themselves.

"What happened to you all believing I'm more than capable of controlling my magic?" I shout back toward Irvette, Zephyr, and Arden.

"We do believe in you! We're just choosing to believe in you from a safe distance! I've already had my fair share of close calls for the day!" Zephyr shouts back.

"Everyone, haul your asses back to where you were. We do not fear our allies," Adrienne seethes, bringing the palm of her hand to her face. "If you fear members of your own squad, how in the realms are you to stand united against any enemy?" Reluctantly, everyone follows their orders with apprehension darkening their eyes.

"I don't think this is a good idea. I failed to master any real control over my magic this morning," I say to Adrienne.

"Relax, my love. This is a controlled environment. I promise I won't allow you to bring harm to anyone here," she assures.

Adrienne approaches me and places a hand on my shoulder. "You've got this," she whispers before stepping back. I grab my shoulder to embrace her phantom touch, hoping to convince myself I am still tethered to my grounding stability.

Conjure flames of lightning fire and then reduce them to a single bolt. Reduce that bolt to a tiny orb of light. I silently repeat the steps of my plan and close my eyes, concentrating on the magic flowing through my veins. I can do this. My magic will obey me. After several moments of deep focus, a stench of iron and faint, distant screeches disrupt my meditation. A blast of white flame escapes from my fingertips and sends me flying backward from being unprepared for the recoil.

The sea breeze grows eerily still. Flocks of birds launch out of the forest in a frenzied pattern as if they can't retreat fast enough. The screeches are suddenly not so distant, and Irvette drops to the ground. Her arms twist and bend out of shape until I hear the snapping of her bones, followed by the pain in her screams. My blood chills to ice.

"Blood mages!" Adrienne shouts. "Prepare for combat!"

Zephyr encapsulates us in a shield of turbulent, howling winds, shielding us from a volley of glowing, violet arrows. Orbs of white light encapsulate my hands as I rush toward Irvette within the confines of our shield. Arrows continue to pour from the sky like torrential rain.

"Blood mages also carry arrows laced with magic-blocking poison. If one so much as grazes your flesh, your magic will be blocked for hours," Adrienne shouts over the winds of Zephyr's shields.

"*Lumithra!*" I shout down our bond in guttural panic as I place my hands on Irvette's arms. She screams and thrashes on the ground as they snap and bend back to shape under the soft glow of my light. After one final snap, she vomits into the iron sand and spews a string of curses before catching her breath.

"Are you alright?" I ask, scanning over every inch of her body as if I have the slightest clue what to expect from a blood mage attack.

Irvette rolls her shoulders back and shakes out her legs, reassuring herself she has control over her body again. "Better than ever and ready to fight," she grits through her teeth with fury surging in her eye. She rises to her feet, and my heart stops when I shift my focus to the skies. Ink-feathered raven griffins covered in bulky armor emerge from the fog carrying cloaked archers on their backs.

Seismic roars answer the ear-splitting screeches, and dragon fire ignites the skies. Lumithra, Sarthon, Tsuna, Fieryn, Sylphira, and Hyrix collide with the raven griffins in sky-shattering rage.

"I can't sustain my shields any longer! Ready yourselves to attack!" Zephyr shouts as his shields shatter, leaving us vulnerable to the threats of poison-laced arrows and blood-wielding. Red, bloody mist taints the skies as our dragons sink their fangs and claws into chunks of raven griffin armor. To my surprise, only a handful of blood mages drop from the skies in the blasts of dragon fire.

I extend my arms and aim a blast of white, electrifying fire toward the skies. Dozens of raven griffins fly straight through the explosion as if flying through harmless clouds. I exert another blast that barely misses Hyrix and Sylphira, causing my knees to buckle and my vision to blur. I've never felt so useless and dangerous in my entire life.

"Their armor appears to be heat and flame-resistant. You and Felix will have to aim your attacks where it's vulnerable around their necks," Lumithra warns.

"Terrific." Needing to execute precise aiming skills after nearly electrocuting two dragons is exactly what I want to hear.

"Blood mages need intensive focus to lock their magic on their targets. Keep your movements swift and unpredictable!" Adrienne shouts to the squad.

All I need to do is wield precise attacks while keeping my movements swift and unpredictable. With swords and daggers, I could handle that in my sleep. With magic from The God of Light, I feel like I've been tossed into the sea without knowing how to tread water.

Lumithra and Sarthon swoop to the ground just long enough for

Adrienne and me to reach our saddles before launching to the blood-stained skies. Zephyr mounts Sylphira, and Hyrix blasts raging fits of fire as he fights his way to Arden.

I watch from above as Arden reaps a stream of iron sand from the earth, lassos a raven griffin's foot, and slams the creature to the ground with brute force. Relief fills my lungs as he takes out its blood mage before it can wield against him.

Lumithra banks a hard left, and I find us flying adjacent to Zephyr and Sylphira. Zephyr has his hands stretched out above him, shielding himself from the downpour of violet arrows and from becoming a puppet of cursed marionettes.

"Hold on tight," Lumithra warns. In unison, Lumithra and Sylphira tuck their wings in, dropping several thousand feet of altitude as my stomach drops to the ground below. Their wings expand again as they weave their bodies in jarring, sporadic patterns that rattle my brain in my skull. How Zephyr manages to stay in his seat, relying on the power of his thighs, rattles my brain with equal force.

"Is flying like this really necessary?" I shout to Lumithra, regretting my decision not to skip breakfast.

"It is if you don't want to become a victim of those blood mages. Swift and unpredictable, remember?" she growls.

Sylphira lets out a spine-shattering roar of rage as a blood mage jumps from its raven griffin and executes a perfect landing on her back. I don't have to be bonded to her to understand she's furious that she can't risk throwing Zephyr by shaking free of her intruder.

"Get me as close to Sylphira as you can! We've got company!"

"On it," Lumithra growls.

"Relinquish the shadow luminary, and be blessed by the holy one," the blood mage's voice strikes like dissonant chords, sounding anything but human. He runs the length of Sylphira's back toward Zephyr, aiming violet arrows for his shield.

"What are you talking about? We don't have any luminaries in our possession!" Zephyr shouts. His arms flinch each time an arrow ricochets off his shield.

"Lies," the mage snarls, now standing within arm's reach of Zephyr. After maintaining his defenses while balancing through deadly flight maneuvers on the back of a dragon, he doesn't have much longer before they give out.

"Zephyr!" I shout through walls of flying, magic-blocking arrows and a sea of raven griffins darkening the skies as I unsheathe one of my daggers. Magic barrels through me with the force of an avalanche and swallows my blade in white flame.

"The stone of Osiris draws near. My senses do not deceive me, boy. Tell me where I can find it before I subject you to The Father's judgment," the mage snarls. Zephyr's shield shatters, and I fling my dagger through the air. Bolts of lightning crackle in the fiery blade as it lands in the mage's chest, piercing him through the heart.

His body goes up in white flames as it falls from the sky with the burning intensity of a dying star, taking my dagger with him. My neck jerks in a jarring whiplash as Lumithra makes a hard bank right without warning.

"We've got more company! Amira! Duck!" She roars.

Lumithra's warning comes right in time as dozens of violet arrows miss me by the hairs of my head. *"Keep low. We've got hundreds on our tail now,"* she grumbles.

"Hundreds?" Bile burns my throat as Lumithra makes another hard bank, flying within inches of the mountains following the shoreline. Hundreds of blood mages, and only six of us. We can only be chased down the beach for so long before we risk burnout. I don't dare attempt turning my head to look behind us, but based on the shrill screeches threatening to make my ears bleed, it feels as if raven griffin beaks are barely missing the back of my neck.

"They think we have the shadow luminary! What in the realms is going on?" I call out to Adrienne in hopes she has the slightest insight on why Eldermoor is attacking Blackthorn amid their extensive operations in Helia.

Silence. Fear strikes me in the gut like a hearty punch.

"Don't shift your focus on unnecessary worry. I can promise you Adrienne is holding her own. The fact we're all still alive can likely be credited to her efforts," Lumithra assures me.

"I'll take your word for it," I respond. If Adrienne can rip the fingers off The God of Death and humiliate him upon his eternal throne, surely she can handle hundreds of Eldermoor's forces.

A small weight is temporarily lifted from my chest as I spot Irvette in the distance, commanding the sea from atop Tsuna. Like an orchestra conductor, she directs the crystal waters to rise and rise until they crescendo, slamming dozens of raven-griffins and blood mages down to their watery graves.

I scan my surroundings without lifting my head above the endless stream of arrows in search of evidence the rest of our squad is alive and in one piece. After spotting Zephyr's carefully controlled tornadoes, Arden's landslides and flying boulders, and Felix's incinerating infernos blazing the battlefield, I'm filled with the reckless delusion that we might actually win this battle.

"Despite their inferiority to dragons, raven-griffins can keep up with our pace for hours on end. You're going to need to wield again to shake some of these death worshippers from our trail," Lumithra orders. *"Brace yourself. I'm going to get us out of this line of fire, and then you're going to strike."*

I fight the tightness of my chest for a deep breath and cling onto Lumithra as tight as my muscles allow. *"I'm ready,"* I gulp.

Lumithra releases a blast of fire and shoots upward into a vertical ascent. The weight of gravity keeps me firmly planted in my saddle and floods me with panic as I become so heavy it feels like I'm about to be crushed into a million pieces. She finally stabilizes, and my mind shifts from fearing my suffocation to frantically scheming an effective plan of attack.

I make out at least twenty raven griffins struggling to climb altitude but well on their way to greet us. If I can't find a way around all their heat and flame-resistant armor to take them out, I'm dead.

"Trust your instincts and strike wisely," Lumithra coaches, blasting her fire as a distraction to buy me more seconds of precious plotting time.

The hairs on my arms rise as I feel the wrath of my magic surging beneath my skin, impatiently waiting for my command. Trust my instincts. Strike wisely. Every bone in my body is rattling with equal parts fear and electrifying currents of power, ready to disobey me if I don't release it within the next few heartbeats.

I unsheathe my sword from my back and command the power of Kallik's light to infiltrate its blade. Tendrils of sizzling, alabaster flames coil around the blade and extend far beyond its tip like rapidly growing vines. Surprisingly, my magic remains tethered to my blade and refrains from exploding beyond my control.

I will fight for hope. I will live to see the next sunrise. I raise my sword and slash it downward in a broad, sweeping motion. Tendrils of lightning-fire branch out like veins and wrap around the necks of every raven griffin and blood mage in line to slaughter me. They don't even get the chance to scream before the flames slice off their heads, and their charred bodies begin falling from the sky like volcanic ashes.

Twenty raven griffins. Twenty blood mages. Forty more souls extracted from The Mortal Realms by the work of my hands. Each body that crashes to the ground pushes the memories of lives I've slain for Rhydian to the forefront of my mind. Am I any better than the soulless killer who raised me? Fearing the answer to my own question pumps this morning's breakfast right out of my stomach, and I vomit over Lumithra's side.

"You executed forty soldiers of The God of Death. Forty enemies ordered to expand the kingdom of The Dark Realms to the ends of Elmoria. You fight for hope, Rhydian fights for greed. You are not your upbringing," Lumithra gently rumbles.

Lumithra makes my actions sound noble, but I feel far from it. I used to kill for Rhydian. Now I kill for The Dragon Knights. If the ending of this war doesn't bring upon an age of repairing the oppressive divide between half-mortal mages and humans born without magic, I'm nothing more than just another force of darkness. Gods, I need Adrienne before I spiral any further.

"Please, tell me you're okay," I beg Adrienne as my body trembles from the sum of power I allowed to devour the blade of my sword.

Within heartbeats, a raven-black blanket of wall clouds stretches across the sky toward Lumithra and me. Sarthon and Adrienne emerge from the thickness of the haze, and I take what feels like my first real breath of air since our arrival on the beach.

"Better than ever, my love," she responds.

Hoards of raven griffins quickly emerge behind them, but Adrienne's shadows slice through them and their mages while her eyes remain focused on me. My heart plummets into my stomach as raven griffin screeches announce the arrival of thousands more Eldermoorians flying from across the sea.

Sarthon and Lumithra quickly drop altitude to dodge the sea of incoming violet arrows while remaining alarmingly calm. I find myself choking on unrelenting waves of sulfur before questioning their composures.

"It's about gods-damn time," Lumithra growls. Sulfur has never smelled so sweet in my life as thousands of dragon knights emerge from above the mountains, colliding with Eldermoor's forces.

Lumithra and Sarthon shoot walls of fire from their maws as Adrienne and I face our enemies side by side. Blasts of lethally honed shadows and white flames incite screams of terror across the smoke-laden skies, clouding our visibility. Fear punches my gut every time a dragon roars, convincing me I struck down their riders. I really wish some wind mages would clear some of this dragon smoke, but perhaps it's the only thing keeping blood mages from twisting our limbs and snapping our bones.

"I thought Eldermoor wouldn't dream of attacking Blackthorn until Helia has fallen. Why are they on our shores already?" I ask Adrienne.

"Based on their numbers, they aren't planning on attacking beyond the beach," she explains while mid-pulverizing a raven griffin. *"Despite their thousands, heading further inland would be a death sentence for them."*

"Then this has to have something to do with one of their mages assuming Zephyr knew the whereabouts of the shadow luminary. Do you sense it at all?" I ask her again.

Adrienne goes silent. Her expression quickly turns from that of a confident Wing Commander to that of a wrathful storm as plumes of black smoke seep from her flared nostrils.

"A wraith general is approaching," Lumithra growls.

"A wraith general?" My heart plummets as something tells me a wraith general will make sea wraiths look like harmless, docile creatures in comparison.

"Osiris released hundreds of his strongest, highest ranking wraiths from The Dark Realms to lead as generals in Eldermoor's army during the last Luminary War. As powerful as you may be, you're not prepared to face one," she rumbles.

"Daughter of Darkness," a low, deep voice carries through the haze as a black, hooded wraith approaches Adrienne on the back of its raven griffin. Its skin is as grey as an ancient corpse, yet smooth and ageless. Her eyes are soulless pools of pitch-black, sending chills through my bones.

"Surrender the location of the shadow luminary, and I'll let your soldiers live. Refuse to give up its hiding place, and I'll turn this beach into a graveyard," the general shrills.

"Get as far away from here as you can. I'll handle this quickly," Adrienne orders. The wraith general lets out a howling shriek as massive wings protrude from her shoulder blades. Thick, obsidian wings expand across the sky like a jar of ink spilled onto a canvas. She rises from her raven griffin, no longer relying on it to keep her airborne. With the breath in her lungs, the wraith creates a thick plume of black smoke, swallowing Sarthon and Adrienne whole. Lumithra takes off, bolting with lightning speed before we're caught in the unholy abyss.

"We can't just leave them out there!" I shout.

"Adrienne and Sarthon are more than capable of handling themselves, and you are in no position to defy her orders," Lumithra fires back.

I look back and watch countless raven griffins filling in the the vast airspace between us and Adrienne, surrounding the perimeter of the massive plume. I'm left with no choice but to resume wielding Kallik's light against Eldermoor until Adrienne hopefully makes quick work of the general.

Alabaster flames and bolts of lightning release from my fingertips, missing more enemies than I strike. Whatever control I had over my magic moments earlier is now gone as my mind becomes plagued with guttural dread. Lumithra sinks her claws into a raven griffin, slamming it into the mountainside before its blood mage can reach me with its cursed puppet magic. I throw strike after strike, draining my energy as I continue to miss more enemies than I hit. *"Mindlessly throwing your light with zero concentration isn't getting you anywhere. Try channeling it with your sword again!"* She rumbles.

"Are you holding up okay?" I ask Adrienne before allowing my mind to focus on Lumithra's advice.

"Right now, I need you to focus on yourself," Adrienne growls in the

tone of her dragon form.

Hearing her voice grants me the focus I need to grab the hilt of my sword and command my tendrils of lightning to coil around the blade. Tresses of electrical flame scuttle down the blade and coil around a raven griffin, slamming it into another. Raven griffins cascade into one another in a rippling domino effect, falling from the sky in unison.

"Looks like you found an element of control," Lumithra praises. I recoil my flames once we find a brief moment of reprieve and soothe my burning lungs with the cool spring air. Wielding this much magic this quickly before my transformation in The Dark Realms surely would've killed me by now.

"Now that I have a reliable technique, can we go pursue the wraith general?" I beg Lumithra as I catch my breath.

Sarthon releases a roar of reverberating rage that ripples across the skies like tornadic thunder. For a moment, his roar drowns out the thousands of dragons, raven griffins, and forces of weaponized nature wielded by the elemental mages.

Adrienne.

"On it. Your healing magic is needed," Lumithra answers gravely.

She roars as she swiftly alters the course of her flight before I catch my next breath. The aerial battlefield rapidly blurs past us in a smoky, crimson haze, yet feels eerily still. My heart plummets with each plunge, twist, and bank as we breeze past enemies and flying arrows toward the massive smoke plume. For Lumithra to so quickly turn around and defy Adrienne's orders…no. I cannot afford my mind to complete that thought. Adrienne needs me stable and in control of my magic.

My eyes water in the sulfurous, salty air as Lumithra picks up more speed, rushing us back to Sarthon. His blasts of fire ignite the sky in the absence of Adrienne's shadows. Something is terribly wrong. Layers of smoke and fog clear just enough for me to distinguish a glowing violet arrow lodged in her chest as her blood spills onto Sarthon's onyx scales.

Her smoky dragon scales disappear from her face and limbs as she fully shifts back into a limp and lifeless half-mortal form.

"Adrienne!" Blistering heat burns me from the inside out as warning strikes of lightning release beyond my control, nearly taking out dragons battling raven griffins a field's length behind me.

"Keep it together!" Lumithra roars. *"You're going to have to manage without your grounding touch. Adrienne needs you in control!"*

Pull yourself together, I tell myself. *Trust your instincts. Strike wisely. Trust your instincts. Strike wisely.*

I feel my glacial blue irises turn white as blinding lights consume my vision. My hair becomes tresses of white fire, burning brighter than the moonlight. Searing heat engulfs my entire frame as I feel myself become one with my flames. I am light. I am a divine, burning light that shines upon death and sends it crawling back to its domain. I raise my arms and aim my reach for the wraith general, releasing torrential waves of electrical flames straight for her head.

My flames wash over the wraith and wipe her from the existence of all the realms, emitting bolts of lightning rather than sparks. Charred flesh blends with the stench of sulfur as battalions of dragon knights rush from behind me, chasing swarms of enemies out over the sea.

"Fall back! Fall back!" Blood mages relay orders to retreat as they flee the obsidian shores in a disastrously erratic frenzy. In a matter of minutes, Tourmaline Beach is cleansed of its invaders, and our forces are all that remain.

CHAPTER 24
The Shadow Luminary

"Adrienne! Are you still with me?" Lumithra and Sarthon rapidly descend as the warmth of my healing lights floods the palms of my hands. The closer we get to the ground, the more I feel like it's moving farther away, as if we will never make our landing. The precious seconds of our descent taunt me for what feels like an eternity.

"Sarthon says her pulse is slow but present," Lumithra relays.

The moment we touch land, Lumithra helps me transfer to Sarthon's back to retrieve Adrienne. Sarthon roars in a tone of protest and blasts rapid rounds of steam as I scoop Adrienne in my arms. *"He knows I'm her best chance at recovery, right?"*

"Ignore his temper tantrum. He's well aware incinerating you will not only prove a fatal outcome for Adrienne, but he would also have to contend with my wrath," Lumithra growls.

His jagged scales dig into my tailbone as I slide down his leg, using all my remaining strength to keep Adrienne from tumbling out of my arms. Smoldering embers, pools of blood, and the poorly masked panic of dragon knights triaging the wounded plague the shores as I carefully lower her to the ground.

"Stay with me, Adrienne. You are not returning to The Dark Realms again so soon."

Removing the arrow from her chest goes against everything I've taught myself about battle wounds. However, working with magic that can mend broken bones, extract poison from the bloodstream, and close gaping wounds changes everything I thought I understood as logic.

Fatigue overtakes my body as I feel energy drain from my body and transfer to Adrienne's wound. By the time her bleeding stops and the hole in her chest closes, my arms give out, and I collapse on top of her.

"Look who found some control over her magic today," Adrienne smirks as her eyes flutter open. Relief quenches my soul as I throw my arms around her and savor the strength of her heartbeat pounding in my ear against her chest.

"Look who singlehandedly took on a wraith general and nearly died," I snap. "Never pull off a stunt like that again. Understood?" I take her in, assessing the progression of her recovery, and notice blood trickling down the sleeve of her flight jacket. I failed to notice the subtle tendrils of shadows concealing her slashed sleeve while preoccupied with the arrow lodged into her chest.

"We should begin searching for the rest of our squad and make sure they all survived this mess," Adrienne sighs as she deflects her gaze from mine.

"Not until I take care of your arm first. It shouldn't take long for me to heal it," I offer.

"You weren't supposed to notice that. It's nothing that won't heal on its own. You need to allow your magic time to rest," Adrienne protests as she backs away from me like a frightened animal. The abrupt panic in her voice raises the hairs on the back of my neck as the shadows concealing her arm thicken. For whatever reason, she doesn't want me anywhere near this particular wound.

"What are you doing? Just let me take care of that," I insist.

"No!" She seethes, pulling away from me as if I'm suddenly her enemy.

"Why are you being so weird? If you don't let me close that up, it's bound to get infected!" I increase the strength of the lights engulfing my hands until they become bright enough to shine through her shadows. My lights shine into her wound, unveiling a stone-shaped mass embedded into her flesh.

"Do not draw attention to this!" Adrienne screams down our bond.

"Is that the-?"

"Shadow luminary? Yes. You weren't supposed to find out like this. No one can know I bear it. Absolutely no one," she desperately pleas.

I choke on all my swarming questions like a bitter, medicinal tonic. Why is the shadow luminary hiding beneath her skin? How is she not thrashing and flailing in insufferable pain from its intimate proximity to her as a shadow mage? *"I don't even know where to begin. How?" Why?"* My throat burns with vile as I stare at the shadow luminary's silhouette beneath her shadows.

"Stop shining your lights on it like a glaring beacon in the night, and help me get this wound closed!" Adrienne lashes.

"You want me to close your wound over it so the stone remains hidden in your flesh?" I ask in guttural disbelief.

"Yes. Quickly. Please trust me," she growls.

Matted knots of dread twist in my stomach as I place my hands on Adrienne's arm and begin closing her wound. It takes all my composure to refrain from passing out as I watch the shadow luminary disappear beneath her flesh, layers beneath her serpentine tattoos.

"Does anyone else know about this?" I ask in secrecy, still frozen in shock.

"Only immortals— the dragons and Niroshen's Elemental Pantheon. And now you. I have been acting under strict orders from Kamaris to bear the stone in secrecy. However, it seems to be becoming less and less of a secret now. Somehow, those blood mages ended up hot on its trail, and now, they at least know the shadow luminary lies within Blackthorn," Adrienne winces.

The exhaustion flooding our bond nearly rips my heart in two. To be burdened with the "gift" of gods-given elemental magic is already difficult enough to live with, but for a goddess to task a half-mortal with hiding a luminary beneath their flesh? How long has Adrienne been carrying it? Months? Years? How is she going to sleep at night now that Eldermoor nearly found her out?

"Does it…hurt?" I ask gently.

"After the first initial months of excruciating pain, my body learned to adjust. It's far from a pleasant experience, but it's hardly one of the reasons for my near insanity anymore," Adrienne shrugs.

"Adrienne! Amira!" Felix and Fieryn descend from the ashen fog before I can ask any further questions. I choke on the dusty trail of soot that follows Felix as he works his way down Fieryn's crimson scales. His black hair is tangled and matted in blood, and lacerations and bruises cover the majority of his exposed skin. His blood-stained armor is shredded in gaping claw marks, yet he appears in perfect condition compared to the thousands of mages being tended to in the triage stations.

"You two look like you've seen better days," he sighs.

"I could say the same of you," Adrienne snorts. "No need to worry about us. We're all in one piece, and I'm well on the mend, much credit to Amira."

"You're lucky my magic can manifest as healing, considering how close that wraith general's arrow was to piercing your heart," I mutter.

"A *wraith general*?" Felix's eyes widen as if shocked Adrienne isn't among the dead.

"Yes, and I lived to tell the tale. Moving on. Do you have a report on the rest of our squad?" Adrienne changes the subject.

"Irvette is assisting with the triage stations, and Lady Rhonwen has apothecaries on the way to assist in stabilizing the critically wounded for transport to the infirmaries. Arden joined the battalions, working on slowing Eldermoor's movement and preventing them from regrouping. He attempted to seek your permission through Hyrix and Sarthon first but was unable to reach you," Felix reports.

"I can live with all that. Any Zephyr sightings?" Adrienne asks.

"Present and at the ready," Zephyr shouts through labored breaths from atop Sylphira as she lands between Lumithra and Sarthon. He slides down her silver scales, drenched in blood, sweat, and soot. "You certainly know how to provide quite the hands-on training experience, Adrienne. Can we perhaps scale back on the realism next time?" Zephyr's teeth chatter as he trembles with a concoction of jittering nerves and crippling fatigue. He collapses to the ground, clenching his severely bloodied and mangled hand, focusing on his labored breaths.

Adrienne opens her mouth, but her words don't come. Our eyes collectively widen the moment we notice the severity of his injury.

"You're certainly not *at the ready*," I reply, stooping down to his level. "Let me help you." I do my best to keep my voice as relaxed and gentle as possible despite his hand appearing like a contorted branch snapped out of place by a violent hurricane.

"You-you should've seen the way I freed myself from that blood mage," he stutters through his pain. "What he managed to do to my hand is nothing in comparison to what I put him through."

"I believe it," I smile weakly as I cup his disfigured hand in mine, putting my healing lights to work. Sweat trickles down my temples, and I grow lightheaded as I transfer my energy to Zephyr's hand. My arms weaken with muscle cramps as his bones realign, and my eyelids grow unbearably heavy as his bleeding slows and then eventually stops.

"That was less than a pleasant experience, to say the least, but I can't complain," Zephyr winces. He gasps in awe as he curls his fingers into a fist and twists his wrist with full mobility. "You're quite the miracle worker, Amira darling. Thank you."

"That's enough miracle working for today," Adrienne abrasively interjects, lowering herself to my level. She gently places my head on her shoulders, and I fall limp into her arms, resting for as long as this moment allows.

"Sarthon just informed me The High Priestess wishes to gather us for an emergency briefing as soon as we can depart for the monastery," Adrienne relays to Felix. "Zephyr, report to the apothecaries and assist Irvette in the triage stations. Amira, I need you to return to the monastery and get some proper rest before you reach another state of burnout," she orders.

"What about you? You took on a wraith general in your dragon form, and gods know what else you wielded on the battlefield. Now you're rushing off to debrief with Lady Rhonwen?" I protest through our bond as Adrienne helps me stagger to my feet.

"Orders are orders. I promise I am still far from reaching the limits of my threshold," Adrienne assures.

"And I promise your secret is safe with me," I mutter. Despite my blood still fuming over her ever-growing reservoir of secrets, my heart still stubbornly swells with unconditional love and empathy.

Adrienne wraps me in a harness of shadows and helps me reach my mount atop Lumithra despite my pitifully weak protests against accepting her assistance. I cave once I realize my legs are as good as dead weight, and I need to save what little remains of my strength for the flight back to the monastery.

"Our conversation isn't over. You're owed more answers, and based on today, I think you're ready to handle them," Adrienne promises in a tone of unease as I grip the pommel on my saddle. Her ashen eyes, laden with the exhaustion of gods-given burdens and secrets she fears to relinquish. The more I study her fatigue, the more desperately I want to be trusted with her scars.

"Our conversation isn't over because I refuse to watch you suffer in solitude for a moment longer. You're owed rest. You're owed companionship," I tell her gently.

Lumithra launches into flight as I clench my weak, shaky thighs against my saddle. Sarthon, Sylphira, and Fieryn follow suit, weaving through the fog and smoke in blurs of onyx, silver, and crimson. *"May every life lost today be not in vain. May their souls find peace. May all of us marching onward find the strength to face the darkness cut out for us. May Elmoria find its harmony once again,"* she grieves as I sense her gaze gravitate to the ground below.

My stomach lurches as I catch an aerial glimpse of the vast casualties stretching across the tourmaline shoreline. Mournful roars of riderless dragons shatter the skies along with fragments of my heart, one piece at a time. With all the war, bloodshed, disease, poverty, and suffering plaguing The Mortal Realms, it's already practically a province of The Dark Realms.

"May no friend journey through these gods-forsaken lands alone," I add. *"May we tend to one another's wounds, leaving no soul behind to wither in the darkness."*

CHAPTER 25
A Goddess of Masks: Adrienne

No matter how many times I've entered into meetings with Lady Rhonwen wearing my mask of calm composure, I always fear she'll eventually learn to see right through it. Withholding a luminary from The High Priestess is an act of betrayal and treason I conceal beneath my flesh every day. Lady Rhonwen has ordered her knights to not only suppress Eldermoor's movements and defeat their armies but to seek all the luminaries and surrender them all to her care. Yet Kamaris made it perfectly clear to me that if I ever voluntarily relinquish the shadow luminary to anyone, my soul will be obliterated.

Pledging to The High Priestess and The Gods of Niroshen should be one and the same, yet I'm damned to serve two very different masters. Lady Rhonwen seeks their council and wisdom to rule over Blackthorn, showing them all her shortcomings, vulnerabilities, and weaknesses, hiding nothing before their thrones. In theory, gods worthy of such worship would offer their transparency and full devotion in return. Instead, they leave their devotees in the dark, unrevealing how they manage Elmoria's affairs and why they choose the methods they do. For one reason or another, they only distribute breadcrumbs of the insight, wisdom, and compassion they're capable of offering while their loyal followers believe they're receiving full-blown feasts.

"Are you alright?" Felix asks. I snap out of my dissociative trance, hardly realizing I've been rubbing my arm without uttering a word to him since our arrival.

"Just struggling to wrap my mind around how quickly Eldermoor managed to send thousands of reinforcements to our shores despite their drastic advances in Helia," I respond. *And struggling to process how they managed to get so close to the shadow luminary.*

I roll my shoulders back, chasing away my chills, and assume the mask of a fearless wing commander. Osiris doesn't know I bear one of the six luminaries his followers are desperately searching the ends of Elmoria for. He would've emptied The Dark Realms of every last wraith and sent every last blood mage in Eldermoor to rip me apart already. However, I need to get to the bottom of how in the realms they got so damn close to tracking it down if I don't want to contend with the Gods of Niroshen for the existence of my soul.

"Thank you for getting here as quickly as you could." Lady Rhonwen shuffles into the dimly lit chamber, followed by the priestesses of her court. Each of her twelve priestesses keeps their gaze on the floor as if delaying eye contact means delaying the inevitable confrontation with our inexcusable failure.

"As the leader of our nation, I confess that today, I have failed Blackthorn. Leaving behind skeletal crews to defend our borders while sending our best to Helia left us foolishly vulnerable to Eldermoor's threats. I confront my shortcoming with great remorse, and hope the gods may mercifully forgive me," Lady Rhonwen confesses.

My stomach roils as her priestesses anxiously sway and fidget with their robes, blankly staring into their reflections on the marble floors. Chances are the gods are emotionlessly collecting the souls of the fallen, unfazed by the tragedies that will haunt The High Priestess for years to come.

"I summoned you and Felix in hopes either one of you might have insight into what might have provoked Eldermoor's sudden attack since your squad was the first on scene," Lady Rhonwen explains.

The shadow luminary burns like a blazing hot coal, engulfing my nerves in scalding flames as I slam my intrusive thoughts down. I want nothing more than to carve into my arm, rip out the shadow luminary, and entrust it to Lady Rhonwen. I want nothing more than to inform her the gods she loves and trusts so fervently hardly consider their half-mortal children as even afterthoughts. I want her to know just how insignificantly they view the humans. I want to relinquish my luminary and fight for Blackthorn, led by Lady Rhonwen— not led by Lady Rhonwen led by the gods.

I stifle my tears before they can form and dig my nails into my palm. "From what I gathered, a battalion of blood mages patrolling over Tourmaline Sea believed they detected the shadow somewhere near our shores. They launched an attack on our squad in hopes for answers, and called for additional aid once they weren't getting anywhere with us," I report. Sticking to the truth without revealing the whole truth is my go-to card that has yet to fail me.

"Do you believe they might be onto something, Adrienne? As the only current descendant of Kamaris, you should be able to sense the shadow luminary better than anyone. Did you feel its call today?" She asks in a tone equal parts hopeful and fearful.

"Eldermoor's suspicion immediately roused my own. However, despite my vigilance, nothing called out to me. I prayed to Kamaris and asked her for signs, and I was given none. It's entirely possible they misinterpreted whatever they believed to be its call. If Eldermoor somehow has enough forces to spare, it's also possible they were looking for an opportunity to preemptively weaken our defenses for once they're through with Helia," I suggest.

"Do you have anything to add, Felix?" Lady Rhonwen asks.

"From a tactical standpoint, burning through their forces just to weaken our defenses would be a reckless waste of resources. If Adrienne couldn't sense the shadow luminary, I believe they simply misinterpreted its call and recklessly attacked before confirming they were truly onto something," he adds.

"Let me add on to that thought. Blood mages may be nothing more than humans who devoted their lives to Osiris, but it would be reckless to underestimate the hand that feeds and shapes them. The God of Death might be capable of crafting blood mages into hounds who can sense the luminaries just as well as elemental mages can. It's a possibility we shouldn't rule out," Felix contemplates.

"The scriptures do state Osiris formerly resided in Niroshen and that he was there when the elemental gods forged the luminaries," Lady Rhonwen sighs. "As reluctant as I am to entertain the thought his blood mages might have sensed the shadow luminary when Adrienne could not, I will not rule out the possibility. I will however, correspond with General Cyrina to devise a plan to withdraw a portion of our forces from Helia and fortify our defenses with more integrity."

Mournful silence fills the chamber as everyone takes a collective moment to process the first massacre within our borders in six centuries. Thunder rumbles the stained glass windows, and rain spills from the clouds as if sent by the gods to wash the blood from Tourmaline's shoreline. This year, Blackthorn's storm season will be accompanied by the roars of grieving dragons and the tears of loved ones left behind. The gods will continue collecting the souls of the fallen and washing the blood off the battlefields as if death is nothing more than a mildly inconvienent mess to clean. Lady Rhonwen will continue her worship and trusting the gods to guide her in the storms, and I will continue my silent, bitter resentment.

Felix snaps his finger, causing several of the priestesses to flinch before the next roar of thunder erupts. His eyes widen with epiphany as he begins pacing back and forth in front of the arched window.

"Is there something you want to share before we dismiss, Felix?" Lady Rhonwen asks.

"I would like to propose a plan for your consideration," he responds. "I would like to make a journey to Eldermoor to study the practices of the blood mages. If I can confirm Osiris is truly gifting them with the ability to sense the presence of the luminaries, perhaps I can learn how he is doing so. If we can confirm and identify their methods, we can fight this war two steps ahead. We can learn to predict their movements and spend more time on the offensive rather than on the defensive. Maybe we could even learn how to sever their abilities to sense the luminaries and implement that knowledge into our warfare."

"That's a rather bold optimism stemming from mere speculations. Not to mention, you would also be recognized as our emissary the moment you reach Eldermoor's borders. Permitting your journey would be condemning you to a death sentence. It would pose a significantly lesser risk to involve our spies in your schemes without your on-the-ground involvement," Lady Rhonwen counters.

"With all due respect, I'm not penning this plan on parchment and tying it to the foot of a winged courier fox just for it to get intercepted. As our emissary, I am well-versed in Eldermoor's culture and know how to pose as an aspiring blood mage. I know how to establish rapport. I know my way around their places of worship. Allow me to correspond with our spies directly to organize an investigative task force. Eldermoor has been advancing far more quickly and boldly than we've been anticipating, and our spies have yet to come up with any real answers as to how they are managing their success. At risk of sounding like an arrogant ass, our spies won't provide us with any intel of real value until I arrive with my unique expertise," Felix argues.

"Felix does have a point. He is an arrogant ass," I scoff as Felix rolls his eyes in my direction. "In all seriousness, wars aren't won without wagering high stakes. The first Luminary War was won on risks and sacrifices, not on luck or by mere favor with the gods. We need an intimate understanding of our enemy if we wish to protect Blackthorn and all that is sacred to the gods from the ploys of Osiris. I am confident they will guide Felix along a path of insight and keep a protectful watch over him."

Sarthon snorts down our bond. *"Listening to you feign such confidence in the gods never fails to amuse me."*

Lady Rhonwen lowers her head and lets out a deep sigh. "I will assemble a team of wind mages to escort you to Eldermoor discreetly tomorrow before sunrise. I want Fieryn to send updates on your condition at the top of each hour. Understood?"

"Understood. Thank you for entrusting me on this journey, Lady Rhonwen. I do not take your blessing lightly. I promise the intel I retrieve will be well worth the risk," Felix assures.

"May the gods reward your bravery with a safe, fruitful journey. May they bless us all with unfaltering strength and wisdom to face the trials before us. You two are dismissed."

We bow to The High Priestess on our way out of the council chamber, and I let out a sigh of relief. *"My feigned confidence never fails to get us what we need,"* I boast to Sarthon. *"We're finally getting a set of keen, competent eyes on Eldermoor, and I deflected the dangerous attention I was receiving. Mission accomplished."* My soul remains intact, and the shadow luminary's location remains a secret, ensuring no one forges The Crown.

"Eldermoor's power may continue to rise and rise, our lands may come to fall, but without The Crown of Luminaries, they will never get Blackthorn and Helia to bow before Osiris. By bearing the shadow luminary, you singlehandedly carry the burdens of the gods on your shoulders, doing more for The Mortal Realms of Elmoria than the gods ever have since they created it. Not a single day goes by where I don't wish I could sink my fangs into their immortal flesh and incinerate their bones to ash. The gods can't remain immune from their atonement forever. One of these days, they will have to answer for their own shortcomings," Sarthon growls.

"One of these days," I agree.

CHAPTER 26
An Ocean of Kindness: Adrienne

The scent of earl grey greets me with a welcoming embrace as soon as I walk through the doors of my room. The stiff tension stored in my muscles immediately melts away at the sight of Amira waiting for me in my bed, sipping on a steamy mug of tea in a satin, sapphire nightgown. "You're just in time. Your tea is finally at a drinkable temperature," she smiles as she points to the extra mug waiting for me on my nightstand.

My heart palpitates like the rain slamming against the windows as I crawl into my bed and curl up beside her. "I do not deserve you in the slightest, my love," I whisper as I rest my head on her shoulder. She kisses me on the forehead and hands me my mug. Tears begin rolling down my cheeks the moment she begins gently combing her fingers through my hair. She is warmth, light, and home, and I am undeserving.

"It's been a long day. You can finally let it go," Amira whispers. She embraces me in an ocean of kindness, reeling me into her arms as I sob into her chest. "You're carrying a lot, and it isn't fair." Her words are soft and simple. Warmly understanding, without demanding me to explain myself. For the first time in ages, I feel like I don't have to hide. I don't have to wear a mask. For the first time in ages, I have permission to break.

Amira's heart beats steady in my eardrums as I collect my breath. Her pulse is the rhythm of home, and gods am I tired of bearing so many secrets and burdens alone. The gentle touch of her hands softly rubbing my back calms my storming nerves, assuring me there is safety in her arms.

"You are owed more answers about why I bear the shadow luminary, and I think you're ready for them. I think I'm ready to give them," I tell her nervously, unfamiliar with what it feels like to be vulnerable.

"You deserve rest, my dear," Amira says as her forehead leans against mine. She wraps her legs around my restlessly shaking leg, and I find stillness in the warmth of her skin. "If telling me your story gives you rest, give me everything."

I take a deep breath, and my mind enters a half-dissociative state the moment I begin to speak. "Years before the first Luminary War, Kamaris found herself hopelessly drawn to Osiris despite a law forbidding gods from sleeping with one another. The law was established in fear that producing too many gods could disrupt the balance of power in all the realms. Despite that law, Kamaris, Goddess of the Night, would often sneak out of Niroshen during the night and venture to The Dark Realms to sleep with Osiris. Eventually, their forbidden love produced a daughter.

"Once the gods learned the child was the product of a forbidden affair, Kallik created powerful shields preventing the gods from traveling across the realms as punishment.

"To Kallik's surprise, the child born of two gods was immune to his shields and could still freely travel without being blocked by his power. The gods grew to resent the child's power, treating her like a cursed threat to their precious, delicate balance. Feeling unwelcome in Niroshen, she spent most of her time in Blackthorn training to become a dragon knight in a search for purpose. Kamaris and Osiris, on the other hand, became devastated lovers, permanently separated by the shields. Osiris retaliated by gifting humans with great power in exchange for their service in his armies. He raised armies of blood mages to seek the luminaries, hoping to place himself in power over every realm. Osiris started the first Luminary War out of heartbreak. Kamaris and his daughter grew to resent him over the atrocities he committed and fought on the side of the Niroshen against his armies of blood mages.

"After the gods nearly lost Elmoria to Osiris and his armies in the first Luminary War, Kamaris feared it would only be a matter of time before Eldermoor would become tempted again by the same lure she once fell for. Turns out she was right to fear the treaty wouldn't preserve Elmoria's harmony forever," I scoff. "In her fear, she sealed the shadow luminary within the flesh of her child to assure no one would ever be able to find all the luminaries to forge The Crown. The elemental gods decided this was a fitting use for the child born of a forbidden affair and condemned the child to eternal exile. If the child were ever to attempt returning to Niroshen or ever willingly relinquish the shadow luminary, the gods promised they would wipe her soul from existence in all the realms."

Amira's face blanches. "So that child was...you," she whispers without retreating her fingers from my hair.

"Yours truly," I admit drily. "Wait until you hear about the timing of my eternal banishment from Niroshen," I laugh through the tears stinging my eyes. "I watched my first love die in the sacrifice that officially ended the first Luminary War. My first love was Nuri, Lumithra's late rider. Funny, right? I watched helplessly as they reached for Kallik's power together and created the shields that prevented the crown from forging on Blackthorn's soil.

"The moment the shields were raised, the luminaries scattered amidst the explosive blast. The shadow luminary flew into my fist as I was thrown hundreds of yards across the battlefield with Sarthon, and Kamaris wasted no time to put her plan in motion. Kallik crossed his shields to collect the souls of the fallen and permitted Kamaris to meet me on the battlefield. I was half-conscious as she carved her knife into my arm and sealed off the shadow luminary. Kallik stood over me, informed me of my exile, and then collected Nuri's soul right before me."

"Adrienne," Amira's voice breaks. Panic frosts over her glacial eyes like an unforgiving blizzard as she's met with scars her magic could never fully mend. "I'm so sorry," she chokes, failing to find words that adequately color the expressions of her heart.

"I don't need your words or your magic, my love. Your very existence is more healing than you will ever know," I assure her as I hold her hands in mine. "If six hundred years of exile, six hundred years of bearing the weight of this damned luminary were the only path that would lead my soul to yours, then I would choose it again and again in every lifetime. You're here with me now, and that's all I need."

Crimson warmth colors Amira's cheekbones as her eyes dart away from mine. I trace my fingers down the lines of her jaw and tilt her chin up, chasing after her gaze.

"To-to think all this time, I've been in the presence of a goddess and—"

I interrupt her with a kiss, claiming her lips like I've waited centuries to find them. She reciprocates my passion, tasting of escape, ecstasy, and earl grey. "And you've never properly worshiped me?" I finish her thought, impatiently desperate to shut her fears and humiliation down. "For one, fuck the formalities. I'd hardly consider that to be true, given how you can never keep your hands off me," I taunt as I graze her ear with my teeth. "However, if you would like an opportunity to worship me, I could really use a distraction right now."

Amira's nightgown hits the floor, and I find myself drunk on the galaxies of maddening desire burning behind her eyes. Her hand presses firm into the small of my back as her breasts brush up against mine. Her warm, silken skin against mine floods me with a high of dopamine, and I fail to understand how the gods adore all the attention that comes with being worshipped and admired by the masses. There is something sacred about being intimately longed for by only one soul.

Insecurities seep into Amira's mind as her tongue dances behind my lips in destructively tantalizing sweeps. I refuse to allow her to believe she is not enough for me. "*Yes, I am a Goddess. I am the Goddess of the*

Shadows. My divinity is hidden in secrecy, and you, my love, are the only offering I desire."

"In that case, I sure hope you can handle what you're asking for," she growls against my lips. She brings her lips to my neck, sending waves of heat rolling down my body like rumbles of thunder. Without warning, she grabs hold of my wrists and forces my arms above my head. "I want shadows around your wrists. Now," she firmly demands. I immediately obey, binding my wrists in ropes of my own shadows. Using my own magic against myself without wasting a damn second to question it.

"Good girl," Amira praises, rewarding me by gently curling her fingers between my thighs. "Now, fasten them to the headboard, and don't you dare break yourself out of that bind," she warns in a dark, commanding tone.

"I wouldn't dare dream of it, love," I moan as she strokes her fingers in slow, figure-eight motions leaving me desperate for more.

"I could spend the whole night worshipping every inch of your divine perfection. The only question is, where should I begin?" Amira cruelly takes her hand away, leaving me shaking in the absence of her touch. "Should I start here?" She asks as straddles me, weaving threads of kisses across my stomach, running her hands down the lines of my curves. "Or maybe here?" She asks as she cups my breasts, tracing over my nipples in light, circular flicks of her tongue. "Or perhaps, here?" She asks as she presses her lips against my jawline, working her way to the corner of my mouth with infuriating slowness.

I arch my back and tug on my restraints, begging her to unleash her full assertiveness. I need the velvet warmth of her lips against my skin more than I need my lungs to fill with air. I need to lose myself in her touch and lose all sense of reality.

"For a goddess, you're surprisingly obedient," she taunts as she breaks her lips apart from mine and slowly crawls backwards until she no longer straddles me. "I think I finally know just where I should begin."

She positions her head between my thighs, and the warmth of her breath already has my nerves throbbing with need.

Amira lets out a low, sexy laugh as I squirm and twist helplessly at her mercy. For a moment, I nearly forget that my shadows submit to my authority and not hers. I could easily break free of my bind and overpower her in less than a second, but gods, I don't have it in me. She pins my thighs down with crushing force as she alternates between swirling her tongue and sucking harshly on my clit. "You're so wet for me," she groans as she pulls away, admiring every inch of my body with her longing gaze.

Her eyes look up to meet mine as she pumps her fingers inside me, curling them back and forth as she muffles my moans with her free hand. I rock my hips in rhythm with her fingers, grinding against the palm of her hand, edging myself on the delicious friction. "You said you wanted a distraction, did you not?" She taunts as electrical pulses tingle on the tips of her fingers, sending bolts of pleasure to my clit.

Amira slides her hand down to my neck, restricting my blood flow as euphoria threatens to take me over the edge. Flashes of blue, lavender, and yellow flicker in my vision as I become weightless, feeling nothing other than my pleasure vibrating through every last neural pathway. Release drags me under an ocean of boundless ecstasy from which I never want to return.

I resurface, and Amira collapses at my side, smirking with victory as she watches me struggle to catch my breath. "I guess I'll allow you to release your bind now," she says smugly. I retract my shadows, and my arms fall limply onto the mattress.

"That was far more than just a distraction, love. That was soul-altering. Healing."

Amira melts into my arms as I struggle to wrap my mind around how her soul found its way to me in an ironic twist of fate. I cherish the sacred moments of her warm skin against mine, finding home within her heartbeat. She's far too pure of a gift to have been sent by the gods. They never would've altered fate for my soul to find such a miraculous refuge. Whatever force of the universe that is responsible for merging our paths however, has my eternal gratitude.

"I know there's infinitely more for us to unpack together, but I hope you know that you are infinitely worth all the learning curves in front of us. I'm ready to bend and break together. I'm ready for whatever it takes to stand by your side," Amira mutters softly.

Somehow, none of the fear, distress, or darkness haunting her heart has had anything to do with fearing me. She fears whether or not she is enough for a goddess, rather than fearing the immortal shadow mage born of The Goddess of the Night and The God of Death. I'm unsure if Amira's ability to adapt so quickly to the presence of monsters should frighten, concern, or relieve me. Maybe all three.

"Be careful what you wish for, Amira darling. There's no coming back from your immersion in the games and secrets of the gods. The depths of what remains for us to endure together are limitless. The consequences that would arise should we anger the gods are irreversible, and you will now be under their constant surveillance."

"I'm no stranger to toxic family trees," she scoffs. "Your burdens are mine, and my burdens are yours. Stop trying to scare me away and accept that I'm here to stay already," she smiles as she kisses my hand.

I pull back a strand of her snow-white tresses and kiss her shoulder. My eyes grow heavy as I hold her tightly against my chest, soothed by the warmth and softness of her skin on mine. She has no idea I have only taken her knee-deep into an ocean of horrors so far. I treasure the gift of her falling asleep in my arms, wishing I could hold her here forever. I allow myself to enjoy this moment of blissful peace, pretending I have all the time in the world before I'll have to drag her all the way beneath the surface with me.

CHAPTER 27
Plagues of Nightmares: Amira

After falling asleep in Adrienne's arms, I wake in my tent, holding my childhood friend, Celene. The dried blood of an assassinated bandit stains her freckled face as she shivers in my arms in the dead heat of summer. "He's going to kill me once he finds out," Celene whimpers. Her words barely escape from her panicked breath as she hyperventilates, still clenching the hilt of her dagger in a death grip.

"Find out about what?" I ask.

"I-I can't take living like this anymore. I delivered that damned bandit's head directly to the knights rather than delivering it to Rhydian. I delivered it to a Wing Commander and told him everything," she tells me as she tremors in my arms.

My heart stops before free-falling to my stomach. "Please tell me you're joking," I beg as sweat starts dripping buckets from my temples.

"I told him about the way we're treated around here. About our punishments, our forced labor, our living conditions…I told him everything, Amira. I thought maybe he would send us help, but something tells me help isn't coming. Sh-should we kill Rhydian? Together, the two of us could stand a chance. Right? I'm right, aren't I?"

I brush a strand of Celene's auburn curls out of my eyes and wipe my tears before they can fall. The last thing she needs to hear right now is the truth. "We can do this. It's going to be okay. We'll kill the bastard and dump his body in the sea. We'll find Casimir, and together, we will flee Blackthorn before the knights suspect murder. You're going to be okay." I promise, despite the pit in my stomach telling me it's all false hope.

Celene's bloodshot eyes, sunken into her skeletal frame, rip into my heart like twisting knives. I will not allow her life to be taken before she's given a real chance to live. My fingers clench onto the hilt of my dagger, trembling with malnourished fatigue. Gods know I'm unfit to stand a fighting chance against Rhydian, fueled by nothing other than yesterday's gruel and fight-or-flight endorphins.

"Celene!"

We hold our breaths as Rhydian's roars rattle the thin walls of my tent like a tornado that's about to rip us off the ground. I grab Celene's hand and attempt to lift us off the ground but find myself unable to move. I'm frozen in place, as if weighed down by a suffocating pile of bricks.

"You ungrateful, worthless bitch!" Rhydian carves his knife through the tent, raging with frenzied bloodlust. "Do you have any idea how much trouble you just cost me?" He laughs hysterically as he spits on the ground. "Do you have any idea how I spent my afternoon?" His pupils dilate, dispelling any evidence that a soul exists behind his remorseless eyes.

"I had to fight for my reputation," he laughs as he takes a swig of liquor from the flask attached to his belt. "All because of some useless, spoiled child! You know what I told them? I told them you're deranged, Celene. I told them you stole the head from my kill and ran off to deliver it to them, along with your delusional narrative. I told them it was your ploy to incriminate me and see my wealth distributed amongst you greedy peasant brats. And...I begged them not to come for you. You should be thanking me," he snarls.

"I-I'm sorry! I promise it won't happen again," Celene whimpers, shaking uncontrollably with a dagger shaking in her fumbling hands.

"Put down that blade, child. You look ridiculous. Do I need to remind you that without me, you are nothing? Who takes care of the orphans, Celene? Who provides them with shelter, food, and hope for a future? Who trains them with invaluable skills that could one day make them great? Does that sound like violence against children to you? Does that fit your twisted, perverted little story?"

"N-no! You're right! I made a terrible lapse in judgment. It won't happen again! I'll fix this, I promise!" Celene sobs.

"Oh, you'll fix this alright. Painting your savior as some deranged villain to The Knights of Blackthorn is a punishment only payable by death. What a gods-damned shame I can't rely on you anymore. Your stealthy prowess was really bringing me some pretty pockets of change. Looks like Amira will have to pick up you're slack around here after you're gone."

I desperately fight against the crushing invisible weight holding me down, but my limbs don't obey my demands. I'm still bound by paralysis as I'm unable to prevent the inevitable. I attempt to scream for Celene to run, but sound doesn't escape from my lungs.

Rhydian punches me in the head, and my vision blurs in an array of hazy colors and stars. Blood spills from my nose, and a sickening thud silences Celene's sobbing. Her head rolls at my feet. Terror still frozen behind her lifeless eyes.

"Don't you ever think of betraying me, Amira. You're my golden child. I can't afford to lose you either," Rhydian cries as he presses his blade against my throat. "Burn her body immediately before the knights decide to pay us a visit and I'm forced to frame you for murder." He spins me around and slices his knife through my back as a reminder that there is never a bluff to his threats.

Electrifying flames boil under my skin, slowly breaking me from my paralysis. Power dances through my veins, screaming to avenge Celene and all the others I lost before and after her. As my power reaches the tips of my fingers, the shredded tent walls behind Rhydian melt away into a sea of dark flames. A portal opens behind Rhydian, unveiling the gates of The Dark Realms. My magic screams as Osiris places one hand on Rhydian's shoulders, stretching his other hand out towards me.

"I can take you away from here, daughter of Kallik. Rule with me, child. Rule with me, and I shall make you a queen. You belong to the darkness, young queen. Forever, forever with me," he hisses.

The flow of my power is immediately silenced as I feel a hand grab hold of my shoulder from behind, ripping me out of my tent and into a quiet room of darkness.

*   *   *

"Amira! Amira, wake up! You're safe. You're with me!"

My magic recoils deep into its well as Adrienne's touch slowly grounds me to the surroundings of her room. "It was just a dream. You're with me. Nothing can touch you as long as you're with me," she promises as she tightens her grip on me.

I run my fingers through my hair, finding it drenched in sweat. Adrienne gently places my head to her chest as my breathing steadies to the sound of her heartbeat. Her scent of lavender and sage slowly returns my pulse to a comfortable pace. The black curtains dance with the breeze trickling into her room as blotches of dawn begin tainting the night sky. Safe. I am safe. I am in Adrienne's arms, far from Rhydian and far from the reach of The Dark Realms.

"I-I'm sorry I woke you," I stutter. "Having to be pulled out of my own head so damn often is mortifying." Knowing Adrienne is unable to shut out the vivid details of my dark inner spirals fuels my guilt like wildfire. Will she ever experience a moment of peace at my side?

"Never apologize to me for being plagued by the darkness of your demons," she responds. "They will never truly leave you, I'm afraid, but you will learn how to bite back in time. Their fangs will sting less as you learn how to clamp down their jaws. I've learned a trick or two fighting through my demons for centuries, and I'm more than happy to help you fight yours."

"A goddess shouldn't have to concern herself with the nightmares of a mere half-mortal," I counter in a panic. Finding myself as the recipient of such profound love is uncharted territory, and I am humiliatingly unprepared to interact with it.

"My divinity doesn't change a damn thing about what you mean to me," Adrienne hisses. "Forget anything and everything you know about the gods when it comes to me. I don't claim them, and they don't claim me. My deepest concerns are the concerns of my love. You have quickly become everything to me, Amira. I want all of you. I want the fire in your heart that hopelessly ensnares me like a spiderweb, and I want the darkness and demons that come with you. I never want to hear you talking like you're beneath me again. We are *equals*."

I'm thankful I'm lying down because Adrienne's words would've knocked me right off my feet. Goddess of the Shadows, unfathomably powerful, hauntingly beautiful, and mine. I lean further into her touch to convince myself she is real— that she isn't a figment of my imagination that will disappear as the sun rises. "Waking from a nightmare to a dream so perfect hardly feels real," I whisper as I kiss her hand softly.

"You're telling me, love," Adrienne chuckles. "Now, get some more sleep before I become more tempted to show you just how real I am," she growls as her lips send waves of tantalizing heat down my neck. "Unfortunately, we can't afford for me to drain your energy dry before the day even begins."

CHAPTER 28
The Departing Ceremony

Adrienne and I walk with the squad through the weeping wisteria gardens as she fills us in on the details of Felix's assignment. The morning fog drapes low to the ground, giving a wraith-like appearance to the bat orchids and black velvet petunias dispersed between the trees. I shudder, half-expecting a wraith to spawn from the ground and lunge for Adrienne's arm. I brush my hand against Adrienne's to keep the images of her confrontation with the wraith general from conjuring flames or lightning.

"How are you holding up?" I ask Irvette, quickly shifting my focus. Dark, heavy rings color the skin beneath her eye, telling the narrative of her sleepless night.

"Oh, you know," she sighs. "I spent the better half of last night begging Felix to take me with him. He insisted I haven't been properly trained in diplomacy, and that bringing me along would risk compromising his entire mission," she scoffs. "Can you believe him?"

"Respectfully, I can," Adrienne interjects. "Being one of Blackthorn's strongest water mages hardly matters when vastly outnumbered in the heart of blood mage territory. Felix knows if an enemy so much as looks at him the wrong way over there, you'd immediately erupt into a hurricane."

Zephyr lets out a chuckle and swiftly receives Irvette's elbow to his ribs.

"He's meeting up with our team of operatives stationed on their soil, so he's not working alone," Adrienne assures Irvette. "Now, as comrades of his squad, you all have the right to be informed of the nature of his missive. We now know the shadow luminary may reside somewhere within Blackthorn's borders, and it appears Eldermoor's blood mages were hot on its trail. Eldermoor wouldn't have dared attacking Blackthorn while Helia has yet to fall unless they had strong confidence they were honing in on a luminary. Felix insisted on leading our operatives in an exploratory missive to understand how they might be sensing the luminaries."

"General Cyrina did inform us that our intel already suspects Eldermoor is strengthening their armies with at least one luminary," Arden recalls. "If blood mages are developing luminary sensing abilities that can rival that of elemental mages, that is worth the investigation."

"Precisely. I fear it's also entirely possible that Felix's suspicions are only the tip of a much larger iceberg," Adrienne adds. "*If I learned anything about my father over the centuries, I've learned his schemes are always layered. I am entirely confident we haven't seen half the power his armies are capable of conjuring against us,*" She tells me through our bond.

Chills trickle down my spine like freezing rain. "What if the six hundred years of peace since the first Luminary War were centuries of scheming? Centuries Osiris spent plotting how to emerge triumphant in a war against armies of dragons and elemental mages?" I ask out loud.

"All the more reason we need our esteemed emissary to investigate the matter," Zephyr chimes in, inching away from Irvette.

"Felix is due to deliver his first report through Fieryn early this afternoon. Hopefully, he'll have some meaningful information to relay. In the meantime, I don't want our squad to divert attention from this morning's departing ceremony. We drop the conversation here and will resume once we have more privacy. Civilians will be in attendance, and the last thing we need is for our whispers to spread rumors, inducing widespread panic through Vespera," Adrienne says.

The weeping wisteria gardens spill into the field behind the monastery.

We put our discussions of Felix's mission to rest and join the masses of a growing crowd, clad in mourning black. Dragon knights, ground forces, priestesses, apothecaries, and seemingly every citizen of Vespera silently gather around a massive funeral pyre. Crows circle the sky above, cawing as the monastery's bell tower counts the top of the hour.

Lady Rhonwen stands before the pyre, adorned in black robes, joined by her court of priestesses. I barely recognize The High Priestess without one of her usual ornate, white flowing gowns embezzled in glistening crystals. Mass crowds continue trickling onto the field as she greets each individual with empathetic warmth behind her swollen, glacial eyes.

"Welcome, beloved children of Blackthorn. Today, we gather in mourning to lay valiant souls to rest. We burn their bodies to liberate them of their earthly burdens as their souls journey onward to eternal peace. In our hour of darkness, we honor their holy passage from Elmoria to Niroshen. May their souls rest joyfully, forever united with their divine mothers and fathers."

My stomach twists and churns as I regret not skipping this morning's breakfast. My mind shifts to Adrienne and her eternal separation from Nuri. How many departing ceremonies has she attended since her loss, taking salt into her wounds time and time again?

"I now ask for your silence as we commence the departing ceremony," Lady Rhonwen addresses the crowd. The soft chatter comes to a lull as a stringed quartet steps forward. They rest their violins to their chins, and their bows strike strands of somber, melancholic chords. Lamenting melodies spill into the air and linger in the fog, flooding the atmosphere with the crushing weight of each delicate note.

A fire mage comes forth, lighting the funeral pyre with bright ember flames. Followed close behind the fire mage, an apothecary pours an elixir vial into the fire, turning the ember flames into a bright, sapphire blue. Sapphire myrrh will waft through the air rather than the scent of burning flesh to honor the dignity of the fallen.

As the quartet of violins continues their song, knights slowly march toward the funeral pyre, carrying bodies on cots covered in white blankets. I hold my breath as I glimpse the line of bodies, seemingly stretching for miles. As a child, I grew up overhearing tales of the dragon knights who call upon the power of the gods and bond dragons. The humans of the peasant slums would always speak as if nothing could break the half-mortals— as if they're as unrivaled as the gods. What would they say now if they were here watching this parade of fallen elemental mages being led to the pyre?

One by one, bodies are placed into the sapphire flames, disintegrating to ash. The ashes scatter into the wind as if Cael orchestrates the breeze to lift them to the mountain peaks and beyond. The God of Wind is believed to be responsible for ensuring the ashes of fallen half-mortals disperse over Blackthorn, while Kun ensures their ashes find rest in the earth and rise again into the birth of new evergreens.

"May the bravery and the nobility of each life honored today never be forgotten. We thank our gods, praising them for the hope of Niroshen's everlasting refuge. We praise them for the sacred, unwavering light that awaits us all after our trials of great darkness," Lady Rhonwen prays.

I reach for Adrienne's hand as my anger for her sizzles beneath my skin. *"May the gods forever regret their vile mistreatment of The Goddess of The Shadows. May it haunt them for eternity and prevent them from knowing true peace."*

A soft smirk curls on Adrienne's lips. *"Blasphemous thoughts, my love. You truly are perfect for me in every way."*

The final body is placed in the sapphire flames as the stringed quartet concludes their song. The fire mage then smothers the flames as tendrils of pyre smoke drift into the hazy skies, and Lady Rhonwen steps forward. "May the gods be with us all as this tragedy fills us with grief so close to the Eve of Eleodora. May we find the strength to worship them with all our hearts and all our minds despite the darkness settling into our lands.

May our grief not hinder our offerings of worship and celebration. May we honor our fallen by persevering with devotion to our Makers in their stead," Lady Rhonwen prays.

"Or…we can honor them by defending our nation and focusing solely on ending this war," Arden mumbles quietly under his breath. Our eyes lock, and I shoot him a subtle yet passionate nod in agreement.

I tune out Lady Rhonwen as the departing ceremony transitions into a sermon-like speech on why times of war and tribulation are the most important seasons to lay down our best offerings to the gods. I shouldn't be too surprised The High Priestess of Blackthorn holds such strong convictions. As a nation of half-mortals wielding the elements of the gods, I would assume they fear the risk of biting the hands that feed us our strength.

Despite the joy and purpose that beams across Lady Rhonwen's face at every mention of the gods, part of me still wonders if at least part of her worships out of fear. Part of me wonders if she senses the glaring apathy that rains down from Niroshen but still leads her nation in worship out of knowing no other sense of direction. I would be lying to myself if I didn't admit that I hope she secretly harbors some level of fear and distrust in the gods. If she did, perhaps she could be challenged. Perhaps her blind eyes could open to the oppressive divide between half-mortals and humans. Perhaps the key to a brighter Blackthorn after this war could be unlocked by demolishing the ancient traditions established under the influence of the gods.

I must have entirely missed the ceremony's ending as the crowds begin conversing and making their way off the field without my ability to recall our dismissal. Irvette grabs me by the shoulder as I'm about to say something to Adrienne.

"Permission to borrow your girl for a much-needed distraction?" Irvette asks, letting out an exasperated sigh.

"Depends on what you're asking to borrow her for," Adrienne

responds skeptically, raising her slitted eyebrow.

"Fair question considering the most recent time I was used for a distraction," I roll my eyes, taunting Adrienne down our bond.

"Relax," Irvette chuckles. "I'm just looking to spend an hour on the town to keep myself occupied, and I could use some company. I'm going to lose my mind if I just sit around pacing the monastery until Felix's first report rolls in. Might as well knock out an errand while I wait," she explains as she readjusts her eye patch.

Adrienne ignores my taunt as she clears her throat. "Fine by me as long as you don't venture too far into the city. I need our squad to remain close by in case our attention is urgently requested."

"Understood, and thank you," Irvette bows. 'We won't be gone for long."

Adrienne dismisses us, and before I can react, Irvette quickly grabs my hand as we begin weaving through the crowd of mourners.

"I don't know about you, but that was quite enough death and despair for one morning if you ask me," Irvette mutters. "What good is surviving this war if we lose our sanity in the process?"

Sanity is such a strange, unfamiliar concept. Sanity is something I have come to experience only recently since bonding a dragon, becoming a dragon knight, and falling in love with a goddess, ironically. I guess now that I've come to taste it, a lesson or two in how to keep it around couldn't hurt.

CHAPTER 29
Distractions

"What exactly are we doing?" I ask Irvette as we descend the long, winding staircase down the mountain to the streets of Vespera.

"The Eve of Eleodora will be upon us before we know it. Something tells me both of us are in need of some new dresses," she replies.

"Dresses? What in the realms does The Eve of Eleodora have to do with dresses?" I ask. The last thing I thought I would be doing after a massive departing ceremony would be navigating the bustling streets in search of a gods-damned dress.

"Haven't you ever celebrated the festival before?" Irvette asks in a perplexed tone. Of all the Eleodora Balls that take place throughout Blackthorn that evening, Vespera's is always the grandest. How does your village celebrate?"

"The Eve of Eleodora isn't exactly a holiday observed by starving humans in disease-ridden peasant slums," I scoff. "Occasionally, humans will venture into the mage towns and attempt to steal holiday food from street vendors to bring back for their bloated children if they're lucky enough not to get caught by a merc for their thievery. Most of them opt to wait until the parties die down and head into the towns to raid the garbage for leftovers. Personally, I've always spent the holiday either in the heat of Rhydian's blood sports or fighting off infections from festering wounds on an empty stomach."

Irvette's cheeks turn bright crimson. "I apologize. I've always known the peasant villages weren't quite as posh as the mage towns, but I never knew they were *that* bad," she admits bashfully. "I've seldom heard of half-mortals traveling to the human villages and have mainly only read brief excerpts about them in textbooks. They aren't discussed very often in the mage towns."

"No need to apologize," I sigh, meeting her with tired empathy. "It's not your fault the human villages are actually peasant slums that are swept under the rug and treated like blemishes that will disappear if you ignore them long enough. If anything, blame your scribes, your scholars, and your leadership."

An uncomfortable lull of silence rests between us as the hairs on the back of my neck rise. "Hold on a second," I mutter quietly to Irvette. We freeze in our tracks as I pick up on the feeling we're being followed. An unnatural, forceful gust of wind confirms my suspicion and whips through my hair, rattling the thin, iron barrier that separates us from falling over the edge of the mountain. I unsheathe my dagger, aiming my blade for the large cloud now spiraling directly toward us.

"Easy there with the blade!" Zephyr cries out as he emerges from the cloud and dispels it right before nearly toppling us over.

"What in the realms made you think sneaking up on us was a bright idea?" I seethe, redirecting the bolt of lightning dancing on the blade of my dagger before it nearly strikes Zephyr.

"Seeing the look on your faces was worth the risk," he smirks. "I decided I'm inviting myself along on this little quest of yours."

"I'm sorry. I don't exactly recall inviting you along," Irvette scoffs. "Don't you have anything better to do?"

"I'm just as anxious to hear from your boo as you, my dear. Shopping with the two of you sounds infinitely more enjoyable than sparring practice with Arden. Besides, you'll never squeeze into any of the boutiques this close to the holiday without an appointment. Not without my renowned rapport with the shopkeeps," he winks.

Irvette's shoulders slump in defeat. "Fine. Only because not having an appointment slipped my mind," she admits under her breath.

"Please tell me you're on your way with some excuse to get me out of this mess, right?" I silently plead with Adrienne. The last thing I need is an hour stuck between Zephyr and Irvette's back-and-forth bickering.

"Why don't you reach inside your satchel and tell me what you think?"

I reach deep into the pockets of my leather satchel to find a bundle of gold coins. Panic immediately flushes through my veins, half-expecting Rhydian to round the corner and rip me to shreds for carrying money I haven't reported to him.

"Relax, my love. I snuck that gold in there for you to buy a dress for the holiday. Get yourself something I'll be spending that evening fantasizing about removing after the ball."

My cheeks flush as I picture the wicked half-smile likely curving on Adrienne's lips at the thought. *"I-I don't know what to say. Are you sure?"* The weight of the gold in my satchel suddenly feels as heavy as a millstone.

"I promise you I won't even notice that gold is gone. I've collected quite the share of earnings serving centuries of high priestesses," Adrienne assures.

"Scarlet is going to be your color, Amira darling." Zephyr pulls me into his arms, interrupting my internal conversation with Adrienne. "I can see it now— a wine-stained rose against a beautiful canvas of moonlit snow. Gods, both of you will be sure to turn every head at the ball this year."

"Save your swooning for the shopkeeps," I hiss, fighting the smile tugging on my lips.

We finally reach the bottom of the staircase and take to the iridescent, sable streets of Vespera. Both tension and anticipation rend the city as we watch people board up their windows and decorate elaborate summer garlands for the holiday in the same breath. They're preparing for the bloodbaths of war to hit the streets, as if hoping somehow their enemies would pass over any home or establishment adorned in festive emerald and gold. I just hope they're putting the same amount of energy into strength training rather than expecting the gods to swoop down and save them in the heat of a battle.

Children laugh as they run through the crowds, toting baskets filled with herbs and flowers to place on homestead alters as their parents continue about their tasks with swollen, bloodshot eyes. Blissful innocence intertwined with grief, apprehension, and a commitment to steadfast perseverance.

"I'm looking forward to the first Eleodora Ball we'll witness Adrienne do more than just brood in her shadows in a corner, I'll admit," Irvette breaks the silence. "Based on the way she looks at you, the sight of you in an Eleodora gown will have her worshiping you like a goddess. Both of you eye each other as if you're literal goddesses."

I trip, losing my footing over an uneven stone in the street, and fall to my hands and knees. I wasn't ready for that comment to sneak up on me and horrifically catch me off guard. Zephyr fails to stifle his laughter while Irvette offers me an empathetic hand off the ground.

"If Adrienne's secret is going to remain safe with you, you're going to have to be a lot less reactive to harmless remarks," Lumithra rumbles.

"Thank you for addressing the obvious," I fire back. At least I can play off my sudden loss of composure as if I'm just a hopelessly lovestruck fool. Literally falling head over heels at the slightest mention of my woman.

"Oh, you've got it bad for the shadow mage," Irvette chuckles.

"That's an understatement," Zephyr snorts. "The chemistry between you two is an undeniable, ionic bond. No one has been able to break Adrienne's impenetrable facade until the day she introduced you to our squad. Don't think I haven't noticed the way you've been acting so refined as if you don't have her shadows wrapped around your fingers."

"Guilty as charged," I admit. "I keep my composure refined so no one will ever find out just where I've had those shadows wrapped," I remark.

I smirk as I glance down, fidgeting with the hilt of my dagger between my fingertips. I think it's safe to say I've more than adequately shifted the attention off my reaction to Irvette's goddess comment.

"You just made me choke on my tea in front of The High Priestess. I hope you're happy," Adrienne scoffs down our bond.

"Don't worry. I'll allow you an opportunity to get me back later. I'll be looking forward to it," I taunt.

Irvette and Zephyr glance at each other, eyes widened as they burst into laughter. "Amira, darling. Nearly taking us out with that silver tongue of yours. Tell me, now. How does it feel to have fallen so deeply for another soul? " He pries.

Zephyr's question strikes a dissonant chord, sending shivers down my spine. Every time I've dared to open even a sliver of my calloused heart to another soul, it has always become a matter of when before they're brutally ripped from my arms. Adrienne forbade Osiris from ever staking a claim on my soul, and she has been forever exiled from Niroshen. The very real possibility of our eternal separation is a nightmare I can't afford to stomach.

"Your magic is stirring, Amira. Reel it in. You're in control," Adrienne assures me.

I almost failed to notice the sparks of electricity dancing on the rising hairs on my skin along with the heat simmering in my blood. I draw in a deep breath of the air filled with floral and herbal offerings, imagining myself in Adrienne's arms. Eyes closed, I grab the hilt of my dagger once again, envisioning I'm grabbing on to Adrienne instead. My magic recoils, and I find myself back in control. Crisis adverted.

"Well done, my love. That was flawless," she praises.

Irvette places a hand on my shoulder after noticing my distress, pulling me into her arms as we continue our walk down the street. I flinch in response, still not accustomed to Vespera's culture of warm embraces. *Patience, Amira. Reel it in,* I remind myself.

"Love is a sacred scarcity," she mutters softly. "I understand your hesitation to speak about it. That's driven by a fierce desire to protect it." Irvette's gentle ocean eye meets mine with waves of silent understanding. An eye that has also witnessed far too many losses within a single lifetime.

"Pardon as I interrupt your tender moment, but we have arrived at the heart of our little quest," Zephyr interjects.

A rose-gold sign labeled The Cashmere Crow hangs from a dark brick shop featuring an elaborate window display of luxurious, glistening gowns. Dresses shimmer in the entire spectrum of the rainbow, outshining the shop's flickering torchlights.

"I can understand why this place is so highly coveted," Irvette gawks, eyeballing the cascading fabrics. An overwhelming concoction of fragrant perfumes seep through the cracks of the iron door, telling of the high volume of business the boutique has seen in the past hour alone.

Irvette opens the door as a cluster of women stumble through the door frame, practically spilling out of the shop. "Mind your manners, would you? Just wait outside like the rest of us had to. You're nothing special," a woman scoffs in a shrill tone. I roll my eyes as they hastily plow back through the densely crowded shop in a gluttonous frenzy.

Countless women packed in the Cashmere Crow clench elaborate gowns to their chests like starved wolves clinging onto prized prey, attempting to either cram into dressing rooms or fight their way to the shopkeep's counter. The last time I witnessed similar behavior was when watching peasants guard butchered chunks of rabbits with their lives. They'd hide their meat beneath their thin, ragged robes in efforts to make it out of the low-stocked meat markets without being stabbed to death over their possession of limited, coveted nourishment.

I'd rather spend the afternoon picking up dragon shit than fighting my way through a sea of pretentious nobles slammed against the doors of over-crowded dressing rooms. Occasional stampedes of patrons toting their bulky garment bags spill out of the shop, double-taking my glowing white hair as they brush against our shoulders. I'm becoming far too tempted to bolt back to the monastery and leave Irvette and Zephyr to the miserably maddening chaos without me.

While centering my thoughts on Adrienne once again to keep the currents of my magic at bay, I didn't even notice that Zephyr somehow managed to work his way through the currents of patrons to the shopkeep's counter. He leans against the side of the counter, fanning his long, sweaty black tresses while unfastening the first few buttons of his ivory tunic. The shopkeep's eyes are instantly drawn to the muscles rippling down his chest as he stares her down with a smoldering burn behind his blazing blue eyes.

"Oh, gods. Do I even want to know what stunt he's trying to pull?" I ask Irvette.

"Most likely not," Irvette sighs. "Normally, we don't like to encourage him, but every once in a while, we allow him to use his quirks to our advantage."

Zephyr leans further over the counter, whispering something in the shopkeep's ear that paints her cheeks brighter than a blood-red sunrise. Within heartbeats, she dismisses a mass exodus of patrons through the front door as Zephyr motions for us to enter.

"What in gods' realms did you say to the woman?" Irvette probes.

"You could say she will be compensated abundantly for clearing enough space to afford you lovelies a proper opportunity to shop without an appointment," Zephyr smirks.

"I don't know if I should be impressed or concerned," Irvette responds skeptically. The sound of her churning stomach rumbles in my ears as she processes whatever ungodly imagery Zephyr has etched into her mind.

"I interpret your disgust as jealousy. You wish Felix was as tantalizing as yours truly," Zephyr bows.

"Oh, please. You know you've got nothing compared to Felix," Irvette counters.

"Perhaps. You've got me there. Maybe I'm a little jealous you get to take Blackthorn's hottest fire mage to bed. Anyways, you ladies can thank me for my service once you're mistaken for summer goddesses gracing us with your divine beauty at the ball," Zephyr winks before disappearing, leaving us to our shopping.

I reluctantly start browsing the rows of dresses with Irvette, refraining from wondering what he said to the shopkeep to disperse her crowds so quickly.

"That 'gone for lunch, be back in thirty minutes' sign on the counter shouldn't raise our concern, right?" Irvette asks nervously.

"I think if we were wise, we would avoid that door to the supply closet like a plague," I warn, nodding toward the closed door behind the counter.

"Good gods," Irvette mumbles. "He owes us a round at The Wretched Owl next so that we can forget about this. Anyways, I think I just stumbled upon a dress practically *screaming* your name."

"I wasn't exactly expecting *my* name to be the one screamed in this shop," I chuckle.

Irvette's laughter fills the shop as she hands me a velvet, crimson gown, dark as a fine wine. "Give this a try before the lovers emerge. We have no way of knowing if we'll actually have a full thirty minutes before the crowds return."

"You've got a very good point," I sigh as I grab the gown and haul it into a dressing room.

It takes a minute to remember how to breathe while adjusting to how tightly the gown clings against my curves. The reflection staring back at me in the mirror feels so foreign, remembering my once raven black hair is now white as fresh snow. My reflection reminds me of the resurrection granted to me by The High Priestess and Adrienne's deal forged in The Dark Realms. I'm no longer the hopeless, gangly, cowardly mercenary I once was. I am an empress, stepping into my new, magical light.

I barely recognize my breasts framed by the gown's plunging, heart-shaped strapless neckline. I almost feel naked staring at the daring, dramatic thigh slit leaving little to the imagination. The way the slit accents my thigh muscles, and the way the skirt sweeps across the ground somehow makes me feel as powerful as I feel when I'm equipped with all my daggers, if not more. I am no longer Rhydian's former mangy dog. I am my own weapon. I answer to no one.

"Well, let's see it!" Irvette calls out. I step out of the dressing room, taken aback as Irvette embodies the beauty of a siren in a sapphire blue gown. I'm convinced her dress is somehow an heirloom passed down from Sirena by the way the sparkling sapphire contrasts the deep richness of her chestnut skin and enhances the vividness her aquamarine braids. The deep blue tones bring out an ethereal glow behind her single, fierce green eye.

"You look stunning," I exclaim before she opens her mouth. "No wonder the waves bow to your command."

Irvette beams with pride as she gives her dress a twirl, admiring the way it swirls like the waves of the sea. She then looks up to me with her eye widening in stunned admiration. "I hate to say it, but damn, Zephyr was right. Crimson was made for you. I can't wait to see the look on Adrienne's face when she sees you in this beauty," she chuckles.

"I think it's safe to say we're both ready to make our selections then," I respond with a grin. By the time we change out of our dresses and place them in their garment bags, Zephyr and the shopkeep emerge from the supply closet behind the counter with matching blush-stained cheeks.

"Ar-are you ready to make your purchase?" The shopkeep asks in a flustered tone. She refuses to look us in the eye as she combs her fingers through her tangled, strawberry blonde hair and smooths out the wrinkles in her dress.

"We're all set," I confirm as Irvette and I place our gold on the counter in exchange for our gowns.

"Thank you for your business. Please come again," she stutters, waving us out of her shop.

"Well, that couldn't have been any more uncomfortable," I mutter to Irvette on our way out the door. I don't need to look back to sense the humiliation further flood the shopkeep's complexion as she hurriedly tries to regain her composure before her patrons notice the "open" sign hanging on her door.

"You're telling me," Irvette rolls her eye.

"I hate to interrupt the success of your outing, but I need you all to return immediately. We have a situation," Adrienne communicates with a bone-chilling urgency down our bond. I glance down at Irvette's engagement ring and my stomach immediately twists into knots. Felix.

CHAPTER 30
No Time to Waste

From Zephyr and Irvette's shared blanched expressions, Tsuna and Sylphira must have relayed Adrienne's message. "I'm going to kill him as soon as we save his sorry ass," Irvette snarls as we clutch our garment bags and take off sprinting as fast as our legs can carry us.

"Lumithra?"

"En route to the monastery. Flying as fast as we can," she confirms.

My lungs burn, starving for air as we race through Vespera's obstructive, crowded streets. I swear the mountainous staircase that leads to the monastery is taunting us, receding further away the faster we pump our legs. "We'll never get there fast enough without our dragons," Irvette huffs.

"I have an idea. You two, grab on to me," Zephyr breathlessly orders us.

Knowing there's no time to argue, Irvette and I grab hold of his waist, trusting his lead without hesitation. Zephyr takes a deep breath, and a large, dense cloud forms beneath our feet.

"Hold on tight," he warns. Zephyr propels his arms as we lift off the ground and find ourselves balancing on the back of a flying cloud. We fly over a choir of gasps of shock and terror, inverting umbrellas over cafe tables and barely evading collisions with storefront signs and awnings.

"Can't you control this thing any better?" Irvette shouts as an abrupt drop in altitude causes us to take out a massive tree branch that crashes down onto a rooftop below.

"You try conjuring your own cloud and steer it with passengers clinging onto your waist for dear life!" Zephyr shoots back.

We finally make it out of the city after damaging numerous homes and storefronts. Evergreens become a blurred sea of dark, emerald pine as Zephyr blasts us up the mountain. Who would've known that standing atop a cloud soaring up the side of a mountain would prove more difficult than sitting in the saddle of a dragon? My thighs burn, threatening to give out while Irvette's feet are somehow firmly planted in an effortless, graceful stance.

"Can the three of you get here any faster?" Lumithra growls impatiently.

"Have you ever tried balancing on a cloud as it rapidly scales a mountain while holding onto a garment bag? We're almost there," I hiss back.

The field behind the monastery emerges on the horizon, bringing a sigh of relief to my trembling muscles. Lady Rhonwen waits for us alongside the rest of our squad and dragons joined by what appears to be a small battalion of wind mages. I hardly notice the moment Zephyr drops us to the ground due to the adrenaline racing through my veins and the restless dread pumping through my heart.

"As you likely suspect, our dragons have not heard a single word from Fieryn. Felix's report is now thirty minutes past due. I am afraid we can assume his mission has been compromised and that his life is in danger," Lady Rhonwen explains, swallowing a lump in her throat.

A gust of wind tosses The High Priestess's moon-white hair around like a snow squall. Her downcast eyes mirror the incoming storm clouds rolling across the darkening skies. Light mist spits out of Blackthorn's fog, providing a soothing coolness to my heat-flushed skin.

"Adrienne, I am entrusting your squad with the task of retrieving Felix and Fieryn and bringing them back home. He planned on assembling his task force in Crystal Bay, so I ask that you begin your search there. You have command of this wind battalion to aid in your discreet arrival and as extra hands on your mission. Bring our emissary home safely,"

Lady Rhonwen commands.

The High Priestess's usual tone of confident assurance, replaced by foreign, grave apprehension, molds my stomach into heaps of burning coals.

Irvette approaches Adrienne, whispering something into her ear that gets her a nod of approval. "I'll be right back. We won't make it a single footstep past the docks dressed like this." She takes off sprinting towards the dormitory quarters faster than rapids spilling into a waterfall without elaborating further.

"Do your best to keep your profile low," Lady Rhonwen continues. "And prepare to fly through some turbulent weather. It appears quite the storm is brewing."

As if right on command, a deafening rumble of thunder erupts across the fog-laden skies, ominously threatening to unleash floodgates from the darkening clouds at any moment.

Adrienne bows and turns her attention to the squad. "To avoid drawing any unwanted attention to our party, we will need to break off into smaller groups once we arrive. Raven griffins have very keen senses, so pairing off will decrease the likelihood of any picking up on our scent. Once we have an eye on Felix and Fieryn, we'll determine whether or not we will need to call for additional aid to assist us in our ploys.

"Zephyr, you will be joining the wild battalion's formation in the skies to help them sustain our cover. Does anyone have any questions?"

"Has there been any consideration to changing our attire, or are we going to storm the docks of Crystal Bay practically screaming that we're dragon knights?" Arden asks

"I've got us covered!" Irvette races back to the party, toting a pile of black dresses, cloaks, and robes, quickly tossing everyone a change of clothing. "Thankfully, our emissary has always brought me back a piece of traditional clothing from Eldermoor during his travels. I'm sure he won't mind us raiding through our little stash. We dress the part and blend in with the crowd."

I quickly remove my tunic and trousers and suck my chest into the slightly too small dress that was handed to me. I carefully conceal my bandolier of daggers beneath the obsidian cloak now draped over my dress. The rest of the squad quickly changes into their blood mage attire, paying no mind to modesty in the heat of urgency.

A resounding roar of thunder shakes the ground, clawing through the clouds now dark as midnight. Heavy, slanted rain spews from the skies. "Get in formation!" Adrienne shouts. Her command hardly cuts across the lashing winds rapidly picking up speed with each heartbeat.

Standing firm on the ground suddenly requires all my strength as the winds threaten to send us tumbling across the field like paper dolls. Vespera's citizens choosing today to board up their shops and homes must have been some sort of fortunate favor from the gods. As for our squad, however, it seems as if the gods are testing us. We couldn't be preparing for takeoff in worse conditions.

"Climb aboard. There's no time to waste!" Lumithra rumbles as she lowers her belly to the ground for me.

I give myself a running start, fighting against the wind resistance as I sprint for Lumithra. My muscles ache and burn as I latch onto her slippery scales, finding climbing my way to my seat taking more upper body strength than I bargained for. My arms become gelatinous by the time I finally reach my saddle. Fighting the lashing winds to keep my floor-length cloak and dress out of my face couldn't be more infuriating. Blood mage attire is not at all suited for climbing aboard dragons in a violent storm.

"Brace yourself, child. I don't think I have to tell you we're in for a rough flight," Lumithra huffs. I clench onto the pommel, ready to give up on repeatedly tossing my cloak out of my face and surrender to Cael's fury. Catching glimpses of the wind mages sustaining just enough of their magic to keep their vision unobstructed makes me wish I was born of a

different god.

"We're not about to let a little weather be the reason we fail to rescue Felix. Let's just focus on getting to Crystal Bay as quickly as possible."

Lumithra doesn't counter.

Zephyr joins the wind mages and their silver dragons flanking our squad, raising up walls of clouds to conceal our rescue party. Any minuscule visibility we once had is now swallowed by thick, fluffy walls of grey.

"Can you see anything at all?" I ask Lumithra without even trying to conceal my mild panic.

"I've flown through thousands of storms in my lifetime and have lived to tell each tale. We'll get through this," she promises.

Lumithra expands her wings, fighting to launch her colossal body into battle against our first enemy encounter— this godsforsaken storm. Fighting for my balance becomes a fight for my life as the winds are more than determined to throw me from my seat as we launch into the unrelenting rain.

Branches snap, and large trees fall to the ground below where we were standing just minutes ago. I flinch at each crackling snap, reliving the sound of breaking bones. The many bones I've broken to maintain the flow of Rhydian's blood money. Rain dumps on us as if we're stuck under waterfalls, creating the sensation of drowning thousands of feet off the ground.

Panic strikes me like a bolt of lightning, and I slip out of my seat. It feels like the winds are about to rip me apart in two as my legs dangle into the stormy abyss. I lose my slipping grip on the pommel as a rumble of thunder rattles Lumithra's bones. The world stops in a heartbeat of weightlessness before my brain registers I've entered into a free-fall.

"Amira!" Lumithra roars.

G forces come crashing down on my chest as I catch glimpses of Lumithra fighting against the storm to chase after me. Her blood-curdling, anguishing roar becomes the only sound I find myself able to focus on despite the deafening downpour determined to pummel me all the way to my death.

Colors flood my vision, and I grow lightheaded from being violently spun like an insect in the claws of a black widow upon her web of death. An equally jarring tendril of shadows wraps around my torso, disrupting my free-fall in a jolting whiplash. I find myself secured in a harness of obsidian ropes, hoisting me through the turbulent gales until I'm gently returned to Lumithra's saddle.

"The only darkness that gets to claim you is me," Adrienne growls.

My heart violently palpitates as I lower my head in an attempt to lessen the severity of my violent bout of vertigo. *"Thank you for never growing tired of saving my ass. I owe you."*

"You can make it up to me by not giving me mini heart attacks, my love. Align your spine with Lumithra's. Lean into her movements. Relax your upper body and shift all your clenching tension to the lower half of your body," Adrienne instructs.

I roll my shoulders back, relaxing them as much as possible as pelting hail slams against my skin like icy shards of glass. I clasp my thighs against the saddle until every muscle in my lower body screams on fire. Lumithra twists and flails, lashing against the winds as they commandeer authority over our flight.

Thunder clamors the atmosphere so violently that I feel my brain rattling in my skull. One moment, I'm watching flashes of lightning illuminate the sable skies. The next, Lumithra roars and all my blood starts rushing to my head. Stars flood my vision for a heartbeat, and when they clear, I have a view of my thighs clenching against her neck above my head. My knuckles, whiter than bones, grasp onto the pommel in a death grip as my stomach rises to my throat. Oh, gods. We're upside down.

"Hang on!" Lumithra roars as she rapidly flaps her wings, shifting all

her weight into rolling against the forceful gusts until we're right side up. *"Are you okay, Amira?"*

"Just fine," I reply through our bond, struggling to take a full, complete breath. *"Is everyone else okay?"* I flinch at every crackle of thunder, bracing myself to be launched in more deadly aerial inversions.

"Everyone is in one piece," she assures me, blowing out a huff of steam. *"Right now, I want you to worry about getting your breath and your shaking under control. We're far from out of the woods, I'm afraid."*

Taking a slow, deep breath might as well be next to impossible, along with controlling my shivers as my soaking wet dress clings to my skin as the rain continues to drench us relentlessly. Lumithra jolts in a brief patch of turbulence, and I release a bolt of lightning before even sensing my magic burning in my veins.

"Breathe, my love. In through your nose, out through your mouth. You handled those maneuvers like a seasoned dragon knight. You're in control," Adrienne consoles me.

The warmth of Adrienne's voice down our bond calms my thundering heart and allows me a moment of sacred comfort to ease out of my hyperventilation.

"That's my girl—slow, controlled breaths. You're in control. You're doing great."

I allow my eyes to close for a moment, envisioning myself in her arms and the heat of her kisses rolling down my neck. *"Keep talking to me like that, and I'm afraid I'm going to get terribly distracted."*

"Not to disrupt whatever it takes to ease your adrenaline, but I need you to stay vigilant. Something isn't right," Lumithra interrupts my brief moment of bliss.

"You mean other than this bastardly storm that threw us into a barrel roll?" I scoff.

The howling winds, hail, and rain come to an abrupt, ominous pause as a foul, rotten stench taints the salty ocean air. The ink-black clouds shift into hues of deep crimson, resurrecting the storm with a newfound fury.

"*Blood mages?*" I ask both Lumithra and Adrienne, taken aback by the blood-red clouds.

"*Not blood mages. Rygor. An ancient storm spirit. I haven't encountered one since the last Luminary War,*" Adrienne answers.

I gulp down the lump in my throat. "*Friend or foe?*" I ask.

"*Rygors slumber in peace unless awakened by sensing threats to Elmoria's balance. Once awakened, they are driven by instinct to slaughter anyone who currently bears or has borne a luminary. They believe in cleansing the world of luminary bearers as they desire to see every stone returned to the earth,*" Adrienne explains.

My blood chills to ice. It's bad enough that Irvette and I have both borne a luminary. Adrienne has one embedded in her very existence.

"*Prepare for combat,*" Lumithra warns.

Thunder ripples like seismic currents through the scarlet clouds. No. Not thunder. An ear-shattering roar. Lightning flickers, and I swear I see the flash of white fangs embedded in a maw the size of a dragon. A quick, breathy cadence of winds mimics the sound of a dog sniffing out its prey.

"*How in the realms do we fight it?*"

"*Immortal spirits are next to impossible to kill. We drain its energy until I can get it through a portal to slumber in The Dark Realms. As long as Elmoria thirsts for the luminaries' power, the creature will not return to dormancy in The Mortal Realms.*" Pain resonates in Adrienne's voice as if sending a creature to The Dark Realms is the last thing she wants to do.

The sniffing winds grow stronger, and the rot-stenched rain grows warmer. Another guttural roar raises the hairs on the back of my neck as the crimson clouds shift into the shape of a giant, vaporous ox sporting gnarled, twisted horns. Our colossal dragons appear as nothing more than horses compared to the rygor. The ancient storm spirit bucks its legs and takes off, charging through the skies, barreling straight for our party.

"As storm spirits, rygors are essentially storm mages. Any element at play in this storm can and will be used against us," Adrienne shouts down our bond.

Her warning comes too late. I call upon Kallik's light and summon a bolt of lightning aimed at the rygor. It catches my bolt between its fangs and chews on it like a bone. The more it chomps on my bolt of lightning, the larger and brighter it grows. I freeze in terror upon realizing it's about to launch the bolt right back at us like a monster-sized, electrical javelin.

Zephyr and the wind mages launch raging cyclones in an effort to distract the rygor and disrupt its aim. It bucks its hind legs, kicking the cyclones out of its way as if they're children's toy spinning tops. Arden and Adrienne throw tendrils of shadows and thick, twisting branches, managing to bind all its legs in restraints.

"We can't hold him back forever," Adrienne grunts as the rygor roars in a beastly rage, desperate to thrash free from its ensnarement. *"We can sustain this just long enough for you to redirect that massive bolt. Channel all your concentration on it. The moment it's unleashed, you call it back to your command. Your light submits to you. Understood?"*

Fear rattles my bones like a desperate prisoner shaking the bars of an iron cage. If I fail, this ancient storm spirit kills us all. I shift all my focus on my branching, fiery lightning, expanding in the rygor's frothing maw. No time to focus on reaching Crystal Bay until that bolt is no longer a lethal threat large enough to incinerate us all. No time to focus on the fact I may very well administer my own execution if I fail to control the bolt once it's back in my possession.

"Understood."

The rygor whips its neck, releasing the bolt from the clench of its jaws. Instinct kicks in as if Kallik himself is guiding my limbs as I extend my arms and reach out for the massive, lethal bolt. Sharp, tingling voltage threatens to burn my flesh as I channel the intercepted lightning into my fingertips. Surges of raw, explosive energy race down the length of my convulsing arms as my muscles spasm beyond my control. Heart-stopping electricity races through the blood in my veins, sending my pulse into a wildly sporadic rhythm. The world around me spins in dizzying, disorienting blurs as the tightness of my chest threatens to distract all my focus.

"Amira! You are in control. You are the mage. Lightning is a muse. Wield it to your command!" Adrienne roars down our bond.

With my entire body now violently working to stop the lethal flow of electricity and redirect it, Casimir's voice echoes in my mind, a reminder of our departing promise. Fight for hope. I inhale the embrace of my excruciating pain and exhale hope in the form of rage. At the last possible second, my massive lightning beam finally submits to my command. I wrap it around my fingers like strands of ribbons and fling it right down the rygor's throat with the flick of my wrists.

An explosive blast of electric fire erupts from the rygor's maw, sending its ox-shaped body of colossal crimson clouds into waves of violent convulsions.

"It's stunned! Drain its energy while it can't retaliate!" Adrienne shouts over the pelting hail and lashing wind gusts. Dragons roar to relay her command as countless blasts of the elements are thrown at the storm spirit. Shards of jagged earth, tsunami-like waves, devastating tornadoes weaponized shadows, and blasts of my white, lightning fire launch toward the beast. It shakes off each blow as if we're just throwing tiny pebbles at a window.

"Everyone is burning out, and this damned beast is regaining its strength. We're never going to make it to Felix at this rate!" I shout to Adrienne as the rygor hurls one of Arden's massive boulders right back toward our party, nearly taking out a wind mage.

"A rygor isn't quickly drained to submission without at least three to

four gods working together. One goddess and a party of half-mortals is an uneven match," she hisses. *"I'm growing quite tired of them leaving me to my cursed demise. As always…I've got this."*

Pools of glowing obsidian overtake Adrienne's silver eyes. Plumes of dark smoke seep from her serpent tattoos and devour her skin whole until the daughter of Kamaris and Osiris shifts into the form of an enormous raven rivaling the size of the rygor.

"If anyone questions anything they may witness, blame it all on the weather. I am not involved," Adrienne relays before disappearing into the thicket of raven-black whirlwinds. Sarthon disappears next, following close behind her to offer his aid and conceal his vacant saddle.

"Quite a few of our mages have suffered their fair share of injuries. Tend to the wounded while I see this through," she orders. *"This storm will be over soon."*

I'm reluctant to leave Adrienne behind again based on what happened when she singlehandedly took on the mage general, but Lumithra and I obey. We make rounds to every mage injured by flying projectiles or reflected attacks while The Goddess of the Shadows battles the rygor in secrecy.

The radiant alabaster glow of my healing lights engulfs my hands as my magic works to mend broken bones and close gaping wounds. Thankfully, none of the injuries are anywhere nearly as devastating as those suffered by the water mages in the caverns. If I were to burn myself out on healing everyone, I wouldn't be surprised if Adrienne sentenced our entire party to an eternity in The Dark Realms to lash out her anger.

Chills scuttle down my spine as a thunderous, gurgling cry nearly slices through my eardrums. The sound of choking and blood spewing from a creature's throat. Without a doubt, Adrienne managed to sink her razor-sharp talons into the rygor's neck. The louder the creature cries, the softer the howling winds become. The rain shifts from that of oppressive waterfalls to a gentle, dying drizzle as it becomes clear power is quickly draining from the storm spirit. My heart nearly stops upon glimpsing Adrienne's raven form through the weakening storm.

"She needs time and cover to shift back into a shadow mage, or everyone is about to learn of her divinity. Get me as close as you can to that fight. We need to create a diversion," I plead Lumithra.

"On it," Lumithra growls.

We fly into the dissipating haze, and I pray to the gods that my magic will manifest into exactly what I need. Beams of sunlight peak through the dying storm as I reach for their light. I catch a beam in my hands and begin shaping it in my hands as if I'm a potter and the beam is my clay. Its warmth dries my drenched, goose-bumped skin as I shape my sunbeam into a massive shield of blinding light. Gasps and winces of pain from the nearby mages become music to my ears as I outstretch my arms, expanding my shield of blinding light to conceal Adrienne as she shifts out of her raven form, and returns to Sarthon.

"Be still," Adrienne commands the rygor. "Elmoria's current state is no place to host your weary heart. In this dark age, you will only know torment in the mortal realms."

Adrienne stretches her arms, summoning a portal to The Dark Realms to open on her command. Catching glimpses of the rotting, obsidian forest I tried so hard to suppress sends my heart racing as my arms above my head begin trembling with fatigue. Control yourself, Amira. Get it together, I tell myself in the middle of dry heaving.

"As Goddess of the Shadows, I command you to occupy The Dark Realms. The energy of the dark will provide you with a bountiful feast in your hour of unrest. I vow to release your spirit to slumber in Elmoria once more upon the last heartbeat that ends this war." Her tone is filled with both unwavering, divine authority and reluctant guilt. The rygor bows in submission and trots through the portal, its crimson horns drooping low in defeat. Sarthon roars to mask the demonic screams that cry out as Adrienne seals the portal shut.

My arms drop limp like deadweights at my side, and my dome of blinding light instantly vanishes. Balmy, rain-scented humidity lingers in the air as gentle hues of cerulean paint over the shades of ominous onyx and crimson. It takes a second before I realize every eye is glued to me in wide-struck awe.

"I've got to hand it to you, light-bringer. Without you, that thing would still be handing our asses to us. We all owe you one," Arden shouts from atop Hyrix.

"I infinitely owe you for saving my ass with that shield of yours. You never cease to astonish me, love."

"I'm sure you'll make it up to me plenty sufficiently once we return from our mission," I smirk.

Adrienne rolls her eyes, returning a seductive half-smile that instantly flushes my cheeks bright scarlet.

"We've wasted enough time. Wind mages, reassemble your formation. We make haste for Crystal Bay," Adrienne orders the party.

CHAPTER 31
Crystal Bay

Trails of charcoal steam seep from the horizon as silhouettes of trading ships mark our arrival to Crystal Bay. My pulse quickens with anticipation as we finally draw close enough to the port where I can make out bits and pieces of conversations on the docks. A pungent stench of rich, burning iron wafts my senses with the sea breeze, churning my stomach with rolling waves of nausea.

"Are you smelling that too?" I ask Lumithra.

My question lingers with a pregnant pause as brewing tension thickens the air. Sulfurous steam and a cadence of low, rumbling growls and hisses emit from every dragon in our midst. Every chest puffs, every tail stiffens, and every pupil dilates with a lethally honed, caged fury.

"That's the scent of freshly spilled dragon's blood, and lots of it," Lumithra growls aggressively, raising the hairs on the back of my neck.

"Dragon's blood?" I swallow. *"There hasn't been a recent battle out this way, right?"*

"Not a battle. An ambush," she seethes through her fangs. *"This blood spill is only hours old, and Fieryn would've been the last dragon to fly near the bay. What you're smelling is dragon's blood burning in fresh batches of incense."*

Bile rises in my throat at the thought of Fieryn's blood burning as incense. What would've had to happen for any enemy to get close enough to a dragon to spill its blood? What does that mean for Felix? The rest of our spies?

"A peaceful, stealthy departure after the completion of our mission is no

longer an option we are willing to consider. No one spills the sacred blood of a dragon without facing the wrath of our legions," Lumithra promises, not threatens.

"The dragons have decided. We will not depart from Crystal Bay without first waging a battle of atonement," Adrienne warns down our bond.

"Lumithra just made me well aware," I respond. *"Let's just hope they keep their rage concealed long enough to not compromise the integrity of our mission."*

Our dragons carefully descend under the concealment of dense wind mage fog into Crystal Bay's shimmering, sapphire waters. My skin flushes with warmth from the collective release of piping-hot dragon steam. If we have any odds working in our favor, it's our legion of livid dragons on standby to unleash molten fury at the first opportunity.

"The next ship will be arriving any moment," Adrienne quietly reels in our attention. *"Once its passengers depart, we dismount and quietly board the ship. From there, we disperse as offloading passengers and begin our search."*

We exchange nonverbal head nods with one another, assigning ourselves to smaller search parties before we make our move. Like clockwork, a large vessel emerges from the foggy haze and waddles toward the dock. Being in the heart of enemy territory hits the moment I notice the large insignia of Eldermoor's crest branded into the violet-stained woodwork—a raven griffin looking up at crystals raining down under a full moon. Our dragons lower their heads and slowly follow the ship's wake in silence as still as night. No one dares to shift in their seats or take more than minimal, shallow breaths.

"Anchor down," a helmsman orders. My stomach drops in synch with the anchor's thud. The amount of Fieryn's blood that had to spill for the incense to be this strong on the docks alone is not a good sign. The scent of her presence is still strong. Either she's incapacitated somewhere

in this town or somehow miraculously hidden in secrecy, plotting to rescue Felix. I hope to the gods it's the latter.

As for Felix…I've witnessed Rhydian interrogate enough of our targets. I've been forced to shadow his tactics and the torturous methods he'd use to get our targets to spill intel on the whereabouts of additional men we were after. If Felix is enduring anything compared to that— I don't allow my mind to complete that thought.

"Felix wasn't carelessly assigned as Blackthorn's emissary. He was selected after proving himself most capable among hundreds of highly prestigious applicants. His resilience burns as bright as his masterful flames, if not brighter," Lumithra consoles.

"Prepare to break," Adrienne orders.

We all raise our hoods over our faces as Irvette quietly raises the waves to elevate us until we become level with the ship. My heart thuds violently in my chest as her waves disturb the stillness of the ship, praying that no one on board suspects our presence.

"The seas are abnormally foggy today. And choppy," we overhear the helmsman converse with a crew mate. Nobody dares to breathe now.

"I'd expect as much after that beast of a storm out there," the crew mate grumbles. "Praise Osiris, our vessel braved the storm unscathed."

"That storm was far from ordinary," the helmsman nods in agreement as he inspects the ship. "The tides are shifting. I can feel it. The tides of this war will soon be shifting in our favor," he croons.

"You sure speak with lofty optimism. Blackthorn still possesses the bulk of the luminaries," his crew mate scoffs.

"I want you to pause for a moment. Take in the scent of the air, my friend. Do you smell that?" The helmsman boasts.

"You mean the dragon's blood incense?" The crewman asks.

"Fresh dragon's blood incense. Fresher than the blood our mages collected from Tourmaline's shore. From the smell of it, I'd reckon the blood burns from a beast caught just earlier today. Osiris is with us, my brother. Victory is on the horizon. Soon, all of Elmoria will learn to praise his name only and forsake all the other gods. The fall of those damned, half-mortal dragon knights is nigh."

"yeah, yeah, I'll believe it when I see it. We've got passengers to offload for now, you know. I want time to polish up the ol' girl before we burn what's left of our daylight," the crew mate scoffs.

The hairs on the back of my neck rise like the high tide. Envisioning all of Elmoria mirroring Osiris's rule over The Dark Realms is a thought I can't afford to process right now. Not if I want to prevent blowing our cover by hurling the contents of my stomach into the bay.

The crew mates open the doors of the ship's quarters, and passengers begin to file out like herded cattle.

"Now!" Adrienne commands, signaling her hand in a forwarding motion.

We bring ourselves to stand and leap from the backs of our dragons onto the ship's deck in the coverage of thick fog. We immerse ourselves in a sea of black robes and follow the crowd, preparing to exit the ship.

"Be careful, my child," Lumithra rumbles.

"Likewise, Lumithra. Next time we reconvene, it will be Eldermoor's blood staining the sea and poisoning the air," I promise her.

Lumithra responds with a carnal snarl of approval.

Adrienne locks eyes with Arden and Zephyr through the crowd as we exit the ship and step onto the dock. She tilts her head to the left as she readjusts her hood. Arden adjusts the mask beneath his eyes and gives a subtle nod back. We keep our distance behind them as they turn down a street to the left of the docks while Irvette, Adrienne, and I stick to the center road. I hold my breath as wind mages break off into their pairs, disappearing into congested alleyways. Our rescue in the Maren Caverns was successful. We survived the surprise attack on Tourmaline Beach and preserved the integrity of the shadow luminary. Retrieving Felix and Fieryn from Crystal Bay is nothing our squad cannot handle.

"Take these." Irvette reaches into her satchel and pulls out three black amethyst crystal pendants. "Basic crystals for protection to better help us sell the parts we play." She hands Adrienne and I each a pendant and secures one for herself around her neck. "They're also symbolic of worshipping Osiris," Irvette adds.

"Since when did you start carrying crystals that symbolize The God of Death?" Adrienne snorts.

"Since about a minute ago. I may or may not have pit-pocketed some pendants from the crowd before departing the ship," Irvette confesses. "If we don't want to draw any attention to ourselves, looking like seasoned blood mages will certainly aid our cause."

"You're damn brilliant," I tell her.

"You learn a few cultural tricks along the way of being engaged to an emissary," she smirks.

Twisting trees bearing leaves bright as torchlight line the cobblestone streets of towering townhouses. We begin carefully scanning our surroundings for any traces of Felix and Fieryn with yellow, glowing leaves crunching beneath our boots.

"I'll admit I never thought I'd see ember oaks up close like this. They bear leaves that glow like luminous embers throughout every season, even through the winter. We were in negotiations to receive some ember oak seeds to plant in Blackthorn in exchange for some of our native spices, but that was before Eldermoor broke the terms of the treaty," Irvette nervously rambles.

As the sunset fades into a dark sheet of night, the streets of Crystal Bay come to life. Vendors wheel portable carts out to the streets selling generous pints of cocktails garnished with elaborate edible floral arrangements. Old crones set up travel sized tents and hammer signs into the ground advertising accurate astrology readings. Children fight their ways into lines to pet a chained pegasus slumped in defeat with injured wings.

"Looks like Blackthorn isn't the only nation gearing up for festivities," I mutter. We nearly collide with a group of minstrels parading down the streets accompanied by acrobats stunning the crowds twirling colorful streamers in sync with graceful front flips and an aerial tricks. We clear out of their path just in time to bump into a group of dancers weaving large fire-lit torches between their limbs with rhythmic elegance.

"If we didn't need to lay low, I'd clear these streets with tricks that would haunt their nightmares for years to come," Adrienne snarls through her teeth.

"The end is nigh! The end is nigh! Good tidings arrive on The Night of the Smierc! The end is night! The end is nigh! Good tidings arrive on The Night of the Smierc!" The dancers chant in between twirling their torches

"Get your tickets! Get your tickets! Night of the Smierc Midnight Ritual! Eighteen and over only." An old, silver-haired woman with a fistful of tickets calls out, making stops to distribute her tickets and stuff payments into her satchel. Her scent reeks that of a masterful blood-mage.

"Night of the Smierc? Does that mean anything to either of you?" I ask.

"Your assumptions are as good as mine. However, knowing Felix, he definitely intended on investigating it," Irvette answers.

An ominous heap of dread settles into the pit of my stomach. Even for a master fire mage and renown emissary, I can't help but to question why The High Priestess agreed to sending Felix on such a deadly assignment alone. I'd pray to the gods the decision won't turn out to be costly, but just the slightest glance at Adrienne and her sleeve of ink serpents masking her eternal damnation reminds me calling upon their aid is a futile effort.

"Over here! Three tickets please!" Adrienne flags down the old woman, signaling her our way with an uncharacteristically warm, inviting smile.

"You said three tickets for The Night of The Smierc?" The woman confirms. Her irises appear glazed over in a perpetually possessed trance, red as a blood moon. She's unmistakably one of Eldermoor's countless blood mages.

"If you could be so kind, madam. My sisters and I would be honored to witness such a special ritual." Adrienne bows and meets the lethal, blood-wielding crone with charm behind her ashen eyes honed like silver daggers as she hands over her payment for our tickets.

Despite her tresses of aged silver and the wrinkles etched into her face, her square posture and the tone of her muscles suggest she is still a threat to be feared. If she had the slightest clue we wield the elements and not blood, we would be as good as dead. That doesn't seem even to faze The Goddess of the Shadows as she carries herself with an effortless, relaxed confidence.

The thought of her contorting our limbs beyond our will causes me to shudder as she fixes her blood-stained eyes on the three of us. "Oh my, I can assure you lovelies are in for a night to remember," she laughs wickedly as she gives us our tickets. "The ritual begins at midnight in the Cathedral of Crystal Bay."

"Word on the street suggests this ritual will be unlike any Eldermoor has ever seen," Adrienne responds. A bold, dangerous statement to pry for bold, dangerous information.

"What fun would it be if I were to spoil the surprises of the evening?" The woman winks. She laughs in a nasal, shrill tone that might as well be a set of nails clawing down a slab of granite. "Praise be to Osiris that our elders were gracious enough to allow the public to spectate such a special sacrifice tonight. The end is nigh," she croons as she returns to the streets, waving bundles of tickets.

"A midnight sacrifice in a cathedral full of Osiris worshippers. What in the realms could that possibly mean?" Irvette's throat bobs. "Felix was intending to investigate this ritual. I know it."

"Should we inform the rest of our party and ask them to search around the cathedral as well?" I ask.

Adrienne's complexion blanches as pale as a corpse. Her eyes widen with panic as her fingers curl into white-knuckled fists.

"Something wrong?" I ask sheepishly.

"I-I can't reach Sarthon. This has never happened before," she mutters.

Irvette and I exchange perplexed expressions as Adrienne pulls the sleeves of her cloak over her hands to conceal the shadows I glimpse seeping from her skin.

"Please tell me everything is alright. Has Sarthon been injured? Did you run into any trouble?" I reach for Lumithra.

Silence.

"Lumithra?"

Our bond is as silent as the heart of the Kanoelani Forest. Knives of ice sting my chest and send blistering splinters into the pit of my stomach.

"Tsuna is silent as well," Irvette mutters.

"What in the gods' realms is happening right now?" I reach for Adrienne.

"Your guess is as good as mine. It appears our bond hasn't been affected in any way," she responds. Her tone comes out harsher than I can tell she intended.

"You don't think this means they're possibly—" I can't even complete my question as if completing it will speak my fear into reality. Oh gods, this can't be happening. I grab Adrienne's hand to stifle the lightning charging under my skin, threatening to compromise our cover by releasing bolts of lethally charged rage.

"When a dragon dies, its final heartbeat is felt as a roar of thunder inside its rider's chest. It is said that the final heartbeat incapacitates the rider with immense fatigue from the weight of grief," Adrienne explains.

"We would've felt their deaths and wouldn't have the strength to stand right now. It appears our bonds must somehow be disrupted rather than severed."

Adrienne's assurance offers little to no relief. Whatever force holds the power to disrupt the bonds between half-mortals and their sacred dragons is a force we are severely ill-equipped to face on our own. I take a deep breath and allow myself a moment to lean my head against Adrienne's shoulder. Her grounding touch is the only source preventing me from becoming one with my white flames, alerting every blood mage in Eldermoor of our presence.

"You're not alone, my love. We're in this together. Whoever decided to pick a fight with Sarthon, Tsuna, and The White Empress set themselves up for royal obliteration," she promises.

"We have no choice but to attend the ritual without the hope of calling for any reinforcements. We'll have to storm it alone. Just the three of us," Adrienne tells us.

"Let's get on with it then. We've got no time to waste," Irvette replies with restless impatience.

✱　✱　✱

We walk in silence as we follow a trail of black robes on the path to Crystal Bay's Cathedral. A dark sea of expressionless, blood-red eyes, offering us glimpses into souls lost somewhere in a sustained, abysmal trance. They march in a uniformed cadence as if an army of one. Do any fragments of their souls remain untouched? Or have they all surrendered their entire essence to Osiris? Even the clamors of their chatter sound as if all spoken in the same pitch of frequency. Adrienne and Irvette subtly tug on their hoods to conceal as much of their faces as possible, and I follow suit. We fall in line with their rhythm, and I pray to the dragons that our deviating eyes have gone unnoticed.

"What are the odds it won't be just the three of us investigating tonight's ritual?" I ask Adrienne, under the concealment of our bond.

Hopefully, the rest of our party caught news of the ritual and are somewhere amid this spine-chilling death march. Even if joining up with them directly would pose too much risk of alerting raven griffins to our presence, seeing that they're safe with my own eyes would put at least some of my mind at ease.

"Arden has the intellect of a future war general. Zephyr always has a trove of wits up his sleeves. The wind mages accompanying our mission have been dragon knights longer than this squad has studied at the monastery. Our communications may have been severed, but our credentials are still very much intact. I trust everyone will make the right calls," Adrienne responds.

"Anyone who has been a dragon knight for longer than the amount of time I've studied at the monastery isn't saying much," I mutter.

"You've been thrown into the field ludicrously earlier than ideal," Adrienne acknowledges. *"Yet, you've already infinitely proven your strength and potential. I'm confident our mission is still in the best hands possible."*

"We can't afford to execute any plan short of perfection," Irvette whispers, interrupting my silent conversation with Adrienne. The glow of the ember oak trees and the light of the full moon cast light into her aquamarine eye, illuminating her rage.

A choir of haunting harmonies woven in a foreign tongue drifts through the breeze as we ascend the staircase to the cathedral's entrance. Adrienne's hand grows ice cold in mine as her muscles stiffen. Her eyebrows raise, and her eyes widen as if witnessing unspeakable terrors.

"They're speaking in an ancient tongue mostly forgotten," she explains. "The blood of Niroshen flows like a fountain. Consume our offering, stain the full moon crimson. Mages and dragons, slain on the altar. Come to the slaughter, consume them, oh, Father."

My heart stops upon realizing just where we will find Felix and Fieryn.

CHAPTER 32
The Infiltration

"Forget the main entrance," Adrienne quietly commands, subtly signaling us not to take another step further. "Felix and Fieryn are the sacrifice. If we want any shot at a successful rescue without becoming blood mage puppets, we need to stage ourselves strategically. We need an aerial infiltration point."

"The roof. We need to get up to the roof somehow. We need to get up there now," Irvette hisses, trembling with a restless fury I fear she won't be able to withhold for much longer.

"I can get us up there if we can break free from this crowd without raising suspicion," Adrienne whispers in the cover of the choir's hymns and the crowd's excitement. "From there, we can scout out the sanctuary and plan our operation," she explains.

"I'll handle the distraction. Follow my lead," Irvette whispers.

"Cursed gods, you've got to be joking!" she screams without warning.

"What's wrong?" I ask, playing the part, genuinely confused where Irvette is going with this.

"I-I don't have our tickets. I must have dropped them along the path somewhere!" she huffs, channeling morsels of her distress into her theatrical role.

"I should've known better than to trust you with anything," Adrienne snarls, following Irvette's lead.

"No use in wasting time hurling insults," I scoff, eyeballing a large patch of dark evergreens lining the perimeter of the cathedral. "If we cut through the woods, we can likely catch up to that crone downtown and purchase new ones and make it back here before missing the start of the ritual."

After earning a handful of snickers and eye rolls from a hoard of unsuspecting onlookers, we venture off the path until we're bathed in the darkness of the woods. To our advantage, the luminescent ember oaks of these woods only grow along the path to the cathedral. The remainder of the woods remain cloaked in a sheet of jet-black night. About gods-damned time, a small tide turns in our favor. We sprint through the darkness until reaching one of the cathedral's towering walls.

"We've got no other choice. I'm counting on you," Adrienne quickly relays down our bond. Within the blink of an eye, she shifts into her large, ghostly raven form.

Irvette's eye widens with bewilderment as she stumbles over her feet several steps backward. "Holy gods!" She exclaims, struggling to catch her startled breath.

"You've never seen Adrienne wield at night?" I ask Irvette with a casual, masked chuckle. *"You'd be surprised what a shadow mage can do when fully immersed in darkness."*

Before Irvette can form a response, Adrienne scoops us up in her massive talons and flies us to the cathedral's roof within a couple of brief, swooping wingbeats. As soon as our boots contact the timber rooftop, The Goddess of the Shadows shifts back into her regular form.

"The sanctuary has to be directly below that skylight," Irvette points out. To my relief, her focus is solely honed on rescuing her betrothed and his dragon rather than questioning Adrienne's sudden shapeshifting. We carefully tiptoe to the skylight and lower our bodies against the lattice woodwork to reduce the risk of detection.

Dense crowds spill into empty the pews below. We scan the rows of pews and heavily congested crowds searching for the sanctuary's altar. Adrienne covers Irvette's mouth, muffling her scream, and my stomach twists into matted knots the moment we find it.

Fieryn's lifeless body lies sprawled out across a massive, dragon-sized altar in a pool of fresh, shiny blood. Lying limp across her neck is Felix's drained, unconscious body, along with six other bodies— the spies he set out to organize. They all lay lifeless across the altar as elders fill gauntlets with their blood and spill it into a massive cauldron.

The sound of Irvette's tears splashing onto the stained glass and the cheers of the congregants below claw into my heart and shred it to smithereens. Adrienne and I throw ourselves around Irvette, working together to stifle her trembling and reel her under control. Attempting to assess the situation proves far more difficult when also actively working to prevent an outburst of a sudden, onset monsoon.

"I promise, I want you to unleash hurricanes and drown the sanctuary out in white-capped rapids," Adrienne whispers to Irvette. "However, Felix won't stand a chance if we strike impulsively. There are only three of us, and thousands of blood mages gathered below. Spare your rage just a few moments longer," she orders in a tone equally blended with authority and empathy.

A blood mage adorned in scarlet robes and heavily layered necklaces ascends the dais to the center of the altar. "Welcome, Crystal Bay, to The Night of the Smierc!" The choir concludes their ancient death chants as the crowd responds with roaring applause. "It is my honor to reveal the prophecy given to me by our father, Osiris. The God of Death is gifting us a new soldier bearing great power. You may have already noticed a shift in the energy stirring in the air this evening," The mage pauses. She allows another wave of applause and gasps in awe and speculation, growing intoxicated by the rising anticipation flooding the sanctuary.

"Yes, yes. There is much to be excited about tonight," she reigns in control of the room. "A handful of our new soldiers have already been released into our atmosphere. Until our gathering, your elders have kept it a secret. You have the lives of the six half-mortal swine on the altar to thank for the successful release of our first six soldiers. Now, you are all invited to witness the harvest we are about to reap from our final two sacrifices," she motions her hands toward Felix and Fieryn. "Behold... Crystal Bay's very first Night of the Smierc! When the blood of our enemies is offered to Osiris, hope is birthed from The Dark Realms!" The mage reaches down beneath her robe, untucking a hidden pendant. "Not only are we blessed to have an altar full of sacrifices, but we are also blessed with power from the gods finally in the rightful hands. Behold... the wind luminary!"

Glimpses of radiant silver light blind my vision as the wind luminary is raised with a fist waving in victory. The glass skylight rumbles as the choir reaches for mallets in their robes and begins pounding on large, orchestral drums, accompanying the roaring congregational cheer. "NOW!" Adrienne bellows.

A blast of shadows breaks through the stained glass skylight as Adrienne crashes down to the heart of the sanctuary. Shards of colored glass rain down from the impact, pouring into the pews of stunned congregants. Pounding drums and floods of applause morph into screams. Screams morph into gasping coughs as Adrienne's smoke consumes the entirety of the room.

"Whatever you do, do NOT disrupt the ritual!" The blood mage hollers through the frenzied commotion. Before I can catch my next breath in the midst of the pluming smoke, I hear what sounds like a lance piercing through scaly flesh. A river of blood gushes down the dais, followed by Fieryn's gargling, anguished roar.

"One more sacrifice down. One more remains!" An elder declares.

CHAPTER 33
Felix and Fieryn

"I've got your back. Go!" I shout to Irvette. Bolts of my lightning rain down like fire into the sanctuary, setting pews ablaze in white flames and invoking screams of terror. Words fail to spill from Irvette's lungs as she lets out a guttural scream. Her eye ignites like an emerald pyre as she she leaps through the shattered skylight, riding colossal waves that transform the sanctuary into a room filled with smoke, fire, and raging rapids.

Thick, pendulant ropes form in Adrienne's smoke, providing me with my infiltration route. I leap through the broken skylight and slide down the shadowy tendrils until I find myself breastbone-deep in Irvette's raging waters. Not what I was expecting.

"I'm not going to be able to strike anyone as long as you and Irvette are also in these waters, or we're all toast," I relay to Adrienne.

A massive wave crashes over my head, thrusting me beneath the surface before I'm given a chance to hold my breath. Rapid-firing currents send me tumbling head over heels, spinning and flailing through the sanctuary as my lungs burn for air. With a stroke of luck, another wave crashes into me, slamming me into a colossal pillar. Adrenaline propels my arms and legs as I inch my body up the marble-smooth column. Dense, smoky air fills into my lungs as my head emerges from the waves.

"There's no reasoning with Irvette right now. I'm going to need you to swim for the dais and reach Felix before he's swept off the altar. I'm currently handling the mage bitch," Adrienne tells me.

Even with my heightened sense of vision, it's almost impossible to distinguish more than faint silhouettes of any figure that isn't right in front of my face. I scan hoards of blood mages firing aimless attacks, bodies tumbling through the water, and finally glimpse the stairs of the dais. Terror and smoke fill my lungs as I take a deep breath and leap back into Irvette's rapids.

"Find the half-mortals and sever their spines!" A low, livid voice roars within a proximity that raises the hairs on the back of my neck. Monstrous waves form into fists, grabbing onto congregants and throwing their bodies out the windows with devastating force. There's no way Irvette will be able to discern me from the others in the blinding haze. I need to make it to the altar before finding myself in the next wave of her victims. Gods, how is it even possible for a cathedral to be so massive?

"Our eldest sister mage is gone! Summon the raven-griffins! Do not abandon your ritual posts! I repeat…do not abandon your ritual posts. Hold your ground!" Another voice roars out.

Ice scuttles down my spine as blaring blowing horns reverberate through the sanctuary. We're good as dead the moment those raven griffins arrive and sniff us out of the darkness. Minutes left to pull this off. Perhaps only seconds based on whatever soldiers will be summoned along with the raven-griffins.

A massive wave rolls in behind me, and I fill my lungs with another large breath of suffocating, obsidian air. I'm swept beneath its relentless force, tumbling through the sanctuary as if I were flying. Debris from broken pews slams into my sides, nearly knocking out my dwindling reserves of precious oxygen. Heartbeats later, I'm spit out onto the steps of the dais. My teeth sink into my tongue as my chin collides with the hard, marble steps, but I couldn't be more relieved to finally hoist my entire body out of the water.

"Forgive us for the intrusion, Father of Redemption. Bless us with the means to fight back. Raise up your smiercs, oh, God of Death," the elders now pray in the common tongue, as if in too much of a hurry to risk blotching the ancient language.

I follow the prayers of the elders, carefully weaving behind them and sticking to where the plumes of Adrienne's smoke are at their thickest. Felix's slow, lethargic pulse guides me the rest of the way to his body until my hands find wet, broken flesh. My hope begins to diminish as his lungs sound to be mostly filled with fluid. His ribs, cracked, bruised, and broken everywhere my hands press down. His chest barely rises and falls as the beats of his heart grow fewer and farther between.

"I need you to stay with me while we let my magic work. Do you think you can do that for me?" My throat bobs as pools of white light engulf my hands. The sight of Fieryn's body at his side pierces my heart with frozen daggers and slams it to the pit of my stomach. To witness a creature as sacred as a dragon, deceased and drained of its blood upon an altar for Osiris electrifies every nerve in my body with ferocity I can hardly afford to contain.

Blood spills from Felix's mouth as he coughs, reeling in my focus. My rage is useless unless I can channel it to heal him first. "Stay with me, Felix. You think you can do that?"

His icy, blood-soaked fingers lightly twitch in my hands in response to my words. "I can work with that," I tell him as I attempt to steady my shaky breathing. "Irvette is expecting you to escort her to the Eleodora Ball. The two of you will be getting married once we're on the other side of this war," I choke as tears sting my cheeks. I may be able to heal his body, but there is nothing I'll be able to do to mend the Fieryn-sized void that will be left in his heart.

Despite my magic bathing Felix in white, healing light, he's hardly responsive. A scorching blast of crimson flame erupts from the cauldron as if summoned to disrupt my efforts. No. No. I need more time. This cannot be happening now.

"Raise us your smiercs, oh God of Death!" The elder mages chant.

Ear-splintering shrieks respond to their incantations, shattering what little stained glass remains as pairs of colossal wings break free of the flames. Felix spits up another pool of blood. The last glint of light drains from his fiery eyes as they darken with looming death.

"Stay with me, Felix, stay with me!" I sob. No. My healing magic cannot have limitations. Not here. Not now. I will not allow death to rip him from our squad. From Irvette.

"Adrienne! Can you stop this! Can you get us out of here somehow? I'm losing him, please!"

A storm of raven-griffins crash into the cathedral before I can focus on Adrienne's response. It's just her and Irvette against a sanctuary of thousands as I fail to stabilize Felix. Now, we're doomed to be plucked out of our hiding and likely offered as the next sacrifice.

"Lumithra! Help!"

Our bond is still hopelessly severed. Hopefully, by now, our dragons at least suspect we've found ourselves deeply, royally fucked.

Irvette. Where in the realms is Irvette? Panic settles in as the waves and currents flooding the sanctuary begin receding. Either she's burning out, or she's already been plucked by a raven-griffin and suffering blood mage torture.

"I can't heal Felix and we can't hold our own anymore. Any sign of Irvette? Arden? Zephyr? Anyone?" I ask Adrienne as the last flickers of hope wilt in my heart like crumbling roses.

"Negative." Adrienne's response is short and breathless down our bond. *"Amira...Felix can't endure the loss of Fieryn in his condition. There is no bringing him back even with the magic of a full-fledged goddess. He's gone."* Her breathing is labored as she sustains the veil of darkness cloaking the sanctuary while likely taking on hoards of blood mages single-handedly.

Felix's faint pulse is no longer detectable. My healing lights diminish beyond my control as an ethereal, ember light takes over. I summon my magic to return to the palms of my hands, but it does not answer. A brief spark of fire flashes in his eyes as his expression of anguish relaxes to a restful peace. Somehow, I know Solaris is holding the gates of Niroshen open, greeting him as he departs from The Mortal Realms. No. No. Not again. I refuse to lose another comrade. Not again.

"Felix! Please! Come back, come back, come back!"

"Amira! NOW!" Adrienne roars.

Two winged, wraith-like creatures fly out of the flaming cauldron. Every muscle in my body stiffens as the elders bow before them, praising Osiris. Their heads lower to the soaking wet altar as fresh blood seeps into the hoods of their robes. "Behold! Our sacred soldiers, the smiercs!" They cheer. The two creatures, the smiercs, expand their dark, feathery wings as they let out deafening shrieks. I strain my neck in an attempt to glimpse their faces, dizzied as I gaze into their towering height. Their faces appear as endless voids of pitch-darkness, resembling a spitting image of the God of Death.

My stomach pitches as penetrating talons dig into my shoulders from behind. My feet depart from the ground, and I find myself flying through the sanctuary as the smiercs leap from the cauldron and disappear from my peripheral. Flashes of violet, ember, and sapphire tint my vision as the talons sink deeper and deeper into my flesh.

"En route to the dungeon with a prisoner," a voice bellows from above. I attempt to call upon my magic, but it fails to answer. My arms tingle like infinite stabbing needles are infiltrating them until they go completely numb. My flailing, dangling legs stiffen like statues as I'm flown through the sanctuary by the talons of a raven griffin.

"Adrienne!" I scream down our bond. She answers in her dragon form, charging after my captor with obsidian wings outstretched and the blinding light of a silver gemstone strung around her neck. The raven griffin's talons start scraping down my shoulders, tearing out pieces of my flesh as Adrienne's roar erupts in waves of cataclysmic thunder.

"Do not drop her!" The deep, animalistic voice coming from above me hollers as I feel myself slowly slipping from the raven griffin's clutches. Pain radiates through my nerves like burning blades as I attempt to thrash free, ripping out more skin with each flailing kick.

"I'm about to get you out of this, and it's going to hurt. Brace yourself," Adrienne warns with another thunderous growl.

My eyelids slam shut as I await to be snatched from the piercing talons dragging down the length of my shoulders, digging into my muscles. Adrienne lets out a bone-shattering roar but fails to grab hold of me. I open my eyes to the sight of hundreds of raven griffins hot on her trail. She latches onto one with her jet-black fangs and hurls it into the frenzied horde. By the time she whips her head back in my direction, she's flanked between two death-lusting smiercs, carnally eager to serve The God of Death. They lunge for The Goddess of the Shadows, joined by an army of seething raven griffins as an arrow lodges into my thigh.

"Adrienne!" Through my fading consciousness, I glimpse her disappear under a plume of smoke, facing the weight of her father's lethally forged soldiers alone.

CHAPTER 34
Dungeons and Demons

"Once a failure, always a failure. Give me one good reason I shouldn't carve you up and feed you to the wolves." Rhydian's voice raises the hairs on the nape of my neck as they graze against the blade of his sword. "Blackthorn's most prolific arsonist is now gods know where because you let his men bind you in a burning barn and leave you for dead. To think I chose to save your sorry ass over pursuing our bounty."

Rhydian spits into my fresh burn wounds, and I flinch at the sting of his saliva. He unsheathes his blade and carves it into my back, torturously slow and controlled. My smoke-filled lungs, unable to scream or pray to the gods to release my soul from my body-turned prison.

"For a bitch with a heart as hard as a stone, you're a damn coward," Rhydian hisses as he cuts his blade back into my blistering burns. Tears stained with my failures sting my cheeks as I choke through the pain.

"Your little friend Celene would still be here if you didn't choke up like a defenseless fawn. I might have chosen to spare her as a reward for your courage." Another slash into my burning back. "Casimir would still be here if the two of you grew enough of a pair to run away. You could've fled to Helia together." Another searing slice of his blade. "And Felix," Rhydian spits, "would still be here if you didn't waste all that precious time fighting that rygor."

This has to be a dream. There has to be a way out. Celene, Casimir, and Felix's corpses stand bloodied and battered behind Rhydian as he continues driving his blade down the length of my back. The sharp precision of his sword spreads pain like a plague until I am one with my pain. Until I no longer have the slightest damn clue who I even am.

"Will you ever learn to control your demons? Or will you always cower before them and drag collateral failures with you? What good is gods-given magic, what good is manipulating forces of nature if you're nothing more than a coward who can't even steer the reins?" Rhydian aims his blade at my neck, and I brace myself to meet my end.

Instead of Rhydian severing the head from my body, I jolt awake and return to consciousness. Dream. Just a dream. However thin the veil may now be between dreams and reality, it was just a damn dream.

* * *

My lungs thirst for a full breath as I'm aroused to the confines of a prison cell with a glowing, violet arrow still lodged into my thigh. Failing to save Felix, Fieryn, and their task force was not a dream but very much a harsh, waking hell. I look down and find my wrists and ankles bound by violet shackles, reeking of rotten flesh and blood.

From the scent of burning blood seeping into my cell and the semi-distant screeching smiercs and raven griffins, this cell has to be located in the cathedral's dungeons. I wasn't taken far. Adrienne and Irvette have to be near. They have to still be alive. My chest tightens with hyperventilating breaths as I pray to the dragons they're somehow still alive.

"Adrienne? Lumithra?"

Silence. abysmal, heart-shattering silence.

For the first time since my magic fully awakened in the Kanoelani, I'm unable to detect the slightest trace of its existence within me. Its absence feels like a missing limb. Breathing no longer feels natural and autonomous without it. Even if I can somehow manage to dislodge the arrow from my thigh, the violet glow of my shackles tells me I won't be getting access to Kallik's light anytime soon. To be cut off from Lumithra, unable to reach Adrienne, and blocked from my magic all at once feels as if my soul has been ripped out of my rib cage, marred to sparse threads, and scattered in front of me on the prison floor.

"Irvette!" I call out, praying to the dragons she's somewhere within these cells rather than dead. Silence.

"Adrienne!"

Agonizing, soul-splintering silence. If anything has happened to them, I will stop at nothing until every damned servant of Osiris is fried into ashen remnants of the parasitic roaches they are even if it burns me out to total depletion. Nothing will remain of this cathedral other than piles of charred bones and rubble if another heart of our squad is no longer beating.

"Keep her alive long enough to get what we need, then I don't care how you end her after that," a voice echoes from somewhere within the darkened, damp corridors. "Oh, and be sure to collect her bloodshed. We need all the half-mortal blood we can obtain for future rituals."

Sweat trickles from my temples as I fight against my shackles, calling upon magic that fails to answer. I scream for it with my soul, desperate to get the realms out of here before confronting my death sentence. Perhaps this is the fate I deserve for all the horrors I've enabled through cowardly submitting to Rhydian's authority as one of his prized ghost assassins. For the decades spent watching children turned mercenaries burn on the pyres without ever rising to challenge him and avenge their deaths.

"Tonight's ritual has been full of many, many, little surprises." A sentry approaches my cell, clothed head to toe in black armor. A mask marked with the runes of Osiris conceals his face as he rattles a long, barbed chain at his sides.

My stomach clenches as the door to my cell slams shut, locking him in with me. His breath reeks of alcohol, causing me to flinch upon instinct.

"You cooperate with me, and your death will be swift and painless. You give me trouble," he chuckles, rattling the barbed chain once more, "I'll drag out your suffering as if you had all eternity."

My muscles stiffen, and the scars upon my back burn in response to the haunting familiarity of his voice. I'm awake. Reality is a nightmare, but I'm awake. This isn't a dream.

"One more thing. Don't bother wasting our time attempting to wield any of your…new tricks. I'm sure you've learned by now that those chains you're wearing are laced with magic blockers. You've always been quite the fast learner." My blood turns cold. I fumble in my chains and dig my nails into the palm of my hand. This can't be real.

"Always such a damn, pitiful coward. I'll give you credit, though. Never thought I'd see cross over Blackthorn's borders." The stench of foul, bitter ale nearly takes me out as the sentry twirls a strand of my hair between his fingers after dropping his barbed flog. "What happened to that lovely dark hair of yours?" His words send currents of ice rippling down my spine as he pulls his blade from its sheath, pressing it up against my throat. "Tell me now, what good was involving yourself in the affairs of the knights without me, Amira?"

Rhydian.

Rhydian, the sentry beneath the dark mask of runes. Rhydian, holding me captive in the depths of an Eldermoorian cathedral, donning the crimson robe of the blood mages. He lifts his mask just long enough to flash me a sinister, twisted smirk. His crooked smirk is familiar yet unrecognizable all at once. Flecks of blood-red now overtake most of his once tawny, beady eyes.

"Was my company not enough for you? Did you grow tired of our numbers thinning out every day?" Rhydian presses his blade against my throat, laughing as I choke. "Damn pity you couldn't save your invaluable emissary. Felix, right? The High Priestess will have difficulty finding a candidate worthy of replacing him," he laughs.

"However, I can't thank you enough for letting him and his dragon spill their blood for our cause. Oh yeah, and his little task force, of course. You all played a pivotal role in fulfilling Osiris's demands for us. Your failure is our bountiful treasure. Our smiercs will ensure Eldermoor cleanses all The Mortal Realms with its righteous authority." Rhydian sheathes his blade and picks his barbed flog from the floor.

My bones shiver. How long has Rhydian had his sights set on Eldermoor? Was he planning on forcing me to join him along his new path? Would I have accepted my new fate as easily as I accepted becoming a dragon knight, or would I have finally fought back? Based on the amount of crimson flooding his irises, he must have made Osiris very pleased with his servitude regardless of how much time he spent in premeditation.

"Bold of you to betray the nation of knights that supplied your wealth," I scoff. "Was all that silver and gold not good enough for you? Or did you just realign your allegiance to the side you believe will win this holy war in your unending thirst for power?"

"Enough!" Rhydian whips the flog across my back. Barbed spikes sink into my tendons, pulling out pieces of my flesh as he yanks it out of me with brutal force. The wind knocked from lungs stifles my scream as his eyes beam with satisfaction from beneath his mask.

"Who's the true pitiful coward then? Who still stands for Blackthorn? For Elmoria?" I snarl through sharp, burning pain as the warmth of my blood trickles down the length of my back.

"You have much to learn, child!" Rhydian seethes. "A nation divided by the worship of countless gods is a nation that will fail. A nation unified under one god, however, can spread justice and prosperity to all. The more I paid attention to the way those damn half-mortals talked about the luminaries, the more I began realizing I'd been wasting precious time serving the wrong gods. Niroshen's blessings are limited to those born of their sacred blood. Osiris extends his blessings generously. He gifts the lowborn humans who seek to worship him with the power to wield blood. A world unified under Osiris would know no divides in power. All would be equal in our Father's eyes."

Wildfires of heat devour my skin, consuming me from the inside out. He robbed me of my childhood, my companions, my peace. He trained me, marred me, molded me into a cursed, calloused weapon. And now, he seeks to see the world bathed in the waters of an authoritarian, sadistic god—a god who promises blessings of great power to all who administer his dark gospel.

"Are you delusional? What possible prosperity do you believe The God of Death would grant Elmoria? Tell me…has he even made you a blood mage yet? How many tricks must you learn before he throws you that bone?" Each word comes out broken and winded through my tightened chest and trembling limbs, searing in bloodied anguish.

As if growing bored with my condition of suffering, Rhydian lashes his flog into my back once more. My hands and knees give out from under me as my stomach collapses into the pool of my blood. My magic still refuses to so much as flicker in response.

The damn bastard captain. Haunting me like a plague, spreading through my dreams and following me to the ends of the earth. To think of all the threats I would encounter in this war as a dragon knight, encountering Rhydian in the flesh has been far from those thoughts. The moment I woke up thousands of feet above the ground on Sarthon's back, I thought I'd never find myself in his clutches again.

"It doesn't have to be like this, Amira. If you choose to cooperate with me, perhaps I can plead a case with the elders to spare you. They welcomed me with welcome arms, after all. I'll warm you up to the deal with the offer of a little intel."

Out of not being ready to endure another lashing, I remain silent. Without having anything left in me to strategize a way out of this rationally, I give a firm nod in agreement. Playing the role of submission he is so accustomed to seeing from me might at least give me the moment of respite I need to cling to my survival.

"Not at all surprised to see you give up so easily," he scoffs. "Now that I have my favorite dog back at my side, you'll get a kick out of this. The only luminary we haven't had the slightest clue how to track is the shadow luminary. Our forces thought we may have sensed a lead on Tourmaline Beach, but now, we know the shadow luminary lies within this cathedral. What a coincidence our smiercs alerted every blood mage in the sanctuary of its proximity the same night you and your knights show up, is it not? Something tells me you know exactly where we might be able to find it. Tell me, and I remove your chains. We'll plead your case before the elders. You will live to see the next sunrise and fight on the side of victory."

"Tell me you're safe. Please!" I scream for Adrienne.

Fear strikes dissonant chords in my blood at the thought of Adrienne bearing the shadow luminary beneath her skin, as well as the wind luminary, fighting against Osiris's forces all alone without a trace of Irvette. A battle between gods, with one of them fighting behind the force of an entire army.

Silence still floods our bond. I have got to find a way out of this. Now.

"Something tells me you've already forgotten my stubbornness so easily, captain. Tell me, Rhydian, what pleasure do I possibly owe to the gluttonous roach who ruined my life?" I spit my blood at his feet. Never again will I give the bastard captain what he wants. Never, will I ever sell Adrienne's secrets to a single soul, no matter the cost. If it means death, then Adrienne's secrets will follow my body to the goblet upon the altar and fade away with my draining blood.

"Perhaps you need a little more convincing." The barbed spikes lash into my back once more, flooding every nerve in my body with excruciating hell. My chest feels as if it's being crushed under the dead weight of a mighty stag as I can barely fill my lungs with air. Never again.

Never again, will I give Rhydian what he wants, even as my blood loss is turning my skin ice cold. Even as I feel my pulse weakening, my vision dizzying, and my breathing growing rapidly shallow.

"Oh, this is much more enjoyable than torturing you with my blade like the good ol' times," Rhydian chuckles. "Come on, Amira. We haven't been apart that long. Have you so soon forgotten I am the one in control?" He drives the flog into my flesh once more, solidifying his message.

"I don't like having to repeat myself. Tell me, child, where might we find the shadow luminary?"

I close my eyes and brace myself for the next flogging, re-living realms of nightmares over and over again as I wonder when the spikes will make contact with my bones. How much more will my body allow me to endure before Kallik comes to greet me at Niroshen's gates?

"I know you've learned by now that I don't make threats. I make promises." Rhydian delivers a bludgeoning kick to my head as I begin choking on the blood spilling from my mouth, clinging to my consciousness by a single frayed thread.

"You tell me what you know about the whereabouts of the shadow luminary, and we get you all stitched up. Fail to come clean, and I promise Amira, I'll flog your soul right out of your body." Rhydian steps on my chest, the sound of my ribs cracking drowning out my faint screams.

I'm sorry, Adrienne.

Tears stream down my blood-stained cheeks upon recalling what little I know of the deal between her and Osiris. With The God of Death unable to claim my soul for The Dark Realms, Niroshen is guaranteed to be my final resting place. The realm eternally forbidden to Adrienne. Finding myself on the brink of our eternal separation hurts far, far worse than any torture Rhydian could possibly administer.

"I'm sorry, Casimir. I am unable to fight any longer."

As long as Adrienne remains the eternal defender of the shadow luminary, Blackthorn and Helia will still have a fool's shot at standing against Eldermoor's rising power. Never again, will I ever give Rhydian what he wants. I fought for hope until the end.

Expecting to enter the gates of Niroshen, the bars to my cell shatter like broken glass as a raging force of shadows barrels through the dungeons. Through my foggy, color-stained vision, Rhydian's barbed flog violently rips free from his white-knuckled grasp. Storms of shadows whirl faster than my mind can process, wrapping the flog around his torso as tight as a tourniquet. The barbs wielded against me just heartbeats ago are now penetrating through the armor over his robes and sinking into his flesh.

"Nobody, and I mean *nobody*, touches my woman." Adrienne's eyes glow like the burning ring of a solar eclipse as she appears like a ghost at the entrance of my cell. Smoky, serpentine tendrils coil around the tangled flog as Rhydian's screams resonate through the dungeons. Another wave of tendrils wraps around my shackles, crushing them to oblivion. Once I'm broken free of my chains, the tendrils rip the violet arrow out of my thigh. Piercing sharp pain from the extraction radiates down my leg as shadows tightly wrap around my wound, preventing more precious blood from draining from my body.

Light as bright as the moon quickly blankets my wounds, bringing soothing relief to the excruciating pain burning every inch of my body. The flow of my magic returning much more rapidly than anticipated hardly feels real. Magic doesn't just instantaneously return the moment it's freed from suppressive poisons. Adrienne was up against two smiercs and an army of raven griffins in her dragon form in the heart of the sanctuary. There's no way it's actually her, standing firm and unscathed at the entrance of my cell, appearing like an unrivaled goddess.

"Not even the armies of the gods can keep me from crawling through all the hells of all the realms in order to reach you," she seethes.

Adrienne's shadows drive the barbed flog tangled around Rhydian's bloodied ribs deeper and deeper. Striking into flesh and bone like an axe to a mine of precious gems. His blood flows like a river as the serpentine shadows twist around his neck and drop him to the ground.

"The wage of treason against your nation is death," Adrienne growls as turbulent, obsidian smoke roars through the dungeon. The clicking of her boots against the stone-cold concrete serves as the cadence of a lethal death sentence. "Typically, treason is punishable by execution in front of The High Priestess. Then, the fate of your soul's final resting place is left for the gods to decide," she smirks. Blood spews from Rhydian's mouth as he thrashes on the ground.

"The wage of child endangerment, abuse, the wage of decades spent torturing my love, is an eternity I get to decide," Adrienne seethes. Her silver irises, possessed by eclipse-like orbs of glowing onyx. Adrienne stomps on Rhydian's chest, his bones cracking beneath the weight of her boot.

"You'll soon learn how fruitless your worship to Osiris truly was as your soul learns eternal torment in The Dark Realms. You'll soon learn how he treats those who submit to his will but fail to advance the works of his kingdom." The darkness of Adrienne's tone is nearly unrecognizable. Her tone is that of an ancient goddess, filled with centuries of rage.

"This kill belongs to you," Adrienne summons me through our bond.

"Thank you, love. I'll take it with pleasure," I respond without hesitation.

It takes every molecule of strength to push through my pain to bring myself to stand. A blanket of white lights still working on mending my wounds. Never again. Never again will Rhydian prey on the vulnerable. Never again will he forge orphans into tortured, stone-cold weapons.

With every healing bone, rattling to my core, lightning dancing at the tips of my fingers, I march toward the bastard captain one last time. Never again will I freeze under the weight of his manipulation.

Rhydian flails and thrashes under the weight of Adrienne's crushing force like a predator of the seas beached on the shoreline. I take one last look in the eyes of the insatiable beast. My lightning morphs into the shape of a giant sword, charged and ready to wield death upon my parasite.

"Never again will I find myself a slave to your authority. Never again will fear be my master. I am in control of my magic. I am in control of my light."

In perfect control over the divine magic within me, I swing my lightning blade down upon Rhydian's chest, executing him in a blast of white, electrifying flame. No threat of my wild magic bucking free of my reins. Adrienne stands unthreatened by my raw power at my side unharmed. My light remains fixated on reclaiming my scarred, fear-driven heart to my authority.

The storm of shadows lashing behind Adrienne recedes as she stoops down to Rhydian's remains of ash and bones. "As Goddess of the Shadows, I commend this soul lingering between realms to enter through the gates of The Kingdom of Death. I hereby sentence this soul to an eternity of slavery to Osiris."

The dark, dense energy ruling the dungeons of the cathedral feels slightly lightened the instant Rhydian's soul enters through the gates of The Dark Realms. The eclipse-like glow behind Adrienne's eyes return to silver as she grabs my hand in silence.

Gone. Rhydian is finally gone. Adrienne catches me as my knees buckle, and I collapse into her arms. Swelling waves of shock, outrage, and fatigue knock me off my feet, hitting me with the force of a typhoon. Its gales so overwhelming, my body is unable to break out in the heavy sobs I desperately need to release. The liberation of closure and the remnants of his legacy that will forever haunt me latch onto me as if trying to tear my body in two.

"Every corridor has been cleared," a dark, flat voice echoes through the dungeon. Swearing I'm hearing Irvette's voice abruptly disrupts the flow of my thoughts. Relief floods my chest as Irvette emerges from the labyrinth of prison cells. Her aquamarine braids matted in blood, her black dress torn to shreds matching my own. A hurricane in the form of a half-mortal, drenched in the blood of the enemies who found themselves in her trajectory of destruction.

"Thank gods you're alright," my voice breaks as I run up and throw my arms around her. I'm so sorry, I want to tell her. The words fail to escape my mouth as if the moment I say them out loud is the moment we have to fully accept Felix is gone. His name is now forged in the scrolls of Niroshen. No amount of love, soul-shattering agony, or gods-given power can bring him back. Felix is gone, yet I still can't bring myself to accept it within the walls of this damned, godsforsaken cathedral. Not here. Anywhere but here.

"No sign of our own anywhere within these halls," Irvette mutters. Her arms dangle limply at her sides as she breaks away from my embrace. The currents of fire that once rippled fiercely through her eye are absent. Her expression is blank and distant as if half of her heart and soul have drifted off to another realm.

Our brief, somber reunion is interrupted by a screeching choir of raven griffins shaking the ground beneath our feet. "That's not coming from the sanctuary this time," Adrienne hisses as she clutches the wind luminary around her neck. An eruption of shrill, wraith-like screeches comes next. Smiercs.

"We need to get the realms out of here. Now."

Clouds of dust and rocks pour down from the stone ceiling above as we sprint down the halls. Any hope of detecting possible escape routes along the seemingly countless passageways diminishes with our declining visibility. My stomach drops as the walls begin rumbling like an earthquake. "Any idea what's going on?" I shout, immediately regretting opening my mouth as I inhale blankets of dust.

"Cathedrals weren't built to be battlefields," Adrienne shouts. "Stop!" A thick barrier of shadows appears in front of Irvette and me, cutting us off from running any further.

The ceiling caves in, bringing down massive chunks of stone and debris, spewing down like a landslide. My heart skips several beats realizing we would've been crushed to oblivion had we taken another step forward. "We could really use an earth mage right now," I yell, coughing up dust from my lungs. With the path before us now obstructed by a mountain of rubble, we're left with no other choice than to stand our ground against our rapidly approaching enemies.

Splintering pain shoots through my temples as the shrill screeches sound like they're now just a few swooping talon grabs away. "Prepare to fight," Adrienne orders.

My limbs tremble with exhaustion as magic courses through my veins, charging my skin with an electrifying burn nearly too agonizing to withstand. None of us are exactly in a position to be wielding more bouts of divine power after the immense forces we've already exerted. Yet we plant our stances firmly, bracing ourselves to fight for hope against the darkness closing in on us.

Adrienne throws up a wall of shadows to throw off the blood mages as slews of raven griffins flood toward us in a carnal frenzy. Thunderous booms and crackles roar under the mountain of rubble behind us as it quakes like a volcano. Whatever is on the other side is about to hit us with the force of an explosion.

"HIT THE FLOOR! HIT THE FLOOR!" Adrienne shouts.

We drop to the floor, shielding our necks from large, projectile stones missing us by the hairs on our hands. Raven griffins and blood mages drop like flies on the ground beside us as Adrienne works to deflect them from crushing us beneath their weight. A flash of green scales flies overhead, catching my attention as Hyrix plows through the flying debris. Arden orchestrates the flow of the stones, slamming them into Eldermoor's forces. Zephyr and Sylphira trail close behind Hyrix, followed by Lumithra, Sarthon, Tsuna. Next, fly in our wind mages and a battalion of Helian pegasus knights.

CHAPTER 35
The Retreat

Lumithra scoops me from the debris-laden floor and hurls me atop her back. The relief of our reunification provides me with a jolting surge of adrenaline that helps me fumble into my saddle. Warmth swells in my heart as I lower myself to embrace her, ignoring the protests of my throbbing muscles.

"Where in the realms have you been?" I ask with tears streaming down my cheeks as we barrel through the dungeons, blasting through stone walls with Helia's forces now in our midst.

"Much to explain, my child," Lumithra rumbles as she makes a hard bank to deflect a volley of arrows. *"We were delayed by a handful of smiercs not long after we parted ways."* Her voice sounds shaky, as if she is clenching her fangs to breathe through waves of pain.

My blood turns to ice upon noticing massive chunks of Lumithra's opal, shimmering white scales caked in thick blood stains. The scent of fresh blood still seeping from her flesh throws my heart out of its rhythm. Her wingbeats sound forced and labored rather than the strong, steady cadence I've grown accustomed to.

"You need to let me heal you."

"No time for that now. Our sole objective is to lose this swarm and retreat. Healing will have to wait. For the first time in the existence of dragons, we finally encountered a foe who matched our strength tonight. If It weren't for Arden and Zephyr summoning Helia's aid, we very well might have met our end," she winces.

"Prepare for impact!" Arden bellows from the frontlines of our forces before I can respond to Lumithra.

"It sounds like he found a weak spot in the foundation to strike. Brace yourself," Lumithra growls, blood trickling down her scales. *"We're getting out of here."*

The White Empress remains a steady force amidst the explosion of stones blasting through the vulnerable wall with catastrophic force. Zephyr and the wind mages shield us from the impact as we leave the dungeon behind in the crumbling dust.

My stomach rises to my throat as Lumithra makes a swift, steep ascension into the star-kissed sky. I call my healing magic to my fingertips, inviting my light to tend to her wounds.

"You're spending your magic foolishly," she roars in protest.

"Based on your level of blood loss, I'd argue it's magic well spent," I counter.

Eldermoor's poison-filled arrows ricochet off wind mage shields as hoards of raven griffins collide with Pegasus Knights high above the ember oak trees. Fiery, winged horses glow like diamonds in the night sky as their riders return Eldermoor's fire through compromised portions of the shields.

"Behind you!" Adrienne warns.

The cry of the smiercs tear through the atmosphere like a knife slashing through linen. The air suddenly becomes denser, as if their very presence suffocates the life around them. Once again, breathing has been turned into a strenuous sport.

Bolts of lightning release from my fists and chase down the winged wraith-like servants of death looming behind us. The damned smiercs evade each and every bolt thrown their way. Blast after blast of preciously spent power, wasted on their swift evasions.

"Any idea how to land a strike against these damned things?" I ask Lumithra.

Silence. Those damned creatures must be clouding our bond again.

Fighting without the flow of battle wisdom from The White Empress is a crutch I cannot afford while fighting against a brand new force of darkness unlike any Elmoria has ever seen.

The smiercs fly toward us, ripping right through walls of dragon fire as if the blazing flames are nothing more than clouds of mist. Lumithra darts across the sky, weaving her body like a thread through a needle in desperation to throw the smiercs off our trail. I grab a dagger from my bandolier tucked under my shredded cloak and aim for the long, bony claws that are now dangerously close to grabbing hold of her tail. My blade manages to strike the claw of a smierc as it shrieks in anger. I duck just in time before it launches a flying lance that nearly makes a clean slice through my skull.

Their dark, ghostly frames make them nearly impossible to spot against the inky night sky. Deadly, invisible predators. No more senseless deaths tonight. I shoot a beacon of white, electrical flame up into the sky, praying the beam will be received as a warning signal to our allies— to guide the trajectory of our forces' retreat.

A sea of pegasus knights comes flying to my aid as if answering my signal rather than evading it. No. "No! No! Turn back, turn back!" My chest tightens, and my lungs seize as I attempt to yell through the suffocating thickness swallowing the air.

Bone-shattering shrieks rattle the stars as the smeircs hurl endless volleys of lances. My heart sinks to the ground below as they effortlessly forge weapons out of their magic and wield them in the same way mages wield the elements. Death flies across the sky in hundreds of sharp lances as cries of stricken knights turn my blood cold. Pegasus Knights continue rushing into the lethal smierc storm, soaring like blazing comets refusing to burn out without an unyielding fight.

Rather than retreating from the frenzy, they continue charging into it, shouting prayers to Aisling, Goddess of Illusions. Prayers, screeches, and screams of the dying throw my head into a violent whirlwind as thousands of large, white moths light up the sky like ghostly apparitions. Their wings produce rapid-firing, strobing lights as they swarm the smiercs, flying directly into their faces.

"Helia's Knights can manifest Aisling's powers?" I exclaim to Lumithra in wonder and disbelief, forgetting for a moment that our bond is still clouded.

Pegasus Knights aim their bows toward the half-blinded smiercs, driving arrows into their dark, leathery flesh. Bursts of black blood spill into the sky as they scream in agonizing pain. Thank dragons, Osiris's army of The Dark Realms isn't indestructible after all.

Wraithly screams send invasive chills beneath my skin as the wounded smiercs retaliate with another volley of flying lances. The vile sound of impaled flesh rouses the hairs on the back of my neck as I catch sight of a lance wedged deep into a pegasus' chest. Within a few short heartbeats, the shimmering winged mare's body shrivels like a wilted wildflower. Her muscular frame, filled with life just moments ago, is now nothing but skeletal remains. The power of one smierc lance, enough to destroy its target to withered oblivion. An entire army of smiercs would easily guarantee Eldermoor gaining possession of the luminaries without much of a fight.

The scream of the withered mare's rider plummeting towards the earth coats my veins in boiling rage. Helia's arrows continue to combat against lances laced with death through the blinding swarms of glowing moths while our mages remain gravely outnumbered by our enemies lusting for our blood and luminaries. Each pegasus knight that engages into descent after their free-falling knight, obliterated by smeirc lances. No more losses. Not today.

I reach toward the light of the stars, commanding bolts of my lightning to fall like rain, zapping smierc lances and frying them to ashes. My vision blurs, and weightlessness fights for control over my body, reminding me that my magic can't tolerate much exertion for much longer. Despite the warnings of burnout, that knight will not fall to his death. Not today.

"After him!" I scream to Lumithra.

Lumithra roars and tucks in her wings, plummeting into a nose dive after the free-falling knight plummeting through the ebony clouds. His long, crimson tresses whip through the wind as his body tumbles in an unforgiving descent.

"Damned fools! We need that one alive! After him, you idiots!" A raven griffin's rider roars.

Blurred, watery eyes and muscles weak and trembling, I'm left with no choice but to strike down the raven griffins brazen enough to chase down the falling knight and claim him for their own. Why they're so devoted to taking this knight prisoner rather than dismissing him as a casualty baffles me.

Lumithra picks up speed, interrupting the knight's deadly descent as he crashes into her back. She doesn't even flinch when the knight grabs one of her wounded scales with a death grip, or when his boots dig into her wounded flesh as he gracelessly crawls up her back toward my outstretched hand.

"Hold on!" I command the knight. Bloodied, leather riding gloves grab hold of my shredded, black dress as his hand finally finds mine. Lumithra pulls out of her nose dive, narrowly missing rows of ember oaks as the knight finally finds his balance.

"My-my sincerest gratitude," he stutters in shock. I can't help but chuckle at his stunned expression as he takes in the fact he's aboard the back of a half-mortal's bonded dragon.

"You can thank me if we manage a successful retreat," I shout breathlessly.

"I do not take the honor of being tolerated atop the back of a dragon lightly," he bows. "I'm Sorin. Son of King Ashe."

My eyes widen. "What's the crown prince of Helia doing joining battalions in battles over luminaries?" No wonder those raven griffins were chasing us down so relentlessly.

"Helia grows closer and closer to falling every day," he responds as he draws his bow and plucks off a blood mage with flawless precision. "My father and I refuse to leave this fight to our people. What good is a leader who watches his kingdom bleed from the comfort of the throne?"

"No wonder Lumithra is so tolerant of my passenger," I smirk. "You will make a fine king one day— assuming we make it out of this alive, of course."

"Well…it looks like we're about to gain quite an advantage," Sorin responds in an inquisitive, hopeful tone.

The lights of the treetops below fade to black as pummeling currents of water demolish the ember oaks. Tsuna's phosphorescent blue scales shimmer above the currents as streams of fire blast from her lungs, igniting the darkness. Branches snap like bones as Irvette raises her arms, unleashing an ocean of fury.

"For Felix!" Irvette's lamenting scream coils around my heart and slices it into shards of glass. Her tears become my own as she orchestrates colossal waves to rise above the trees. Her pain saturates every last droplet as hurricane-force white caps stretch to the stars, devouring slews of Eldermoor's forces. Sky turns to ocean as raven griffins and blood mages asphyxiate in torrents of rage.

"Godspeed to Tourmaline!" Adrienne shouts as she emerges with Sarthon through the walls of waves, parted just long enough to let them through. Bathed in enemy blood, the glow of the wind luminary still shines from the chain around her neck. Helia's forces fall into formation along with our own as we make haste for the refuge of Blackthorn's borders.

A Felix-and-Fieryn-sized void sinks into my chest as I turn my head over my shoulder and take in the vacant air space adjacent to Arden and Hyrix. Irvette and Tsuna fill the gap, and I forget how to breathe as our squad adjusts to our smaller formation in silence.

"Their deaths will not be in vain," Adrienne seethes down our bond.

Ominous rumbles of thunder shake the ground below as if an echo of Adrienne's promise. Our attention collectively shifts from Eldermoor drowning in Irvette's aerial waves to the Crystal Bay Cathedral haunting the night sky. Towering walls quake and groan as plumes of dust and smoke seep from the cathedral's rapidly crumbling foundations. Centuries of laborious, perilous construction and Eldermoorian history come crashing down from the clouds in a torrential downpour of stone and glass. Fire bathes the massive mounds of rubble, transforming the demolished cathedral into a funeral pyre of vengeance.

"You didn't think I'd allow their bodies lay confined in the walls of that damned cathedral, did you? I made sure to destroy them. May our comrades rest in triumph," Adrienne declares.

The sense of accomplishment stirring in her somber, silver eyes as she watches the cathedral's spire crash to the ground sends chills of awe and terror down my spine. Adrienne, Goddess of the Shadows, lured hoards of Eldermoor's forces back into the cathedral with the wind luminary as bait before bringing it down on them. Adrienne, Goddess of the Shadows, wielded wrath and darkness to bring down a centuries-old monument sacred to our enemies.

"A cathedral of dark rituals shattered to oblivion in honor of our fallen," her voice breaks in wearied torment. Never again will Adrienne see Felix, as his soul now rests within the gates of Niroshen. The gates forever sealed to her as the cost of her secret, eternal burden. Another cherished soul lost in the collection of loved ones she'll never embrace again. Centuries of loss after loss in an endless, torturous cycle.

Thoughts of Kallik coming to collect my soul for Niroshen one day creep up on me like a blistering fever I am in no condition to fight. Fatigue slams into every aching muscle and bone in relentless, shivering waves as I envision Adrienne one day, holding my lifeless body in her arms. Not even a goddess can alter the inevitable fate of a half-mortal. Love is now the inflicting curse of my mortality.

"Such dreadful thoughts are not serving your mind any fruitful purpose while your body is on the verge of burnout," Lumithra warns. *"Please rest your eyes, Amira. Between myself and the crown prince, we will not let you fall. Rest while you can, child. You will be in no shape to combat the darkness ahead of us if you continue down the path of spiraling."*

The ghost of The Crystal Bay Cathedral weighs down on me like an anchor, ready to drag me to inescapable depths of soul-depleting exhaustion. Lumithra's reins in my blood-stained hands quickly become as heavy as a mighty broadsword. With no energy left to form a coherent response or plummet deeper into my living nightmares, my body slumps against Lumithra's scales as I allow sleep to carry me the rest of our flight.

CHAPTER 36
The Aftermath

Since returning from Crystal Bay, The Blackthorn Monastery has morphed into a bustling infirmary filled with apothecaries tending to the wounds of pegasus knights and their winged mares and stallions. How so many of them managed to endure the flight back to Blackthorn in such critical conditions is nothing short of a miracle. Study halls and corridors have become overcrowded with occupied, blood-soaked cots, and as many medical supplies and elixirs the apothecaries have managed to track down from their supply reserves.

It takes me several full minutes of walking through the triage stations before realizing hundreds of civilians share the cots alongside our injured allies, wounded in yesterday's storm that feels more like ages ago. Conversations regarding squads of dragon knights and ground forces working to clean up debris and tend to damaged structures with restless haste pull me from my jaded trance.

"The High Priestess says Osiris is working against the blessings The Eve of Eleodora brings to Blackthorn. She says Vespera must be restored and ready for the celebrations with no delay," I overhear an apothecary mutter to a mage as they tend to a screaming child with a severely mangled arm.

"In just two days? We'll be lucky if we get through treating even half of our wounded by then. How in the realms are we supposed to restore the city in just two days?" The mage blurts in panic.

The hairs on the back of my neck rise upon overhearing the urgency Lady Rhonwen is placing on redecorating the town in festive marigold and emerald. As blankets cover bodies to be sent to the pyre, I overhear more and more pieces of orders to rebuild lavish altars in time for The Eve of Eleodora. Apparently, not even death can displace The High Priestess's priorities of worshipping the gods.

The reality of The Eve of Eleodora taking place in just two days feels like a hearty punch to the gut. Two days from now, we're expected to don our festive gowns and celebrate the sun and earth gods and goddesses as the monastery opens its doors to the public to spend the day worshiping, feasting, and dancing. Two days from now, we are to dance the night away at the Eleodora Ball and waltz through the weeping wisteria gardens with hearts filled with joy. The thought of appeasing the gods that couldn't bother lending me a hand to save Felix and Fieryn sends bolts of lightning sizzling through my veins.

Finding myself in no mood to mimic the cold apathy of the gods, I redirect the rage coursing through me to assist in healing the wounded. The last thing Adrienne needs to worry about is me frying up the monastery while she's stuck in Crystal Bay debriefing meetings with Prince Sorin and Lady Rhonwen.

"I know you'll ignore my request, but I would like it to be made known anyways that I would prefer it if you rested," Lumithra tugs on our bond.

"I could ask the same of you," I mutter.

"Dragons heal faster than humans and half-mortals. I can also assure you that The High Priestess has healed me sufficiently. The sun will be rising before you even make it to your bed, and I would like to see you resting before then," she growls.

"Right now, I just need to concentrate. I'll rest after every cot is cleared. Unlike the gods, I'm more than happy to intervene in times of distress."

My focus returns to the bloodied knight on the cot before me. The gaping wound in his abdomen sealing under the white lights engulfing my hands. The purple, shriveled flesh surrounding his grazed lance wound slowly returns to the color of healthy, viable skin.

"You're doing great. Your healing is progressing at a promising rate. Can you tell me your name?" I ask, attempting to distract him from as much pain as possible while an apothecary pours an antibiotic elixir directly into his closing wounds.

"Other brothers and sisters of mine were not as lucky as I am," he winces as he grits his teeth.

His words sting like freezing rain as the dark circles under his bloodshot eyes grow heavier before me. The weight of the internal wounds far beyond what I can heal will remain with him for the rest of his life, all because allies who did not know us by name chose to come to our aid.

"I'm sorry for all that you've lost," is all I can say as I avoid making direct eye contact like the plague. How many of his lifelong comrades rushed toward my warning beacon rather than away from it? Bile rises in my throat, wondering how many lives might have been spared had I never lit that warning at all.

"Our losses would've been far more catastrophic if Eldermoor managed to acquire the wind luminary and harvest its power along with those new beasts of theirs," he shudders. "We purchase Elmoria a fighting chance to return to the refuge of peace, one bloody battle at a time. Thank you for patching me up. May the light of justice prevail."

We exchange weak smiles as he brings himself to stand and limps away to seek out his comrades. No point in telling a knight who has lost much during the twilight hours that he should sit still and let the magic fully settle. Not while he's driven by a determination to ensure the deaths of his brothers and sisters won't be in vain.

"I hear you are to credit for saving Helia's crown prince," Arden calls out as he approaches me through the crowds. His black tunic is torn to shreds, revealing fresh scars and bruises across his dirt and blood-stained chest. His wavy, chestnut tresses, matted in dried blood, frame his grief-laden eyes as he places a hand on my shoulder.

Don't credit me for anything when I failed to reach Felix and Fieryn in time, is how I want to reply. However, now is not the time or place to wallow in self-pity.

"I take it you and Zephyr are to credit for summoning Helia's aid in the first place. How did you manage to orchestrate such a grand scheme?" I ask.

"The moment we realized our bonds have been cut off, we knew confronting the ritual relying on our squad alone would turn out to be a death sentence," Arden sighs.

"So, we did what any intellectual half-mortals would do," Zephyr interjects as he catches up with us, matching Arden in bruises and blood stains.

"You didn't happen to notice that poor pegasus mare chained down like some circus prop down at the docks, did you?" He asks with a half-chuckle. "We may or may not have set her free and asked her to find us help. Lucky for us, she flew us right into Helian Battalions, more than willing to come to our aid as we frantically explained our situation. If it weren't for the pegasus knights, we also wouldn't have been able to help our dragons ward off the smiercs they encountered."

"Looks like the two of you are a damn ingenious duo when you put your wits together. You should collaborate more often," I smirk.

"Please, don't encourage him," Arden scoffs with an eye roll.

I'm hit with a surge of bewildered amusement and awe as I take in the sight of Arden and Zephyr before me. Not long ago, I could hardly stand being in the presence of these damn nobles. Not long ago, I fantasized about escaping my newfound fate, never seeing their faces, and never seeing any of the faces around this monastery ever again. How quickly all that has changed. From noble brats to squad mates, to trusted comrades, to now…brothers.

Perhaps it's sleep deprivation and a painfully empty stomach. Perhaps it's the weight of losing Felix and Fieryn juxtaposing the weight lifted from Rhydian's death. Something strange has gotten into me as I find myself unable to resist the urge to pull them into my arms and squeeze them tight. Where words fail to form an explanation, tears sting the fresh wounds on my cheeks, saying all that needs to be expressed.

"I knew you would eventually come crawling into our arms," Zephyr whispers.

"Shut up!" I snap. "I-I'm just thankful you're both alive," I choke on my words. To my surprise, Zephyr refrains from making additional remarks, and Arden leans into the embrace without pushing me away.

"Eldermoor does not get the final word," Arden mutters. "From here on out, our squad fights for Felix. For Fieryn. In their memory, in their honor, we will fight for hope. We will see our way to the other side of this war, eliminating every threat to Elmoria's balance in our wake."

"In their names, we fight for hope," I whisper in agreement. "For all who have fallen in the dark, we fight for hope until the light prevails."

CHAPTER 37
Faith vs. Works: Adrienne

In all the centuries of my existence, I have never seen such depths of my father's power manifest into a single weapon forged against The Mortal Realms. I would much rather take on an army of wraiths and rygors singlehandedly than face a single smierc ever again. Unfortunately, it won't be long before thousands of them infest the skies. At this point, I'm unsure of what I wouldn't give to turn every damned smierc against Osiris and wipe his existence to oblivion. I'm unsure of what I wouldn't give to make the gods taste a fraction of the suffering they've inflicted upon me since my eternal banishment from Niroshen.

"Adrienne? Did you hear my question? Adrienne?" Lady Rhonwen's sickeningly sweet voice claws into my mind, reeling me back to our conversation.

"Get your head together," Sarthon grumbles. *"Believe me, I am more than ready to help you plot vengeance against the gods. However, the sooner The High Priestess is brought up to speed on the events of Crystal Bay, the sooner you're out of here."*

"Forgive me, Lady Rhonwen. May I ask you to repeat yourself?" I ask as I bow apologetically.

"Your squad has more than earned your share of grace. I'm sorry, Wing Commander. I cannot even begin to fathom your unique pain of witnessing such tragic events."

Prince Sorin stands beside me with a solemn stare behind his crimson eyes. Our eyes meet in silent understanding as his own losses weigh heavily upon his shoulders.

I take a deep breath and remind myself not to roll my eyes at Lady Rhonwen's weak empathy. I take another deep breath to remind myself not to laugh at the fact she thinks she understands. The High Priestess may have wells of knowledge and spiritual wisdom, but she will never understand why I will never find a fraction of closure to my grief.

It truly is almost laughable. I've spent centuries serving under high priestesses who have never detected the goddess standing at their sides. Each of them believed that being gifted with Elethea's rare healing magic blessed them with special insight from the gods— as if possessing the ability to heal rather than destroy cloaked them in a sacred, pleasing innocence. However, as Goddess of the Shadows, I find their arrogant, perceived innocence immensely repulsive.

"What have you learned from your time in Crystal Bay? What rumors have you learned to be true of the new creatures now being weaponized against us?" Lady Rhonwen reiterates the question I missed while fantasizing about the gods' suffering.

"Felix was right to be deeply concerned with Eldermoor's more enigmatic developments. Crystal Bay has been conducting rituals to offer sacrifices to Osiris in exchange for smiercs. They offer the blood of slain dragons and half-mortals, and The God of Death reinforces their armies. Together, they conspire to wield The Crown of Luminaries to extend the rule of Osiris to all Elmoria."

The cadence of Lady Rhonwen's pulse remains surprisingly calm for a high priestess receiving news of exactly how our enemies wish to destroy the most prized creation of the gods. Yet again, high priestesses tend to hold firm to the belief their gods will always come through with unwavering salvation in their personal favor. Pitiful, pitiful foolishness.

"Wretched fools," Lady Rhonwen scoffs. "To believe they can defile what The Gods of Niroshen created with the limited power of The God of Death will only lead to their demise."

"With all due respect, Lady Rhonwen, while it may appear as one dark god against all the might of Niroshen, I urge you not to underestimate Osiris. The most recent smiercs born in the flames of their altar have been promised to rapidly produce more offspring. Between whatever blood of our slain Eldermoor acquired from the shores of Tourmaline, along with the smiercs likely breeding more enemies as we speak, we have an inevitable disaster on our hands," I counter.

"May I also add, Lady Rhonwen, smeircs are unlike any evil we have ever encountered," Sorin interjects. "We've seen a wide array of their powers, and I fear we haven't even seen the entire surface yet. They disrupt the bonds between your mages and their dragons, cutting off their communications. They produce an unbreathable thickness to the air. Half your energy depletes just from simply breathing in their presence."

"To add to what Prince Sorin has already mentioned, they also fly through walls of dragon fire and emerge unscathed," I hiss. "They wield lances laced with dark poison that immediately withers the flesh of their targets. A direct hit kills instantaneously. Even being grazed by one of their lances is enough to inflict critical wounds, as you've seen since our arrival. The wounds you tended to on our dragons…have you ever seen dragons in such critical conditions?"

"Adrienne! Breathe, Wing Commander! Take a deep breath," Lady Rhonwen orders. "There is no need to fret over even the most unforeseen of our trials!"

It takes a full second before I realize my cheeks are flushed red as smoldering coals. Shadows seep from my clenched fists as I invite my anger to flow freely through my veins.

"Do not be dismayed, Wing Commander. Do not fail to understand the unfailing love of the gods who light our paths. No unholy magic, no poisoned lance, no creature or any force of darkness will ever be enough to smite our faithful armies," Lady Rhonwen preaches in fearless confidence.

Perhaps it's fatigue. Perhaps the centuries upon centuries spent quietly, eternally suffering under the weight of the shadow luminary finally removes the bit from my tongue. "I am not the one who fails to understand the gods," I snarl as surges of dark smoke escape from my fists and shatter the stained glass windows.

Sorin and Lady Rhonwen's eyes widen as they cower in terror, shielding their heads from flying shards of glass. I peer into Sorin's mind, sensing paralyzing fear and hesitation as he debates whether or not he can intervene without my shadows slicing him to death. I claw my way into Lady Rhonwen's mind, discovering her finally filled with the disturbance and rage I've longed for her to feel. Her anger fills me with a satisfying, intoxicating high I desperately need to savor to the last drop.

"The gods of Niroshen care about one thing and one thing alone—Elmoria. Their half-mortal descendants, and those who pick up swords, bows, and axes to wield against the forces of Osiris, are seen as nothing more than disposable, replaceable guardians of their masterpiece!" There's no stopping the anger spewing off my tongue. Nothing good ever comes from suppressed, immortal wrath.

"I command you to control yourself at once!" Lady Rhonwen bellows over the plumes of obsidian smoke now tearing through her chamber in violent, lashing gales. Shadows growl and spiral with tornadic force as furniture turns into lethal projectile.

"The gods would hold no reservations in allowing each and every last soul fighting for Elmoria to die in this war if that's what it would take to save their precious world. Their precious artwork means more than any of us could ever mean to them. We are disposable!" I scream from the top of my lungs as I exhale tendrils Lof shadows.

It's been six hundred years since I have last allowed tears to roll down my cheeks. I almost forgot the sensation. Centuries of locking my anger in a cage, now released like a feral beast. The melodies of Lady Rhonwen's singing chandelier cease as tresses of sable smoke slice through its suspending chains. The flames of torchlight starve out as it crashes to the floor, bringing down chunks of the ceiling along with it.

"Please!" Lady Rhonwen gasps in between unrelenting coughing fits. The sight of The Prince and The High Priestess now knocked to the ground, choking on the thickness of the swirling smoke, doesn't even faze me. An eternity of rage, an eternity of loss after loss, spiraling beyond my control. Thoughts of bringing the entire monastery to the ground in the same fashion as The Crystal Bay Cathedral become increasingly tempting with each passing second.

"Our lives will not be spared by faith alone! The gods do not care about the souls separated by the veils of our realms. To them, we are nothing but disposable, replaceable weapons. We are all insignificant! Unless we fight Eldermoor with actions screaming louder than faith, we will continue to hemorrhage in losses unceasingly!"

Massive, serpentine shadows spill out of Lady Rhonwen's chamber and into the corridor like a sea of unyielding wraiths. That's what I truly am to my core as the daughter of Osiris— a divine wraith. A goddess of shadows and curses.

"Adrienne! Snap out of this! You already destroyed the cathedral. The monastery must stand strong, or our forces stand no chance," Sarthon roars.

"Our forces? Who is truly for us? If neither The Gods of Niroshen nor Osiris? Or their divided pawns of The Mortal Realms?" I hiss down our bond. I now want nothing more than to rip the shadow luminary from beneath my flesh and throw it like a bone for Elmoria to fight over like packs of starved, feral dogs.

"For the sake of Elmoria, she's disposable." Memories of Kamaris's voice play my agony like a shrill violin. The memory of lapsing in and out of consciousness through the excruciating pain of the shadow luminary imbedding into my flesh feels as if just moments ago. After growing accustomed to the eternal, burning sting of its presence beneath my flesh, my suffering has now resurfaced to the forefront of my mind. A visceral scream escapes from the top of my lungs as the throb of the shadow luminary reminds me of Nuri, of Felix, of all the souls I'll never walk beside again.

I close my eyes to shut it all out— as if sinking deeper into my darkness will somehow nullify my pain and silence this storm. My mind replays Nuri's soul ascending into Niroshen, forever beyond my reach. Her soul-shattering scream rings in my ears as the formative light of Blackthorn's shields impales her through the heart.

"Adrienne!"

White mist infiltrates the darkness behind my eyelids, pulling me from drifting further down the frigid sea of nightmares.

"Adrienne!"

The white mist grows brighter and brighter, consolidating into a bright, white light as a force of warmth slams against my icy, shivering skin. A warm, healing embrace wraps tightly around my chest as a familiar heartbeat chases my frigid, stinging pain away back to its dormancy.

"Adrienne! Listen to my voice. Come out! Climb out of this, love. You are here, and you are with me!"

Amira's fierce yet gentle voice calls out to me through the howling squall of shadows. Her forehead pressed against mine. My eyes open to her striking, glacial eyes of blue-tinted moonlight. Her touch transfers relieving waves of heat into my icy blood, calming my chattering bones. The vicious cyclones of raging shadows dissolve the very moment she smiles at me.

"My love, the only goddess worthy of her divinity. You do not walk your path alone. With every heartbeat I have left, I'll be with you for every step."

My heart melts like molten metals prepared to forge a blade in response to her enduring, unwavering love. Her desire to give me everything, to give me all of her, is a gift I will never fully fathom. A gift I will never fully deserve.

Amira tightens her embrace, paying no regard to The High Priestess or The Crown Prince of Helia still lying on the ground, catching their breaths and trembling in shock. The groans and commotion of the triage stations several levels beneath us send chills down my spine. I would be no better than the very gods I vehemently despise if my outburst facilitated their deaths.

"I'm supposed to be the one who grounds you," I grimmace, surveying the catastrophic aftermath of my explosion.

"We're supposed to ground each other. Goddess or not, your burdens aren't meant to be carried alone."

Amira seals our secret conversation with a gentle, passionate kiss. The brush of her lips against mine cleanses me with undeserved relief. Undeserved healing. Gods, I wish we were alone so I could take her right here. As much as I wouldn't mind further desecrating Lady Rhonwen's chambers, Sorin doesn't deserve to be dragged into these affairs any deeper. Especially not after all he has lost lending his battalion to our aid. Reluctantly, I break away from her kiss before giving in to my impulses.

Amira makes her way across the room, offering Lady Rhonwen a hand as she pulls her from the debris-cluttered ground. Prince Sorin rises to his feet and dusts himself off, retraining from engaging in any eye contact.

"You must not hold the pain of my Wing Commander against her. This briefing is never to be held against her. Am I clear?" The authoritative tone of Amira's voice echoes through the chamber as she confronts Blackthorn's High Priestess with reckless boldness.

"How strong can faith truly stand unless forged under trials? Is faith without doubts even true faith at all?" Amira scoffs at The High Priestess. No doubt, she was raised with the courage of a mercenary in the lawlessness of the peasant slums.

"One more word, and you might find yourself in another cell for the extent of your poor etiquette. I'd very much prefer not to see you shackled

in restraints that aren't my own ever again," I warn.

As expected, Lady Rhonwen's fair complexion is now canvased in scarlet splotches. The anger I sense buzzing in her mind like a swarm of hornets has my ears ringing as I rush to Amira's side, placing myself between her and The High Priestess.

"I do not want to become the next child of the gods to act on brash, regrettable impulses," she hisses between clenched teeth. "This briefing is over. You are all dismissed. IMMEDIATELY."

I elbow Prince Sorin, snapping him out of his frozen panic, and signal him to follow us out of Lady Rhonwen's storm-torn chamber with haste. We briskly descend the spiral staircase, not daring to utter a single word until reaching the bottom and relocating ourselves to the opposite wing of the monastery.

"Forgive me, Prince. Typically, I conduct myself just fine without unleashing demonic shadow storms. What you witnessed back there was inexcusable," I apologize as I attempt to regain a fraction of my diplomacy. "It's been a particularly bad day."

Amira gently rests a hand on my back. A reassuring reminder she isn't going anywhere. Despite all the horrors I've shown her, all the horrors I've recruited her to endure, and the ones I have yet to confess, somehow, she is still with me.

"Respectfully, if my father addressed our concerns with a response like Lady Rhonwen's, I can't say I would easily refrain from lashing out at him…to say the least. Not that you need my opinion, but I believe your anger was justified."

"For a son of royalty, your energy is refreshing, Prince. I almost wish I could offer you a spot on our squad if it were an option," I smirk.

"As honored as I would be to serve alongside your squad, my father wouldn't be too pleased with me if I don't return with my battalion by tomorrow. I need to bond with another pegasus in as little time as possible and return to leading our aerial forces. Earning enough of one's trust to ride one into battle typically takes months, and I have less than days to work with," Sorin chokes, fighting back the tears forming in his eyes.

"Anyways…I have critical information to relay to you that we didn't get a chance to discuss during our briefing. I know things are tense right now, but Lady Rhonwen will need to be informed right away."

"I'll see that The High Priestess receives word. What do you have to report?" I ask.

"We've lost another vital port to Eldermoor's forces just days ago. We sent out missives to Blackthorn through our courier foxes. Based on the lack of response, however, I fear they may have gotten intercepted. Despite the might of your forces fighting alongside us, we're finding ourselves on the brink of defeat. Eldermoor has been catastrophically outnumbering our combined forces, and now, with the smiercs joining their ranks, it will take nothing short of a miracle to prevent the collapse of our kingdom. Helia is falling."

Obsidian steam seeps from the pores of my skin as I process the details of Sorin's bleak report. "Not a single word of this has come through on our end," I mutter. With Osiris's smiercs now infesting our skies, the age of winged courier foxes relaying missives across our borders might as well have come to an end.

"Do you think Lady Rhonwen would deploy more dragon knights to Helia, given the circumstances?" Amira asks sheepishly as if already knowing the answer.

"With the Eve of Eleodora clouding all sense of her logic, I wouldn't count on The High Priestess to be making any rational decisions right now," I scoff. "Between Felix, myself, and General Cyrina's missives, The High Priestess has been informed time and time again of the weight of the threats stacked against us. Yet as the threats stack higher, she's busy putting down her swords and picking up the roses of her foolish, weaponless faith."

"Correct me if I'm wrong but to my understanding, Blackthorn now has possession of the light, water, fire, and wind luminaries. Four out of six luminaries in the land of the elemental mages," Sorin interjects. "That should certainly be enough to rack catastrophic havoc upon Eldermoor's armies, even with their smiercs. Is there any hope The High Priestess would permit her knights to wield them in battle? For the sake of preventing Helia's collapse?" The tone of his plea carries the intensity of a lover frantically searching for anyone to save his dying beloved. A prince who loves his kingdom, watching it crumble beyond his ability to alter the fate of its defeat.

The pain flickering in his eyes compels me to claw into the darkness torturing his mind as I watch the deaths of his people play out like morbid, unshakeable omens. His deepest fears, a promise of what's to come if we fail to turn the tides of this war within the next waking sunrises.

"I wish I could say you're the first to suggest that strategy," I sigh deeply. "Using the luminaries to aid us in battle has been proposed to Lady Rhonwen on multiple accounts by multiple wing commanders, generals, and high-ranking officials. Myself and Felix among those who begged for her consideration. She stated to use the luminaries in battle would be to desecrate Elmoria's sacred heirlooms. She holds firm to her belief using their power for our gain makes us no different from our enemies and would lead to the corruption of Blackthorn, posing us just as equal of a threat to The Mortal Realms' balance."

The crimson flicker of hope behind Sorin's darkened eyes smolders to ash. The infestation of my father's imperial reign upon The Mortal Realms feels more and more like a future we can only delay rather than prevent. Osiris will channel as much power as his blood mages can withstand to execute his will. He will stop at nothing to ensure his armies retrieve every last luminary using those smiercs as his damned puppets.

"Without using the luminaries we've acquired to our disposal, The veradis spirits will need to be called into action. You and I both know the

hour is coming for you to unbind them from the Kanoelani and command them to our ranks," Sarthon rumbles.

"I'd much rather force The High Priestess into relinquishing the stones even if I have to pry them from her pious fingers myself," I hiss.

Lady Rhonwen insists on fighting ancient, dark magic conjured by Osiris with faith in the deadbeat gods. With festive feasts and altars. Meanwhile, my mind is frantically searching for any solution that avoids unleashing the Kanoelani spirits and enlisting them in our armies. The thought of leaving dragon hatchlings vulnerable without the protection of the spirits makes me want to rip out all my teeth one by one. Lumithra would likely rip them out for me in protest, and I can't say I'd blame her.

"At this point, playing by Lady Rhonwen's rules is a guaranteed death sentence," Amira scoffs, fidgeting with the hilt of her dagger. "Those damn smiercs are breeding and multiplying Eldermoor's armies as we speak. We won't allow Helia to fall without a proper fight," she snarls as a concoction of dangerous, reckless schemes brews behind her glacial eyes.

"What exactly is running through that devious, beautiful mind of yours, my love?"

"Oh…you know. For the sake of defending Elmoria as we know it, I think I'm ready to commit treason," Amira responds casually.

"I'm going to need you to elaborate. Any scheme that involves you carelessly throwing yourself to the verge of death again, however, I vehemently forbid," I warn her.

"Get Helia through two more days, Prince, and I'll see that we arrive at your borders with all the luminaries we possess. The High Priestess no longer has a say in the matter. I decided I'm taking them off her hands," Amira ignores me as she addresses Sorin.

Sorin's jaw drops agape as his brows raise in stunned perplexion. "My kingdom has always known dragon knights to be faithfully sworn to their high priestesses no matter the cost. Yet you're telling me that as a dragon knight, you're just jumping to the decision to defy her direct orders?"

"Correct. However, I wasn't born to be a dragon knight. You see…I was born and raised as a lawless mercenary peasant. A starved, feral, killing machine. And I'm just reckless enough to undermine a poor leadership decision to save us from ever having to see Osiris bear The Crown of Luminaries," Amira smirks.

Tendrils of shadows trickle down my spine in surges of anger and seep from my fists as I process Amira's gravitation toward her hasty, lethal impulses. I'm unsure if I am more upset with her willingness to propose such a deadly scheme or the fact that I don't see a better solution than committing the level of treason she's suggesting.

"While your proposal is the only solution I'm willing to accept right now, Elmoria isn't worth saving if you're ripped apart from this realm," I seethe down our bond. *"However, I am only accepting on one condition, and one condition only."*

"And what might that condition be?" Amira challenges.

"The moment I so much as fear things are about to go south, I'm unleashing every bit of my divinity that it takes to pull you out of harm's way. If that means Helia falls, and that Osiris has his way with Elmoria, then so be it. I refuse to allow any other god to steal what soul belongs to me."

"You worry too much, love. I wouldn't have proposed any scheme I feared I would be incapable of handling. Don't forget I can't afford to lose you just as much as you can't afford to lose me. That being said…I'll accept whatever condition it takes to give my plan a fighting chance," Amira responds with a soft smile that makes me forget how to breathe for a moment.

"We'll get our hands on the luminaries," I promise Sorin reluctantly. *"Don't you forget for a single heartbeat that, again, your safety is my first and foremost priority. And before you even ask…no. Not a single damned thing will possibly change my mind on the subject,"* I remind Amira as I stroke the small of her back with my shadows.

"In that case, I will be delaying my return to my forces to assist in your operations," Sorin declares as a glimmer of light returns to his eyes. "As Crown Prince of Helia, you have my deepest, most sincere gratitude. I do not take the weight of what you are plotting lightly. Whether we succeed or we fall, I will stand with you to the end," he bows.

"We have ourselves an agreement then," I sigh. "We will steal the luminaries and rally the might of their power against Eldermoor. Unfortunately, this means we must act with haste. Time to move on to developing our strategy."

CHAPTER 38
Schemes of Secrecy: Amira

Having gained the agreeing support of both Adrienne and Sorin with relative ease is equally as relieving as it is terrifying. An immortal goddess who fought in the last Great War and the Prince of Helia stand in agreement that betraying Blackthorn is our best shot at saving Elmoria.

The Rosemary scone I scarfed down in a hurry after oversleeping roils in my stomach as Lumithra hits a turbulent patch of winds in the hazy morning skies. Deciding to involve the squad in our treasonous schemes was a decision that kept me awake well into the twilight hours of the night. However, planning to steal heavily guarded sacred luminaries as a party of three would likely be a recipe for cataclysmic failure. Today, we're exposing our plans in the secrecy of the Kanoelani, and inviting them to join us. Today, our squad will either decide to stand by our side as we betray our nation together, or turn against us and expose every last bit of our plan to Lady Rhonwen. Elmoria's future now rests solely on how they will choose to align.

Rays of beaming sunlight penetrate the fog and stroke my face with summery warmth as I take in the sight of our formation. Tsuna, Sylphira, and Hyrix spill breathtaking hues of aquamarine, silver, and emerald scales across the dense, charcoal fog. The half-mortals sitting in their saddles, the friends I can no longer stomach imagining a life without. Will this be our last flight together as tightly-knit comrades? What would Felix think of our plans to commit treason after earning his prestigious title as Blackthorn's emissary? Is involving our squad to any capacity a deplorable dishonor to his memory?

"If it's any consolation, the Felix I knew wouldn't stand for Lady Rhonwen's abysmally poor judgment. As Blackthorn's most loyal dragon knight, fighting for an Elmoria in which Blackthorn could thrive would mean more to him than the orders of his high priestess," Adrienne assures with profound confidence.

"Let's just hope the others will feel similarly then," I respond as I swallow the lump in my throat.

"Easy, Lyra, easy!" Sorin tightens his grip on his new mare's reins, bending her head and neck to the side to stifle her wild bucking. After sending his recovered knights off to defend Helia, Sorin decided to hold a mare back who lost her rider at Crystal Bay. Attempting to bond with her mid-flight seems to be going just as arduous as he mentioned it would be. Lyra's hind legs thrash and flail in desperation to shake off her new rider like he's an unwanted parasite as her shrill whinnies send goosebumps down my spine.

"Are you alright back there?" I shout in his direction. The Prince wasn't exaggerating at all when he mentioned the stubbornness of an un-bonded pegasus. Lyra flails her ember wings in heated protest as she continues fighting against Sorin's control of her reins.

"I expected nothing less than a turbulent flight from this one," Sorin grunts. His scarlet tresses are drenched in sweat from exerting every muscle in his body to avoid being thrown from Lyra's back and getting kicked by her hooves on the way down.

"I will not stand for this young mare's deplorable behavior," Lumithra grumbles.

Lumithra pulls back her speed and meets Lyra with a menacing warning growl through her clenched fangs. Her violet, iridescent eyes meet Lyra's, challenging them to submission as she releases a warning blast of fire from her breath. Lyra flinches and bucks around the flames, startled into willful obedience. She bows her head to The White Empress, submitting herself to Sorin's command as he takes flawless control over the reins.

"*Careful now, or Helia might try to recruit you to command all their stubborn pegasi into willful submission if that's all it takes,*" I chuckle. The shock overtaking Sorin's expression might suggest his temptation to ask for such a favor.

"*We don't have time to spare on the hot-headedness of resilient pride,*" Lumithra grumbles. "*Any creature that joins our cause will quickly learn their spirits will be better spent working against our enemies than wasted on fighting against their riders.*"

"*Now, if only you could will the smiercs into submission as well,*" I mutter.

The ethereal, haunting melodies of the Veradis Spirits send chills scuttling down my spine as their tunes stir through the mountainous fog. The last time I flew over The Kanoelani, I was a prisoner awaiting deadly trials, restrained atop Sarthon's bed of obsidian, jagged scales. The shadow mage that once drugged me with a hallucinogenic elixir and threw me to the fate of the forest now has an eternal chokehold on my heart and my soul. Despite the drastic turn of my fate since my last trip to The Kanoelani, returning to the sacred, spiritual grounds churns my gut with waves of unsettling dread.

"*Are you sure the spirits won't be disturbed by a cluster of half-mortals and The Crown Prince of Helia plotting treason within their sacred forest?*" I ask Adrienne sheepishly.

"*Choilleich, The Matron Spirit, is expecting our visit. Our party will be met with gracious hospitality, as the spirits know I come to prevent their call into battle. They know my desire is to prevent exposing our hatchlings to this war,*" Adrienne assures.

Shades of ashen fog bleed into clouds of emerald the deeper we descend into Kanoelani's thick, spiritual haze. Eyes of ancient, immortal spirits flicker like fireflies in the silhouettes of large, winding evergreens as we land into a bed of glowing, sage-green moss.

"Welcome to our council chamber, the heart of The Kanoelani," Lumithra beams with pride.

My heart skips a beat as I admire the mossy meadow, encircled in towering vines and knobbed trees veiled in thick, emerald blankets of fog. Distant babbles of flowing streams and waterfalls provide the only soundscape amidst the haunting tranquility. The heart of the Kanoelani feels more like an island, detached from the rest of The Mortal Realms—a secluded gem well-suited for protecting delicate secrets.

Our dragons nestle their claws into the glowing moss, making themselves at home. Even Lyra appears to be adjusting to her strange surroundings with ease. Despite the looming presence of spirits watching us like inquisitive crows hidden deep within the trees, I have never witnessed Lumithra or any of our dragons more at peace. The spirits among us are their kin.

"Lady Rhonwen will expect us to be available to assist in last-minute festival preparations later today, so we have little time to give to our emergently pressing discussion," Adrienne rallies the attention of our squad. "I brought you here because what we are about to discuss cannot be overheard by a single soul not present in this forest. Understood?"

"Understood, Wing Commander," Arden responds, masking any skepticism or perplexion with a calm, collected composure. Zephyr nervously fidgets with the laces of his tunic while Irvette casts a blank stare, unfazed and stoic as a statue.

"With smiercs rapidly multiplying into Eldermoor's armies, their power grows stronger with every heartbeat. Prince Sorin has informed me that the attacks on Helia now have them on the brink of total collapse. Their losses have been insurmountable despite the aid of Blackthorn's alliance. Without possessing the bulk of the luminaries, Eldermoor is still draining our magic faster than our forces can recover. Helia is hours away from becoming a vital victory. Once Helia falls, Eldermoor will storm our borders with nothing stopping their advances toward acquiring our luminaries. Osiris is hours away from claiming all of Elmoria as his own," Adrienne addresses with seething anger commanding her tone.

"How is The High Priestess responding to the severity of Eldermoor's advances on Helia?" Arden asks with his arms folded across his chest.

"Lady Rhonwen is under the belief honoring The Eve of Eleodora is a sufficient weapon against our enemies despite smiercs breeding their armies as we speak. Her response is merely faith without action," Adrienne responds with sharp disgust in her tone. "If we don't take matters into our own hands, Eldermoor will stop at nothing until Helia's court is overthrown and handed to Osiris. From there, they will stop at nothing until The Crown of Luminaries is placed upon the head of whomever they deem will be their chosen vessel to host his spirit within their flesh. The luminaries responsible for the birth of every mountain, every living creature, every grain of sand, and every last molecule of Elmoria's composure will be used to usher Osiris into a vessel that will rival the power of all the gods. The leadership of our High Priestess is failing us."

Adrienne pauses, stroking her hand over the serpent tattoo that conceals her secret curse with fear behind her silver eyes. If entire smierc armies storm the gates of Blackthorn, it will only be a matter of heartbeats before they find the shadow luminary and tether The God of Death to flesh and bone. I grab her hand to prevent myself from releasing lightning storms provoked by the horrors of everything that would mean.

"What I am about to propose is more than enough to strip me of my title as Wing Commander. Should you choose to accept a role in this operation, you will be committing treason," Adrienne warns.

"I thought you said we had to keep this brief. Go on with it." Irvette pleas Adrienne in a tone of rage intertwined with grief without allowing a moment of silence to linger. "Whatever you need from us, consider it done," she growls. Arden and Zephyr remain silent as the color drains from their faces.

Adrienne takes a deep breath, paying no attention to their deafening silence, or to Irvette's immediate, zealous agreement. "I am asking our squad, with Sorin's aid, to steal the luminaries under Blackthorn's protection tomorrow during the Eve of Eleodora. Should you choose to accept this operation, we will then fly for Helia's borders, bearing the power of four luminaries against Eldermoor's forces. If I believed we had any other option to prevent the collapse of their kingdom, we would not be having this discussion. However, if we don't harvest the power of the stones within our reach, Elmoria will fall. My friends, are you willing to join us in defying the orders of your High Priestess? Are you willing to put the fate of The Mortal Realms into the hands of our squad?"

The lull of silence feels like heavy bricks stacked against my chest as our squad exchanges nonverbal glances, somberly processing Adrienne's commission. Waiting for the tension to lift from the meadow might as well be as difficult as riding out the stinging squalls of an unrelenting blizzard.

Arden forges a rock in the palm of his hand, tosses it into the air, and catches it. The rock repeatedly smacks back into his palm at a steady tempo. His eyes follow the rise and fall of his stone, deep in thought. "The luminaries are heavily guarded day and night within the monastery by rotations of renowned squads. It would be a damn shame if we had to volunteer to miss a portion of the festival to take a shift," he casually scoffs as he continues tossing and catching his stone. With the twist of his wrist, the stone forms into the shape of a sword right as he catches it in his fist. "Treason it is," he sighs with a smirk.

The devious smile in his earth-toned eyes floods my heart with relief. Our rock of reason and logic, our rock of order and obedience, is capable of defying orders after all.

"Who knew the earth mage with rock-hard abs would also possess a mind equally as admirable? You're quite the total package," Zephyr smirks as he rustles his fingers through Arden's chestnut curls.

Arden's eyes meet mine with a burning glare as I fail to stifle my laughter. "A total package forever out of your league," he scoffs, pushing Zephyr away.

A blend of relief and satisfaction beam in Adrienne's eyes as she takes in the sight of her squad before her. A squad that has shed much blood, shared much grief, and grown so much as a unit in such a short amount of time. Her squad before her, Helia's Crown Prince, and myself, all willing to brand targets on our backs to fight for a fool's shot at hope.

"Looks like we've got ourselves our next assignment," she beams with hope. My knees weaken at the curve of her wine red lips as they take the shape of her rare, soul-melting smile. For a moment, my thoughts drift to all the unholy ways in which I want to experience that smile all to myself. My heart skips several beats as I plot my own merciless schemes of buying us some much needed distractions before setting out to put an end to this war.

"Anyone have the slightest clue how we're to go about convince Lady Rhonwen to give our squad a shift on guard duty? Guarding the luminaries is an assignment traditionally granted to squads with years of active field service under their belts," Irvette interjects.

"I don't know exactly know how in the realms Lady Rhonwen would dream of considering it after my outburst," Adrienne mutters to me.

"We'll think of something. The squads you've trained in the past have gone on to serve as renown knights among our battalions, and she has been impressed with our squad's performances out in the field, right? That all still has to count for something," I shoot back.

"Leave persuading The High Priestess up to me," Sorin interrupts our silent conversation. "I've got a trick or two in my arsenal that may be of use."

"What? Like sending hundreds of those glowing moths of yours to swarm her until she agrees to assign us to a shift?" Zephyr jeers.

"The Goddess of Illusions has gifted her devoted pegasus knights with far more illusive magic than just one simple trick," Sorin responds patiently. "Allow me to demonstrate what I have in mind."

Within a heartbeat, Helia's crown prince disappears in a spontaneous cloud of marigold haze. Seconds after the haze forms, it dissipates, unveiling an orange, bushy-tailed courier fox. Long, feathery wings stretch out from its shoulder blades as Sorin's crimson eyes beam back at us with a wink.

"Something tells me you have much to experience fighting alongside our knights, my friend," Sorin chuckles. He nuzzles his chest with his nose, and a letter strung by a necklace of tweed and vines appears around his neck after another brief puff of haze. "Perhaps a correspondence from General Cyrina would get us what we need. I've fought alongside her enough times to gather that Lady Rhonwen seems to defer to her input quite often."

Adrienne stoops down to Sorin, skimming over the magically crafted letter addressed to Lady Rhonwen. "Impressive…this penmanship is nearly identical to General Cyrina's." Her eyes widen with satisfaction upon reading over the lines of the message. "You certainly do not disappoint, Prince. This letter should do the trick."

"Now that we're all on the same page, we should prepare to head back," Adrienne addresses the squad. "Today, we keep our heads down low. We decorate altars, prepare offerings, and decorate the monastery halls in emerald and marigold. We play the part of submission. Tomorrow night, however, we bear our claws and fangs. We steal the luminaries on our watch at the mausoleum and fly for Helia's borders. Tomorrow night, we celebrate the Eve of Eleodora by obliterating Eldermoor's forces. May The God of Death remain eternally bound to The Dark Realms."

Sarthon lets out a thunderous roar of agreement, followed by the rest of our dragons echoing passionate, roaring war cries. Even Lyra whinnies along as if one of the colossal, fire-bringing beasts. Her body stands so tiny next to Lumithra's, yet she appears entirely unbothered by the staggering difference in height as she puffs out her chest with pride. *Good. We'll need all the fearless, fiery spirits we can acquire for the trials ahead of us.*

The battle roars and whinnies come to a pause as a whirlwind of rustling leaves stirs the stillness of the surrounding thickets. A pair of glowing green eyes slice through the fog, stirring my nerves with unease. Orbs of white light encapsulate my hands as I reach for the hilt of a dagger.

"Stand down!" Adrienne commands, placing her hand on top of mine. "She comes in peace, not as a foe!"

"You mean to tell me you're familiar with this thing?" I utter as the ground beneath us rumbles like rolling thunder.

"Relax," Lumithra interrupts. *"It's just Choilleich."*

Adrienne chuckles as I release my grip on my dagger and allow my magic to recede back into my veins. *"Your dragon isn't the only immortal that goes way back with The Matron Spirit."*

My knees buckle, and I nearly lose my footing as a massive, wolf-like creature emerges from the thicket, standing only a little shorter than the dragons with antlers composed of large, winding branches. Wildflowers and rows of ivy, intricately woven into her thick coat of leaves. While Lumithra has described Choilleich to me before, laces of fear and admiration intertwine around my heart as I take her in with my own eyes.

"Brave warriors of Elmoria," Choilleich's voice floats like an airy melody, reverberating through the meadow with chilling beauty. Her drifting scent of wildflowers and honey soothes the restlessness in my nerves as I still myself in her presence. "The risks you are willing to take to defend your homelands, to defend Elmoria, are not about to unfold before I extend my sincerest appreciation," she rumbles.

"You wield your magic and your weapons as nobles, not as ill-hearted traitors. Forgive The High Priestess, for her judgement is clouded. To possess even one luminary, is to carry an all-consuming burden. Lady Rhonwen currently possesses a double-edged sword, as does every knight tasked with guarding the luminaries. On one end, standing in proximity to their divine, sacred influence drastically heightens their strength and power. On the other end, the luminaries also seep poison into one's mind, as they were never meant to become the affairs of mortals or even half-mortals. As the luminaries constantly cry out to their Creators, her instincts to defend them will only intensify. Her judgment will continue to dwindle as long as she oversees their protection," Choilleich explains.

As livid as I am with Lady Rhonwen for triggering Adrienne down her torturous spiral, a small part of me is relieved knowing she is not entirely herself. Hopefully, wielding the luminaries to put an end to this war will also lift the spiritual fog that clouds her mind.

"The luminaries were never meant to become the affairs of those without full, immortal divinity," Choilleich continues. "Once your squad takes the stones into your own hands, you'll begin to endure personal battles against your mind and flesh."

The Matron Spirit bows before our squad, lowering her antlers to the ground of glowing moss. Swarms of butterflies and fireflies depart from her antlers, multiplying by the hundreds as they disperse to the skies. Rainbow blurs of rapid, fluttering wings and flickering golden lights fly around our bodies like intricately woven threads as necklaces suddenly appear around our necks. The trail of butterflies returns to their perches atop Choilleich's branchy antlers as she raises from her bow and observes us with fierce gratitude behind her glowing, green eyes.

"To thank you for your efforts in sparing the call of a god from summoning my beloved spirits to the bloodshed of this war, to thank you for the weight of the burdens you are about to bear, I leave you with a parting gift."

My eyes are drawn to the beauty of the emerald pendant that now lies between my breasts, strung by a silver chain. An intricate design of shimmery, silver branches are wrapped around the pendant, as if designed to protect whatever sacred magic lies within the strange gem.

"It-it's like a heartbeat," Irvette gasps in astonishment as she delicately cups her pendant. Upon closely examining my own necklace, I notice the swirls of emerald glow in a steady, rhythmic pulse.

"I leave you all with tokens of my spirit," Choilleich explains. "Should death try to claim you, may my spirit offer you sacred protection. May it be a light of hope when all hope seems lost. As long as you bear my pendant of life, my spirit will be with you."

Adrienne steps forward, revering a deep bow before The Matron Spirit. "Thank you for your blessing. May we wear our tokens well and restore harmony to our lands. Choilleich's eyes take her in as she embraces her old, familiar friend. How long has Adrienne's divinity been one of the secrets guarded by the spirits of the Kanoelani?

Choilleich and Lumithra take their turn with a meaningful farewell as we climb into our saddles and prepare for our departure.

"Time to return to the monastery before we're missed," Adrienne orders.

Sorin shifts back into his princely form and takes his mount atop Lyra as we ascend into the late morning sky. He tucks his pendant from Choilleich under his tunic and secures his magically crafted letter of deception into his supply satchel as the ground below disappears in the layers of fog.

"*Do we really believe this plan can work?*" I ask Adrienne. A long pause of silence chills the warmth of the air as I await her calculated response.

"*I've seen you suffer in The Dark Realms once, and I refuse to see it again. I refuse to watch you suffer under Osiris's reign upon The Mortal Realms, and I refuse to watch the gods take any more from me than they already have. I refuse to accept any other alternative other than securing an Elmoria worthy of hosting my love,"* she growls.

Obsidian darkness seeps into the wispy, summery clouds surrounding Adrienne and Sarthon, echoing the darkness expressed down our bond. Tendrils of smoke trail from her inked serpents. For a moment, I almost wonder if Adrienne's rage alone could be enough to put an end to this war.

CHAPTER 39

For Eternity

"If I ever have to weave together one more godsdamn floral arrangement or pour one more glass of wine in my lifetime, I think I'm going to lose what remains of my sanity," I complain to Adrienne after finally reaching the end of a long day spent adorning altars and preparing the monastery for tomorrow's festivities.

Adrienne chuckles as she pulls my body closely against hers. Her bare, smooth skin against mine under her silk comforter offers much-needed respite after spending the entire afternoon feigning unwavering obedience to Lady Rhonwen without letting my anger slip out in uncontrollable flames of lightning.

"Every year, the Eve of Eleodora reminds me why whiskey is my vice of choosing. I may be the only deity who prefers it over wine," she scoffs.

I press my back against Adrienne's slender, muscular frame, inviting her to tighten the hold of her arms wrapped around my chest. Her scent of lavender and sage sends tingles down my spine as her lips softly graze against my neck.

"To think I've spent all day preparing offerings for gods that mean little to me feels blasphemous. I would've much rather spent the day worshipping you instead," I tease as I swivel my hips against hers.

"Is that so?" Adrienne lets out a dark, sensual laugh, sending waves of heat down my neck as I run my fingers through her silky black tresses. To be tangled in her immaculate web of divine beauty is a thrill I will never tire of seeking.

"I will gladly take your devotion, my love," Adrienne growls as she slides a hand up to my neck, lightly restricting my blood flow. A pathetic moan escapes from my mouth as I melt into her chokehold and roll over onto my back.

Adrienne's body follows until I find her heartbeat on top of mine. My pulse slams inside my chest as I trace my fingers down the lengths of her curves. Her lips forcefully claim mine as she grabs hold of my wrists, throwing them above my head.

Black ropes of shadows bind my wrists in place, and my eyes close as her teeth bite into my lower lip. "Should we make this last forever?" She taunts as she works her kisses down my neck and my chest until the heat of her breath hovers over my breasts.

Forever. The one thing I don't truly have to offer.

Waves of pleasure threaten to consume me as she swirls her tongue over my nipples. Forever.

Behind my closed eyes, seeing Rhydian's battered corpse on the floor of the prison cell takes me out of my realm of euphoria and into a realm of panic. An unshakable nightmare unfolds before me as I lose my sense of reality.

Rhydian's bloodied, broken neck snaps back into place. Life returns to his eyes as pools of black swallow his irises. "You may have won your battle against me, but your time will come. Mortality is a cruel, cruel thief, Amira."

"No," I whimper.

Rhydian's voice growls in my ears and for a moment, I witness my frail, wrinkled corpse on the floor of the cell. Strands of moonlight hair now aged in silver. Adrienne hovers over my body, her tears crashing to the floor.

"One day, your bitch will lose you forever." Rhydian's corpse stands behind me with his knife to my throat.

"Shall I end your pitiful life now, as you have ended mine? A soul for a soul, perhaps?" Rhydian's voice carves through my brain as the blade pressed against my throat feels all too real. "What a damn shame, an immortal goddess falling for a mere half-mortal confined by her expiring flesh."

"Amira! Snap out of it! You are safe! You are with me!" Adrienne shouts down our bond, pulling me out of my spiral.

It takes a full moment for me to process I'm sitting up in her bed with her arms wrapped tightly around me, slowly coaxing me back to reality. Her embrace, the only force preventing my magic from channeling the moonlight into razor sharp beams of mass destruction.

Making note of the grand sable walls of her chambers laden with shelves of dark flowers and ancient trinkets, the starlight seeping in from her balcony, along with the soft touch of her skin, work together to fully convince me I am safe. I am in the present, rather than the torturous distortion my brain conjured.

"Rhydian is dead. He can never touch you again. You're here. You're with me." Adrienne's tone is firm, yet gentle as she leans my head against her chest.

"I'm-I'm here with you…for now," I choke. "What happens if our mission fails and we fall? What happens if I fall?"

Tears roll down my cheeks in embarrassment over how soft and breakable I've become. I've never been one to break down so easily. I've never been one to fear death. My whole life has been spent cheating death, flirting with it, and letting it edge me. Sometimes even begging for it, demanding it to stop stalking me, and finally come claim me.

Now, just one glance into Adrienne's sterling silver eyes, and I'm reminded that I want to live. I want my ice-laden heart to continue thawing in her presence, no matter how uncomfortably vulnerable it makes me. Not only do I truly want to live for the first time in my life…I want forever.

"I've selfishly been putting this conversation off longer than I should have. Not only are you ready, but now you need to know everything,"

Adrienne breaks the silence, looking at me with an expression filled with both empathy and dreadful anticipation. Her heart pounds like steady drums in her chest as she hops down from the bed and wraps herself in a black, satin robe.

"This conversation needs to be held somewhere lingering ears can't possibly follow. Come with me," she beckons, handing me an extra robe.

"We're not going back to the Kanoelani at this hour, are we?" I ask, sensing my own pulse racing in restless apprehension.

"I know better than to wake Sarthon at this hour for anything less than a catastrophe," Adrienne scoffs. "We're actually going someplace a little more personal to me."

Adrienne pulls back her violet floral rug, unveiling a wooden door starkly contrasting the dark marble floor. She unfastens its latch, revealing an entrance to a stone staircase spiraling to depths beyond what my eyes can discern.

"Goddess of The Shadows, or Goddess of Secrets?" I scoff. Of course, Adrienne's chamber wouldn't be complete without an entrance to some sort of secret passageway.

"Perhaps both," she winks. "Don't be shy, my love. Follow me."

A soft, purple glow illuminates our path as we descend the spiraling stairs. Wafting scents of earthy cedar wood and the aftermath of a fresh, summery rain grow stronger the farther down we travel. I shiver as a sudden drop in temperature prickles my skin in goosebumps beneath the thin, satin fabric of my robe.

"Why not tell me whatever you want to communicate through our bond?" I ask, focusing on my footing as the steps grow slick in musty-scented water.

"A change of scenery is never a bad idea after your brain concocts traumatic horrors. Besides, maybe I just want an excuse to finally take you to my secret lair," she shrugs.

My heart nervously flips in my chest in response to the playful darkness in Adrienne's tone. We finally reach the bottom of the staircase as it spills out into a massive, phosphorescent cave. Infinite purple amethyst gemstones carved into the cavern walls shimmer like galaxies of lavender starlight. The ceiling above and the ground below, all bathed in breathtaking, sparkling amethyst crystals.

Our skin appears to have a soft lavender tint as we're submerged in what feels like an entire realm of its own. If the Kanoelani belongs to Choilleich, her spirits, and the dragons, this cavern realm belongs to Adrienne. Despite the briskness of the air, it feels as if a large blanket of healing warmth is wrapping itself around me, injecting an intimate sense of peace directly into my veins. The restlessness in my heart steadies, finding comfort in an aura of intense healing.

"What-what is this place?" I whisper, nearly too mesmerized to speak.

"You could think of it as an alcove of healing, solitude, and refuge. I discovered it centuries ago beneath the monastery when I first sensed a strange swell of energy seeping from the floors of my chamber. None of the high priestesses or anyone in their courts has ever mentioned it to me, seeming unaware of its existence. So, I claimed it as a secret lair to get some time alone to myself."

Adrienne grabs my hand, leading me deeper into the cave of glowing amethyst. We trek through ankle-deep pools of crystal waters and weave through mazes of shimmering stalagmites until reaching a massive pillar of amethyst. My jaw nearly drops to the ground as my eyes trace over the tower of pure, lavender gemstone stretching to the heights of the cavern ceiling.

"This is unbelievable," I gawk in admiration, approaching it slowly as if moving too quickly would vastly disrespect its beauty. I reach out and touch its jagged surface, and my hand immediately glows in the white lights of my magic. Tendrils of warm, revitalized energy surge beneath my skin as if the crystal is not only drawn to my magic but tugging on it and charging it by the power of its unique chemistry.

"I figured this place would interact fondly with the magic of a light mage," Adrienne smirks. "While I can't exactly soften the blow of the deal that brought your soul out of The Dark Realms, the least I can do is come clean within hidden, healing alcoves of amethyst."

"Nothing can be worse than the threat of losing you for an eternity. I think I can handle anything else just fine," I counter confidently. Perhaps I'm finding myself at more peace than I should be, but the last thing I want right now is to suggest removing ourselves from the comfort of the warm, healing buzz easing my nerves.

Adrienne exhales, releasing smoke through the maws of her inked serpents as she fidgets with her robe. "The sight of you suffering at the hands of my father, the idea of you as an eternal slave to his torment in a realm that would take me ages to single-handedly destroy, drove me to desperation. I refused to pull you out of The Dark Realms without ensuring Osiris could never stake his claim on your soul again, so I agreed to the terms he required."

Adrienne rolls her shoulders back, exhaling tendrils of smoke from her shaky breath as she nervously twists her wrists. "Osiris agreed to return you to The Mortal Realms and forever exile your soul from his realm under the condition that you lose your mortality. The bond that allows us to communicate through our souls? A side effect of your soul becoming tethered to mine. I allowed The God of Death to abolish your mortality and fuse your soul to mine…for eternity. Your heightened senses? Those are not a side effect from the wounds Lady Rhonwen healed. They are simply a part of your existence as an immortal being."

Adrienne pauses, and the lull of silence hits me with the force of pummeling deep-sea waves. A rush of jitters scuttles down the lengths of my arms and into my fingertips. A thrill of terror and excitement flips in my stomach like flocks of frenzied crows.

"Did you know about this?" I ask Lumithra, too stunned to gather my

words to respond to Adrienne.

"I've known it from the moment you woke in Lady Rhonwen's chamber. I hope you can forgive our silence. It was never my truth to unveil, and Adrienne wanted to wait until she was confident you could withstand such a heavy, complex reality."

With the amount of light that seeps through those stained glass windows, I likely would've been at risk of setting blazing white flames to the monastery just as a reaction of pure shock.

"Please, find it in your heart to forgive us," Lumithra pleads. *"With Adrienne being the only source capable of grounding your magic, she was not in a position where she could risk losing her ability to prevent your magic from exploding into fatal tragedies."*

Adrienne approaches me with caution, cupping my face in the trembling palms of her hands. "I hope you can understand my delay in coming forward, my love," her voice shakes. "While technically tragedy could still claim you for Niroshen, death is no longer an inevitable, inescapable future for you, Amira. It is merely a threat that no longer stands a chance against you. Through the wells of power that reside within you, and through my vow to defend you with my every breath, death will find you eternally untouchable."

Lumithra and Adrienne expect me to be seething with boiling anger, but instead, my heart is filled with endless fields of elation. In an outburst of pure euphoria, I throw my arms around Adrienne's neck and claim her lips with passionate force. The warmth of her smooth skin against mine, combined with lips sweeter than wine, fills me with an exhilarating buzz. "You've got to stop fearing my reactions to your deepest, darkest revelations," I taunt as my heart threatens to burst out of my chest.

Whether credit is due to the soothing aura of the crystal caverns, how jaded my brain has become over the years, or the overwhelming relief our love can finally know unbreakable hope, immortality doesn't frighten me. Especially now that Rhydian is rotting away in the torment of The Dark Realms.

"I admit your utter lack of disturbance is a bit unexpected," Adrienne confesses as her porcelain complexion flushes with rose-colored warmth.

"Well, maybe I'm a little disturbed you brought me all the way down to this secret lair where no one can hear us without giving me a proper taste of what an eternity with you will look like," I challenge. I lean my back against the pillar of amethyst and slowly pull a sleeve of my satin robe off my shoulder, hoping my message gets across.

Adrienne slowly leans against the pillar, firmly placing a hand above my head. She grips my chin with aggressive force and tilts it up to lock my gaze into hers. "Be careful what you wish for, my love. I fully intend on taking my time with you down here. Do you wish to submit to my mercy?" Her dark, seductive tone sends throbbing waves of desperation between my thighs.

"Please, do your worst," I beg as my legs nearly give out beneath me. Adrienne slides her hand down my neck, placing me in a light chokehold as tendrils of shadows caress my skin and strip me of my robe. Picking right back up where we left off in her bedroom.

Adrienne wedges a thigh between my legs as her teeth scrape my earlobe, sending twinges of pain and pleasure down the lengths of my body. Her silken, breathy kisses trace my jawline to the corner of my mouth as I grind against her thigh, craving as much friction as she'll allow me to have.

"So eager now, aren't we?" Adrienne growls as she works her kisses down to my breasts. My back arches off the pillar as her tongue alternates between swirling concentric circles around my nipples, and biting down on them when I least expect it. "You'll need me to carry you out of these caverns after I'm done thoroughly destroying you. How does that sound?"

"Divine," I whimper.

"That's what I like to hear. Now, on your knees," she orders, pointing a finger to the ground.

If Adrienne thinks I intend to submit without putting up a fight, she's horribly mistaken. White, wispy flames engulf my hands as I cool them to a warm, gentle temperature rather than conjuring my usual lethal infernos of lightning. My goddess is about to wish I had never learned such refined control over my magic.

Obediently dropping to my knees, I grab onto her hips and caress her upper thighs with my swiveling, gentle flames. As the touch of my magic tauntingly works its way up between her legs, I worship her skin through waves of depraved kisses. Brushing my lips against her thighs, I kiss over the lines of her tattoos, admiring the centuries of stories in the form of ink.

"Every inch of your skin is a divine masterpiece, and now I have an eternity to study your beauty. An eternity to explore your mystery."

I work my kisses up to her abdomen as my hands explore the lines of her back. Her breath hitches as I command the flames swirling between her thighs to taunt her where her nerves are most vulnerable. Adrienne moans as my flames produce sensations of warm, rippling currents, grazing over her clit in a torturously slow rhythm.

"I could listen to you make that sound all—" a black rope of shadows forms behind my teeth, cutting off my speech mid-sentence.

"Did you really think I would let you win so easily?" Adrienne laughs darkly.

Ropes of obsidian smoke wrap around my torso, forming an intricately designed harness around my chest. Another set of shadows latches onto the harness, extending between my legs and forming an additional tightly fastened rope against my clit.

Adrienne tugs on a fistful of hair from my scalp, forcing my gaze to fixate upon her towering over me. With her robe now draped on the ground next to mine, nothing is left to obstruct my view of her mesmerizing perfection.

"Just for attempting to take lead, I'm afraid I'll have to punish you," she growls. "Shall I have my way with you, my love?"

"*Please*," I beg her through our bond after a pitiful attempt to mutter words through my gag.

"Just look at how vulnerable you are." Adrienne tugs on the rope between my legs, moving it back and forth. I thrust my hips, grinding myself against the movement. My thighs shake as I indulge in the sensation of burning friction wickedly teasing me with both pleasure and pain.

"*More, please, more,*" I beg pathetically.

"What a greedy little thing, "Adrienne teases as she tugs on the rope faster, increasing the tension pressed up against me. Without warning, the rope begins vibrating.

"*Gods, you're unfair,*" I whimper as I roll my hips with the rhythm of the steady pulsations, moaning as I draw dangerously close to release.

"You're so beautiful when you squirm and struggle at my mercy," she growls.

The vibrations cease as Adrienne stops tugging on the rope. I scream into my gag, hopelessly feral as the threat of release cruelly recedes like the tide from the shore.

"I'm not letting you finish so quickly now, love. Where would the fun be in that?"

Adrienne lowers to her knees, wrapping me in her arms. I fight against the ropes tying my hands behind my back, desperate to break free and ravenously consume her. My legs still shaking from the residual pulsating friction burning between my thighs.

"I don't need altars adorned in my honor," she whispers in my ear as she kisses down my back.

"I don't need my name worshipped by the thousands. There's only one set of lips I desire to hear it upon."

My teeth clench down on my gag as she runs her nails down my back, leaving her mark as she digs into my skin. The sting of Adrienne's nails is an exhilarating rush, as if overwriting the years of scars etched into my back with her claiming mark. Part of me wishes her mark would remain as permanent as Rhydian's scars.

"I can truly leave my mark on you, if that's what you wish. I can carve symbols in ink, in honor of my love that marks you for eternity," Adrienne whispers down our bond as if having read my mind.

"I would love nothing more than your symbols over my scars. To be permanently marked by your ink would be an honor."

My heart accelerates at the very thought of Adrienne carving visible, permanent evidence of our love beneath my skin. Even if our immortality is sworn to secrecy, the thought of all Elmoria knowing I am hers and she is mine is enough to melt away at the fortress I once believed was impenetrable.

"You're going to look immaculate with my mark on your flesh, my love."

Colors swirl in my vision and my lungs fill with screams of pain as Adrienne shifts her nails into claws, penetrating my back with ink. The searing pain of her claws at work, suffering at the mercy of my goddess lapses in waves of ecstasy. To have her pain washing over the pain once inflicted by Rhydian is a healing redemption.

"You're mine for eternity." Adrienne trails breathy kisses down my neck as she works on her mark. "Mine to love. Mine to protect. To mark. To pleasure." Her dark, seductive tone interrupted by a stream of velvet kisses is more than enough to thoroughly destroy me.

Adrienne flashes me a wicked smile, reveling in my ungodsly desperation. "Perhaps I shall reward you for being on your best behavior for me."

Vibrations return to the rope between my legs, teasing my clit with pulsating friction. As if that wasn't nearly too much to take, thin, feathery, trails of shadows graze circles over my nipples. My gag is now doing little to nothing to muffle the humiliating moans escaping from my mouth in response to euphoric, sensory overload.

"Almost there. Look at how strong you are, Amira. How beautiful and helpless you are, all tangled up in my web." Adrienne tugs faster on the rope between my thighs, rubbing it harder and harder against my throbbing clit.

"My offering, bound and gagged, making the most beautiful noises I've ever heard."

With one of Adrienne's hands carving ink into my back with razor-sharp claws, her other hand tugging on the rope with endless increasing intensity, I am intimately, vulnerably surrendered to her mercy. Release washes over me in cleansing waves of unholy, divine pleasure.

"And, finished." Adrienne withdraws her claws from my back as the restrictive ropes disintegrate. As the last set of ropes fades away in obsidian mist, I immediately collapse to the ground. My shaking limbs are heavy and useless dead weight as my jaws loosen and adjust to being freed from their bind. I would be more than content to lie here in my fatigued bliss, soaking up every last drop of this afterglow for an eternity.

"Told you I'd thoroughly destroy you," Adrienne smirks as she extends a hand to help me off the ground. I fall into her arms, stumbling like a fawn figuring out how its legs work on a frozen pond.

"I'll thoroughly remember this when I retaliate," I barely manage to respond. Forming words through my breathlessness is near impossible. "Perhaps tonight even, if you're lucky."

Colors flood my vision and my head grows light as I bring my lips to Adrienne's, desperate to kiss her with reckless force. Desperate to destroy as I have been destroyed.

"Slow down there, my love. Even an immortal won't so quickly recover from such intimate acts with a goddess. We need to get you back upstairs and replenish your energy," Adrienne counters. "Some lemon cake and a lavender calming elixir should do the trick."

My stomach grumbles as it becomes more and more difficult to ignore my depleted blood sugars. Begrudgingly, I comply and retract my plans of retaliation. For now, they will have to wait.

"Before we leave, would you like to take a look at your back?" Adrienne motions toward the reflective pillar of amethyst.

For a second, I almost entirely forgot about Adrienne's ink work on my back while coming down from the biggest release I've experienced in my life. She drapes her arms over my shoulders, and holds me steady as I confront the reflection of the masterpiece written over my scars.

A constellation of stars stretches down the lengths of my back, with the biggest ones blanketing over a wolf with an ethereal glow I have no idea how Adrienne managed to capture through her ink. Its eyes and fangs glimmer like diamonds, catching reflections of the lavender amethyst. Between the stars and the glowing wolf, each stunning, intricate detail has been carved so vividly that I'm convinced this work of art has a life of its own.

"Beautiful doesn't even do justice to describe it," I whisper in total awe. It should be no surprise that an immortal goddess is capable of producing such immaculate art, yet I can't help but take in Adrienne's work while frozen in stunned mesmerization.

"Beautiful doesn't do justice to describe the masterpiece that you are. It's nice to finally see you looking at yourself in a fraction of how I see you," Adrienne beams with pride.

"I couldn't trace over every scar, but that was never my intention or desire. Doing so would have felt like a discredit to the storms you've endured," she explains. "Every inch of you is profoundly beautiful, my love. And every scar, a story of your resilience. I felt a creature as rare and enduring as a moon wolf would suit you well."

"A moon wolf?" I ask. "I've practically grown up trekking Blackthorn's mountains and forests and have no idea what you're talking about," I confess.

"The moon wolf is an incredibly rare species, symbolic of hope and strength throughout ancient folklore. It's possible you may have encountered one without knowing it. They're masters of survival, only revealing their unique properties when facing substantial threats. I, however, have had the honor of witnessing moon wolves weather the harshest storms time and time again. Their coats absorb the energy of the moon, and it charges them with enough strength to take down slews of wraiths as if they're nothing but injured hares. They hold their own against the dark with their cunning prowess, and the light of the stars and the moon keeps them warm in even the harshest blizzards. If there's any creature worthy of representing the beacon of hope and strength that you are, it's the moon wolf."

I allow myself to fall deeper into Adrienne's arms, indulging in the oxytocin running through our veins as we embrace each other skin to skin. "I'm afraid I don't even know where to begin in expressing the depths of my gratitude for you," I tell her.

"Your existence is far more sacred and precious to me than you'll ever know," she responds. "Fight by my side, and together, we will see an end to this war. From there, we will rebuild. We'll fight until we eradicate the divide between the peasant slums and the riches of Vespera. We'll fight until the luminaries can rest in undisturbed peace, and until leaders can rule the lands of The Mortal Realms without their obsessions over the gods clouding their judgement. The journey will never cease, but I refuse to settle for eternity without fighting for a realm worthy of being your home."

CHAPTER 40
The Eve of Eleodora

Summery beams of sunlight seep infiltrate the darkness of my eyelids and warm my skin, waking me from potentially the deepest sleep of my life. I trace over the inked lines of my back, still raw with throbbing pain, reassuring myself last night was not just a dream.

I focus on the sunbeams and redirect them from Adrienne's face, buying her a few extra moments of rest. My slumbering goddess, innocently wrapped up in my arms, as if she didn't destroy me with torturous, chemistry-altering pleasure in the depths of her secret amethyst caverns. Thinking about the events of the day we are about to face, I tighten my grip around her torso and pull her body closer against mine. Savoring every heartbeat, praying to the dragons we'll return safely to this bed of ours after putting an end to Eldermoor's tyrannical rampage.

"We'll make it out alive, my love," Adrienne whispers softly as she stretches her arms. "The nights ahead of us are infinitely countless." She brings my hand to her lips, brushing my skin with a soft kiss.

"How long have you been awake, eavesdropping on my distress?" I scoff, pulling strands of her hair back to kiss her neck.

"Despite my assurance of our survival, I'm afraid I won't truly rest until the flames of my father's influence are reduced to ash," she mumbles in her low, groggy morning voice.

Adrienne sends tendrils of shadows to pull back the curtains, officially inviting the summer morning into her chamber. Our chamber now. The peace of the rain-scented fog, melodic cawing crows, and bustling courier foxes grazing the mountainous horizon makes it difficult to imagine our allies across the sea spending their morning drenched in bloodshed, struggling to hold down the thinning lines of their remaining forces.

My stomach churns as I struggle to comprehend how anyone in Blackthorn is supposed to carry on with jubilant celebration today while Eldermoor slaughters its way through Helia's pegasus knights and our dragon knights. A fight against blood mages, wraiths, and smiercs won't last much longer without the might of a single luminary.

"Do you think Sorin will succeed in convincing The High Priestess to assign us that mausoleum shift?" My mind drifts as I watch a courier fox whirl through the morning fog, welcoming the warmth of the air into its fiery-orange wings.

"He'll be reporting to us at the breakfast banquet, so we'll find out soon enough. Speaking of, we should be getting into our gowns. It's customary to dress in formal attire for the entirety of the festival. The last thing we need is to further aggravate Lady Rhonwen today of all days," Adrienne sighs.

"The last thing I need is to spend an entire day in an uncomfortably tight dress after what you put me through last night," I roll my eyes as I collect my wine-red ball gown from the armoire and head for the bathing room.

"If it's any consolation, keeping my hands off you all day will be far more torturous than what that dress will put you through," Adrienne smirks. Color flushes my cheeks at the thought of her salivating over me all day as I lace the strings of my corset.

At least Choilleich's glowing, emerald pendant dangling above my strapless cleavage makes quite a beautiful statement piece, fitting for a summer celebration. The swirls of green still beating in time with The Elder Spirit's pulse takes a slight edge off my restless nerves, reminding me of the comfort of having her support today.

Despite no longer truly needing my daggers, I still fasten my bandolier to my thigh, allowing my array of blades to peak through the slit of my dress. Many experienced mages still opt to carry weapons, often using them as vessels for the magic they possess within.

I emerge from the bathing chamber to find Adrienne's silhouette cloaked in obsidian smoke, concealing her frame as she slips into her gown. "Almost ready," she calls out. My heart fumbles its rhythm the moment the smoke clears, and I'm met with the most lethal form I've ever seen her in.

Adrienne slowly closes the distance between us, clothed in an onyx gown that will without a doubt, be the death of me. Her lacy, plummeting neckline floods my head with an endless stream of unholy, insatiable desires. Her smoky, semi-sheer skirt laden in glistening sparkles cascades down her towering legs, framing her tattoos with a daringly high slit above her left thigh. She might as well be clothed in the stars of the night sky, with the threads of her gown singing of her ethereal beauty. Her smoky eyes widen as she takes me in, as if entirely unfazed by her own stunning divinity. The sultry expression on her face suggests if we don't head down to the festivities this instant, we'll spend our entire day tangled up in dark indulgences.

"Just the very sight of you alone is plenty of retaliation from last night," Adrienne gapes in awe. Warmth rushes to my cheeks once again as her eyes study every inch of me, temptations swirling in her ashen irises. "However, if you don't snatch me away for a moment of alone time at some point today, I may never forgive you." She smirks as she brings her lips to mine, kissing me with a taunting gentleness that makes my knees buckle.

"I'm afraid I wouldn't forgive myself either," I whisper in agreement.

Adrienne's lips part for mine as I claim them eagerly, with flames of magic roaring in the pit of my stomach. Shadows at her fingertips trace the sparks of electricity dancing down my spine. Our magic intertwines as my fingers comb through her midnight black, wavy tresses, and then claw into her back.

Adrienne moans and grabs my waist with possessive need. Her scent of lavender and sage intoxicates me right along with the danger of her body pressed firmly against mine. My hands explore all the delicate, dangerous ways her dress clings to her curves as I reach the slit that allows me generous access to her upper thigh. My heart sprints out of my chest as I curl my fingers upwards and trace them along the muscles of her silken, smooth legs, intoxicated by the scent of her arousal.

"So wet for me already," I growl down our bond. Understanding our need to keep things brief, I waste no time summoning electrifying currents at my fingertips, pumping them in and out as her walls clench against me.

"Please," Adrienne whimpers as I rock my fingers back and forth, teasing her clit with light, rippling shocks at a torturously slow rhythm. I cover her mouth to stifle her moans as she rocks her hips in sync with the palm of my hand. After just a few carefully-timed thrusts, I have her breaking free of my hand over her mouth, muffling her screams of release into my neck as her body thrashes against mine.

"Will that hold you over until I can properly take my time with you?" I taunt.

Adrienne casts me a burning glare, muttering a string of curses as she slowly steadies her breath. "You better properly finish what you started later if you know what's good for you," she hisses.

We both laugh and exchange one more long, passionate kiss as she reels me into a hug that steals the breath from my lungs. "We'll be back here before the next sunrise," I tell her. "And then, we'll take the proper time to worship one another, tangling endlessly until the morning light."

Adrienne smirks in agreement as we take a deep breath before heading out the door. Hand in hand, holding each other close as we brace ourselves for the trials that await us.

*   *   *

Botanical garlands of emerald ivy and marigolds hang from the tall ceilings of the dining hall. Morning light trickles through the stained glass windows, filling the room with tints of a soft, rainbow glow. Large crowds work their way to large banquet tables adorned with candles, bouquets of wildflowers, and rose gold dining platters. From dragon knights, to priestesses, to civilians from all over Blackthorn, guests mingle and savor in the flavors of an over-the-top brunch all donned in their finest festival attire.

The tables usually reserved for Lady Rhonwen's priestesses have been cleared off the dais as a stage for renown minstrels providing worshipful ambiance. A choir accompanied by a harpist and a stringed quartet perform melodies in celebration of The Eve of Eleodora over the bustling commotion of the dining hall. The religious choruses set my blood boiling while the hauntingly beautiful melodies threaten to move me to tears. Being overtaken by such a divisive contrast of emotions is enough to nearly destroy my appetite.

"Espresso elixirs, ladies?" A scullery maid courtesies, balancing a platter stacked with glasses of fizzling iced espresso beverages, topped with a lavender rosemary garnish.

"Much obliged," Adrienne lowers her head in a light bow, and grabs two glass goblets from her platter before politely dismissing the cheery maid on her way.

While I've heard rumors of what Eve of Eleodora festivities were like amongst fellow dwellers of the peasant slums, nothing could have prepared me for the magnitude of this spectacle, or the sea of blind eyes. Not a single expression in the room appears to be even the slightest bit bothered by the distress of our allies, and knights of our own, fighting for their lives in Helia. The overall atmosphere of extravagant celebration punches me in the gut like potent medicinal herbs.

"How? How in the realms is everyone roaming about seemingly so carefree? How are so many gathered together, unbothered by the endless bloodshed just across the Tourmaline?" I ask Adrienne.

It takes every morsel of self-control to retract the sizzling, miniature bolts of lightning dancing atop my curled fists. Every morsel of self-control to not flip every banquet table and command every beating heart to follow us to get our hands dirty despite holding no authority to my name.

"The influence of Lady Rhonwen's faith is not to be underestimated. The faith of The High Priestess, especially when puppet-queened by the power of the luminaries, is potent enough to intoxicate an entire nation," she responds.

"Even the half-mortals?" I ask in disbelief.

"The half-mortals who have not taken the disciplines of grounding and meditation as essential, daily practices are more susceptible to falling under such influences. That unfortunately seems to account for more mages than I expected. All the more reason we cannot afford to draw any unnecessary attention onto our squad today."

"Ah, there you two are." Zephyr makes his way through the crowd, adjusting his marigold vest layered over an unbuttoned, ivory tunic. His emerald pendant rests on his bare chest, beating in sync with the gems around our necks. I can only hope the matching gems of our squad will pass as festive jewelry, rather than tokens signaling of a looming rebellion.

"If I wasn't acquainted to you ravishing beauties already, I would've easily mistaken you for queens. Perhaps goddesses even."

I chuckle nervously and choke on my sip of espresso elixir, accidentally inhaling a sprig of rosemary before I intended. It takes a series of humiliating coughs to chase it all the way down my throat.

"She's still learning how to interact with flattery. Never mind the manners of a former merc," Adrienne jeers.

I send a spark from my fingertips to send a light, pinching shock to the small of Adrienne's back, causing her to flinch and stifle her wince of pain.

"Sorry. Still working on my manners," I scoff. Adrienne's cheeks flush as I throw her a subtle wink.

"I can't save our seats all day. Come with me before we have to fight the townsfolk just to dine alongside our squad," Zephyr huffs.

We follow him to our seats at a banquet table, Arden and Irvette already seated and tearing into their meals. My stomach rumbles at the wafting aromas coming from the caramelized onion omelette and lemon ginger scones on Arden's plate.

The generous feast sprawled out before us indicates this is no ordinary brunch hour. Honey-glazed hams, arugula salads topped with smoked salmon and vegetables freshly picked from Vespera's gardens, fruit tarts with sweet buttercream, rosemary-roasted carrots topped with crumbled goat cheese, and blueberry cheesecake, to name a few of the selections.

"Anyone hear from that prince yet?" Irvette inquires flatly, mid-shoveling a forkful of omelette into her mouth.

The sight of Irvette nourishing her body graces me with a sense of relief. Based on the dark circles beneath her eye and her paled complexion, it's evident she has hardly slept or eaten since our return from Crystal Bay. Even if she's only focusing on her strength for the plans ahead of us, I'll accept whatever it takes to see her taking care of herself.

As if right on command, Sorin approaches our table with a forced, weak smile resting across his freckled face. Something feels off. Something about the heaviness of the bags under his fire-orange eyes tells me something is horribly wrong. Adrienne throws me a glance in concern, confirming she senses it as well.

"I've got both good news and bad news, and prefer to start with the good news first," he greets us. "Lady Rhonwen is adhering to the advice

I forged from General Cyrina. Your squad has been requested for guard duty in the holy mausoleum at sundown. I even have her summons in writing, addressed to Adrienne."

Sorin hands Adrienne a thin scroll of parchment addressed to her as Wing Commander Adrienne with the formal orders for her squad.

"Well done, Prince," Adrienne praises, reading over the lines of our assignment. Our first small victory.

"I'll give credit where it is due— hiding the luminaries in the mausoleum where Blackthorn's former high priestesses rest is ingenious. No one would question why such a sacred burial ground is so heavily guarded," Arden processes out loud.

"On with the bad news, Prince," Irvette interjects, sipping her espresso elixir.

"Of course," Sorin clears his throat. "I received a rather grim missive from my father's court this morning. It mentioned thousands of winged wraiths unlike any he has ever seen, slaughtering through our forces by the masses. Since our time in Crystal Bay just days ago, the smiercs have already multiplied their numbers to the size of a small army. Mayavin, the capital city of Helia, is all that remains unoccupied. Once her walls are breached, Helia will be forced to surrender."

My bones chill to sheets of ice as I hear the anxious lump traverse down Sorin's throat. The more dragon and mage blood Eldermoor spills, the more smiercs they receive from The God of Death in exchange. How many casualties did it require to supply thousands of smiercs within just a few short days?

"There's not a chance in any of the realms I'm waiting around all day for the night shift. We need those luminaries now," Irvette growls as her glass of espresso elixir breaks between her clenched fists. She quickly transforms her spilled drink into ice before it has the chance to spill into her lap.

"Helia cannot afford the cost of our squad making any rash

impulses," Adrienne interjects. "Requesting an earlier shift will only invoke suspicions and possibly compromise the entire mission. If we're found out, it will be our squad fighting against every single knight in Blackthorn rather than Eldermoor's smierc armies. With the masses of Lady Rhonwen's knights swooned under her impaired influence, we have to treat today as if we are already in the heart of enemy territory. We need to lay low and refrain from striking until planned if we want any shot at victory," she orders.

"Look how good we did last time we were in the heart of enemy territory," Irvette seethes. She slams her fist on the table, and our drinks shoot out of our cups like small geysers. The cyclone of rage confined in her aquamarine eye screams waves of confliction— knowing Adrienne is right while at the same time, refusing to accept it.

"Believe me, I wouldn't waste a damn second at this festival if I had any confidence in any other alternative," Adrienne hisses, choosing not to fight the pools of obsidian overtaking her smoke-toned irises. "We will not let the darkness win. Just a few hours of laying our heads low. A few hours of playing by Lady Rhonwen's rules before we play by ours. One Elmoria under Osiris is our flame to smother, and we will extinguish it with perfection."

"Just a few hours of playing nice with our best table manners. Nothing our squad can't handle," Arden winks.

"The fate of the world…resting in the hands of our best behavior. What possibly could go wrong?" Zephyr smirks, catching the eye of a blushing scullery maid passing our table. He summons tendrils of wind to deliver a bouquet of marigolds from our table to her platter as he gives her a slight head nod. She collides with another maid while caught up in her flustered distraction, causing every glass on both platters to spill onto the floor.

"Gods help us all," Arden mutters, slapping a hand over his face.

Additional maids come by to collect our empty plates and clean up the shards of sticky glass as our squad parts ways to begrudgingly engage with the rest of the festival.

"The High Priestess will be making her rounds soon, starting in the gardens. We need to engage ourselves in some of the rituals if we want to earn her good favor, and I know just the place to start," Adrienne tells me as we make our exit.

Crisp bonfire smoke dances with the earthy mist the moment we step out of the dining hall and into the weeping wisteria gardens. Knights and civilians alike gather around dozens of bonfires flickering with lively orange and scarlet flames. Prayers and protection incantations are recited through the gardens as bundles of rosemary and folded up pieces of parchment are tossed into the flames with expressions of unwavering hope.

"It's custom to cover one's head in a crown of summer blooms when praying by flame to the sun and earth gods," Adrienne sighs as she snags a couple of floral crowns hung from a willow branch. We place crowns of ivy, dahlias, and lilies atop our heads and seek out the least crowded bonfire we can manage.

"Are all deities so needy of such elaborate validation?" I scoff while fidgeting with my itchy crown.

Adrienne sneaks curls of shadows up my dress, teasingly caressing my thighs before dissipating. The brief sensation is enough to make my knees buckle, nearly causing me to lose my footing in front of all the crowds. "Not nearly as needy as you, it seems," she smirks.

The light crowd gathered around our bonfire briefly nods at our arrival before diving back into their prayers and incantations. The chants might as well be fingernails scraping down a tablet of slate, causing my spine to shudder in response to the dissonance.

"Bow your head and close your eyes. Meditation is also an acceptable practice if you wish to avoid participating in the clamor," Adrienne instructs down the bond.

Even if I have no true intentions of prayer, and every intention of faking my meditation, finding myself surrounded by worship makes me feel like a lone wolf cornered by invasive predators. As I close my eyes, the thought of connecting with any god other than Adrienne when I haven't attempted to commune with my own father, Kallik, is laughable.

My relationship with the God of Light begins and ends with channeling his magic, and nothing more. His role in Adrienne's banishment from Niroshen and his poor judgment in entrusting my childhood with Rhydian are more than enough deterrents from ever desiring to commune with him. My staged meditation turns into meditating on the sadistic complacency of the gods, and suddenly I feel the burn of my magic boiling in my blood.

Shrieks of terror interrupt my inner spiral as the familiar heat of my white flames sears my skin. I open my eyes, finding the once blood-orange bonfire now flickering in flames of white. Rather than crackles of sparks and embers, mini bolts of lightning spew out from the white flames.

"What did you throw into the flame?" A civilian gasps.

"Just a bundle of rosemary, I swear!" Another one answers.

The white flames engulfing my fists aren't even brought to my attention until Adrienne grabs a hold of me. The white, electrical flames vanish, returning the fire to its original hues of orange and scarlet the moment her fingers interlace with mine.

"Perhaps it was an answer to our devotion. The veil between Blackthorn and Niroshen truly is said to be thin today, and my prayers were answered through flames of miracles. Blessed be!"

Fools. Ignorant, naive fools.

"Forgive me for not grounding you sooner. The collective horror those mortals felt at first was truly delectable, and I was admittedly savoring the moment," Adrienne confesses.

Rather than being concerned over the fact that I unknowingly bathed the bonfire in my lightning flames, I can't help but laugh at the reactions Adrienne also found herself enjoying. *"I can do it again intentionally this time and give them a real spectacle if you'd like,"* I offer.

"Allowing that would be quite tempting if we could afford the attention that would draw," Adrienne admits.

Our conversation is interrupted as we pick up on Lady Rhonwen's floral scent wafting through the smoke and burning rosemary. Fragments of her airy voice catch the attention of our ears in between the clamors of the garden celebrations. Thankfully, the mortal civilians gathered at our fire have returned to a state of diligent worship, likely praying my jolting white flames don't make another appearance.

Adrienne refuses to release her physical contact from me, not taking any chances of another theatrical episode playing out before the approaching High Priestess. My anger toward the gods, still stirring the heat in my veins.

"What a delight to behold, the two of you paying your due respects to the gods," Lady Rhonwen chirps inquisitively. A swarm of butterflies flutters in my gut, wondering if she can sniff out my resentment towards the gods like a bloodhound sniffing its prey."I hate to interrupt such curious worship, but I must confirm that my message has reached you. I have yet to hear your response to your squad's assignment for tonight, Adrienne."

"My apologies, Lady Rhonwen. Sending my confirmation must have slipped from my attention. In reflection of my outburst the last time we met, my mind has been preoccupied with using today to reconcile with the gods. To invite them to challenge my perspective, and to hone my faith in renewed strength," Adrienne bows.

"Aren't you quite the actress," I snicker down our bond.

"You're fortunate General Cyrina holds such high faith in your squad's performance," Lady Rhonwen scoffs. "If you wish to maintain your title as Wing Commander or wish to remain allowed on monastery grounds as an instructor at all, I suggest your squad doesn't so much as allow anyone to look at the mausoleum the wrong way tonight. Are we clear?"

"Crystal, Lady Rhonwen," Adrienne responds.

"Very well. Considering the esteemed work of your squad and the rapid progress you've made in mentoring Elmoria's only light mage, I can see why it would put General Cyrina at ease to assign you to the most critical shift tonight. Do not disappoint us. May the gods bless you," The High Priestess scoffs as she dismisses herself curtly.

Her threat toward Adrienne stings my chest like icy daggers as she continues strolling through the gardens, greeting the other bonfire gatherings in a warm, hospitable tone. *"We can't afford to find out what the gods will do to you if you're stripped of your positions at the monastery. There has to be another way to stop Eldermoor's tyranny without stealing the luminaries. I know your power is next to unrivaled in The Mortal Realms, but we can't afford you angering all the gods. Should we reevaluate our strategy?"*

Adrienne cups my face, gently brushing her fingers through my hair. My slamming pulse finds a sense of regulation as I regulate myself in her eyes of soul-cleansing silver.

"No need to spiral, my love. I'm well aware of all the risks and sufficiently prepared to contend with the potential obstacles. I'm no stranger to provoking the gods."

Unbothered by our audience, Adrienne's lips meet mine with a decadent delicacy that shifts my mind from an endless spiral of worry to escapist lust. My heart skips a beat as tendrils of shadows caress the small of my back, serving as an extension of her intoxicating touch. If there's even the slightest possibility we won't make it out of tonight alive, we'll sure as realms make every damn kiss count.

As Adrienne's tongue entwines with mine, I intentionally command the dancing, electric sparks at my fingertips to possess the fire with my snow-white flames. With the bonfire's flames now under my authority, I wield them to weave around us like decorative, blazing garlands. Flames bright as a full moon, responding to our reciprocal, intimate love for each other. Flames that could never ignite in the desperate embers of one-sided communication and admiration.

The moment we untangle ourselves from our heated embrace, the flames return to a carbon copy of the dozens of mundane bonfires burning throughout the gardens. Adrienne and I relish in the sight of speechless jaws dropped and eyes widened in disbelief.

"Forgive me for the theatrics. If we're going to fight for a brighter Blackthorn, its people need to see far more displays of mutual, reciprocal love. How can we expect our nation to extend compassion to every soul within our borders and beyond while the gods leave theirs parched?" I ask Adrienne.

If Blackthorn doesn't learn to be loved so it can love, impoverished peasant slums will continue to exist. Mortals without divine lineage will never be seen as equals to the mages. Orphans will remain a forgotten afterthought, vulnerable to the hands of monsters like Rhydian. If the worship of the high priestesses continues to leave them blind to the vast divide separating the famished from the thriving, every drop of blood shed by our knights will have been spilled in vain.

"Keeping my father off the throne of The Mortal Realms is just the beginning," Adrienne sighs. *"The fight for hope is a layered, never-ending war— a war I only have in me with you at my side for eternity, light-bringer."*

CHAPTER 41

Tears in the Garden

The closer we get to relieving the evening shift at the mausoleum, the more it feels like a dangled piece of bait being dragged further and further out of our reach. A savory, mouth-watering taste of hope dangling on such a breakable string. Hope has never felt more dangerous to crave, and dismembering Eldermoor's tyrannical rampage by wielding the luminaries is truly only the beginning.

Crowds trickle from the gardens to the monastery in congested masses to commence The Eleodora Ball— the final itinerary item to check off before assuming our night shift. Adrienne gathers our squad around an unoccupied fire, allowing us one final chance to review our plan.

"My father should have sent another missive by now," Sorin shares with disheartened eyes, scanning the skies for any courier foxes. I follow his gaze to the silent sunset, feeling slightly unsettled by the blood-red light sweeping across the darkening horizon.

"Our squad has been permitted to excuse ourselves from the ball early. Our dragons are already close on standby as well. It won't be much longer until we're storming the gates of Helia," Adrienne assures. "Any questions or concerns regarding the task ahead of us, please voice them now before we go dance like the unsuspecting, compliant dragon knights that we are."

"Eldermoor will be reduced to a fragile condition if our plan succeeds, but how do we guarantee they never seek The Crown of Luminaries again? Winning this battle hardly feels like winning the war if there's no guarantee armies of smiercs will stop rising," Arden contemplates as he sharpens the blade of his axe with a whetting stone.

"The God of Death does not perform hefty, lethal miracles without a hefty, lethal asking price. From what we've gathered, smierc rituals are impossible without the fresh spilled blood of dragons and half-mortals. Once we wield the luminaries' strength to sever their armies, it will take ages before they can regain enough strength to contend with our forces. We will have ages to fortify our defenses, rebuild Helia, and prepare for their return to power," Adrienne answers. "Next question."

"Then what will we do with the luminaries after we wield them? We can't exactly waltz up to Lady Rhonwen as traitors and hand them over to cloud her mind again or toss them in the sea. Blackthorn has all but the shadow luminary. One stone short of forging the Crown. Who's to say none of our minds will become clouded by wielding so much sacred power?" Irvette asks, fastening her braids into a tightly-knit bun.

Adrienne scoops the pendant in her palm, stroking her thumb over the swirling, emerald pulse. "If there's any sufficient protection against the call of the luminaries, it's in bearing tokens of Choilleich's pure, ancient spirit. The Matron Spirit has preserved The Kaneolani in a pacifist, innocent reign since Elmoria's beginning, even through the last Luminary War. Even if we were to cross paths with the shadow luminary, we have sufficient protection. As far as what will come of the luminaries after our use, I have already made arrangements for their safekeeping. That is all you need to know," Adrienne answers firmly. "Any other questions?"

"Well, that's a little cryptic even for our dark and brooding Wing Commander," Zephyr snorts. "No need to be the hero and bear that burden alone. How can we help you protect them once this is all said and done?"

"Do I need to remind you that even if we are successful, we'll all be enemies of Blackthorn for directly defying The High Priestess?"

Adrienne hisses. "I refuse to risk sharing such critical intel should any of you find yourselves detained for interrogation before I can reach you. "No. Further. Questions," she orders.

No one dares to challenge Adrienne as her silver irises darken. However, I've learned how to read The Goddess of the Shadows like a sacred tome and know exactly where she intends to hide the luminaries.

"Since you're bound to me for eternity, this secret is ours to keep. You and I will fly the luminaries to the Kanoelani the moment Eldermoor's forces are wiped clean," Adrienne communicates down our bond, confirming my suspicion.

Adrienne abruptly shifts her attention back to the rest of the squad. "A return to Blackthorn will be out of the cards for the foreseeable future. We will be hunted down to the ends of Elmoria, deemed as additional threats to its delicate balance. Any information you possess can and will be used against you should any of our knights track you down. You will be tortured until you break, and then executed as if you were never one of their own."

Grave silence lingers in between the crackling flames as we all lock eyes with one another, silently acknowledging the price to be paid. "My kingdom may be in a state of shattered oblivion, but you have my word that Helia will welcome you with open arms. You will find yourselves safe and harbored in secrecy among what remains of my people," Sorin's voice cracks in time with a branch snapping in the flames.

Within the hour, we'll become traitors to the Nation of Blackthorn. Every half-mortal before me has devoted years of bloody, grueling training to attain the titles they're about to relinquish. They've spent years honing the discipline of their elements until repeatedly breaking their bodies to near burnout. Years of sparring in deadly matches on the backs of dragons, rivaling one another, while sharpening their unbreakable camaraderie. Within the hour, they will sacrifice it all.

Arden brings himself to stand, sheathing his axe at his side. "Let's go enjoy one last dance, shall we? One last waltz through the monastery as welcomed, cherished dragon knights." His earth-toned eyes glisten with the glow of Vespera's lights at the bottom of the mountain.

"Not a single ruler over any kingdom, nation, or over any of the realms can truly strip you of your title as dragon knights," Adrienne declares. "You have all fought too damn hard to hand the fruits of your bloody labor over so easily. Not a single ruler can strip you of the title you earned through the courage, the resilience, and the passion that burns in each of your hearts. It is no longer just Blackthorn that you serve. Rise, my friends. Rise up, as the first Dragon Knights of Elmoria."

We rise to our feet as an orchestral melody spills out of the Grand Hall's entrance, signaling the start of the ball. Irvette's gaze remains intently fixated on the fire. She leans into its warmth, reluctant to depart from its familiar comfort.

"You're not confronting tonight's ball alone. Shall we, friend?" Arden asks gently, offering his arm to her escort into the hall.

"He should be here," Irvette responds softly, wiping her tears onto her dress while remaining frozen at the fire. The weight of Felix's absence crashes over me in pummeling waves once again watching his betrothed, fierce warrior of the seas collapse into Arden's chest.

"He should be here," Irvette's voice rasps as she buries her head further into his chest, unable to bare the sight of the fire any longer. "He should be here," she sobs uncontrollably.

"He should be," Arden whispers. "He should be."

I join Adrienne, Sorin, and Zephyr in embracing her as she embraces her hurricane-force grief. Looking over Irvette's shoulders back into the fire, I can't help but to imagine Felix, Casimir, and Nuri, all standing together on the other side, promising that their spirits will always be with us. Divided by the realms, but eternally tethered in the love our souls share.

Irvette wipes her tears and takes a deep breath as she releases herself from our arms, linking herself to Arden. "Now is not the time to break," she utters. "When my time comes, my soul will crawl back home to his. In the meantime, I need to find my strength. I need to fight for the Blackthorn and the Elmoria he longed to see. And…I need to know I'm not in this alone."

Zephyr places a hand on Irvette's shoulder, meeting her with gentleness in his cerulean eyes. "My beautiful friend, you are many, many things. A hurricane-like force to be reckoned with. An ocean of kindness. A river that never runs dry of clever wit. Of all the things that you are, Irvette, alone is not one of them. Not a single one of us is alone, in fact. We've been forged under the trials we've shared, and together, we will share the fight for hope."

CHAPTER 42
Omens: Adrienne

While making our way up the steps toward The Grand Hall, a jarring, knife-like pain shoots into my arm without warning. For a split second, I almost wonder if I've just been shot at with an arrow.

"Everything okay?" Amira asks concerningly.

Gods above. It takes me a full moment before realizing I just winced out loud over the shadow luminary throbbing beneath my flesh like a second, piercing heartbeat. It's been at least a couple of centuries since I could hardly endure the daily torment. Up until just moments ago, I nearly forgot about the ages when my pain was far worse than just an eternally irritating, dull ache.

Amira's eyes widen once she tracks the source of my agony. "*What would be causing a reaction like this? Why now?*" Her voice wavers with alarm.

"*Not a damn clue,*" I grimace, scanning my senses for any trace of smiercs, raven griffins, or blood mages. Nothing. Nothing other than the festive fragrances of smoked meats, burning herbal incense, perfumes, and body sweat.

My brain feels as if it's being split in two as I ascend another step toward the hall. Each and every step feels more and more like descending into an ocean of knives. Before I know it, I'm hunched over in a ball, writhing in agony as if my whole body is about to implode. "*You're not picking up on any threats, are you?*" I reach for Sarthon, trembling in a cold sweat.

"*The skies couldn't be any more clear. All is peaceful, almost to an unsettling extent. That being said...I wouldn't be surprised if you're experiencing omens of threats yet to present themselves. We must remain critically vigilant,"* he growls.

"Reassuring as always," I mutter.

Either I'm experiencing some sort of strange omens, or possibly a form of punishment from the gods for my premeditated treason. Relinquishing my proximity to The High Priestess and marking myself as an enemy of Blackthorn isn't something they'll allow me to get away with so easily, even if it is in the name of protecting the very world they created through those damned stones.

Perhaps this plan could've been avoided altogether if any of you high horses chose to intervene a little more invasively, is what I want to scream to Kamaris. However, no amount of communing with my mother or with any of the gods would turn them into empathetic deities. Nor would it ignite a sudden desire in their hearts to start personally caring for their descendants and devotees.

Along with the shadow luminary tormenting me from the inside out, contemplating what kind of goddess I would have become if I had never been banished from Niroshen causes bile to rise in my throat. Was getting my arm carved open like a holiday turkey and stuffed with a sacred stone what it took to keep me from succumbing to the ways of their sadistic apathy? Perhaps eternal damnation to The Mortal Realms as a sacrificial lamb at their disposal became my saving grace.

Another wave of acid triggers a state of violent dry heaving. I immediately enclose myself in a chrysalis of shadows to prevent anyone from witnessing me potentially discard all the contents of my stomach. Amira quickly follows, stepping into the shadows, stooping down to my level.

"You're in no condition to be heading into that room right now. We're getting to the bottom of this, especially before dealing with the mausoleum," she orders. "Let's start by getting you someplace a little more quiet."

Before I can find it in me to protest, Amira scoops me in her arms as if I'm as light as a feather and rushes us down the stairs, all the way to the field behind the monastery. "I'm not sure how much I can do for you, but this is worth a shot," she tells me. My vision is now so blurred from the pain that I can hardly focus on her words as she gently lowers me to the ground.

Orbs of blinding white engulf Amira's hands as she brings them to my temples. Her touch manifests as pools of ice, instantly dulling the inferno of blades infiltrating my body until the pain recedes. I slowly regain my composure and arrive to a realm of euphoria, soothed by the intimacy of her magic coursing through me.

"How are you feeling?" She asks, placing her forehead against mine. Her wintry scent of peppermint, blended with the lingering, soothing waves of her magic, triggers a humiliating rush of arousal.

"A little too good if I'm being honest," I confess as heat rushes to color my cheekbones. Despite having been mended up by a plethora of healers in my life span, nothing could have prepared me for the unique side effects of Amira's magic. Anytime her magic interacts with mine, my nerves become pathways to sparks of pleasure. Every fiber of my existence longs to intertwine with hers.

"Do you have any idea what happened?" Amira asks as her eyes critically scan me for any external wounds or any evidence as to what may have triggered my pain.

Discussing possible explanations as to what provoked my sudden onset shadow luminary attack is the last thing I want to do with my first moment alone with Amira since dawn. Despite knowing I should be giving what happened more thought, caressing her with nothing other than my shadows throughout the day has been a form of masochistic torture. I need to appreciate how immaculately her curves cling to her dress with my bare hands.

"All I know is that you're eternally bound to me, my love. Any time your magic touches mine, keeping my hands off you takes insurmountable restraint, I'm afraid. And last I checked…it appears we're all alone."

Amira's crimson lips curve into a playful smirk, instantaneously filling me with a warm buzz. Wisdom says we should make our appearance at the ball before our absence is noticed. However, wisdom also says there will be consequences to the state of my sanity if we don't take full advantage of this moment.

"We have shown restraint all day, haven't we?" Amira asks as she tauntingly walks away, relishing in my need for her.

"We have, and I'd prefer it if we released a little tension before rewriting the future of the world," I beg. My request is practically a desperate plea for Amira to hold nothing back and act upon every desire that's been swirling through that beautiful mind of hers all day. I slowly lean back against the monastery's sable-brick walls, leaning into its shadows. "Do your worst," I challenge.

Amira takes the bait, swaying her hips in a confident swagger as her glacial eyes lock intently onto mine. A winter storm on a summer night. How the very essence of light herself longs for me despite my wicked darkness is a privilege that will cost an eternity attempting to fathom.

"A gorgeous, lethal goddess, already melting for me." Amira leans against the wall, placing her hand above my head. "Oh, I'm going to have so much fun with you." Her boldness in using such a dark, authoritative tone with me nearly melts me to my core.

My mouth parts for hers as velvet lips crash into mine. The taste of pomegranate mead on her lips is so sweet, I can hardly breathe. My knees buckle as I surrender to a series of long, gentle kisses as her breasts press firmly against mine. Galaxies swirl behind my eyelids as Amira's breath runs hot on my neck, her teeth softly scraping against my earlobe. The longing to feel her bare skin on top of mine becomes damn near maddening the moment she cups my breasts in her hands with an aggressive need.

Amira's hands slide down my body as she drops to her knees in a stoop of slow, controlled elegance. "I'll go semi-easy on you. Can't exactly take away your ability to walk tonight," she growls. Her eyes of crystal ice lock onto mine as she sinks her teeth into my inner thigh, nibbling and licking her way up higher and higher through the slit of my dress. I conjure a dark cloud of haze to offer us more concealment as Amira begins to rub the palm of her hand against the satin fabric of my underwear.

"Bashful now, are we?" Don't want anyone else to see how pathetic you look melting for me?"

Gods, if she were to talk to me like this all the time, I would never be able to think straight. Her hand firmly presses into the smooth, slippery satin of my underwear, making the friction irresistible. I let out a soft moan and grab a fistful of her moon-white hair, yanking her head back as my hips grind against the satisfying friction of her hand.

Amira whips herself free of my grasp and shoots me another one of those lethal, playful glares. "You're a needy little thing, so wet for me already," she growls. Without warning, her free hand sends sparks of electricity to my nipples, sending jolts of pain mixed with pleasure rippling through my body. I form a rope of shadows to cover my mouth in a desperate attempt to stifle my humiliating moans.

"Let it out, love, I've got you," Amira coaxes. My underwear drops to my ankles as she begins circling my clit with painfully slow strokes of her tongue. She then forms a suction around it with her lips, sucking on me in a steady rhythm as her tongue flicks up and down with the perfect amount of pressure. "Please. Please, don't stop," I beg as my trembling thighs nearly give out beneath me.

"As you wish, love."

Her tongue swivels in figure eight motions as she continues sucking on my clit, inducing every nerve between my thighs to throb in aching pleasure. Suddenly, I'm seeing colors I forgot even existed outside of the Mortal Realms as release consumes every last inch of my body. Amira embraces me as I collapse into her arms, screaming into her chest in a frenzy of breathless convulsions.

"That's my girl," she praises.

"There you two are. We were looking everywhere for you," Zephyr calls out as he rounds the corner of the monastery with Arden and Irvette. Amira quickly rises to her feet, abruptly smoothing out the wrinkles in her dress, as I have less than a heartbeat to come down from my waves of ecstasy and regain my composure.

"Damn, that was close," I mutter.

"Close? I'm pretty confident that I finished you," she fires back with a chuckle.

"It's finally time for us to relieve the evening shift. Everything alright out here?" Zephyr asks, interrupting my ability to retaliate.

"We just needed some air to clear our heads for a moment. All is well. Where is Sorin?" Amira redirects.

As if waiting to be cued, a tawny owl swoops down from the fog, perching his talons on Zephyr's shoulder. Sorin's scarlet eyes meet ours as he ruffles the light mist out of his feathers. "Any extra company joining your watch would certainly raise suspicion. Until we're ready to depart for Helia, I'll be maintaining this form," Sorin explains.

"Like it won't raise any suspicion if anyone overhears us conversing with an owl," Arden scoffs.

"Then let's keep this interaction brief," Sorin retorts. "I'll establish my post in the evergreens near the mausoleum to keep watch. In the event that I suspect even the slightest sign of potential conflict, I will signal for your attention."

"Sounds like a plan to me," I respond. "Before we proceed…let me give you one final reminder. This is your last chance to turn a blind eye and walk away from this mission, should you find yourself not ready to become an enemy to Blackthorn. I will hold no ill feelings toward anyone who wishes to stray from the path of treason."

A resounding silence answers my warning as Arden, Irvette, and Amira all look at me as if I had just asked them to jump off a cliff and fall on their swords. "If you're looking to get rid of us, I'm afraid you're going to have to put forth a much more solid effort," Zephyr snorts.

"Zephyr is right," Arden adds. "Stop wasting your time wondering whether or not we are with you, and start focusing on guiding us well, Wing Commander. Guide us well, as Dragon Knights of Elmoria."

In my six centuries of guarding the shadow luminary in the protective halls of the monastery, I would have never imagined leading a squad of dragon knights on a mission that directly defies the orders of their high priestess. As an unknown goddess…Goddess of the Shadows, I would have never imagined leading souls under my command beyond the humble role as "instructor." I can only hope that I will guide them to a future that stands a fighting chance. I can only hope that I will serve as a goddess worthy of following. "It's settled then," I exhale. "Time to head to the mausoleum."

CHAPTER 43
The Mausoleum: Amira

The briefing from the afternoon shift is kept mercifully brief as we relieve their watch. No incidents to report. The sickening pain of the light luminary's call would've prevented me from paying much attention to any critical information. Its blaring summoning slices into my skull with the grasp of razor-sharp talons, leaving me short of breath. Part of me is tempted to channel magic to soothe my throbbing nerves, but knowing I need to save my entire storehouse for Helia is reason enough to show restraint.

From a quick glance around the room, everyone from our squad, along with the mages of the afternoon watch, all appear to be on the verge of collapsing to the ground and curling into fetal positions. I couldn't even begin to fathom what it would be like to be stuck with a luminary beneath my flesh for centuries.

"Your mind can serve as either your greatest weapon or, as your downfall," Adrienne instructs as the afternoon shift clears out. "Shifting your mental focus off the luminaries and onto the element you wield can make or break your ability to withstand your torment. Meditate on your element long enough, and you'll eventually grow accustomed to the call of its luminary."

"Or, I can focus on the chills this place gives me. Whose brilliant idea was it to hide the luminaries here? If I end up contracting some sort of curse, I swear I will never let any of you live it down," Zephyr winces. His voice reverberates through the mausoleum as he struggles to stand on his two feet.

Vibrant glows of the luminaries flicker from atop casket lids, lined along ivory walls canvassed in cobwebs. The very stones that forged Elmoria into existence, all residing within a holy mausoleum. The balance of our world, resting on dusty tombs of Blackthorn's late high priestesses, makes my stomach churn. These terrible, beautiful stones were never intended to reside in the hands of men— mortal and half-mortal alike. The sooner we can send them off to the Kanoelani, the better.

My gaze fixates on the light luminary, flickering in an orb of glowing white on top of the tomb of Lady Petra. Somehow, it's difficult to believe this is the same stone I intercepted off the shores of Tourmaline. Despite the downpour of searing blades digging into my skull, something about its glow feels unfamiliar. Skepticism floods my senses, whispering this can't truly be the light luminary, but I shut the thoughts down immediately. Now is not the time to lose my mind to irrational paranoia. This is the light luminary— the stone forged by Kallik to fill this world with light and electrical energy.

"You're all ready to retrieve us, correct?" I reach for Lumithra, nervously searching for some distracting sense of comfort. Anything to assure me all will go smoothly and according to plan.

"All of us are in position, at the ready," she confirms.

The faint stench of sulfur seeping in from the entrance to the outdoors provides further reassurance our dragons are nearby. Within minutes, we'll be on our way to Helia, putting an end to this war, no matter how unbelievable it may feel.

Arden peers out from his post at the entrance of the mausoleum, waiting for Sorin's "all-clear" signal. After a few excruciating seconds of silence, I flinch as the coo of an owl catches me off guard. "That's Sorin," he confirms.

"We need to make this quick," Adrienne orders. "Grab the luminary of your element and head for the exit. As far as the fire-"

"On it," Irvette interrupts, having already grabbed both the water and fire luminary. If the weight of bearing the water luminary is still clawing away at her mind, the stoic expression on her face doesn't show it.

One by one, we grab our luminaries and make haste for the exit. Despite the sensation of flaming hot daggers impaling my brain, our plan is in motion. Our operations so far are running smoothly as planned.

"Headed your way. Ready for us?" I reach for Lumithra as I sprint past the aisles of tombs.

Silence. Lumithra fails to respond. The scent of sulfur lingering in the air, now hauntingly absent.

Not a single dragon awaits us as we exit the mausoleum and step out into a sheet of darkness. Vespera's shimmering lights below have all gone out. Music and laughter are no longer seeping out of the doors of the Grand Hall. Piles of smoke and fading embers are all that remains of the bonfires. It's as if the entire capital of Blackthorn is holding its breath under the crimson clouds infiltrating the night.

Sorin swoops down from his perch in the evergreens with eyes that appear as if they've just witnessed an army of ghosts. "We've got company at Vespera's northern gate," he chokes.

My bones chill to ice the moment we make our way to the precipice to survey the gates on the horizon. A frontline of cavalry knights lurks still as the night, silently awaiting orders. A wall of clouds shifts in the breeze, unveiling Eldermoor's scarlet raven-griffin crest, waving across large banners. As the moonlight continues to disperse through the fog, silhouettes of catapults and battery rams emerge from the cloak of darkness.

"How didn't we sense them coming?" I ask Adrienne, hardly believing the sight of an army stretching back through the trees as far as our eyes can see.

"The only logical explanation I can speculate is by the power of the smiercs. Something tells me we're still far from understanding the surface level of their capabilities," she responds dryly.

"Apparently, we can add covering the tracks of an entire army and dimming the lights and music of an entire city to their list of abilities," Zephyr mutters in shock.

A wave of nausea rushes over me as I entertain the strong likelihood that our dragons are catastrophically outnumbered, fighting through hordes of smiercs as we stand frozen at the sight of a silent army.

"Helia won't hold up for much longer, if it even still stands at all," Sorin chokes.

The sound of weapons unsheathing, mounting horses, and rustling commotion confirms the knights and mages within the monastery and Vespera below are now well aware they're dealing with far more than just an eerie blackout. The pain from the light luminary in my satchel claws into my skull, making it a resounding effort just to stay planted on my feet.

"FIRE!"

The bellowing command of an Eldermoorian General disrupts the silence as thunderous booms of battering rams begin bashing into the city's stone walls. Explosive cocktails are catapulted over the walls, chasing panicked and confused civilians out of their homes, aimlessly fleeing for their lives from the destructive blasts of impact.

Half-mortals and calvary knights spill out of the monastery by the masses. Thunderous waves of hooves clatter down the steep cobblestone stairs to Vespera, rushing into the heart of the explosive blasts. Mages hurl forces of earth, fire, water, and wind over Vespera's walls while frantically calling out for their dragons. Not a single one answers.

"Until we get sights on our dragons, we fight alongside the ground forces. Don't utilize the luminaries until you receive my order. We still don't fully know what we are dealing with," Adrienne commands. "Be mindful of your exertions."

"How does Eldermoor have enough troops to spare on invading Blackthorn with the amount of destruction they've been imposing on

Helia?" Arden asks in between volleying massive boulders over the walls, sweating profusely under the weight of the earth luminary.

"Either their forces are drastically larger than any of us calculated, or Helia has fallen hours ago, and they wasted no time in coming for the luminaries," Adrienne responds bluntly.

Slews of Blackthorn's arrows and violent forces of nature fly over the northern gate, picking off Eldermoor's troops like flies. If there is any advantage we have in this surprise attack, it's our hold on the high ground. How long we can continue to hold it without the aid of dragons however, is a thought I do not have the stomach to entertain.

Eldermoor returns our volley with a concoction of explosives and arrows, firing them mercilessly into the heart of civilian territory. While some civilians are spared under the protection of shields, others drop to the ground like limp rag dolls. Vespera, known for its shimmering lights, lush, moss greenery, cobblestone and rainbows of wildflowers, now cries in pools of blood, debris, fire, and ash.

For every innocent woman, child, and defenseless man I witness drop in the blood-soaked streets, I answer in strikes of lightning. Bolts of pure fury, frying every Eldermoorian troop I can set my sights on until they become nothing more than charred ash. Sorin fights by my side in owl form, casting hoards of murderous hornets to swarm the enemy forces.

A battle horn sounds over Eldermoor's troops as severed heads are catapulted into the war zone. Heads still garbed in helmets bearing Helia's crest. Heads continue to pour into Vespera by the thousands, and thousands. Eldermoor's message confirms Adrienne's suspicion as sobering truth. Helia has fallen. Blackthorn is next.

Color drains from Sorin's feathery face until his tawny feathers grow white as a skeleton. Whatever flicker of hope that glinted in his eyes earlier this evening has morphed into guttural terror. Severed heads continue bombarding the city, slung by the masses. Without warning, he takes off into swift flight straight into the heart of the war zone.

Sorin becomes a tiny spec nearly impossible to distinguish in the midst of smoke plumes, along with the commotion of Blackthorn's knights racing to save the remaining civilians left in the town.

"Looks like the battle for Elmoria is on Blackthorn's front. Wield your luminaries! Now!" Adrienne commands.

I concentrate on the light flowing through my veins, directing its energy into the light luminary now clenched in my fist. My intentions set on decimating the army ravaging Vespera, turning the waves of its forces to clouds of dust. If we emerge from this battle still perceived as deceitful traitors, then so be it. I'd rather live hiding in the shadows of a free world than live in the light of a world devoured by the dark reign of Osiris. This ends now.

Streams of searing magic beneath my flesh as I channel all the power I can relinquish to the authority of the light luminary. Adrenaline-fueled rage keeps me standing tall as the might of its power repeatedly slams into my brain like a battering ram. With my fists now bathed in alabaster flames, I speak my intentions into the stone one last time, hoping this will all be over in a matter of heartbeats.

Jagged lines form on the smooth surface of the light luminary, branching out like cracking ice on a frozen lake. Before I take my next breath, it shatters in the palm of my hand, sending me flying backwards upon impact of a spontaneous, explosive blast. A cloud of mustard-yellow gas erupts from the fragments of the stone, starving my lungs of air as my pain becomes impossible to endure.

Mages rush past me, racing bloodied civilians to the refuge of the monastery, choking as they charge through the plumes of yellow smoke. Many with severed and missing limbs. Irvette, Arden, and Zephyr, nowhere to be found amid the plumes of suffocating gas.

"What just happened?" I ask as the ringing in my ears throws all my senses in a disorienting whirlwind. The ground feels as if it's spinning violently beneath my feet as I stumble toward Adrienne.

Thousands of our forces are now lined at the gates, fighting against waves of Eldermoor's soldiers climbing over the walls while choking on the yellow haze. No evidence of the luminaries executing even a fragment of their world-shattering power.

"The stones were fakes," Adrienne snarls between her teeth as her shadows race through swarms of enemy soldiers, executing them by asphyxiation. "Those were counterfeit gems loaded with chemicals used in concocting explosive elixirs. I should've seen this coming," she seethes.

Pools of black devour Adrienne's ashen irises as she shifts into the form of a dragon composed of obsidian shadows. She lets out a deafening roar and flies down the mountain to the heart of Vespera within mere heartbeats.

"*Adrienne! Wait!*" My heart plummets into my stomach as she disappears into the night.

Another wave of ear-shattering roars rattle the skies above. Only this time, they're not coming from Adrienne's dragon form. Sulfur and freshly spilled blood thicken the air as a forceful gust of wind rushes over me, pummeling me back into the ground.

The wind gets knocked out of my lungs the moment I spot a massive smierc with claws sunken into pale dragon flesh, tumbling across the sky, only a few feet shy of grazing the ground. Their bodies soar over the valley, bound together by the smierc's life-draining claws. A final cry of fire erupts from the dragon's dying breath as its colossal body crashes down on the wall of the northern gate.

Eldermoor's forces stampede through the compromised wall, launching their full-blown ground invasion as swarms of smiercs, blood mages, and raven-griffins plague the night sky. Blazing behind them in blasts of fiery rage, come legions of dragons, shattering the atmosphere with their guttural roars.

CHAPTER 44
The Luminary War

"Lumithra!"

I stumble to my feet, frantically surveying the sky for a streak of opalescent, shimmering scales. For a second, I forget my cry to The White Empress is a futile effort. The pathway of our bond is unquestionably obstructed by the thousands of smiercs infesting the night sky.

Fool. I was such a careless, reckless fool for exerting so much of my magic into a decoy luminary my instincts warned me not to trust. Rather than fighting Eldermoor with fatal bolts of lightning fire, I'm left with no choice other than standing my ground with my sword and daggers. At least I'm still a lethally trained mercenary, with the art of spilling blood as one of my earliest muscle memories.

"I'll keep as many smiercs occupied as I can manage. They know what I have. Something about the air feels lighter, and I would wager all my gold on it being the severing of our shields. If any of the smiercs so much as glimpse The High Priestess, it's all over. I need you to join the mages defending the path to the monastery," Adrienne orders.

Her message hits me like a volley of poison-laced arrows I find myself entire unprepared to embrace. *"What do you mean? How are the shields possibly weakening? And you can't possibly hold that many off on your own! Especially with them knowing what you carry,"* I seethe. *"Where are you? Let me rally aid your way!"*

"Now is not the time to defy my orders," she growls. *"The luminary beneath my flesh is not a decoy, and I am not a mere half-mortal. We're short on mages. Defend the monastery. Now."*

By the time I lift my head from cutting my blades through hoards of enemies, a blood-curdling roar rattles the skies as Adrienne soars directly overhead. If I hadn't known better, I would've mistaken her for Sarthon. The last time I saw her like this was under torture in The Dark Realms, assuming I was half-hallucinating the true monstrosity of her form.

"There. You've seen with your own eyes that I am fine. Now, go defend the monastery," she orders before swooping back down into the heart of the city.

A suffocating wall of luminescent shadows releases from her breath, charring the flesh of two smiercs flanked at her sides. Their shrieks rattle my bones as their winged bodies collapse into the rooftops of Vespera below. That's neither an ordinary display of her shadow wielding, nor ordinary dragon fire spewing from her maw in blasts of obsidian flame. Despite the vast distance that now separates us, I can feel the heat of her fire reddening and peeling away at my skin.

"What in the realms did I just witness?" My jaw drops as buckets of sweat drench my hair.

"Shadow fire, my love."

Hundreds of smiercs now gravitate towards Adrienne like moths to the light of a pyre. I hold my breath as the dark angels of death swarm her until she disappears from my sight again. Her blasts of shadow fire continue incinerating their bodies to ash as smiercs fall from the sky like snow. Adrienne can hold her own, and I need to obey her as my wing commander and goddess.

The mages that have reunited with their dragons defend the monastery from the air, battling swarms of blood-mages and their raven griffins, defending the towers with blasts of earth, wind, water, and fire. Between the bodies of mangled blood mages and contorted dragon knights dropping from the sky, it's impossible to distinguish who has the upper hand.

Wing commanders shout orders to their squads along with whatever lower-ranking dragon knights have found themselves absorbed in the disorganized, aerial brawl. Relief floods my veins the moment I spot Irvette and Zephyr in their midst, alive and fighting atop Tsuna and Sylphira. If our mages have any hope of defending the monastery, it's having Irvette and Zephyr among their ranks.

The concoction of falling ash, blood-mist, and the clanging of weapons and falling horses draws my attention back to the ground. "All will bow before The Dark One!" A soldier shouts, charging after me with his sword shaking in a flawed form. I shank him in between the plates of his armor and kick him square in the chest, sending him tumbling down the path away from the monastery.

Shank, kick, repeat. I commit the sequence to muscle memory, occasionally exerting sparks of electricity to charge my blades when faced with larger opponents. There is something oddly satisfying about murdering soldiers clad in full, protective armor in nothing other than my crimson ball gown.

Bloody mist continues to spew from the skies as dragon knights and blood mages call upon the power of their gods to tear one another to shreds. "Father, Osiris, help us!" A soldier cries out with his eyes on the jet-black sky. Icicles slam down like a rainstorm, impaling him in the head right before my eyes.

Upon closer observation, the cluster of icicles appears to be lodged into a mangled, battered blood mage corpse turned human pin-cushion. His eyes still open, widened with terror. Two more bodies drop from the sky, immersed in spears of ice, impaling enemies around me as they crash to the ground.

Tsuna's cries of rage, followed by incinerating blasts of her flame igniting the darkness, reveal Irvette is the mastermind behind the brutal, icy slaughters. It shouldn't come as a surprise that she has regained enough of her strength to fight with the vengeance she desperately needs to wield. Yet at the same time, I can't help but to stand in awe of her power.

Enemies continue charging up the path to the monastery by the masses, severely outnumbering the forces fighting at my side. Bodies collapse to the ground like deformed, discarded puppets as blood mages collect their bloodshed into vials. All the decadent festival meals threaten to spill from my stomach. Not nearly enough of my magic has recharged to defend myself from joining the next waves of slaughtered marionettes.

A loud, sudden *whoosh* signals me to quickly drop to my knees, evading an axe aimed for my neck by the hairs on my skin. Nothing other than sheer luck can explain how I managed to reflexively sink my daggers into his abdomen before my head was nearly wiped clean off my shoulders. Either sheer luck…or maybe the blessing of Choilleich's pendant dangling around my neck. I rise to my feet and throw a small bolt of lighting into a cluster of blood mages, buying myself seconds of survival. My arms tremor and my knees weaken as my body begs for more time to recharge. How much magic did I throw into that damned decoy?

"We have sights on the light mage! Keep her alive, but barely. We'll need her conscious for interrogation," a blood mage bellows, raising the hairs on my neck and sending shivers down my spine. Within a heartbeat, I fall to the ground in a state of heavy paralysis. My limbs fail to move despite my screams of desperation. My magic burns beneath my flesh, and screams to retaliate to no avail. My body is nothing more than a severed vessel, unable to unleash its wells of fury.

My lungs seize, unable to scream as a crimson hooded blood mage plants a boot on my sternum and presses a blade to my throat. I try desperately to scream, imagining releasing the white fire from my breath and incinerating him to ash. Not even a whimper escapes from my breath.

"Here's how this is going to play out," he growls. Colossal cobblestone boulders slam into his head before he can finish his sentence, crushing him upon impact along with swarms of enemies caught in the sudden blast. My suffocating paralysis lifts, leaving me as weightless as a feather as my lungs gulp down the cool air in a starved frenzy.

As the dust of the debris dissipates, I'm met with familiar earth-toned eyes and curly, dark brown tresses. "What a damn, pathetic fool to think he could lay hands on you," Arden seethes as reaches for my hand and helps me off the ground. What little remains of his beige dress shirt has been shredded into bloodied scraps, revealing an abdomen coated in layers of soot and fresh wounds.

I laugh nervously as I rise to my feet. I've never been more thankful to see him in my life. "We couldn't possibly be dressed any worse for the occasion," I chuckle as I rip the lengths of my gown with my dagger to free up my mobility.

"We're at quite the disadvantage," Arden huffs as he catches his breath. "Raven-griffins have most of our dragon knights tied up in the skies, leaving the ground accessibility to the monastery dangerously vulnerable."

"I've gathered that much already, I reply as I stab the neck of an approaching soldier who assumed he could take advantage of my blind spot. "Any sighting of Hyrix yet?"

"What does it look like?" Arden scoffs. "He's alive. He's somewhere. They'll find us." Through a series of flawless punches, spear-shaped rocks fly from his fists into the temples and eye sockets of enemy soldiers.

Hopefully, our dragons appear before we draw the attention of any smiercs. Adrienne can only entertain the majority for so long, even with her draconic shadow fire, and we can only hold down the monastery for so long.

Eldermoor's ground forces storm the path in endless waves as Arden and I hold down our defensive positions. Covering each other's weaknesses, we fall into sync as a well-calculated, lethal fighting machine.

Wielding axes and daggers when energy needs to be conserved, and blasting forces of earth and lighting when vital for survival.

"How Lady Rhonwen left Blackthorn with a skeletal defense force baffles me," Arden scoffs as he dislodges his throwing axe from a bloodied neck.

"A few extra hands would be nice," I mutter as I duck below a sword aimed for my own neck and drive my dagger into the achilles of a soldier twice my size. It knocks him off his feet just long enough for me to finish him off before giving him a chance to counter my attack.

Rumbling wheels and thundering hooves rapidly grow increasingly louder amid the explosives and forces of catastrophic nature demolishing Vespera. Bile rises in my throat as Arden and I take in the sight of Eldermoorian battalions and battering rams stampeding straight for the monastery. Thousands against our hundreds. Without any of the true luminaries anywhere to be found, failure closes in on us like an inescapable plague.

"Cover me!" Arden shouts.

Without needing him to explain, I position myself to deflect attacks thrown in his direction as he sheathes his throwing axe and widens his stance. In the corner of my peripheral, I glimpse him conjuring towering walls of stone from the earth, raising them high above the rapidly approaching battalions. Sweat drips from his dirtied brows like rain as he molds his walls into the shape of a massive barricade.

"This should buy us some time. Take out that battering ram and as many knights around it as you can," Arden orders.

"On it!" I confirm.

Archers instinctively swarm to scale Arden's wall, plucking off Eldermoor's cavalry knights as I climb to the top as quickly as my muscles allow. The moment I steady my footing, I unsheathe my sword and command tendrils of lightning to coil around its blade. My body aches in protest as I bring my blade down, aiming directly for the soldiers toting the battering ram. Vertigo threatens to disrupt my balance as I watch my lightning swallow my targets in white flames.

Eliminating the battering ram hardly eliminated our crisis. Knights abruptly dismount their horses, racing to scale the wall faster than my magic can keep up with picking them off. I wield bolt after bolt with the support of my blade, but it's not enough. My arms burn with agonizing fatigue as my grip on the hilt weakens.

"Amira!" Arden screams.

Before I can process his alarm, the wall beneath my feet begins rumbling like an earthquake. An ear-splintering shriek knocks me off my feet as I find myself tumbling head over heels down the collapsing barricade. Chunks of jagged debris crash into my head and my ribs, expediting my fall with pummeling force.

"Amira!" Arden's screams are faint as if he's miles away. My vision blurs to a disorienting haze as I distinguish a massive smierc towering over me. The world around me freezes in time as its faceless silhouette looms over me in dead stillness. Finding myself on the verge of burnout, I hardly have the strength to flinch upon noticing the crown of blades atop its head.

"Foolish, foolish child," the smierc laughs. His voice is so heavily muffled, it sounds as if it wasn't built for communicating with the inhabitants of The Mortal Realms. "Fighting on the wrong side of history. Unfortunately, I take no prisoners of war. My sincerest apologies, but The Goddess of the Shadows won't be able to come after you this time. At least you can send Nuri her regards."

The smierc lifts the crown from his head and reverses it, pointing its blades directly toward me. I don't even have a chance to scream before he drives it into the center of my chest.

CHAPTER 45
Niroshen

"Wake up, daughter." An unfamiliar, yet familiar voice wakes me from my unconsciousness as I awake to strange, blurry colors. Some familiar. Some, unlike any I have ever seen in my entire life. As my eyes slowly adjust, I realize I'm no longer on a battlefield. My ears ring in the alarming absence of smiercs, dragons, and explosions.

I appear to be in a large, oval throne room, adorned with large, rose-gold shimmering pillars supporting a ceiling painted in unrecognizable colors. Large glass windows compose the entire room, revealing a forest laden with golden mountains and waterfalls, as if the outdoors is painted in the hues of sunset. Winged courier foxes flutter around the golden forest without messages tethered to their necks. Owls, dragons, and unfamiliar creatures roam freely in harmony. The more foreign colors and creatures I observe out the windows, the faster reality settles in. I'm no longer in The Mortal Realms. I'm in Niroshen.

"NO!" I scream as terror fills my lungs. "Adrienne! I have to get back to Adrienne! Take me back! Take me back to Adrienne!" My cries come out in panicked, mucousy, dry-heaving snobs. It wasn't supposed to end like this. I cannot be dead. I was supposed to spend eternity with Adrienne in Elmoria. I will not accept an eternity without her. My limbs thrash as I punch the rose-gold marble floors beneath me, screaming in protest. "Take me back to Adrienne!"

"SILENCE!" A voice bellows from a cloud of white fog atop the dais of the throne room. "There is much we have to discuss, Amira, and we have very little time." A man descends from the cloud of fog, clothed head to toe in blinding white. Long white tresses cascade down to the mid-length of his back. My eyes squint upon glimpsing his, glowing in orbs of pure light.

"Spare your tears, my daughter. You came close to death, but you are not dead. You have Choilleich to thank for that."

I look down and notice her emerald pendant is still around my neck. I clutch it as if it will disintegrate if I don't protect it with a death grip. "How can I trust you? How can I trust any of this?" I scream.

"You have no choice, daughter. I am Kallik, God of Light. Divine Blacksmith of the Light Luminary, and you are my daughter. You share my sacred bloodline."

Seas of blazing anger boil in my blood. I want nothing more than to kill him. I want to kill him for placing me in the care of Rhydian. I want to kill him for his absence from my life. I want to kill him for letting me learn of my lineage through an accusation of treason and traumatic trials in a spiritual forest, rather than ever attempting to reach me himself. My fists erupt in orbs of white flame in response to my anger, despite knowing there is no killing a god upon his throne in his eternal realm.

"God or Light or not, I don't care who you are. I don't care that you rule over the elemental gods of Niroshen. You will never have my respect. Not after your hate-filled silence. How could you? Why is this how we meet for the first time? Why does it take me nearly dying to finally exchange of formalities?" My questions spew out in an incohesive rage of sobs.

"Your anger is valid, my daughter. There are more pawns at play than you know. Now is not the time to address your questions, although I promise those will be all well addressed in time," he responds coldly. "Like I said, you are not dead. I can't hold you here forever, and we have critical matters to discuss."

A crack of lightning strikes the ground of the golden forest, rattling the floors of the throne room. "Your mother is in grave danger. And because of it, so is all of Elmoria. You must reach her before the smiercs conform her to Osiris's will."

"Excuse me. Did you just say my *mother*? Of course! Of course, now is as good a time as ever for you to reveal a branch of our family tree to me!" I seethe in disbelief.

"You won't let me talk unless I give you some context, so I'll stop wasting my time. You're as stubborn as they come, Amira," he grumbles.

"You didn't truly believe your hair turned as white as The High Priestess as a mere side effect of her restorative efforts on your physical body, did you? You've seen her heal others before. Not one of them has had that effect. Adrienne has been under the impression that your physical transformation was a side effect of your immortal transformation, but she is mistaken. Because you and Lady Rhonwen share DNA, you inherited some of her likeness as your magic's response to recognizing hers.

"Lady Rhonwen is your mother, and despite her imperfections, she loves you fiercely. Leaving you in Rhydian's care was not a decision she made lightly. Children of high priestesses are vulnerable targets, viewed as political pawns for leverage. With tensions with Eldermoor increasing since your birth, your mother did not want to risk you ending up as collateral in international affairs. She kept her pregnancy a secret from the public, and sought out Rhydian's assistance. He promised you would be in the care of an affectionate, fierce protector, and swore to conceal your identity as her daughter. She had no way of knowing his true colors."

"And you didn't bother intervening the moment you first noticed his true colors?" I hiss, fuming out of my temples.

"Our communications with Mortal Realm dwellers are complicated. Plus, I knew how Rhydian would shape you. I knew he would hone you with the skills necessary to survive Elmoria's trials to come."

Immortal bastard.

"The luminaries are powerful, influential stones, designed with the power to erect worlds from nothing. Such luminaries cloud and corrupt the judgement of their mages, especially those who possess more than one at a time. Your mother has all but the shadow luminary in her possession. The moment The Elder Smierc reaches her, Elmoria will belong to Osiris."

"Then I demand you release me back to Elmoria this instant so I can put an end to this. How in the forsaken realms am I supposed to distinguish which one of those wraithly swine is The Elder Smierc? Care to enlighten me, *almighty* father dearest?"

"The Elder Smierc is the all-knowing smierc. The first smierc Osiris gifted to Eldermoor and the final pawn in their game. He's the one who sent you my direction, and has already extracted the shadow luminary from Adrienne since your time here with me. Adrienne can't hold him off forever, especially while adjusting to losing her luminary," Kallik responds in an unfazed, flat tone.

A storm of lightning erupts from my fists, sending a torrential downpour of bolts straight toward The God of Light. "You bastard! Send me to Adrienne *NOW!*"

Kallik catches my bolts in one hand and dissolves them all into tiny sparks while hardly moving a muscle. "Quit your insufferable yapping and I can finish telling you everything you will need to know to have a fool's shot at saving our world and your beloved," he roars.

"The Elder Smierc is temporarily acting as a vessel for Osiris's soul. He can't contain it forever, and needs to transfer it to a powerful, deceivable host from The Mortal Realms. He plans to make The High Priestess the new, eternal host. Blackthorn's shields have already collapsed under the smiercs' power. If The Elder Smierc succeeds, he will use The Crown of Luminaries to inhabit Lady Rhonwen's body and begin his eternal, imperial reign.

"Before I return you to Blackthorn, I wish to bestow more power upon you. With the power I seek to give, you will ascend to the status of a goddess. All I ask in return, is that you humble yourself before me," Kallik offers.

I swallow the endless depths of my rage and bow before my father. "I will accept whatever it takes to give Adrienne a fighting chance without hesitation. I humbly ask you to transform me with your power."

Kallik's blinding white eyes lock onto me as a pool of light engulfs my body. I fill my lungs with a deep breath and find myself levitating off the ground as I exhale. Surreal weightlessness consumes me as I ascend The God of Light's throne room. My body, lighter than vapor. My moment of tranquility is short-lived as alabaster flames pour into every fiber of my existence. My magic aches in searing growing pains as surges of power branch through my veins like wild lightning fires. I try to scream to release fractions of my anguish, but fire fills my lungs, burning them from the inside out. My vision fades to white, and then the pain recedes into the waves of weightless floating. I open my eyes the moment I'm returned to the ground, awakening as a vessel of divine power.

"Amira, Goddess of Hope. You are to return to Elmoria and put an end to this war," Kallik declares, summoning a portal to Blackthorn. "I hereby authorize your passage into The Mortal Realms. Fight for her lands. Fight for her balance. Fight until the darkness is displaced."

Without hesitation, I step into Kallik's portal and enter into a jet-black free fall. Raven-griffins, smiercs, and dragons fly by me in a bloody haze until my fall is broken by a sea of glistening, opalescent scales.

CHAPTER 46
A Crown of Luminaries

"Lumithra?" I reach down our bond, looking for any evidence that our encounter is real, and not imagined.

"Welcome back to The Mortal Realms, Goddess of Hope," she responds with a small blast of fire to further ground me in reality.

I lower myself to embrace her as far as my arms can reach. *"You have no idea how relieved I am to be reunited with you. I don't even know where to begin. There's no time for me to bring you up to speed right now, but we need to reach The Elder Smierc as fast as we can,"* I spiral as my heart sprints in my chest.

"No need to explain anything, my child. I've seen and heard everything you were shown in Niroshen," she responds gently. It just dawns on me that Lumithra is flying away from the monastery. Away from Lady Rhonwen. Away from where Adrienne likely had her confrontation with The Elder Smierc.

"Adrienne!" I call down the bond, only to be met with silence.

"She's been severely weakened, but she's still alive. Fighting The Elder Smierc alone," Lumithra hisses. *"He overpowered her and extracted Lady Rhonwen from her chamber. They're headed to the woods as we speak."*

"How long was I with Kallik?" I scream as my heart plummets into the pit of my stomach. For Adrienne to have fallen victim to The Elder Smierc, she must have been holding him off for hours.

"Time passes differently in Niroshen than it does in The Mortal Realms," Lumithra responds in a sobering tone. The night sky transitioning to shades of twilight makes me spew vomit into the woods below. Hours. I

was gone for hours.

The trees appear as blurred brush strokes as Lumithra races us through the woods as fast as she can carry us. We soar until we find Sarthon sprawled out on the forest floor with an unconscious Adrienne at his side. My chest is met with a suffocating weight as my world crashes down on top of me.

I jump from Lumithra's back before she makes a full descent and take off in a maddening dash for Adrienne. The world around me doesn't exist. The forest might as well be a chamber of silence despite the war still raging in full force. *"Adrienne!"* I scream as I finally reach her and place my hands over her chest. Her pulse is faint, but present. She lies limp on the ground, back in her human-like form. Far too much color has drained from her complexion. Far too much magic has been depleted from her body, even for a goddess.

I call upon my healing magic and grab hold of the gaping wound in her mangled arm. The cut runs so deep that I can see her bones. *"You're going to pull through this, love. I'm here now."* Glimpses of Felix's lifeless body on the altar flash into my mind as I beg my magic to work faster. Too late. I am here far too late.

"An injury that severe will take days to recover from if she's lucky enough to survive under my reign." A sinister voice chuckles over my shoulders, rattling my bones in icy shivers. "She truly gave all she had, and then some. You should've seen the look on her face once she realized I sunk my blades into your flesh."

I turn my back to the sight of The Elder Smierc, holding a limp, unconscious Lady Rhonwen in his skeletal arms. "You want to know what's really frustrating? That pendant around her neck is the only reason she's still alive at all. I threw attempt after attempt to destroy that damn thing, yet it remains unscathed. Taking care of Choilleich will be my first order of business once I take my throne."

"Your reign will end before it even starts," I hiss as I spit on his feet.

The Elder Smierc chuckles. "Ahh, yes, yes. A new star has been born. What are you now? The Goddess of Hope?" he laughs. "A goddess you may be, but you pose no threat to me."

The Elder Smierc uses his free arm to shoot a rapid fire of poisonous arrows from his gnarled claws. Lightning snaps from my fingers as I break each arrow like twigs. Lumithra positions herself behind me, reaching for him with her lethally honed fangs as violet arrows graze over her scales.

"I can't afford to lose you!" I hiss in warning. *"You're of little use to me here. I need you to rally our squad. Rally as many of our surviving forces as you can,"* I order.

"I'll comply only because I sense just how much power Kallik has gifted you, and you have yet to learn your new burnout limits. I'll bring as many reinforcements as I can gather," Lumithra growls as she blasts off into the twilight haze.

I take on The God of Death in the body of The Elder Smierc with my new heightened strength as The Goddess of Hope, matching his attacks blow for blow. A battle between two gods. "Don't get too cocky now, little love. I have eons of experience on you. You're not nearly as powerful as you think you may be," he scoffs.

"Is that so?" I challenge, casting my gaze upon the light of the moon and the stars. I extend my reach toward the skies, harvesting the energy of the light above me. I welcome massive orbs of light into my hands, molding raw power into the shape of a massive moon wolf. It charges after The Elder Smierc with a life of its own, pummeling him to the ground and sinking lightning-charged canines into wraithly bones.

A foul stench of burning, rotten flesh stirs in the fog as The Elder Smierc fails to successfully counter the electrocuting fangs dripping in black, inky blood. I've never been more relieved to hear the agonizing shriek of a smierc in my life. Osiris's vessel writhes on the ground as my moon wolf gnaws his bones, pinning his wings down under its massive paws.

"Are those eons of experience serving in your favor right now?" I scoff.

"Naive fool," Osiris growls in blood-boiling fury as he spits on the ground. "Do you really think you can contend with The God of Death?"

Icicles scuttle down my spine as The Elder Smierc latches onto the moon wolf and consumes it through its faceless void. Faster than I can wield my next attack, tendrils of shadows coil around me, forcing me high above the ground before slamming me back down with bone-crushing force. Splotches of indigo and violet taint my vision upon impact as my body tremors in violent fits of dry heaving. Despite sensing my heightened healing magic rapidly tending to my fractures, paralysis holds me in place. I'm unable to move a muscle. Once again, I'm stuck on the ground, writhing in excruciating agony.

"What an appropriate audience for the execution of your mother as you've known her," he laughs.

Tears stream down my cheeks, but the sobs don't come. Shock possesses my body as my lungs feel as if they're collapsing within my shattered rib cage. "Let the ritual commence," The Elder Smierc croons as he lays Lady Rhonwen on the ground beside me. His body then collapses to the ground as an endless rope of black smoke spills out of his maw. Osiris's soul. I fail to so much as bring myself to my knees as his soul spills into Lady Rhonwen's chest, restoring life to her body.

The High Priestess levitates like a limp marionette, tugged by invisible strings hoisting her high into the twilight sky. Clothed in white, with irises black as the night. She takes one look at me and my arms snap like twigs as they're forced behind my back under the authority of her blood magic. "Bow before The Dark One," she snarls through her teeth in a wraithly voice far from the delicate, melodic tone I've come to know.

"Mother, stop! It's me! Your daughter!" I attempt to scream from under the suffocating weight of The God of Death's blood magic pinning me to the ground. The words mother and daughter feel like foreign, unwelcome objects on the tip of my tongue, but perhaps calling out our relation to one another may somehow break her out of her trance. Perhaps the strength of a mother's love for her child could be enough to dispel the death spreading through her like a disease.

Lady Rhonwen reaches for the pocket of her cloak, extracting a handful of glowing stones. My effort to reach for any maternal bond suppressed deep within her consciousness was futile. The High Priestess is gone. My head convulses in familiar twinges of pain, recognizing the magic of the light luminary cutting into my temples like scorching hot knives. The stones in her hands are, without a doubt, the true luminaries.

"No!" I scream from the depths of my soul. I have failed. I failed Blackthorn. I failed Elmoria. I failed Lumithra, and the squad. I failed Felix and Fieryn. I failed Casimir, along with every friend I lost to Rhydian's mercenary camp. I failed Lady Rhonwen. I failed Adrienne.

The High Priestess's body ascends higher into the sky as a beacon of blinding light. Her body disappears behind an explosive plume of opalescent colors, sending Adrienne's unconscious body and me flying head over heels upon impact of the blast.

"Death to Elmoria! Death to Elmoria!" Osiris's chants hit me harder than every rock and tree I collide with while tumbling through the dense forest like a rag doll caught in an unforgiving storm.

The plume lifts. Levitating amid the morning fog is a faceless man adorned in black robes that were once white. His large, muscular silhouette, darker than midnight under a new moon. Not a single fraction of evidence that his body once belonged to Lady Rhonwen remains. Upon his head, a crown of devastating, hypnotic beauty.

The rich soil beneath our feet turns crumbles to rotten, blackened ash. Life rapidly drains from the evergreens faster than my devastated heart can beat. Blackthorn's emerald mountains drain to withered black as I watch my world take on the spitting image of The Dark Realms.

I freeze. Unable to sob. Unable to scream.

A hoard of smiercs descend from the sky, bestowing a large, obsidian cape upon Osiris's shoulders as they make their landing. "Behold, The Dark One!" They shriek in victory, bowing before their god upon the ground of ash and bones.

"Master, we've come to escort you to the monastery. We humbly ask that you oversee the construction of your new throne," one of his smiercs growls.

"Very well, my spawnlings," Osiris responds.

"Would you like us to take care of those mage scums before we depart?" The smierc asks, waving a long, bony finger to Adrienne and me."

"Those mage scums are goddesses. As ill-equipped to contend with me as they may be, discarding them isn't so easy. As long as those two bear the pendants of Choilleich, not even The Crown of Luminaries can touch them. Scheming the downfall of The Elder Spirit is my first order of business, so their days are already numbered. Leave them be for now," Osiris snarls. "Return me to the monastery, spawnlings. I wish to establish my throne room immediately."

"Very well, Dark One." Another explosive blast of multicolor plumes erupts as Osiris and his smiercs take to the skies. Smoke fills my lungs as splotches of black flood my vision until waves of weightless drifting devour me whole.

*　*　*

I awaken atop Lumithra, glimpsing a fully awake Adrienne, and Sarthon flying beside Sorin and Lyra. As my eyes slowly readjust to consciousness, I then spot Irvette and Tsuna, Arden and Hyrix, and

Zephyr and Sylphira all tightly-knit in our formation. Beams of sunrise bathe us in warmth as I slowly realize we're among thousands of dragon knights, many with displaced civilians and human soldiers as extra passengers. Blood spills like iron-scented rain from the squads flying above us. If it weren't for being surrounded by a sea of suffering, I'd almost assume we were all among the dead flying over the golden skies of Niroshen.

"*For now, The Kanoelani remains the only fragment of Elmoria Osiris cannot touch with his influence. We are on our way there to reconvene,*" Lumithra explains.

"*What do you mean?*" I ask with half of my brain tuned in to Lumithra, and the other half lost in a numb, frozen trance.

"*Osiris may have established his Elmorian throne, but the veradis spirits and the dragons refuse to accept defeat,*" Lumithra growls. "*We are not retreating as an act of surrender. We are retreating to establish our base and organize our forces. Whether The God of Death realizes it yet or not, this war is far from over.*"

Choilleich meets us as we descend into the deafening silence. Masses of veradis spirits in the form of vapor wolves stand behind her, heads lowered in somber grief. Not a single word is uttered as knights dismount and begin silently establishing triage stations to tend to the wounded. Aches, groans, and sobs flood the silence of The Kanoelani, but still not a single audible word amongst an entire army.

*   *   *

Hours of silently assisting in the triage stations pass as morning turns to afternoon. Within the next few moments, Adrienne and I are due to join The Elder Spirit in addressing what remains of Blackthorn's army and its surviving citizens. With all of Blackthorn's high-ranking generals missing in action including General Cyrina, Choilleich has declared Adrienne and me as the new commanding generals under her spiritual authority.

A nauseating concoction of sorrow, guilt, and shame stirs in my stomach as we make our way to the top of a large hill to address the thousands below us. My heart shrivels and crumbles to dust as Choilleich's eyes meet mine. The weight of her pendant around my neck crushes my chest like a millstone, suffocating me under the weight of abysmal failure. Blackthorn and Helia have fallen. Eldermoor reigns in victory. The Kanoelani may stand firm as our refuge for now, but it won't be long before Osiris's forces evolve and bring death upon our sacred forest. With The Crown of Luminaries, it won't be long before Elmoria's last oasis of hope is drained of every drop and reduced to lifeless wastelands. My body breaks out in violent tremors as The Elder Spirit begins her address to the crowd below.

"The God of Death will proclaim that the age of balance is gone. While it may be gone, it is not beyond our reach. Whether The Gods of Niroshen arise to reclaim their masterpiece or leave it to wither, our council will fight for Elmoria. Together, we stand. Dragons, spirits, mages, and mortals.

"Nothing lasts forever. Elmoria's foundations may have been decimated, but that doesn't mean new foundations can't rise from the ashes. Today, we mourn our infinite losses. We grieve. We let ourselves feel the weight of Elmoria's death, but we don't let it smother us. Tomorrow, we reconvene. We fight for our emergence into a world rebirthed in hope," Choilleich proclaims to the masses.

My heart races like an avalanche picking up speed as it barrels down a mountain. Hours ago, I watched helplessly as Osiris established his reign over Elmoria. Now, I'm one of the commanding generals leading the fight to reclaim our lands. To say I am the least worthy candidate of such an accolade is an abominable understatement.

"The Elder Spirit does not bestow her trust upon others lightly. You are more than capable and worthy of the titles you bear, light-bringer. You are not your failures, nor did you fail Elmoria. You are hope, you are love, and you are mine. We are in this together," Adrienne consoles.

Adrienne laces her fingers between mine as Choilleich signals for me to speak my piece. I bow before The Elder Spirit and take a deep breath, feeling the heaviness of the thousands of eyes locked onto me. Eyes filled with grief, fear, and fatigue. Every set of eyes before me shows me glimpses into souls worth fighting for. Souls worth defending, protecting, and leading. As The Goddess of Hope, I refuse to allow despair to have the final word in their lives. As I step into my divinity, I refuse to surrender to apathy.

"Elmoria must endure. Tomorrow, we fight for better. We fight for brighter. And when we rebuild, Elmoria's cycles of oppression will come to an end. Tomorrow, we fight Osiris, and demand the gods to answer for their apathy. Tomorrow, we fight for hope." Inhale the flames and shadows of unbreakable tenacity, exhale defeat. We will prevail. We will live to see the next sunrise.

Acknowledgements

This book started out as an impulsive thought after playing "The Black Eagles" playthrough of Fire Emblem: Three Houses and romancing female Byleth with Edelgard. I thought to myself, "I wish more authors would write dark fantasy stories including sapphic romances." That impulsive thought turned into my own personal challenge as I started daydreaming about the plot for A Crown of Luminaries. Daydreams turned into my passion project over the past two years.

There are so many people I would like to thank for their supportive involvement in my self-publishing journey.

My husband, for encouraging me to follow my dreams, and for being just as excited about this project as I have been. He has become the inspiration for many of the best traits of my main characters. His unwavering support and patience have made profound impacts throughout my writing journey.

My friends and my family, for always believing in me and taking my silly little ideas seriously since day one. If any of you have read the pages I explicitly marked for you not to read, I am not responsible for the emotional damage certain scenes may have caused.

My cover designer, Muhammad Kaleem, and my map designer, Khayyam, for capturing the visuals in my head and bringing them to life. I tremendously appreciate the art of your crafts, and working with you both has been an honor.

Olivia King, for taking on the project of bringing a graphic audio narration of A Crown of Luminaries to life. Thank you for always being an incredible friend and an incredible human being. Having your voice and your talent as a part of this story is an honor I am infinitely thankful for.

My beta readers, Johanna Marian, Chad Wimberly, and Olivia King, for volunteering their time on a brand new author and for giving my writing a chance. Thank you so much for sticking with me and for your critical, valuable feedback and support. This story wouldn't be what it is without you all.

And thank you, for giving me a chance as well. Thank you for journeying to Elmoria and beyond with me. Thank you for following Amira, Adrienne, and the squad along their journey to fight for hope. This is not the end of their story.